Shoot the Moon

* * *

BY

PATRICIA STEELE

Dear Sheryl –
Thank you for your
support! I hope you
enjoy my book when
you read it ♥.
Take good care —.
Patricia
2009

RoseDog 🐾 Books

PITTSBURGH, PENNSYLVANIA 15222

ISBN: 978-1-4349-9195-9

Printed in the United States of America

First Printing

For more information or to order additional books, please contact:
RoseDog Books.
701 Smithfield Street
Third Floor
Pittsburgh, Pennsylvania 15222
U.S.A.
1-800-834-1803
www.rosedogbookstore.com

Dedicated to everyone in the health insurance industry who truly cares about what they do, to everyone who believes in the power of love and especially to my husband, J.D. and our children who have thoroughly supported me along the way.

"Beware how you take away hope from another human being."
—Oliver Wendell Holmes

Chapter 1

✳ ✳ ✳

Callie jumped as if she'd been stung when the phone's buzzing caught her mid stride near her office door. "Damn!" Slapping the door knob testily, she leaned across her file-strewn desk and grimaced before quickly glancing at her small gold watch. Lassoing her impatience from her voice, she answered. "Good afternoon... This is Callie Beauvais."

"What's going *on*, Callie? The voice was strident and tense.

"Caroline. I'm on my way downstairs to the party now...You beat me." Callie laughed quietly, knowing how Caroline loved a party.

Silence reigned.

"Caroline? What.........?" Callie was instantly concerned. "Are you all right?"

"No, I-am-NOT-all-right," Caroline Phillips spit out. "I valued our friendship.... through thick and thin, remember?"

Callie blanched. ".....Caroline," she whispered urgently. "Of **course** I do. What are you *talking* about?" Her free hand lifted to her tightening throat, clearly stunned.

"Steven's on the warpath about today's press release Lee guided me through. He asked me why I changed my mind about the contracts. I tried to calm him down and told him there were no quick answers.... I just needed to study it further to form a confident decision." Caroline sniffed loudly before continuing in a low voice. "He ranted and raved about Lee being too cautious.... Then he told me I shouldn't listen to you either, of all people........" She sniffed again.

"Why on earth would he say that? I'm headed to the open house now; let's talk right away." Callie's heart raced.

"No, I'm at home, not in the building. I left early. I have to resolve this with him. He's arriving any minute." Caroline's taut voice broke suddenly. "I've already tried to cajole him into low gear, but I couldn't.

That's why I told him to come here. The last thing I need is a scene at the party. And he.... said something else that I can't quite get my mind around, Callie." Caroline's voice petered out like air leaking from a balloon.

"What, Caroline? You're scaring me. You don't sound like yourself at all." Callie pressed the phone to her ear and felt the hair rise along her forearms.

"He said you couldn't be trusted. Steven told me everything about you two. I can still be so naïve sometimes, it makes me sick...."

"Why would he say that..........?" Callie's brow creased in mystified anger.

"He told me why!" Caroline cried.

Callie's blood pressure shot up and her throat clogged. *I'm sleeping and this is a Nightmare!* "He-told-you-why....?" she repeated slowly, her voice waiting for answers.

"Yes. You and Steven," Caroline whispered into the phone. "He said....."

Callie's intake of breath sounded loud in her ears. "What **about** me and Steven, Caroline? What are you trying to say?" She slumped down onto the edge of her desk as she felt a headache begin to erupt behind her eyes.

"I **told** you! You-and-Steven". The words were enunciated, clipped and low.

Callie knit her brow in confusion as a fragment of understanding dawned. The room became small and surreal.

"Yes, Steven told me!" Caroline's voice rose in pitch like a loud whisper.

".....that he and I.........? That's a lie! Caroline. A damned lie!"

"Oh Callie....." Caroline said with a loud sigh, sounding angry and hurt.

"For God's sake, will you let me speak?!!" Callie's frustration mounted.

"We will later. Right now I have to concentrate on the drug card and Canada. I let Paul push me around when we were married and I'll be damned if I'll let Steven do it too. I'm sick about this and it's turning into a monster.

"Caroline. Stop and listen to me. How can you believe..........?" Callie stuttered with frustration.

Caroline Phillip's voice sounded flat as she blew air from her lungs. "He's at the door now, Callie."

"What......" But she was talking to air. Caroline had hung up. She shook her head before replacing the receiver, staring at it for a full minute before moving from the desk. Numbness dribbled into anger as her eyes narrowed. *Something stinks at Larkspur but one of us has to make a showing. Damn. Damn. Damn. I'll go down there and play the hostess for Caroline but then I'm going to set her straight and slap Steven stupid when I see him. The lying jackass!*

A few moments later, Callie stood in the midst of the crowd, dazed and oblivious to the Pacific Northwest's miraculous sunshine and chattering people. Steady conversations reverberated through the large room, but despite the sea of faces, she felt utterly alone. Caroline's distraught words snaked through her head like yarn being clicked through a crochet hook. Closing her deep brown eyes a moment, she inhaled deeply. Her stomach hurt. Caroline's accusation put her in a fog as she felt the beautiful room close in on her.

She reached for a crystal flute of champagne and raised her bubbly glass in the air, knowing everyone expected a little speech. She stretched her lips in a semblance of a smile as her eyes moved around the room, nodding acknowledgements and raised her glass high. The room hushed around her.

"Thank you so much for being here today. I salute you! Without all of you working hard to enroll new members and your wonderful service to our current members, we would not be what we are today. Caroline Phillips couldn't be here because she was called away for a mini-crisis, but I thank you for her and all of us here at Larkspur Insurance Company. We have loads of food and unlimited champagne. Eat and drink. Today we are here to serve you and hope you always remember what a valued group of people you are to us. We can't survive without you —- our agents. Thank you."

Callie sipped the chilled Champagne, forcing the golden liquid over the lump in her throat. Agents swarmed around her and hugged her shoulders, tapped her arm or nodded their thanks over the rims of their own glasses.

"It's starting to feel like spring, Callie," Marsha Smithson murmured as she stood beside her and munched on a stuffed mushroom. "Portland in springtime is my special place to be." The woman's eyebrows arched as she munched on a pickle wrapped around a piece of ham and grinned at Callie before washing it down with champagne. "Larkspur really does treat us agents well and we appreciate you too."

Callie's brow creased as she finished the champagne and smiled at the woman; she wanted to lose herself in the crowd, so she slipped into the jostle of people wandering around her.

Portland, Oregon is called *The City of Roses*. And for good reason. Millions of roses bloomed throughout spring, summer and early fall with varieties beyond the imagination. They scented the air, in the Portland Rose Garden high above the city and in nearly every garden. More rain than sunshine was the secret. Portland had been deluged with drizzling rain for weeks; its inhabitants doled only short spurts of fickle sunshine, a sacrosanct promise of spring. But today was different. Today's bright sunlight generated a delicious spring fever as people wandered into the elegant atrium of Larkspur Health Insurance Company for the annual Broker's Cocktail Party.

Callie's chest hurt as she glanced around, saying hello and smiling to the blending of men and women who made her job worthwhile. She was a private, but positive woman, who typically faced each day as a new adventure. New faces. New hopes. New friends. But today, her fingernails raked through her silvery bangs, scraping her scalp slightly. *I can't believe I'm just standing here calmly. I feel that empty loss again just like when I lost Francois. After his death, Caroline was my rock.* She felt the first uninvited tear as her eyes filled and she swiped her cheek angrily. *I will act like an adult and I'm sure this will iron itself out. I'm taking it all too seriously.* She sniffed.

Suddenly a smiling waiter stood next to her and held the serving tray aloft, offering several flutes of sparkling champagne. Gratefully, she smiled, placed her empty one and lifted another glass, gripping the stem tightly like a friend in a storm. She squeezed her eyes shut a moment, sniffed slightly again and glanced at the chilled liquid. She stood, mesmerized by the tiny sparkling bubbles swimming in her crystal glass, then glanced up at her surroundings as she inwardly chafed at the bit, wanting to slip out unnoticed. But with Caroline missing, she knew her duty lay inside this room.

The room was large. Pale blinds, neatly pulled back from the large windows allowed the sunshine to dip and dance through the clear glass. Old Portland décor covered the walls with large photographs of the city at the turn of the century, when motorcars and streetcars littered the downtown section along Broadway. Some of the "grandfathers" of the city were easily recognized, since many local street names, schools and buildings carried their names. But Callie didn't notice any of it.

Quickly gathering momentum, the men and women gravitated toward the aromatic buffet table and hovered there as black-coated waiters materialized in various corners of the room. The sound of ice clinking against crystal ricocheted in the room amid buzzing conversations. But Callie heard only her own mind chatter.

No! Her mind screamed defiantly. *This isn't like Caroline at all.* She was angry at her childish reaction. Instead of the professional she had become, she felt like she was twelve. *Caroline.* Her friend who had always been there for her in the past through what they'd jokingly called 'thick or thin'.

A loud thundering in her ears gave her pause as she glanced out the sun-streaked windowpanes. But there was no thunder. No dismal rain. "Thick or thin....." she murmured, shaking her head mutely, eyes far off as her heart beat thickly within her chest.

Callie turned with a start when she felt a warm hand on her arm.

"Are you talking about yourself? You are hardly **thick**." The deep, cajoling voice cut into her thoughts, a chiding seesaw-sound, followed by quiet laughter.

Smiling slightly into her glass, she took a deep breath and turned toward the man in front of her. His kind eyes stared into hers, delving into her soul. She closed her eyes and sipped some champagne. "Hello Derek."

"Hellooooo...? I see a 'doe in the headlight look' on your face, lady." Derek stared at her, waiting for her normally-quick response.

She laughed softly, made a miserable attempt at a smile, and glanced around as if she'd been dreaming earlier and Caroline was nearby. She felt his closeness and strained away from him, leaning into her aloneness again. *Please don't be so nice. My heart is still broken in so many pieces. I just want to be alone....and I want to leave.*

Derek Leander saw no encouragement on her pale face, and continued in soft chatter, his voice deeper. "I have never seen you look so pale and lost, Callie. Anything I can say or do to make you feel better?" His gray-green eyes waited. A look of dismay and a faint sad smile touched her features in response.

Callie shook her head slightly and patted Derek's arm. "Thanks, Derek, but I'm fine." She fought tears, nodded imperceptibly in his direction, and moved away, leaving him with a thoughtful look on his face as he tracked her with his eyes.

She glanced back at him and liked what she saw but knew better than to entertain the idea of allowing a man into her private life. *What private life*, she wondered?

Derek Leander wasn't a tall man, standing at 5'9" in his stocking feet and weighing 175 when he was soaking wet. However, his confident stance emphasized the force of his thighs, the slimness of his hips and his athletic physique belied his small stature. A swath of wavy dark hair fell casually on his forehead, curling just slightly. His eyes continued to follow her as he slipped his hand inside the pocket of his smooth, expensive suit pants and studied the back of her head.

Leaving San Diego had been difficult for him, since he'd left a grown daughter behind and friends he'd cultivated over twenty years. But despite his initial despair at leaving southern California, being the eternal optimist, he'd moved to Oregon six months earlier to be near his ailing father. It hadn't taken them long to regain the closeness they had always shared and his new life grew more appealing every day.

The opening at Larkspur fit his needs as their Internet Web-site guru, and it was a nice surprise and very comforting to see his old college roommate, Steven Roget in the management team. He hadn't quite believed the coincidence of being part of his world again. Thirty years was a long time to lose track of someone and he saw some changes in Steven that perplexed him off and on, almost like there were two Stevens. One was a nice guy and one lost and angry.

However, it was like coming home when he saw his office and the knowledge that his father was just across town. It seemed right. His new co-workers made him feel welcome from the start. Especially Callie Beauvais. He was warmed by the camaraderie he'd immediately felt upon first meeting her and the impact she seemed to have on others. His thoughts slipped around her. He could see her in his mind's eye when he'd first met her; a friendly woman with a quick smile and a great sense of humor, she greeted people with "Good morning" first, before she allowed business to enter their conversation. She'd actually hold her hand out in front of her like a time out gesture in a football game if someone tried talking business without first saying, 'hello.' She was just so damned nice and that intoxicating smile.... His mind wandered and he admitted that having his office near hers was an added incentive to begin his workdays.

Derek felt a spurt of uneasiness flow through him. *Something is definitely dampening her spirit. I wonder what's fueled such sadness today.* Now, watching her worm her way through the crowd in the large room, he saw that she spoke to no one, but instead, walked purposefully toward the large double doors. Then, he caught and studied her reflection in the floor-to-ceiling mirror and grimaced at the pain etched on her features. Her nutmeg-colored hair was short and curly, with a natural silver streak woven through fluffy bangs that hugged her forehead. Dark eyes sparkled beneath long eyelashes that appeared much too long to be real and her sun-kissed complexion was jotted with freckles. She pursed her pink lips tightly as she passed through the doorway, and shook her head slowly as if to be rid of a fleeting shudder. Then she was gone.

He wanted to follow her. Instead, he sighed and lifted a second wineglass off the passing waiter's tray. Nodding his thanks before taking a slow sip of the amber liquid, he stared at the empty doorway and knew in his gut that his attentions would not be appreciated. He lifted his glass in a silent salute. *Another time then*, he mused.

Callie sucked in her breath, waved at a man giving her the high sign and escaped the crowd and Derek, relieved. *I don't want him to touch my heart. I can't. His proximity makes me feel way too warm. My God, there I go again, sounding like a kid. I wonder when and IF I'll ever really feel like an adult?* She snorted an instant as a stabbing pain pinched her head and a great heaviness invaded her body. She moved quietly down the long hallway and away from the noisy party sounds. *I have to get to Caroline and set her straight. That damned lying Steven!*

Caroline's disjointed words seared into her mind again as she slipped back to her office as unobtrusively as possible. Lifting her black-leather purse, she shut down her computer and shuddered involuntarily before rushing blindly toward the elevator and her car. Mentally struggling to understand the conversation she'd had with Caroline made her throat tight and pressure build in her throat. *Why would Steven lie to Caroline? She never misses making an appearance. It's so important to her. She loves that part of her job. He must have been madder than hell. He's been acting so weird lately. Sometimes he can be such an ass. I can't believe she fell for his line in the first place. Not Caroline, woman of the world. And, why today and that bald-faced lie??* Callie's questions cascaded around each other, begging for answers.

She forced order to her jumbled thoughts by ticking off the high points in her brain as she shifted her little red car out of the basement parking lot. Callie was Supervisor of Sales and Caroline was the CEO of Larkspur Insurance Company and they made a fine team. Making decisions for their covered members as a group, and working closely with their agents and brokers, Caroline had always backed Callie's ideas wholeheartedly until Steven joined the company two years earlier. Callie's thoughts faltered at the coincidences that niggled at her mind. *Steven. Why would he make this kind of trouble? The possible merger was nearing signature time and he was a minor stockholder.* She tried to steal her mind from tossing the blame into his corner but his name kept popping into her head like a ball ricocheting back and forth in a wild tennis match. She saw softness sneak out of his overall snotty attitude sometimes, but more often, his actions revealed a hard chameleon-type stranger. *And Caroline fell for him like a ton of bricks with his smooth-talking ways and good looks.*

How in the hell could Caroline think I was after Steven? She knows I shy away from relationships like the plague. She knows me! Their friendship spanned three decades and it was the one thing Callie had always been absolutely sure of. A complete trust that today shook and trembled. *Caroline just wasn't herself and this whole thing is absurd. Her professionalism always dictates her actions and that's why she is so perfect for Larkspur. She makes people sit up and listen, takes stock and makes things happen.*

Her mind rambled as she drove away from the building. *I always assumed Steven liked me; we've spent a lot of time together, but it was always just business. It wasn't **like** that. Cripes!! Why are relationships so hard to understand and enjoy? That's why I don't need one,* she thought as she reemphasized the promise she'd made several years earlier. *Francois. He made me feel complete and at home with myself. Oh, God, I miss him more than I can believe. I won't go there. Why did you take the boat out that day? You knew the storm was coming fast.* Her mind screamed her anger and veered away from the past as she headed toward Caroline's. *And then losing Mom the next month.....* Today, missing her mother sliced across her brain and meshed with the pain swirling around inside her head. *Don't cry! I refuse to cry! Caroline can't really believe this. Steven's not even my type. Well,* she thought shortly, *what IS my type? What a bunch of golden crap!* Her stomach shook with anxiety and frustration.

Callie drove north on Twelfth and then east on Alder, heading toward the Morrison Bridge where it crossed the wide Willamette River. Oblivious to the charming view she always enjoyed, she kept her eyes glued to her windshield and sped across its span. *I won't lose hope in a friendship I've always trusted.* She tossed the possibility out the window as she rolled it down to let in the spring-like air cool her face. She took a deep breath. She smelled the river and saw boat traffic below, idly wondering what it would feel like to be down there with the wind blowing through her hair in wild abandon. She was surprised at the soft image, since she had not been in a boat since Francois died.

Despite her resolve, ready tears brimmed and flowed down her cheeks and great shuddering sobs rushed up from deep inside. Her chin quivered and her soft contacts swam in her eyes. Sniffing deeply, she pulled over onto the shoulder of McLoughlin Blvd. and killed the engine. Swallowing big gulps of air, she pulled out one of her mother's hankies from her purse and wiped her face. "I won't stand for this stupidity," she yelled, hitting the steering wheel as she reached for the ignition again.

Tense emotion reeked through her Audi, when her cell phone rang, startling in the stillness. She placed her shaking palm over her heart, cleared her throat and forced normalcy to her voice. "Callie Beauvais" she answered woodenly.

"Callie. It's Steven. I *think* I just shot him."

"You THINK you just shot him, Caroline? My God!!" Callie could hear Caroline crying and Steven yelling in the background and her mind froze a bump. "I'm on my way now and I'm not far away." Swiping at the tears on her face, she blew her nose loudly, stunned at the turn of events as curiosity married fear and she listened breathlessly.

"YES —- hurry. He's going to hurt me. Cal, I just know it."

"Oh God, Caroline —— I'm coming————-." She tossed the phone onto the passenger seat as she heard two sharp blasts. *My phone's still on!! And that wasn't my car backfiring!* Horrified, her foot slipped off the accelerator, then quickly adjusted as she tromped down again and sped toward the Milwaukie Avenue exit, raced a few more blocks, twisted the wheel right onto Carlyle and left on 13th. Her little car careened into Caroline's driveway at 40 mph, bumping the edge of the curb, jerking her body like a rag doll and banging her head into the headliner. Oblivious, she downshifted quickly, slammed her gearshift into park, and ripped the door open as the little car rocked wildly on its tires. Then, fed by adrenaline, she slammed the door and fled at a dead run toward Caroline's front door.

Skipping up the sixteen cedar steps, the faint perfume of lilacs slid past her as she reached for the door. Dismayed, she found it wouldn't open; everything was silent. Rushing around to the bay window, she looked into the living room, shading her eyes with her hand. *Now what? Call 911. That's it. Why didn't I do that first?* She screamed inwardly. Blindly, she rushed to the car, grabbed her cell phone, and frantically dialed 911.

At the sound of a woman's disembodied voice on the other end, Callie managed to beg for help in barely controlled sentences.

"Please remain in your car, ma'am. You should see the police and an ambulance right away." *Ok. The ambulance and police. That's good. That's good. Soon.*

A few seconds later, frustration fueling her movements, her hand jerked the car's handle upward and she bolted for the house once again. *Remain in my car? Hell no, I can't remain in my car.*

Lunging toward the front door a second time, she rammed herself against it and pushed hard with the palm of her hand. The heavy, leaded glass door lurched open, stunning her momentarily. She grabbed the knob before it banged against the wall fearing the noise and the broken glass. *I was so sure it was locked!*

She heard a whimpering sound and realized it was her own. She immediately lifted her left hand to her mouth to muffle the noise she couldn't harness and tiptoed across the parquet flooring. Reaching the tufted carpeting, she tentatively touched the handrail leading upstairs and craned her neck upward. *Damn. Are they up there? I can't see anything.* Her mind raced. *How could such turmoil all happen in one day? It's as surreal as a movie.*

She paused only a moment in indecision as she fought more unbridled tears and quietly toed off each of her shoes. *That's it——I'm going up there.* Straightening her shoulders and bending slightly forward, she began a quiet ascent; each step calculated and deliberate, her heart raced near her throat and short, gasping breaths made her body quake. Suddenly, upon hearing the blessed sound of sirens, she lunged up the last three steps in one giant leap. The view at the landing when she turned the corner stopped her cold.

"A good head and a good heart are always a formidable combination."
— Nelson Mandela

Chapter 2

✳ ✳ ✳

Caroline's strawberry blond head lay against the wooden doorframe, one leg bent and the other splayed crookedly in front of her. Blood trickled down her forehead and one cheek; a bruise darkening her right eye and cheek bone. She was alone. Eyes closed. Her body still. Callie glanced around quickly before bolting to her friend's side and fell swiftly to her knees. She cradled the pale head into her neck and shoulder, as her sobs reached up and filled the air between them.

"Callie......I can't...."

Callie jerked her head back quickly and stared down at her friend. "You're alive!" she whispered brokenly. As soon as the words left her mouth, she saw Caroline's gray eyes fill with fear and focus beyond Callie's left shoulder, nodding her head in warning.

Alarm knifed through Callie, realizing she wasn't alone after all. She twisted around slowly and took a deep breath before feeling an unnerving calm invade her body.

"Well...........if it isn't little *Pollyanna*...." a deep voice barked.

"Steven! What have you done? Why have you hurt her like this??" Callie turned toward Caroline again in a protective gesture that wasn't lost on the man behind them.

"Aren't we just full of questions, *Ms. Beauvais?*," he sneered as he studied her.

Callie stared at him and shook her head in disgust. Steven Roget was over six feet tall and athletically fit. His dark blonde hair fell over his forehead, which usually had the appearance of hair-salon perfection. But not today. Sunshine glinted off his hair from the hall's skylight, making it gleam like dark gold as he advanced on the two women slowly, towering over them. Blood was spreading along his pants leg near the knee. Dragging his right leg painfully, he pushed deeply against his left side with the palm of his hand. Her heart sank as she saw the small silver gun held limply in his other hand. She glimpsed uneasiness and a fleeting sadness in his eyes. As he advanced, she gripped Caroline close to her chest and smiled as she heard the sirens screeching in the background.

"What did you do —— involving the police? Damn. *SHE* shot *ME*. *I'm* the victim here.... I just tried to stop her from......" His blue eyes sparked as he moved his gun to his forehead and closed his eyes in a brief display of uncertainty.

"....Steven! *STOP LYING*! You know I was just defending myself," Caroline burst out hoarsely as tears slid from the corners of her eyes. She looked at Callie and whispered, "It was his gun, Callie —- When I told him I wanted to re-write the merger contract because the Board and I didn't want to include all the LEXUS doctors, he went ballistic. He started yelling about the Midlothian Merger making us all rich ...and he was sleeping with you behind my back and....Oh, Callie," Caroline whispered urgently. "I'm sorry. I believed him for only seconds. I didn't think it out before I jumped on you. Forgive me —— He said that you and he...e...were———— and he said you wanted ———-and———-but I really KNEW wasn't true—— I I *knew* it...." The words rushed in a torrent, beseechingly. Caroline's shaking hand swiped at her running nose as she sniffed again and gripped Callie's arm tightly.

"Shut up, I can't think!" He moved the gun handle against his cheek, as if it held the answers and his face became mottled with rage as he glanced between them and the sounds drawing nearer with each second.

Callie leaned toward Caroline, "Shhh now. You're going to be all right." *Where is that ambulance that woman promised?* Her thoughts stumbled wildly. *It's taking too long.*

Caroline was getting delirious. She gripped Callie's arm again and mumbled, "The stairs are bouncing around.... and I'm cold, Cal————————so cold."

"Shut up, Caroline!" Steven yelled again and stood directly over them, his gray- striped suit bloody and soiled. His rasping voice and flushed face spoke volumes as he jerked his pale, maroon tie to half mast. He used his gun hand to pull it free from his pale shirt as his eyes pinned the women with an unblinking blue stare.

"*YOU* shut up, Steven. What is going on with you? Are you so money hungry that you'd beat up a defenseless————?"-?" Callie questioned his sanity edged with panic, as she sat on the floor beside Caroline, and tried to articulate recently-learned Tae Kwon-Do martial-art moves.

"*DEFENSELESS!!!?*" he shouted. "You call her defenseless? Hell, she was pushing me OUT and I worked hard to get the Board to let Midlothian IN. What's wrong with letting a few HMO docs get added to the plan? What could it really hurt? AND it's worth thousands, maybe millions and she GETS COLD FEET. Everyone knows with the cost of prescriptions skyrocketing, there's money being made and I intend to have my share. The

Ace-Deer prescription contract would be the icing on the cake!" Angrily shaking the gun in their faces, Steven's out-of-control ranting echoed in the hallway.

Suddenly, stomping feet running up the front steps drew his attention away from the women for an instant and Callie angrily kicked her right foot straight into the bloodiest part of his pant leg.

"Aaaargh........." He hissed and rammed downward, slicing the air with his gun.

His blotchy face, now so alien to the women, made Callie's breath catch, but she was faster than he was; jerking out of his way, she twisted around on her butt. Shooting her legs out in front of her in a fighting stance, as she'd been taught to do in her new Tae Kwon-Do classes, she fought back rhythmically. She never imagined in her wildest dreams that she would be tested so soon and the reality of the situation shot adrenaline through her like a cannon ball at the front lines.

'Don't try anything wild, Callie,' Master Bettencourt had admonished her only the week before, 'you know just enough to be dangerous—- to yourself!!' Regardless of Master Bettencourt's instructions, she kept kicking wildly as men's voices penetrated through Steven's bellowing. Feeling a sudden burst of energy spawned by anger and frustration, she gulped a lungful of air and screamed down the stairwell, "COME HELP US!!!" Her kicking feet continued to pummel Steven as naturally as if she'd already earned her black belt.

Steven recoiled from her piston punches and felt a purple haze overtake him as he lunged forward to strike back. The barrel of his gun inadvertently struck the crown of her anklebone, eliciting a crunching noise. A hideous pain shot up her leg. Clenching her jaw, her eyes drilled holes into him. "You are absolutely cuh—-**razy**...." She yelled.

"Oh no, I'm not! I just wanted...." He faltered a second. "*Callie*, stop —— I really don't want to hurt you too!" His voice sounded almost tearful as he turned quickly toward her as she staved off the blackness that promised to engulf her.

Then, suddenly losing his footing in their tangled legs, he fell against them. In the melee, trying to right himself with his outstretched hand, the gunmetal tip of the silver gun slammed into Callie's cheekbone and instant pain blanked out the sounds of Caroline's scream. As Caroline yanked Callie away from Steven, Callie fought for lucidity, despite the excruciating pain in her wet face and she sluggishly wondered if it was tears or blood.

The abrupt movement ripped through both of them and Caroline cried out suddenly, as her legs, purple and oddly swollen, sent spiraling, painful jabs upward into her hips. Despite her aching contortion, Caroline continued to hug Callie in a caring embrace, her curling fingers spasmodically digging into her arms. As fear invaded Callie's senses for another wild moment, she stared at her friend's legs again. *Oh my God!*

Suddenly, the blessed sound of long-overdue footsteps thumped up the stairs and a stranger's clipped words were tossed around like angry pistons. "Lady....are you .....? Hey, mister..... Look out!.....Damn it!"

Seeing the medic's white pant legs running up the carpeted stairs, Steven rushed toward them. Lunging forward, he knocked them half way back down the stairs. The men, black bag and white towels were flung into the wall as Steven vaulted past, in two wild leaps, his wounds no deterrent; blood spattered in his wake.

Simultaneously, the angry men scrambled to right themselves and stared at the open front door, temporarily dazed. "Man! Guess that's one less for us to patch up, right, Rudy?" His dark jaw clamped down tightly, his eyes flashed with outrage as he grabbed his bag and towels a second time.

The other man shook his face in alarm and spun forward as the women moaned above him. His dark eyes filled with concern as he jogged up the stairs, his big feet brushing the carpet quietly.

Sobbing quietly, Caroline stared beseechingly at Rudy, as he shook his head.

"My God, Miss." He blew out a breath. "My name is Rudy and I'm here to help you," the large man said quickly, trying to decide who to help first. Dropping to one knee, his eyes moved rapidly from one to the other; he painstakingly calculated the damage as he performed standard triage procedures with clinical and compassionate attention.

Caroline tried to turn her head in his direction, but a searing pain convulsed her. Instead, without moving her head, she swung her eyes toward Callie and disengaged one of her legs to ease the pain in her own.

"Get the leg splints, Mason," he said, anxiously. "It looks like we'll need two before we can get them into the ambulance."

Mason was skinny and agile, with black hair as curly as an SOS pad. His caring mocha face reappeared almost instantly, his smile gentle. He began wrapping wounds to prepare the women for moving as Rudy ran back downstairs, looking for the phone.

"Send the police to 3075 S.E. 13th. Yes, directly across from the school. FAST. We have a gun-toting man on the loose. He's been shot. Yes." He paused, listening. "Blonde hair, about 6 feet tall, gray suit, pink shirt, tie flying loose. Yep. Real professional looking but he just victimized two women. We're here now. He just ran out the door and since he's been shot there should be a nice bloody path to follow. Yes. My name's Rudy Stocker, Riverside Ambulance. Oh, wait! I hear the police sirens outside now —- Thanks!'"

Caroline's legs throbbed and shock settled around her again. "Callie, are you ok?" Caroline whispered near Callie's ear and brushed dark, curly hair off her friend's forehead. Straining to see her face, her own pain slowing her movements, she waited for an answer.

Pain stabbing through her head, glazed eyes looked at Caroline. She tried to smile. *My friend's back—— - A good heart and a good head.* "I'm ok. Through thick and thin…Caro….” Closing her eyes a moment, she felt Mason prod her ankle softly. Then everything went black.

"Some cause happiness wherever they go; others whenever they go."
—Oscar Wilde

Chapter 3

✳ ✳ ✳

Six months later.

Callie heard a click and lifted her head as Caroline poked her heart-shaped face around the corner of her office door, "How about a latte across the street with a bowl of Three Lion's famous Hungarian Mushroom Soup? I'm buying. I have good news about the merger..."

"You're on," Callie answered with a warm smile as she closed the file she'd been studying and grabbed the sweater slung over the loveseat beside her. "You sure are walking better, my friend." She felt good about the advancements they'd both made as they continued to heal, each trying to release their own measured anger.

Caroline nodded. "I'm trying to toss the cane and still going to that masochistic physical therapist three times a week. Lord, I'm sick of this but you know what? I am really starting to feel better and my nightmares have nearly stopped." Caroline gripped the wooden handle of the cane and stabbed the floor for emphasis, making a dimple in the hallway carpet.

The mention of nightmares invited a quiet moment in shared retrospection before Callie spoke. "He's still in jail, honey. He will be for some time. You know that. And I think of him too —— every time I push my foot into these low, ugly shoes."

"Yes —- I know what you mean,"" she looked down at Callie's ankle, still slightly swollen and grimaced, "but it doesn't take away the sadness, or the fact that I was so dimwitted. He appeared to be such a nice guy and how he could manipulate me that way. ..... You'd think my constant fight for independence living with Paul for so many years meant nothing. I should take a page out of your book and stay clear of the animals."

"We are just human, after all, aren't we? Come on, Caro — let's eat." The elevator whirred to a stop and their stomachs rumbled, halting further conversation.

Three Lions Bakery was nestled into the corner of S.W. 12th and Morrison Streets, an eatery frequented by locals and tourists. Its European atmosphere and French pastries were well known and its proximity to the Metropolitan Area Transit light rail, known as "MAX", enticed everyone with its aromas, crunchy breads and mouth-watering pastries for a short break or lingering lunch. The counter's glass cases were filled with difficult choices; stuffed croissants filled with a number of meats, cheeses and tomato-pesto. The espresso machine hummed all day. On Friday afternoons, pastry items were sold at half-price and the line of people snaked around the corner and down the sidewalk like a drunken acrobat. Someone from their office managed to sneak down weekly since chocolate croissants were their weakness. They froze well and the microwave melted the chocolate to drooling expectancy on Monday mornings.

The enveloping aroma of coffee and hot bread buffeted their senses as the women stepped through the glass doors and foraged for space inside. Sitting down at the small round table covered with white linen and smelling the fresh-baked croissants, pastries and cookies should have taken their mind off their earlier conversation. But it didn't.

"I'll have a non-fat, single latte and a bowl of your Hungarian soup with those delicious herb sticks, Lou." Caroline handed him the unopened menu, and linked her hands under her chin, propped her elbows on the small bistro table, and looked at Callie. Smiling, she crossed her legs automatically, and then grimaced as the pain shot upward. "Damn, I keep forgetting." Settling herself again, she felt the comfort of the room and glanced at the new artwork displayed on each wall with interest.

Lou chuckled and noted the order as he gave both women napkins and glasses of iced water, a slice of lemon dancing inside. "What about you, Callie?" he said, turning and smiling at her, pen poised and writing before she opened her mouth. His apron looked clean but smelled of garlic and bread. He pulled two paper-wrapped breadsticks from his large pocket and placed them between the women. "For starters," he said and slipped away toward the kitchen.

"One of these days I'm going to surprise you, Lou." Callie called after him, as she reached for the iced water and arched her eyebrows above the rim of the glass. She felt it drip onto the table in front of her as she chuckled, "But not today."

Lou laughed at their predictability as he slid behind the cook's galley to process their order. He'd managed the bakery café a long time and enjoyed the camaraderie with his new and favorite regular customers.

"One of these days I'll surprise him and order one of those fat croissants stuffed with meat and a plate of those chocolate cookies or a cream puff and a triple latte. Maybe that will wipe that smirk off his face."

"Callie." Caroline interrupted with comfortable laughter in her voice.

"Yes?" Chocolate-brown eyes returned to settle on dusky gray.

"As I was saying....Obviously I have thought about Steven a lot, and I know I should get rid of these angry embers ripping through me. Someone told me once that twenty minutes of unwanted stress subtracted twenty four hours from one's life." Head shaking, she inhaled deeply. "If that's true, I'm on my last leg." Her eyes widened, "no pun intended. And you know I dread every birthday as I fight this old-age stuff..."

Callie chuckled. "You were vulnerable, Caro — at a time when you were free to do as you pleased after divorcing Paul. Your kids are on their own...... and besides, you deserved to have some fun. And Steven gave it to you. Remember, you did have fun with the man. It's just that we couldn't see through him. I truly think he went a little insane. You weren't alone; I was duped too. It was like he was schizophrenic or something. And what about Derrick?" She crumpled her napkin and brushed the breadcrumbs off her skirt.

"Yes," Caroline smiled and looked imploringly at her friend. "What *about* Derrick? He spends quite a lot of time in your doorway and your face lights up when you see him. If you didn't realize I noticed, well —- I did."

"Just friends," Callie responded quickly. "Besides we are talking about Derrick's disappointment in Steven and their long friendship. He told me the other day that Steven called him. He's in therapy and professes sorrow for ...well..... for all he put us through and he's been trying to get an early release. He has to call collect and not many people will accept the call to talk to him, I guess. So, Derrick lets him talk." Callie carefully smoothed out the napkin again, as if trying to push out the wrinkles of her anger.

"Well, I do not want to ever see the man again. I hope he stays in the full year!" Caroline's voice was clipped and her features hardened. "You know I'm not one to hold grudges but between Paul and Steven. Well, let's just say I'm making an exception." The freedom she enjoyed since divorcing her husband had laid her feelings bare and the rawness didn't disappear easily. Eyes on the table, she crunched down on the rest of her bread stick and watched pieces fly across the table to scatter onto the floor.

"Caroline. I know. What news did you have to share about the merger?" Callie asked, determined to change the subject. Her own broken ankle and injured cheekbone had some complications and discussing Steven over lunch was not her idea of a good time. No more high heels for her; at least not for some time and low pumps even hurt her. *Would this swelling ever go away? And when can I chew a steak again with this jaw?*

"Yes, the Midlothian Merger." Caroline smiled wanly and accepted her latte as they clicked their cups and saluted one another with outstretched arms.

"Well? Tell me! Now what happens?" Her features became more animated.

"Okay. The Board is meeting this afternoon. The LEXUS HMO group still wants to be involved but we have a new slant and some great ideas since Derrick's involvement as the newest Board member. They are going to discuss how it would work if we changed our insurance company status from "company" to "plan." What that means is that we can offer health insurance to our members through Larkspur Health *Plan* and still retain the existing providers as our participating network."

"Then we don't need LEXUS at all?" Callie rushed at her.

"We are not forced to utilize the LEXUS group within our own health plan. But, this is the great part, Callie. We don't have to use all of the LEXUS providers. We pick and choose doctors to fill vacant holes in our current provider network."

"So we won't be locked into LEXUS then?" Callie's thoughtful smile lingered.

"That's right. This way, competing insurance carriers can "rent" LEXUS as well. And we don't have to worry about their questionable practices having a negative aspect on the marketplace." Caroline sat back and smiled as she sipped her latte, burning her upper lip slightly. "Whew! Lou boiled it this time. What do you think?"

"So you mean LEXUS doctors would be a network of providers that we would just use to offer specific docs and facilities, without contracting with the whole LEXUS crew so we can cull out the ones we don't want to be associated with in the beginning?"

Caroline nodded, blew on her latte and took another tentative sip.

"Oh —- I like it. Yes, our agents will like it too because they'd have the ability to offer some of the docs on other carrier's plans and we'd still retain groups with our own docs. Derrick thought of this?" Her smile broadened in approval.

"Yes. Inter-Web, the internet company he worked with in San Diego, was involved in procuring agreements between providers and insurance carriers and setting up the documentation and differentiating between the Commercial, Indemnity and Self-Insuring providers. Their company also did a check and balance report to ensure all the criteria was met in the testing processes before a provider was allowed to join any network. We liked the idea and with his Internet experience, we are seriously thinking of asking him to help us form and monitor our new HMO network. It's to our advantage to get a move on and allow us to gain a better foothold in the insurance community and updating all of it onto our Larkspur web site."

"But we're already bullish on HMOs. What————-?"

"I know. I know. We've always wanted to create a competitive method of delivering healthcare but not at the expense of our members. All this negative hype on television and other news media bites my butt because they generalize and downgrade all HMOs and you know Larkspur's mission statement." Caroline slapped the table with emphasis as she finished her diatribe. "Steven didn't know what he was talking about."

"I know. We act as a third party payer who sets up the contractual agreements with the physicians and hospitals on one hand and offer the benefits on the other," she said thoughtfully. Callie moved aside, allowing Lou to set her steaming bowl of soup down and accepted the second paper-wrapped herb sticks happily. "Oh, these smell good!"

"They are good. I just dipped them in my soup back there and tried one myself. Try it. By the way, you are both going to have birthdays soon, so I'll have free chocolate croissants in the case…" Lou was proud of the good food he served and his friendship with the women, so he hovered and lifted a questioning eyebrow at them, cocking his head.

"Yes," the women responded simultaneously and laughed at each another.

"Free croissants! I don't count birthdays anymore, Lou, but for you, I'll make an exception," Caroline said in an aside whisper.

Callie's eyebrows lifted to meet Lou's broad wink.

As they ladled hot soup into their mouths and crunched on bread sticks, their minds wandered back to Steven's ranting about the prescription issue. It was a day riveting their brains with unanswered questions.

Moving the bread around in her mouth thoughtfully, Callie glanced through the glass windows at the leafy, green trees and brightly colored blue and yellow pansies. Their little faces smiled from their giant, colorful cement pots around trees planted in the wide sidewalk. *It's almost like being in Paris. Mmmmm. French bread, a latte in my hand and potted flowers. Oh, I do miss Provence, Cendrine, the family…and….* She paused, smiling to herself as she ladled another spoonful of soup. Caroline's words broke into her reverie.

"Callie. A favor?" She laughed as she saw Callie's spoon stop mid-stream.

"Oh, oh. Do I want to hear this, Caro? Her face cracked into a Vivian-Vance smile as if listening to a nutty Lucille Ball. She watched Caroline pause. "What is it?"

"Absolutely." She snorted. "I'd like you to be the keynote speaker at the next agent's meeting." She watched Callie's eyes squint toward her.

"You know I'm not fond of public speaking and I do it very reluctantly." Callie said through a mouthful of bread. She continued to chew slowly. "What's the subject?

"The prescription war." Caroline stated with fervor.

Callie drew her eyebrows together and pursed her lips. "Hummmpf…oh boy."

"I know. I know… but you work closest to your reps and the agents and get feedback from them monthly with employer annual group plan renewals and the pharmacy costs keep skyrocketing, nearly doubling! Our premium rates have reflected a minimal 17% increase on top of their annual increase due to claims experience. How many more times can we ask our agents to tell employers our cost of doing business increased so we have to share the rate increases with them?" Caroline's eyebrows winged meaningfully and her gray eyes blinked before focusing again.

"Well, you are right about that, Caroline. Our persistency rate isn't as good as it once was but don't you think the merger with LEXUS —— at least how you outlined it — will make an impact on the prescription costs?" Callie finished her soup and set it aside, placed her hands on the table and folded them, waiting.

Caroline took a deep breath. "We got a copy of a letter today. A homegrown Oregonian now living in Virginia wrote the letter. Her husband is on Medicare. The man has arthritis and takes a generic medication called Meclofenamate. He's taken the medication for over twenty years. But that's not the main issue." She sipped her coffee.

"In 2004 they paid $65 for 500 pills at the old Drug Emporium, now Longs Drugs by Washington Square. Then they moved to Virginia and in 2005, he was quoted by six different pharmacies for the same number of pills between $106 and $250 around Williamsburg. She even called Longs Drugs here in Portland and they told her it increased from $65 to $100. That is a ridiculous cost differential. In just one year? I want to know why. We aren't the only insurance carrier who's facing this problem. This morning, I called the woman and you know what else I found out? The pharmacy that sold her 500 pills for $106 in 2005 was recently purchased by another drug chain. That same prescription will now cost them $225. That is absolutely unacceptable. I want NAHU to help us fight this."

"NAHU is the association for health underwriters for the *agent* community," Callie said slowly, digesting Caroline's story. Her mind reeled.

"I know that, but you know what? They get things done. **You know** NAHU has their senator's ears and each state has their local health underwriters association. Invariably there are agents in each association with good senator relationships who make sure our issues are heard. **You know** they meet annually at a Capitol Conference in Washington, DC. They meet in groups with their senators and **you know** they have their own lobbyist— — if they can afford one. Portland's lobbyist used to work for Blue Health and she is excellent. She has a funny name .....hummmm, I can't remember it now. So, you see? We must show the agent community that this is our war too."

Callie laughed aloud at Caroline's earnestness. "Hey, lady, you're preaching to the choir. I'll do it. I'll *do* it."

Caroline reached over and squeezed Callie's hand. "I knew I could count on you. It's Tuesday at the MAC club, 7:30 a.m., with breakfast. Now back to the other matter."

"What other matter, Caro?"

"Derrick."

Callie's dark eyes studied Caroline thoughtfully before she scraped her chair backward against the wooden floor. Averting Caroline's eyes, she reached for her purse, "Another time for that one. I'm not ready to discuss my feelings for him," she whispered, face flushed.

"So you *do* admit having feelings for him?" Caroline grabbed her own purse and cane, turned around to follow Callie out of the café, and nearly ran into Derrick Leander as he raised his arm in mock surrender.

"Hello ladies. Fancy meeting you here," he drawled while swinging his eyes toward Callie.

Blushing, Callie's eyes grew wide as she turned a questioning glance toward Caroline.

Caroline shrugged her shoulders in response and side stepped the patrons waiting for their table.

Smiling a nervous goodbye toward Derrick, they both moved toward the door.

"Well," Derrick whispered. "Well, well, well —." Clutching his turkey croissant and coffee, he walked toward the narrow cement benches at the MAX turnaround on 11th Avenue. The light rail train had just departed down Yamhill Street and a breeze beneath blue skies embraced him.

An older man with scuffed shoes and socks twisted around his ankles held a newspaper in one hand while munching a hotdog with the other. Receiving an answering nod before joining him on the bench, Derrick's face split into a bemused smile. He bit into his croissant while hazy daydreams Callie inspired in him took firmer root.

"Rather fail with honor than succeed by fraud
—Sophocles

Chapter 4

✳ ✳ ✳

The Multnomah Athletic Club, commonly known as the MAC club, is situated in S.W. Portland near Larkspur's offices. Its elite membership had access to swimming, tennis, workout rooms, a lounge and two separate restaurants. First-class meeting rooms were strewn along the two floors offering catered food and all the amenities required for conferences and meetings, large or small.

In the past, Callie and Caroline had shared an exuberant walk with other staff members. Not today. Their still-healing injuries continued to confine their movements to cars or MAX. Despite an Oregon drizzle slowing her down, Callie arrived at 7:15 to find Caroline already near the podium talking to her secretary, Lana. She was arranging papers with one hand while taking quick sips of steaming coffee with the other, blonde hair bent close to pale red.

Callie watched Caroline sip her black coffee while jotting notes and scanning papers in front of her. Looking like a model, with her short-blonde hair hugging her face and diamond studs in her ears, Caroline Phillips exemplified her CEO status, exuding both a provocative and seriousness to her demeanor. Despite shoving her reading glasses up onto the bridge of her nose every few seconds, she endeared others to her with her quirky elegance. Her firm control at the monthly forums always filled the room to capacity with independent agents who arrived, eager to listen to Larkspur's meaty agendas. Now, Caroline's gray eyes scanned the room quickly, before bending toward Lana.

Well my friend. You'd think I'd be used to speaking in front of all these people, but oooooh—— nono. Pondering the food table, Callie felt butterflies as big as birds dive bomb inside her stomach. The delicious aromas intensified her hunger and her stomach yawned. Smiling at the older woman in front of her, she reached for the stack of warm ceramic plates.

"This is a great way to start the day, Mona, but if I did it every day, I'd be in bigger trouble than I am already," she said as she speared a large, nutty-bran muffin, bite-size pieces of cantaloupe, huge strawberries, bananas, scrambled eggs and tiny pieces of ham. She reluctantly bypassed the bacon and frosted breakfast rolls.

"I know you enjoy your daily walks, Callie." The woman glanced downward. "When's the ankle going to let you get back to it?"

"I wish I knew, my friend. I wish I knew."

"Good luck then. This food's burning a hole in my plate." The woman laughed softly and moved away from the string of men and women waiting their turn in line.

All I need is to add more beef to these hips. Yes... If only I can start walking again! My skirts are getting snug. But, dammit! It's hard to pass up sweets and my glass of wine in the evenings. It used to be so much easier to keep the weight off.... I hope I can hold all this food down when I get up to the podium. Her mind rambled. She glanced around for an empty chair before seeing Caroline pointing her finger vigorously to the front table. Callie nodded, smiled at her agents and Larkspur employees as she balanced her breakfast plate and wove her way to the front of the room. "Whew. Made it! Now, I need coffee!"

Lana reached for the pot and placed it into Caroline's outstretched hand. She poured the hot, steaming black coffee into Callie's cup and squeezed her shoulder. "You can do it, kid. You always sound relaxed even if we know you aren't."

Callie rolled her eyes at Caroline. Forcing nonchalance, she dug into her breakfast like a football player eating his last meal before Super Bowl. Eyes trained on the food, she ignored the barrage of nerves doing the tango within.

"It looks like Callie hasn't eaten for a week," Lana joked, eyes filling with warmth before flattening momentarily. She breathed deeply, her face strained, troubled.

Caroline laughed. "She still stays skinny too."

"Yes, it's rather disgusting." Lana forced a smile.

Callie grinned at their banter, as she chewed silently, trying to stabilize the fluttering inside. Several insurance agents joined them at the large round table, keeping conversation flowing and the coffee pot empty.

Suddenly, Caroline was at the podium. *Here it comes*, Callie thought. She wiped her mouth with the linen napkin and pushed her plate aside. Moving her tongue gently to the front of her teeth, she tried to snag any leftovers. All she needed was food in her toothy smile when she faced the crowd.

"Good morning, everyone. Thank you for joining us this morning and hopefully you get enough to eat —- if you leave hungry, it's your own fault," she said with an open smile that encompassed her audience.

The crowd chuckled as they reached for coffee, juice or the remainder of their food.

Caroline's eyes scanned the room. "As you know, Larkspur is committed to providing the highest possible level of service to our agents, employer groups and members. We have focused on improving our service in recent weeks, and we believe our actions demonstrate our initial success in this area."

The group nodded in agreement and sipped coffee; their eyes trained on Caroline as she continued.

"In response to the feedback from our agents, we have recently examined some of our pharmacy policies to ensure that they are as simple and consistent as possible for our members, particularly as they initially join Larkspur and make the transition to a new pharmacy plan. We've listened to the angry arguments about Ace-Deer prescriptions."

"Well, **that's** good to hear." the man nearest the podium mumbled.

Caroline smiled and nodded toward him. "Over the past several months, we have been evaluating the future needs of the product development areas of our drug card option. Given the current market conditions and our future business needs, we have decided to make a significant change at Larkspur. Until final decisions are made, I can tell you that we will soon be a full insurance plan, utilizing our own providers. To enhance our plan, we are negotiating with a well-known network of providers. And we will add some specific specialist providers and one more hospital that will certainly boost your client's accessibility as well as, I hope, your sales."

"What about the prescription fiasco? The high rates? The messy administration that some carriers are having with Ace-Deer?" The questions were hurled toward the front as they digested her opening statements.

Caroline waited a moment, watching the men and woman nod, commenting to one another, waiting for more details. "I can't tell you more than that until the negotiations are finalized but we have listened to you and Ace-Deer is not part of the picture. Most of you know Callinda Beauvais. As Sales Director and Vice President of Larkspur's Northwest Region, I fully trust that Larkspur will continue to benefit from her optimistic approach, her unwavering commitment to Larkspur and to our members. She has demonstrated extensive knowledge, skill, and success during her long career in the health insurance industry and I am very pleased she will remain with Larkspur as we move forward in our quest for a drug card that works for everyone."

Many eyes turned toward Callie as she nodded and smiled. Derrick saw baby's-butt pink color staining her cheeks. Her youthful appearance belied the fact that she'd just turned fifty the year before. He'd heard about the fifty black balloons delivered to her office and the antics involved when she was determined to take them home in her Audi by stuffing them into the back seat and only popping one of them. *I seem to be focused on Callie a lot,* he thought. As dad would say, 'she trips my trigger.' *Damn Steven for hurting her. And, what changed him so radically?*

"Many of you know that Callie managed Sales and Marketing for eight years at Blue Health after a sabbatical in France before I lured her over to Larkspur. Callie has been a real asset for us. We tried to bring her on board several times but her loyalty to Blue Health was remarkable. I applaud loyalty, but glad our perseverance finally paid off."

Callie began to feel like a fish in a glass bowl and glared at Caroline, who got the message and invited her to join her at the podium.

Finally! Callie took a deep breath and shot a saccharin smile at Caroline. The audience's applause scattered Callie's thoughts briefly as she turned to face them. Wearing black jet earrings, a slim black skirt and polka-dot bolero that fit over a lacy chemise, she faced the bevy of faces and waited for silence.

With her heart accelerating, she glanced at the expectant crowd and gently surveyed the agents that filled the room. *I know my business and they know I know my business so relax!* With strengthened resolve, she laid Mrs. Dalton's letter down on the podium in front of her and began.

"Thank you, Caroline. Thank you, too," she murmured, smiling at the men and women who waited for her to begin. "I am going to read you a letter that we recently received. It mimics your grumbling and we've taken it to Larkspur's heart. Once I share this with you, we will tell you how we plan to fight the *prescription war*, which as you know, has been a firestone of controversy."

She watched many of her agents move slightly forward in their chairs, secretly pleased at their attention. "But first let me explain how I feel about the problem we are all facing today. Like many Americans, I have watched the pharmacy war for some time. I know the costs have risen dramatically over the past year alone for everyone, regardless of age. I have listened to my peers discuss the reasons why, as a health insurance industry, generic drugs continue to climb the ladder in cost right along with name brands."

Murmuring comments disrupted her presentation for a moment. She waited a beat before she continued. "As your liaison, we have consistently listened to pharmaceutical suppliers cry their lament over the high cost of making drugs and trying to recoup these costs by cost-sharing with the consumer. The reality is that this is big business. As such, the drug industry has helped to create an inefficient-money making system, and some doctors have added to the problem. Three specific instances put me on this soapbox even before the prescription crisis."

1 "My mother was on Medicare when she died last year. She had a sinus problem. Her PCP prescribed *Prilosec* to combat acid reflux disease. It costs about $100 for a 30-day supply. Mom didn't have acid reflux and at that time, didn't have a drug benefit. She stopped taking the pills after one week when no change occurred. The

doctor prescribed the drug to a woman without drug coverage and without regard for the cost involved to 'try'. WHY?

2 One of my seminar speakers in Washington, D.C., last spring stated that lower-priced generic drug sales hurt pharmaceutical companies because too many generics were being purchased. So, these name brand suppliers are buying out the generic suppliers. Do you know how many generic suppliers are still in business? I can count the number on one hand. Obviously the drug monopoly is alive and well.

3 Now to Mrs. Dalton's letter that was sent to our senator.

Callie read the lines, explaining the huge cost increases she'd discussed with Caroline a few days earlier and finished with the last page:

Before Part D kicked in, America penalized its senior population the moment they turned 65 by dropping Rx benefits when 52% of all drug costs were being paid out of pocket. Even if seniors could afford the monthly premium, the coverage includes a doughnut hole with no coverage. Why, as a nation, can't we revere our seniors, instead of financially crippling them? Part D helped, but we must change our priorities.

Please fight the graft that is going on in the pharmaceutical industry today by suppliers, doctors and others, Ms. Amburgey. Many seniors are being forced to choose between food and medicine. Your proposed plan hopes to fortify and renew Medicare and return the pride and independence that we have fought for nearly 300 years to win. We need help.

Sincerely, Mrs. J. Dalton"

Callie laid down the letter and removed her glasses. The room was silent for a moment before conversations erupted around her. She raised both hands to stop the flow of words cascading over her as she stared down at the expectant crowd.

"Now, you are asking what we are going to do, aren't you." As an escaping silver-streaked curl fell over her forehead, she pushed it aside and tilted her head, listening to the questions hurled in her direction.

"What about Larkspur's rates?

"This price gouging is all over America."

"Where does Larkspur stand?

"Why can't the government intervene?"

"Now we know why pharmaceutical companies keep buying out generic companies."

"How many generic companies are left now?"

The questions flooded Callie's brain. Again, she waited. She watched Derrick's attempt to soothe people around him and glanced toward her, nodding his head questioningly. She smiled at his sensitivity and shook her head against a sea of intruding feelings.

"We don't have the audacity to tell you we have all the answers. As we said, the drug industry is big business. There's no doubt about that. The sad news is that each time our actuaries do their job, you receive the renewal rates that the State Insurance Commissioner's office approves. Then, drug costs soar again and we are back where we started from. So, we'll explain what we are contemplating; Caroline?"

Caroline joined Callie at the podium.

"Thank you, Callie. How many of you wonder why prescriptions in England, Canada, Germany and Mexico are so much less expensive than we pay in America?"

A hundred voices rose in unison.

"How many of you would be interested in a select drug card available through mail order with two co-payments for a 90 day supply for all generic and name brand prescription drugs, without a strict formulary? And costs would decrease?"

Again, many voices burst forth as perplexed confusion reigned.

"I thought importing from other countries was still illegal?" Jarrod Galt asked. He was an agent from Albany concerned about his large employer groups in the Willamette Valley. "I would love the idea if it's legal but, what would it take?" His red hair stuck out in puffs; freckles covered his pale skin. His eyes held a gleam of interest.

The audience was stilled by the query before erupting in another frenzy of questions. Caroline held out her hands to quiet them.

"Jarrod, you can't possibly believe that Larkspur would offer this alternative if it wasn't legal, do you?" Caroline gripped the wooden podium and locked eyes with the man until he looked down to study his coffee cup.

Suddenly, nervous laughter escaped from those who had been thinking the same thing. Legality, of course, was of utmost concern. Even with their Errors and Omissions insurance coverage, agents and insurance carriers must be careful with the many laws and guidelines they faced daily.

Derrick stood up. Querulous eyes turned toward him, including Caroline's. He felt the intensity of the crowd as they held their breath.

His voice was low and deep, requiring the group to refrain from their whispered comments and lean toward him. Being a member of Toastmaster's had taught him to project authority and silently thanked his mentor as he began to speak. "Please let me step in for a moment, Callie and Caroline?" With their answering nods, he looked steadily all around him, making eye contact with several of the more intense questioners.

"I returned from Washington, D. C. recently. I had the letter from Mrs. Dalton with me as well as many of your comments to discuss with our senators along with our lobbyist, Tillie Tooter." Laughter caught him off guard a moment before he smiled, his eyes crinkling with humor. "The name may sound whimsical but believe me, she is an intelligent woman with a serious cause. We met with Senators Wilding and Amburgey as a team, even though they are on opposite sides of the fence. But on this issue, with the rising drug costs, they agreed with one another and went to the crux of the problem."

"Legality is our question, Derrick," he heard a man interject. Faces automatically turned toward his voice and back again, awaiting Derrick's rejoinder.

"Yes, legality. The drug cost issues have long crushed our society. When the idea first germinated for Larkspur to use a Canadian drug card, we immediately called our lawyers. Yes, it is legal with the process we chose. We are now a full-fledged insurance plan and therefore, we will soon be offering this gem to our members and Larkspur will stand apart from the marketplace." Derrick let out an audible sigh. He studied the audience's response before sitting down, pleased to see they listened intently to every word he had to say.

Caroline gently gripped the microphone and took a deep breath. "Thank you, Derrick. I know this is an entirely new concept but I'm gambling it will work. We will not pussyfoot around the issue. You will be told when the contract is signed. I promise you, this marks the first of many good things from Larkspur. Thank you for attending today and remember we intend to challenge any obstacle." She straightened to her full height of 5' 6" and felt her pores whisper steam as she banked the papers in front of her.

The occupants of the room stood up simultaneously, akin to an umbrella opened to stave off giant raindrops. Applause drowned out further conversation. Both women, still at the podium, felt their muscles relax and an excitement the applause assured, replaced their previous tension.

Minutes afterward, the room began to empty and excited voices responded to Larkspur's idea as the men and women headed in different directions to share the news.

"You did well, Callie. Thanks again." Caroline touched Callie's arm and squeezed it gently.

"Well, I'm glad it's over, Caro." Callie walked back to the table. She pressed both palms flat on the linen tablecloth and studied her gold and diamond ring before swirling the now-cold coffee in her cup. Her face softened. *Mom you would have loved being a fly on the wall today.*

"It's just beginning, honey." Caroline whispered as she gave instructions to several of her assistants and to Lana Potts, her secretary. "I need to see the serving supervisor to check the tally for their morning's breakfast statement." Caroline knew her limp was a little more pronounced than the day before, and needed some Aleve, but she left her cane propped up next to the podium nevertheless.

Lana Potts was a smart and efficient secretary. She enjoyed her job and her employer, although she'd initially fought against both. She had been happy with her management position in Salem, forty-five miles south of Portland, during her pregnancy and her fervent hope had been to remain at home when little Frankie was born. Then her world collapsed around her.

She'd been forced through Larkspur's open door in exchange for keeping her world safe. She'd kept her silence during the two years she'd been Caroline Phillip's secretary, but it was becoming increasingly difficult. She'd been pleasantly surprised to like and respect Caroline. She worked diligently to remain indispensable during the day, while cringing at the daily deceptions. But her major concern was focused on keeping her boys safe. Fear that it might not be impossible raged within her.

Today, Lana's ginger-colored hair brushed her collarbone and her greenish eyes withheld their usual sparkle. With heaving chest and shaking hands, she walked around the perimeter of the room, stopping nonchalantly at the podium. Quickly thumbing through the papers, her clear eyes followed her employer surreptitiously, noting that she was leaning on a side table while examining the cost breakdown across the room. Then, she glanced briefly toward Callie. Nobody seemed to be paying any attention to her. Then, nervousness sliced through her as she saw Derrick dodging the crowd and winding his way toward the front of the room.

Lana's heartbeat raced and stumbled. She quickly found what she was looking for and stuffed it into her day planner. Inhaling deeply, she crushed her leather binder to her breasts and moved to join the throng as they left for their various destinations.

"Every problem has a gift for you in its hands."
—Richard Bach

Chapter 5

* * *

"Okay, my intentions were good but we all know about the road to hell and all that. So, basically, I just laid another paver down on that infamous walk way." Lee Carle leaned over and pulled some papers out of his brown, worn leather briefcase before chuckling at the expression on Caroline's face.

She stared at the man blankly, brows knit.

"Hey, Caro....." Lee smiled reassuringly.

"You know, Lee, sometimes you really trip me up, even after all these years." She was thoughtful a minute as she ticked the years off on her fingers. "It's been twenty years since we worked together on that board of governor's convention in Seattle. Remember when I invited you to join the round table discussions?" She grinned at the memory.

How could I forget? Lee's mind misted. Her hair was longer then, her eyes a brighter gray, a few pounds slimmer, but still Caroline. He'd known Paul Phillips, watched her struggle with his infidelities, watched her fall apart and helped put her back together again. He was more than her legal counsel at Larkspur; he was her loyal friend and one she called her knight in **legal** armor.

She'd told him, "You can't be my knight in **shining** armor because I've learned that those knights are usually untrustworthy and invariably fall off their horses." And she'd meant it, even before Steven's duplicity.

"Yes, of course I remember and it's been a long and special friendship." *Yes, a special friendship, but.....*

Caroline studied the lean, olive-skinned man, standing at 5' 10 weighing about 185. His hair was a rich brown, peppered with gray that matched his neatly coiffed mustache and short beard. Her 'truth meter' registered an unflappable trust in him as her legal resource and good friend. She reveled in the calming effect he had on her.

"Don't tell me your trip to Toronto was useless, Lee?" She shuddered inwardly at the thought with more than a twinge of disappointment. She waited for him to tell her about the meetings he'd concluded, half in anticipation, half in dread. She knew the contract with the pharmaceutical company would mean salvation for Larkspur.

He looked at her a moment before answering.

"Lee, yesterday's paper indicated that.........." She shuddered again.

Lee leaned forward and lowered his voice, his eyes studying her with a curious intensity. "Do you remember when I told you I had a feeling that there was someone feeding information to the Premier Insurance execs? Well, I was right."

"Oh God.... No." She stared.

Lee nodded, trying to concentrate on something besides the softness of her skin and the length of her lashes. "Yes, I read the Oregonian and yes, somebody is obviously privy to some very confidential information. Someone at Premier has contacted Robert Dubois."

"What? How could they know about S/K? We have been diligent with our secrecy. Are they pulling their contract option?" Her mood veered sharply to anger.

"No, that's the good news. Robert said he'd given you first offer and unless he was forced to do otherwise, it still stood. They are in the same timeline mode as you are. If the paperwork is finalized by November 1st, they are ready for your January 1st start dates. The drug card will have a tiny chip imbedded in it. Remembering, of course, the agreement is for mail order only; but the first time the prescription is filled they must go to their local pharmacy to begin the process. After that.... Viola' .... The members will order it via telephone or over their internet site."

A thrill of frightened anticipation touched her spine. She leaned forward and shrewdly pinned him with her look, "Who contacted him from Premier and what's the bad news, Lee?"

Lee chewed the inside of his cheek briefly before answering, his voice filled with depth and authority. "Robert wouldn't give me names. But, since the issues are no longer speculative or uncertain, Robert stated we should find our mole before moving forward. He wants an above-board, honest relationship and if everything he sends to you is under scrutiny by an unknown entity, he wants full disclosure before being allowed to proceed."

She felt screams of frustration at the back of her throat. Standing abruptly, she paraded back and forth like a bent and limping pendulum. She sputtered with indignation and turned back to Lee to see him forming a T with both hands in front of his face, mimicking a time-out signal.

"A mole inside Larkspur? It's abhorrent for me to play detective here. Many of the employees were employed long before I was hired. There are only a handful of new hires within the last three years and .... Lana, Callie, Derrick. And... They have strong characters and wouldn't sabotage this for us. I know it and I don't doubt their loyalty.

"Has anyone been acting different lately?" he asked, seriously.

"Not really. There are only a couple of people close to me and I don't worry about them at all! Take Lana for instance. She's a mature single mother with two children, responsible, on time and efficient. And she's also my friend. She leaves every Thursday afternoon about 2:30 to visit her sick mother in Salem, but that's fine with me. In fact, I'm surprised she hasn't lost work due to sick kids. She couldn't be the one..." She was sure of it, despite Lana's quiet attitude lately.

"We have to find out, Caroline. There is definitely a problem here and you have to fight it to save your Canadian drug card concept. You know that." He finished lamely.

"Oh, Lee... You're right, I know that. I don't want to be put in this position but we worked too hard to arrange this prescription deal. With that plus the LEXUS docs and facilities, the ball should be in our court. Dammit! This is not fair! I want Shelton-Kent prescriptions to cover our members. Steven fought it before, but who's fighting it now and why?"

"Over him yet?" A brief frown marred his features.

"Over him?" Her brow furrowed. "Steven? Lee, I was over him long before my first bullet slammed into him. I didn't love him and it wasn't a shocking discovery to admit it. When I think of his betrayal and lies, especially against Callie, just so he could manipulate me .... Well, it's something I'm not proud of. I was needy and he made me feel special and beautiful."

"You *are* special and beautiful." Lee was stunned as the words slipped out and his lids came down swiftly over his eyes a moment, before returning to meet hers.

Caroline's anger evaporated, leaving a seed of confusion. Caught off guard, hearing the vibrancy in his voice, she experienced a gamut of conflicting emotions. Her thoughts stumbled at the invitation in the smoldering depths of his eyes, before they cleared and held hers. The room grew still.

To break the sudden sweet tension, Lee continued, "I'm serious, Caroline. You need a kind, honest man."

"And where do you propose I find this gentleman? An advertisement tacked on the wall somewhere?" she asked softly, feeling a twinge of disappointment.

"Good men are out there, my dear. You just need to look. A national survey on the news last night shows that 75% of the divorced people in the nation remarry." Lee's emotions steadied slightly; he mentally shook his head and tried to reel in his mind.

Caroline watched the emotions scurry across his face, "Oh, they *do*, do they?"

"...do what?" Lee's forehead wrinkled a moment.

"The survey. Hallooooooo? Lee, where are you?" She walked around to the front of her large desk and leaned against it. Her navy blue, slim skirt inched above her knee, one leg stiff and the other bent. She was thoughtful for a moment, then looked down to meet Lee's steady gaze. Time slowed. *What's going on here?*

Then, without a word, she held one hand toward him and glanced at her watch with the other. "Come on........." She pulled him up beside her and slipped her arm through his, temporarily brushing aside interesting questions in her head.

He grabbed his briefcase, and they walked in tandem to the door.

"Let's get this over with and alleviate the anxiety yesterday's Oregonian article is causing all of us." Her voice returned to their typical camaraderie and she arched her eyebrow toward him.

"Yes, boss." Lee felt the warmth of her fingers through his sleeve and relaxed.

Laughing, she pulled open her office door.

Lana jumped away, startled.

"Lana, are you all right?" Caroline's voice filled with concern.

Lana bobbed her red head up and down and reached for some files next to her computer. "Yes, I'm fine...you're headed for the Board meeting? I was just going to remind you it was time." She smiled quickly at Lee as he tipped his head slightly, studying her a moment.

"Yes. It's almost two o'clock. Has everyone arrived and found their way to the conference room?"

"Yes. Shall I take notes?" she asked hopefully.

"No. Gary Ives will do that, as usual.

"Well, I thought **this** time..." Lana's words died.

"What, Lana? Have I missed something?" Caroline was at a loss.

"No, it's nothing." Lana turned to pick up the phone again, curtailing further conversation.

"Caroline Phillips' office. How may I help you?" Lana's eyes remained averted and reflected a fierce tenseness before turning toward Caroline. "I'm sorry. Ms. Phillips has just walked into a meeting. May I take a message? Yes, Dr. Reed. Yes.... Premier Insurance Co." They watched Lana write down a phone number and break the connection after sending a worried smile toward them. Her hand was shaking as she replaced the receiver and rested the note in Caroline's outstretched palm. Her eyes lifted to Caroline's again only briefly before she turned back to her computer.

Lee and Caroline exchanged questioning glances.

"Del Reed? I wonder who he's loyal to... us or Premier? The only reason we retain him as acting Medical Director for surgical request reviews is because he's fair but he seems so indifferent and sometimes downright grumpy. Just recently, he tried to get us to contract with the full LEXUS provider panel. He doesn't seem to understand the word, 'no.' My God, that's all I need. What do you think he wants now.......... To give me a hard time over the newspaper article too? "

Caroline's mood changed abruptly and it was the businesswoman once again who continued down the hallway, Lee in tow. The tensing of her jaw reflected her deep frustrations as they walked into the conference room together. She nodded at the others surrounding the eight-foot mahogany conference table.

Lee kept his own counsel about Del Reed. He was nonplussed. The large glass windows lent a sense of freedom, because the building next to them sported a large helipad. He replayed a previous conversation in his mind when Caroline fantasized about flying away from reality into Portland's wide blue yonder. *And I'd go with her in a heartbeat.*

Caroline glanced out at the helipad and allowed a brief smile to touch her lips and glanced at Lee, also remembering her fantasy, which usually enhanced her mood. But today, somehow, the light and airy feeling was missing. Today there was an air of bafflement and she could feel it permeate the large room, as if tiny crystals were tinkling and ready to crash around her.

"Gentlemen...and ladies." she began, nodding to the two ladies, Patricia Harwood and Linda Carlson. Thank you for attending this impromptu meeting to discuss the Oregonian's disturbing article in yesterday's paper about our Canadian pharmaceutical firm and the Premier Insurance Co. I've asked our legal counsel, whom you all know—— Lee Carle, to join in our meeting.

She touched his shoulder lightly. "Lee has just returned from a meeting in Toronto with Robert Dubois and I'd like to give him the floor. And, no, we have no idea who leaked this information to the press."

Lee gloried briefly in her light touch and smiled at the small sea of faces waiting in anticipation and consternation before him. Placing his hands, palm down, on the table as he studied each face around the table, he explained in fine detail from beginning to end the conversation he had just shared with their CEO.

He waited until the comments and questions died down. "First, we must keep uppermost in mind that the person responsible for passing on such sensitive information to Premier must be caught, chastised and one would hope – arrested for theft. At this point, all we know is it must be someone who may have infiltrated Caroline's confidential system.

I have asked James Garnett, from a reputable investigative firm that I have used many times before, to help here. I will leave it to Caroline to decide how to deal with the spy when the time comes." Lee's voice was firm and final.

Caroline watched everyone as they shook their heads. Breaking the silence, she asked, "Do I have your vote to continue in this vein, then? We must have the perpetrator in order to continue and settle the contract with Robert. I refuse to bend to whoever it is, without fighting back, and tackling Premier really is the rub."

The room erupted in "Ayes" all around, but the disgruntled Board was far from relieved. Derrick spoke quietly to Patricia and Gary, just before they grabbed their belongings and followed the other Board members out of the large conference room. He glanced over at Caroline, nodded at Lee, and left to return to his own office.

As Derrick walked down the long hallway and approached the copy room, he nearly collided with Callie, who was in deep conversation with two of her sales reps, Elaine Rose and Janet Crow.

"Whew! Almost gotcha...." He grinned, a deep dimple in his left cheek. He held his hands up to steady both of her shoulders briefly and inhaled the gentle, sweet scent of her perfume. His heart stumbled. *My God, she smells good.*

Callie laughed out loud before shaking her head and moving aside with the women. She floundered a moment before the brilliance of his look and then turned away to continue her conversation. For just an instant, she glanced back to see him wink broadly. Feeling her flesh color, she turned around again. She found Janet and Elaine looking at her with knowing smiles. "What?" pretending confusion, her eyes widening with false innocence.

"You are watermelon red, Callie." Janet snickered.

"Well, it is warm in here......" Elaine said, trying to come to her rescue.

"Right, it's warm all right." Janet responded, stealing a glance down the hallway.

Janet Crow and Elaine Rose were two of three health insurance sales managers at Larkspur and they met their goals and deadlines systematically each month like perfectly-wound clocks. Each agreed that working with Callie Beauvais boosted their confidence level, since she listened to complaints and gave exceptions when warranted. Callie went that extra mile to support them in meeting their goals; the expense account and car was an added incentive but she made their job fun as well.

"Betsy Haydon is doing really well, Callie. She's definitely going to be an asset for the small groups. We saw her in action the other day at the Babbitt Financial employee meeting. She asked us along for moral support and for a critiquing session afterwards, so we left with good feelings."

"Oh —- good news. And where,"" Callie dropped her voice conspiratorially, "was the critiquing session held?"

Janet and Elaine glanced at one another sheepishly.

"Well, Jakes, of course. It was 4:20 or so and happy hour....." Janet murmured.

"But we did **not** put the wine on our expense checks, we promise!" Elaine piped in.

Caroline had taken Callie's advice to lift morale by rearranging furniture; replacing dreary drapes with vertical blinds opening the breathtaking view from the wide windows. Many of the surrounding buildings had stone edifices with curving architecture to modern pinkish slate. The Hilton Hotel lay eastward and the west hills lay splayed on the other side, with the port authority far to the northeast. Often, the noted Portland rain was part of the view, but when the sun shone brightly, smiles replaced the gloom.

Today was one of those bright, sunny days in late September and Derrick was feeling especially blessed as he left the women. He whistled softly as he headed toward his office. *Dad's finally been diagnosed. Surgery will make him feel so much better. Callie seems to be more aware of me. I can see emotions... Steven's last phone call sounded positive even if we had to clear the air with mental fists. His therapist challenged him with counseling sessions that might shorten his jail time and he can have a second chance. Now someone's leaking information.... Damn! And to Premier!* Negative thoughts overran positive as his mind wandered. *I can't blame them for trying to jump on the bandwagon but let us get on first, for God's sake. It's only fair!* He strode down the second hall and walked toward his desk when the intercom broke into his thoughts.

"Derrick. It's Sophia on line two."

Derrick's hazel-gray eyes were tender as he picked up the phone. Her voice seemed to regenerate his mood as the warmth in his smile echoed in his voice. "Yes, that's right. Yes, he is better. Thanks for asking, honey... How are you doing and when are you coming to see me?" Answers followed questions as Sophia's voice prattled on. "Yes, darlin' .... No...... Of course....." Placing the phone back in its cradle, he sat back in his chair, contemplating the woman on the other end. He picked up the 5 x 7 color photo on his desk, missing her.

"Real Knowledge is to know the extent of one's ignorance."
— Confucius

Chapter 6

* * *

Doctor James' patients would have blushed to hear his expletive as he slammed the receiver into its cradle. *This is the third time this month that one of my surgical requests has been sent to the medical review board. How hard can it be to approve surgery when the patient's test proves beyond a shadow of a doubt it's Acid Reflux Disease? Carl Leander is popping Tums day and night and the needless delay on this case is another pain-in-the-ass decision that is making his life a daily hell.*

When his office manager gave him the slip of paper displaying the red mark in the 'pending' slot of his surgical request earlier, his blood pressure rose like a hot poker. *When will this stupidity end?* He grabbed the slip of paper off Carl's file again, picked up the telephone and angrily punched in the numbers.

He snapped, "This is Dr. Sam James. When does the next review board meet?" Anger ripped through his mind.

"Well, they met yesterday, so they'll meet again next Thursday, doctor," the voice responded kindly, trying to ignore his rancid tone.

"Oh, great! Thanks." *Well, that blows the reserved operating room I'd hoped to push Carl into on Tuesday morning.* The doctor was sullen, mulling over the remaining files before him.

Doctor Samuel James, III sat back in his chair and sucked in his cheeks like a fish starved for air. His Larkspur contract forced HMO rules on him that weren't so far fetched four years ago because he still had some decision making ability and liberal control over his practice. He closed his eyes a moment. *Then, a year ago, my LEXUS contract was the ball-breaker. Now, with the additional requirements shooting across my desk daily since I joined the LEXUS panel with Larkspur.... Well, they say LEXUS "sort of" joined them—-words and more words.* He'd argued against the anti-HMO arguments in the past, but lately, he wanted to hobble the managed care idea altogether. He crumpled a piece of paper and tossed it toward the wastebasket beside his desk. He missed it and grunted.

Sam had always put his patients first. His medical training, logic and experience had taught him when to operate and when to use alternative methods. He didn't try to beat the system by operating just because he felt like it and let the insurance company pay the bill, regardless of the patient's need. He was a damned good doctor. But lately, he was being squeezed from both sides like a plump orange with his patients dripping through the cracks like orange juice.

Disgusted, he reluctantly lifted the phone again and dialed Carl Leander. His fingers gripped the end of his glass-topped desk strewn with papers, files, pencils and various objects pushed into a wooden case. The ends of his fingers tapped the top of the glass as he stared at his medical degree hanging on the wall. Then, he picked up one of his pencils, tapping it up and down in time with his dangerous mood and waited for Carl to pick up the phone. The pencil broke.

"Yes?" Carl Leander asked tentatively.

"Carl, Doctor James here. We've had a slight delay. Can't do your surgery on Tuesday morning after all and I'm sorry about that. All the paperwork involved, you know... but I will contact you on Friday to set up a firm date and time. I hate putting it off but couldn't push it through in time for Tuesday. How does that sound?"

"Well, it isn't good, doc. Now that we know what this pain is all about, I want to get it over with." He grimaced into the phone, but his confidence in Doctor James far outweighed his desire to rush into the operating room prematurely.

"Well, Carl —- guess you can just keep the Tums handy in the meantime, huh?""

"Yeh, doc. Thanks a bunch," Carl tried to joke but his thoughts were gloomy and the doctor knew it. "Talk to you on Friday then?" Carl sighed with disappointment.

"Yes sir. Back at you then, huh?" *This delay is bullshit, but telling Carl the reason would just open a can of worms,* Sam told himself as he tried to calm down.

Carl Leander had always led an active and remarkable life. When his wife died four years earlier, he had returned to Portland from Santa Barbara, so he and his brother, Ted, could share some good times, memories and companionship while growing old together. He didn't see seventy-four as old yet and his older brother, Ted, agreed. "Damn! The youth is wasted on the young," they'd say and laugh uproariously.

He'd steadfastly refused to be a burden to his son, Derrick, but was overjoyed when he decided to move back to Portland from San Diego the year before. *What changes have occurred in just one year,* he thought. He'd missed the family and friends he had left behind but having lived in Portland for the first forty years of his life, it was automatic for him to return to his roots when he was alone. And he'd not regretted a single day of that decision. It also gave him the opportunity to be as melancholy as he wanted to be without others telling him that Sara was gone —- *they had to remind him? Never! We'd almost made fifty years together. A very good fifty years. And God—- I miss her.* Many of their memories lay all around him, especially with Mount Hood's majestic view a memorable reminder of their early times together.

Now, with a constantly burning gut and relentlessly chewing on chalky Tums, he was disenchanted with the medical community as a whole. He wanted to get on with his life, but he'd trust the doc and wait until next Friday. Exhaling loudly, he turned back to his newspaper and began to read the Oregonian from front to back, as was his custom each morning over his hot coffee. He poured in his usual dollop of cream and slapped the spoon around inside the cup trying to stem his disgruntlement.

An article on the inside of the third page caught his eye as he read the headline, "Larkspur's Execs pull out the Plug Attempting to Be the First with Canadian Drug Card." His eyes scanned the article and smiled when he read his son's name in the text. *The new prescription deal sounds great but it won't help me. Why is it that other countries revere their elderly and America lost them in the cracks where health insurance is concerned? Now that we are older and we need the drugs, they cut it off. At least we have the new prescription rider.*

His face matched his whining thoughts before returning to the article and reading how Derrick was working to make the plan viable. His mood lifted. He dialed Larkspur's number, and then punched in Derrick's extension. His smile broadened as he heard his son's voice on the other end. "Hey, son —- am I interrupting anything?""

"Hell no, Dad. Good to hear from you. What's the news from the doc?"

"As a matter of fact —- they've delayed the surgery until at least after next Friday instead of Tuesday morning and I'm not sure why. Doc James just said something about the paperwork and that kind of ...... well, anyway —- that's not the reason why I called. Just read about you in the paper, big shot. Nice to see your name in print, son. It was sure more positive than the one the other day when Premier Insurance obviously wants in on your deal. Anyway, how's it going there?" Carl chided Derrick for not keeping him apprised of the excitement he knew dogged his son's footsteps daily since Premier stepped into the picture.

"Dad, you know I can't go into any details. Remember, you shouldn't believe everything you read in the paper. Those reporters print half-truths and ad-lib. It will be nice when I can get back to my real job....like finishing this Web site. This undercover stuff isn't really for me."

"What undercover stuff?" Carl's eyes widened in astonishment.

"Well, dad......."

Hmmmpf....well, ok.... When are you coming over to see me? The neighbor lady brought a casserole yesterday with lots of mushrooms and peppers in it and there's no way I can eat it by myself. You know Ted hates mushrooms."

"What neighbor lady....? Oh, you mean Alice across the street?"

"Yep, she's the one. And don't start in, son." Carl chuckled because he knew what his son was thinking.

"You think maybe she thought if she made the casserole big enough, you'd invite her in to share it with you..... c'mon, Dad. Are you *that* old?" he challenged with a slight snicker in his voice.

"Hey now, young man!" Derrick could hear the old man's glint of humor returning and they talked a moment more before ending the connection.

Carl went back to his paper and Derrick sat with his hands locked behind his head as he thought back to his father's words. "Delay and paperwork," he repeated. He tapped his keyboard and grimaced. *Was it the age-old HMO runaround? Well, just because I work here doesn't mean I can get involved with the medical issues and referral process... unless I'm pushed into it, that is.* Derrick returned his attention to his monitor and the website he was updating for Larkspur when he heard a voice behind him. "Derrick Leander?"

The tall man stood just barely inside the doorway with his knuckles tapping on the doorframe, peering in at Derrick, a question in his dark blue eyes. "Nobody is at the desk out here but I see this is the right office. At least that's what the name plate tells me." He gestured with his hand and lifted his eyebrows, requesting entry.

"Oh, sure." Derrick got up and walked toward him. "How can I help you, I'm Derrick Leander." He reached out his hand to invite the man inside and the stranger grasped it firmly.

"James Garnett. I understand you are working closely with Ms. Phillips on the current prescription issue and...."

"James Garnett! Of course, Lee Carle's man. It's nice to meet you. Please have a seat." Derrick gestured toward the chairs in front of his desk, and closed the door. Eric was still not at his desk so he set the do-not-disturb button on his phone.

The men faced one another, each waiting for the other to begin.

James Garnett's lined face looked steadily at Derrick before choosing his words carefully. "I know this is going to be a difficult job and Ms. Phillips hates the idea, but you and I both know we have to find out who's behind this. I know there must be more than one person involved. I just *feel* it in my bones. I'd like your help here, but forgive me, but I have to assume everyone is guilty until proven otherwise."

"Go on." Derrick met his accusing eyes without flinching. "How do you propose we begin then? And then.....once I've cleared myself in your eyes, we can get to work." Derrick bit his lip and stared into the man's eyes.

The detective was thoughtful a moment. "What's your history here, Derrick?"

"I've been at Larkspur less than a year but I've seen good things happen around here. My main job is to create and maintain our website and I'm damn proud of what I've accomplished here. And I'm now in charge of putting together the HMO network using a new provider base. So whatever you need to do or say to get me cleared as one of the bad guys, just do it so we can get on to the real joker in this story, ok?" Derrick's features felt tight and strained. *This is bullshit.*

James hesitated, measuring the man in front of him for a moment. He saw a quiet strength in the man and noticed that he dressed with a casual, but professional quality that many men couldn't quite carry off. His gray suit almost matched his eyes and was offset by the white shirt and darker gray tie that looked classic, but fine. His own Dockers and collared-golf shirt sat on his own frame like a basketball player, with more fabric than meat. He'd always been slender and looking across at Derrick now, made him wish he'd eaten more spinach as a kid. He smiled at the thought and continued, answering Derrick with a hint of rebuke.

"I'm not here to shoot you, mister, I'm here to help but you would be the first to wonder why I didn't start with you, now tell me if I'm wrong on that one." Eyes stared down the other.

"Okay —- you're right. You're just doing your job and I applaud your tenacity." He pulled his chair closer to his desk, pushed his keyboard farther away to one side and loosened his tie. "Let's dig in. Where do we start? Assuming I pass, you understand."

James' lips twitched as they nodded to one another in a silent touché.

Later that day, seeing Derrick and Eric talking earnestly, Lana approached them. She wore her bright, shoulder-length hair clipped at the nape of her neck, as her peach and cream-colored dress fell softly around her knees and her pumps quietly moved across the carpet. She nervously pulled at her collar before interrupting their conversation.

"Hey, Derrick, who was that tall guy I saw leaving your office this morning? He sure didn't look familiar." Lana dropped the files onto Eric's desk and stood beside it for a moment, lingering beside the men as they finished their computer-lingo discussion.

"Oh, just a guy who needed some help with their system. What's going on, are you *shopping* for a man or something?" Eric turned around, grinning, and leaned on his desk leeringly toward her.

"No, Eric." She rolled her eyes. "Just curious."

"Well, if you *are* shopping, I want to be first in line," Eric said glibly... "I'm going up to the Mission Theater on 17th tomorrow night to see the 6 o'clock movie. It's an English movie and...."

"Sorry, Eric", she retorted. "I pick up my boys from daycare right after work and even if I *was* interested, I can't change the schedule, so perish the thought." Her tone of voice belied the fact that she liked Eric, but inner turmoil dictated her actions.

Derrick raised an eyebrow and hid a smile before wandering toward Callie's office. He hoped to catch her before lunch. The room was empty. *Why did I refuse her invitation to join the crowd for a drink after work tonight? Hell, just because Millie made me bleed, doesn't mean all women will. And Callie doesn't seem the type to....Well, Millie didn't either. In the beginning anyway...... What do they say, twice burned, twice shy? Yeh,* he thought... *that's it, but God, I don't want to go through that again!* He turned away from the doorway and closed his eyes a moment to inhale the discreet, delicate scent of her perfume. *And that sexy scent drives me nuts.*

As Derrick walked slowly back to his office, Lana's voice called out to him. "Caroline wants to meet with you right after lunch today," a thawing note in her voice.

He saw Eric watching her with a puppy-dog look.

Romance can be hell, he thought. "No, that's good. Tell her I'll be there a few minutes after one." He watched her swish away from them and wondered why she kept herself so aloof and mysterious, always keeping people at arm's length. He knew she was single with two little boys at home. *Well, that was probably the answer.* He returned to his computer.

James Garnett held his notebook in the palm of his hand. *He's flipping pages like a T.V. detective,* Caroline thought as she tried to concentrate on what he was saying. His voice filled in the morning's blanks as they waited for Derrick. She touched her gold bead and pearl bracelet, playing with the white treasures, as she listened to him. *I am so anxious to get this over with.*

"I have talked with seventeen of your employees so far. I have all the notes Lee gave me along with my questions and hope you can fill me in. Oh, Derrick Leander and the Claims Department are cleared. All nice folks, by the way," he continued. "There are three I'd like to check further, especially those people closest to you but I'll need a couple of things. Your secretary seemed very busy so I'll talk with her soon. How do you keep track of outgoing calls and the outgoing FAX log and what about Email messages in house and outside?" A pad was on his lap and a yellow pencil poised in his hand, in dire need of sharpening. His bushy eyebrows arched slightly, waiting.

A couple quick knocks on her office door gave her pause. The door opened, admitting Derrick into the large office. Books lined the room on two sides and matching loveseats mirrored each other in front of her oak desk. A four-foot urn held a huge, flowering plant and bright blue candleholders bordered a picture of Caroline's adult children. It was a welcoming room and Caroline's smile did the rest.

"Oh, it's you." Derrick's silky voice held a challenge.

Caroline looked up quickly.

James let out a long, audible breath. "Yep... it's me. Back like a bad penny."

"Derrick, James needs some backup facts and I'd like you to work closely with him, without Eric's involvement." Caroline wondered at his tone of voice.

Derrick gave Caroline a look and then focused on James. "Is Eric on the bad-guy list?"

"No, it's just that the less people involved, the better. Everyone I've interviewed so far thinks I'm doing a survey for a new software invasion."

Derrick's chest heaved as he shook his head. "Yes, you're right. Guess we got off on the wrong foot. Friends?" He reached out to shake James' hand again and then pulled up a chair next to the loveseat, littered with papers.

"Ok, this is what I need on these three folks plus this list." He pointed to the pad and pointed it in Derrick's direction. "I need Emails, FAX logs and long distance phone logs. How fast can I get it?"

"Whoa —- it's a tall order. This is Friday....one o'clock. Is Tuesday at noon soon enough?" Derrick tried not to look as disgruntled as he felt.

"No. Monday morning about nine o'clock is better. Can you do that for me? Any sooner isn't practical and I know that's pushing you already, right?" His confidence in Derrick had been cemented with their first handshake but he also knew he was treading on thin soil. He knew these people were his friends, but he had to get answers.

Derrick's brow furrowed in surprise.

"Can't you put your social life on hold for the week end?" he jibed and saw Derrick's eyes darken.

"Just kidding, Derrick. Come on. Loosen up."

Caroline looked from one to the other. "Hey! you two. This is important but it's certainly not worth killing each other over." Her face was etched with concern.

"Right." They spit out in unison, a tentative friendship seemingly short lived for the moment.

"The information will be available Monday morning in my office." Derrick said as he stood up, looking sheepish. The room suddenly seemed warm, a little small to house both men.

James Garnett gathered his papers, shoved his notebook into his shirt pocket and shook Caroline's hand, holding it longer than necessary. Derrick rolled his eyes as James walked to the opened door.

"Derrick, wait a moment longer, please. I have a couple of issues from Claims to go over with you. The website is freezing on the provider network now that we've added some of those LEXUS docs." She moved deeper into her chair and nodded goodbye to James.

Derrick seriously considered the complaints as she showed him the memos she'd received that morning.

"Ok, let's see what we can do. Hadn't heard there were problems but we'll iron them out. Did I tell you how much help Eric's been to me on this project? I'd like to hire someone to work his desk so he can assist me on some other jobs, if we can fit it into the budget?"

Caroline smiled at his intensity. "We can discuss it later, Derrick. The matter at hand keeps my mind so occupied it's hard to fit much else in but I'm sure we can work something out for you."

LATER, after Eric left and the building was emptying out, Derrick welcomed the silence and surcease from the wild, wooly day he'd encountered. He settled back in his chair, cradled his head with linked hands and stared at the ceiling. He thought about the information James wanted, hoping for peaceful solitude, when the stillness was interrupted by the opening and closing of nearby doors. He hurried out to the hallway to see if it was Callie. She'd been noticeably absent all day except for her brief, "Let's get together for POETS DAY wine at Jakes" that encompassed him along with five other co-workers that morning. *Which I said no to like an idiot*, he thought now.

"Lana."

"Hello Derrick." Her purse dangled lopsidedly, her arms around several files, as she headed toward the elevator. "Well, so much for the computer system guy. I know he was in Caroline's office with you..... Is she helping him with his system too?" she said quietly, sarcasm underlying each word.

He tried to temper her statement with amusement. "Why should this guy get you so riled up and what's with all the files? Are you working at home on a week end?"

She flinched. "I don't like being kept in the dark. I work for Caroline. I should know what's going on. And yes... I am working at home a little this week end." Her eyes slid away from his and she tapped the elevator button.

"Well, it's a shame you have to do that since you have two little boys who are undoubtedly hoping for some quality time with their Mom," he answered, seriousness creeping into his voice as he watched her face flush slightly. "Go home, Lana and spend time with your boys. They'll be grown up soon and you won't have them around to play with. I know how fast that time can fly. It seemed like yesterday that my daughter was that age. Leave the files here. I'm sure the work can wait until Monday, can't it?" he said as he moved toward her.

"No," she said, wariness in her voice, fighting tears.

Derrick stared after her a moment as she hurried into the opened elevator. Then, he turned at a snail's pace toward his office and a job he looked forward to with loathing. He took a deep breath; let it out slowly.

"Laughter is the shortest distance between two people."
—Victor Borge

Chapter 7

No matter how much he told himself he was only following orders, Derrick felt like a burglar, trespassing into hidden closets best left closed as he pulled up the Emails for James. *A hacker. Yes that was what I've felt like ever since I started this rotten project.* Not since he and Steven were roommates at University of Oregon in Eugene had he felt so sleazy. Steven had always been an ace at it; he hadn't even needed the software to retrieve information. He'd begged Derrick to join him as he crept into computers where he didn't belong all those years ago. But Derrick could never see its entertainment value and felt the irony of doing a job that Steven could have done with his eyes closed. *Steven, the BS artist. Okay, enough,* he thought, *back to work.*

Six months' logs of Emails, phone calls and FAX output was one of the biggest jobs he'd been given in years. *Six months!* The paperwork piled up and the stacks surrounded him.

He wondered how long it would take James to decipher the printed words and phone numbers. Getting the phone numbers was the easy part, due to having access to the phone company's accounts payable. Jackie Chapman had given him everything he needed. Yellow highlighters littered the floor. His eyes hurt, his shoulders ached and his head was throbbing. It was almost 8 o'clock on Sunday night when he printed the last page.

"My God, what a mess," he murmured into the quiet room. He sat back in his chair and stretched his arms out on the armrests, switched off the computer and swiveled around to gaze outside his window.

Portland's nightlights intrigued him and the cityscape made him glad once again that he'd moved back. He could see tiny lights flickering everywhere, the MAX train flitting down the tracks toward the Willamette

River and miniature cars rushing across the bridges. *So many bridges to cross over one river.* He stared, enthralled.

He couldn't chance Eric finding the mess, so tired though he was; he pushed himself out of his chair, feeling aches and pains rushing around his body like a Virginia lightning bug on a hot night.

Twenty minutes later, banker boxes taped and stacked neatly along one wall, he grabbed his sweater and left his office. Ignoring the elevator, he skipped down the stairs to rev up his inner motors, fighting the aches in his legs and swinging his arms like a locomotive. Swinging around each floor landing, he managed to reach the basement where his Ford Explorer was parked; He keyed the ignition, backed out of his space and headed out, honking to open the automatic garage door before driving up the ramp and into the slightly drowsy Portland night.

He flipped open his cell phone, dialed Caroline's home number and left a brief message, "Hi Caroline. This is Derrick. The information is boxed up in my office for James. I've highlighted Emails and phone calls. Maybe we can find the mole with it, but who knows? I'll be in a little late tomorrow but in plenty of time to meet with him at 9:00. Good night now."

He clicked off and popped on the CD player to enjoy Michael Allan Harrison. As the piano music floated around him, his muscles began to relax and his head slowly stopped pounding. At that hour, the narrow, tree-shrouded streets were deserted and he headed home.

Doctor Del Reed watched his wife, Lorrie, as she poured his coffee while half-listening to her chatter. His mind was on Steven Roget and the job he promised to do.

"............then, we would get on the cruise ship and be on the water nearly two weeks. We dress up one of the nights and we might be able to eat with the Captain. And we will get our picture taken in our fancy clothes. Mary and Todd have one in a nice 8 x 10 folder and everything looks so special and glittery." She filled her own cup and sat across from him at their dining room table. She let the sunshine lightly caress her face as she closed her eyes and wrapped her hands around her steaming cup.

"Two weeks?" Del said, baffled.

"On the water. Yes. The cruise, remember? Del, where are you? You have been so wrapped up in your work lately. What is it?" She implored him, pushing her curly silver hair behind her ear, waiting for an answer.

"Nothing that concerns you, hon. Sorry I haven't seemed enthused about the trip but I will be. I promise you that. Soon. We'll talk about it soon." He rushed through the paper and lifted his cup for one last swallow.

"It's our time now, Del. I can only garden and clean so much and darn it! Retirement is around the corner. Did you tell them yet?" She could see his face turn pale and the telltale signs of frustration enter his eyes. "Ok......ok. I won't pester you but the cruise is set up for February and this is already the end of September, remember."

Del sighed and smiled gently at his wife as he walked to her chair. His hand touched her cheek and she lifted her face for his kiss. "Sweetheart, we are going to have the time of our lives. We will really be able to talk when we hit the ocean and we can read all the books we want and get sunburned and take pictures. We'll do it all. But, I have to get to work now. You make the plans and we'll do it. Just like I said," he promised.

"Well, I can hardly wait," she answered, her eyes sparkling. "I know Premier's fighting Larkspur for that drug card, Del. I hope you don't get yourself in a stew over it. Let the others work on it. Your time is almost up there anyway..." She let the words run out of steam when she saw his eyes turn flat. "Ok... I'm pestering again. Go to work then."

Lorraine Reed stood at the kitchen window long minutes after she watched her husband drive away. Pondering his changing moods and secretiveness over the past few months, she drank more coffee, now cold. She grimaced as she set it on the counter. "What is it, Del?" she whispered to the chickadees flitting around the bush outside the glass. "What is keeping your mind so worked up?" The beauty of the Indian summer, which usually brought peace to any chaos in her life, was suddenly dulled by inner worries.

Derrick was awake at 6:30 on Monday. He began mulling over the situation. With his mind churning, he recognized the futility of trying to get back to sleep. *Shit! I might as well get up!* He took a quick shower and stopped at Starbucks for coffee and a sweet roll before heading to work. The elevator deposited him on his floor by 7:30. He strode into his office, hung his coat and noted he'd beat Eric to the office. That didn't happen often.

Sighing loudly, he bit into the roll and sat down with his coffee before glancing toward the boxes he'd stacked neatly the night before. Suddenly, blood draining from his face, he jumped up sloshing burning coffee onto his hand. The boxes were askew and the papers had been ripped into like a chisel against plaster. He bent over the mess, speechless, before turning toward his desk once again. He quickly wiped up spilled coffee, mumbling at the papers now dripping with brown sludge. Grabbing the phone, he dialed Caroline's extension. No answer.

He got up quickly, locked his door behind him, and hurried down the corridor past Callie's office and around the corner to Caroline's. Lana wasn't in yet. Caroline's door was closed. His mind was a riot of anger and questions. Then he remembered James' business card. He dug it out, jogged back to his office, unlocked it and closed it hastily before grabbing the phone a second time.

Voicemail again! James' card also showed a cell and pager numbers. Derrick's fingers zipped out the number. "Come on, James. Come on........."

One ring and the business-like voice answered, "James Garnett."

"James, thank God... Derrick. Please get over here fast. I finished the work for you last night and I just got to my office. Looks like somebody beat you to it and it's a mess." Derrick spit out words as he glared at ripped boxes and felt his muscles cramp.

"How the hell? I can be on my way in five minutes. I'll cancel my first appointment. I'm on the Burnside Bridge now." James punched it, sliding through yellow lights all the way up to 10th before he hit a red light. Trying to avoid any more lights, he twisted right, next to the old Daisy Kingdom building and then left again on Couch, sped up to 13th, crossing Burnside by the skin of his teeth and jerked into a parking slot just a block away. Touching his holster beneath his hounds-tooth jacket, he hurried into the Larkspur building and joined Derrick a few minutes later, puffing like a steam engine. "Man! I need to spend more time at the athletic club," he said, staring with distaste at the mess.

The four boxes were 24" by 30". They were each sliced neatly with a sharp instrument, papers pulled out of the shredded openings as if someone was in too much of a hurry to cut the tape and open the boxes from the top. Literally torn from the sides, papers hung down to the navy carpet.

The men looked at one another and shook their heads. James put his hands on his hips and struggled to remain calm as he shook his head in bafflement.

"Dammit~ who the hell knew what you were doing besides us? Wait! Come to think of it, Lee said he told everyone at that last board meeting what I was doing. He gave them my name too, didn't he?"

"Yes, I guess he did," Derrick answered slowly, sickened at the inference.

A knock at the door stopped the men mid-sentence as they both turned to see Callie standing at the door. Her dark hair was in curly disarray as she inched into the room. Smiling at Derrick, she held a cup of coffee gingerly and lifted a Three Lions Bakery bag with a tantalizing aroma of fresh baked goods in the air toward him. Seeing the boxes, she dropped her arm and looked at them questioningly.

"Come in, Callie. Please shut the door behind you. Have you seen Caroline yet this morning?" James' voice sounded drained.

She shut the door with her hip, put down the bakery items on Derrick's desk alongside her coffee and joined them. "What on earth?"

"Callie. You've met James already, right? And you know he's trying to find out who is trying to rip Larkspur. These boxes were filled with information he needed that I worked on all damned weekend and this morning—— this is how I found them. And I just left them all neat and tidy less than twelve hours ago!" His voice shook with rage.

"Well!" She shook her head furiously in disbelief. "Who is *doing* this?" She reached up and pushed the silver strands off her forehead, staring at the mess and back at the men.

"Well, that is what we'd hoped these boxes would give us...and that's probably why they were slashed up." James said heatedly as he stepped toward her and asked again if she'd seen Caroline that morning.

"No, I haven't," She shook her head and looked up at Derrick before walking over to sit down, lifting the coffee to her lips. Sipping slowly and thinking hard, she shook her head once again. As her subtle perfume filled the air, the trio silently stared at the ripped papers before them.

"I left her a voicemail message last night as I drove out of the parking garage, telling her the boxes were here and the stuff was ready for you, James. That was about 8:30." Derrick's voice was perplexed and distant.

"And she wasn't home?" Callie was surprised. "She told me she was going to curl up with a glass of Chardonnay and a good book to help get her mind off this whole thing. It's funny she wasn't home."

Derrick smiled suddenly at the enormity of the situation, "You mean ha-ha funny?" He tried to catalog his emotions when he watched her answering smile. He couldn't.

Callie laughed shortly, "Noooo, not ha-ha funny, idiot, but let's go find her. What should we do, James, lock the door or ...."

"I want you to open the boxes, Derrick, and see if the phone logs are there. I have a feeling that is what might be missing and if I'm right, somebody went to a hell of a lot of trouble to stop us from finding out who called who and where and when... and if that's all that's gone, that's the good news because we can get a FAX of the billing statements with a simple phone call. If it's Emails, we'll just have to get back in there and reprint them...unless, of course, it's someone here and they've managed to delete what they can only assume we're looking for to hide their butts. Not a problem there... but it bites to try to figure out how they knew you were working in here late on this. Derrick, did you see anyone around on the week end or late Friday?"

In his minds eye, Derrick revisited Lana's strange departure Friday night, closing his eyes and trying to think. He backtracked over the weekend without coming up with anything further to add to the dilemma. "Well, Lana Potts was around. That's all I can think of, but I doubt Lana....."

"Don't doubt your instincts."

"Shit." Derrick's head started pounding again. Remembering his half spilled coffee, now partially cold, he picked it up and drank the remainder in one long gulp. His phone rang beside them and he reached for it quickly.

"Derrick?" It was Caroline. "I know James is due to arrive any time. Glad to hear about your finishing up the....."

"Caroline. Please come down to my office quickly." James and Callie stared at the phone, hearts racing.

"Well...? Ok, I'm on my way."

Barely two minutes later, Caroline's anxious face filled the doorway. Cracking the door open, she saw the calamity. She stared at Callie in the chair beside the desk, Derrick behind it and James beside it.

"The information you needed, right?" She stood with the cane handle braced under one hand as she looked at the people staring back at her.

"Right," James and Derrick snapped as one.

"Caroline, James thinks it might be a Board member. Remember when Lee told all of us who would be investigating this issue? And of course, James was here Thursday and Friday interviewing people," the men shared a bemused look, "everyone on his list.... I'm going to go through the boxes to see what's missing. James and I'll do that. Please get a list of the Board members for James."

Caroline's look of dismay encompassed everyone in the room. She sank down into the remaining chair and held her head with one hand and tapped the large jeweled pin on her blue suit's lapel with the other. She stood up with rock-firm determination but couldn't hide her agitation.

Callie joined her before looking back at Derrick and James, "Is there anything I can do to help? I feel like a third wheel but I'm sure I can do *something!*"

"Thanks, Callie. Let me and Derrick go through this and see what's missing. Then, if you can gather what I think may be missing, we have a job to do again. As soon as we're done here, we'll take you up on your offer." James' voice was soft and reassuring. "Caroline, please tell Lee what's happened. I have a feeling we'll be at this for quite awhile and we'll need his help too."

Caroline and Callie left together after watching both men grimace, joint anger spurring them on. They'd already dropped to their knees to open boxes before the door closed behind them.

"So, my friend, where were *you* last night?" Callie teased, sipping her coffee and looking at Caroline.

"What do you mean? I told you a good book, a glass of wine........... and then I zonked out about 8 o'clock and slept on the couch all night. In fact, I can't believe I didn't even hear Derrick's call. Guess I was more tired than I thought or too much wine. I felt great when I got to the office....except for the crick in my neck.... at least until Derrick called. This is making me so sick to my stomach. You'd think our lives could run smooth now, wouldn't you?" Caroline rubbed her neck briefly and shook her head. Her leg seemed inordinately heavy as she pulled it along with the aid of her cane.

"Why are you limping so much? Hurting more than usual?" Callie's voice was worried.

Caroline groaned. "The therapist pushed a bit too hard yesterday and I thought I'd die from the pain. He's worried that maybe something isn't healing right. It's just what I needed, hummmmm?" Caroline's brow danced and her eyes flashed. "I nearly had this cane tossed into the realms of old history too."

"Right." Callie followed Caroline into her office. Her black slacks and matching tunic were new and the colorful scarf set off her flushed cheeks as she voiced her concern. "I'm due at a meeting with the sales reps but I can be a little late." She followed Caroline into her office.

"Hey, wonder why my computer's on? I'm positive I shut it down Friday night. Good Lord, I'm losing it, Callie." A green light shone on the monitor, but the screen was black, due to the 'safety sleeper' Derrick told her about, hiding the desktop icons. She tapped the space bar and watched the screen lighten up slowly. "What's that? What's BE A HOST mean? I should know more about this thing. If Derrick hadn't forced me to have one for office Emails, I wouldn't have one at all." She turned to Callie.

Their brows knit together as they stared at the screen. "I don't know. Maybe it's just a glitch." Callie said thoughtfully. "I know Derrick has had Eric working on some of the others in the big room, maybe he did something in here too. Click the exit button..." she said as she reached over to tap the mouse and the colored box disappeared.

"Well, as long as I still have Email. It's a wonderful thing, but it's frightening that Derrick was able to access all those deleted Emails. I meant to ask him how he did it this morning but with all the excitement, I forgot." Caroline looked at the stack of files on her desk and glanced toward the door to see if Lana had arrived yet. "I'm earlier than usual. She's always at her desk before I arrive; she really spoils me."

"I must go, Caro... Janet and Elaine are probably already there and the small group department's new sales rep is undoubtedly there too. Any more reforms happening and we'll have the room filled up with specialty reps, won't we?" She backed out of the room and glanced at the monitor once again, frowning.

The phone rang beside Caroline and she was somewhat surprised to hear Janine's lilting French voice.

"*Bon jour*, Caroline. Sammy's at 4:30 as planned?"

"Oh, Janine. I am in the middle of......... Yes, of course. I know we must get this business taken care of and we've already postponed it twice. Order me a glass of wine if you arrive before I do and I'll do the same for you..." Caroline smiled briefly.

"Excellent, *mon ami. Abiento*." The phone clicked.

Caroline sat down to lasso the uneasy feeling floating inside her head; her stomach fluttered and fingernails tapped against the desktop. Something didn't feel right and it hadn't for some time. The files ripped apart in those boxes looked like something out of a movie. *How in the hell did someone know they were there? And they had to get in with a key....* Her fingers drummed against her cheekbone, as if she could pound out the message and clear up the confusion through Morse code.

Well, I'll open the mail, answer Emails, and return Friday's phone messages, she thought grimly. Dr. Del Reed's message was on top. His name grated on her nerves. "Why does that man put a sour feeling in my head? " *Oh, and revise the letter I started to the agent in Eugene who'd sent such a nice thank you letter about Elaine.*

Glowing with pride, she set aside the letter to give Callie. She sorted through the papers on her desk, found the letter, and decided some good news was in line for the day since it had started out so fiercely. She headed for Callie's office, the letter squeezed firmly in hand, as she mentally went over the long list she had stuffed into her schedule that morning before her lunch appointment.

THREE hours and too many uncountable swear words later, papers were strewn on the floor in little stacks around Derrick's office. Staring at each other in complete frustration, both men shared the floor beside the boxes and thought in silence.

"Okay, you can't find a damn thing missing and there aren't any phone calls to Shelton-Kent's number in Toronto or to Premier as far as you can tell?"

"No, I had all the phone statements and they showed the extensions with corresponding long distance calls. They're all there! And nothing! Ripped a bit, but there! And the Emails — that new software program, *Spector 3.1*, allowed me to pull up the deleted Emails. It took me all damn weekend since there were so many on that list of yours.........." Derrick exhaled deeply and looked straight at James, leaving the rest of the sentence unsaid.

"Well, you know what I think, Mr. Leander?" James said as he pulled himself up. He brushed off his pants, and stretched out in a chair, knocking off the small white paper bag on the corner of the desk. "Whoops....... Sorry." He bent over, wrapped his fingers around it, and handed it to Derrick.

Opening it, Derrick found two chocolate croissants. "Oh, so that's what Callie brought in this morning and in all the...." Looking at James, he pulled one out and gave him the bag. "Here. Have some breakfast and tell me what you think, Mr. Garnett."

As James reached inside the bag, Derrick looked at the fresh croissant a moment and smiled before biting into the crisp chocolate.

Munching on the corner of the butter-layered crust, James stuffed a third of it in his mouth. "God... this is good. Never had one of these before....." he mumbled between bites, his mouth full. Derrick nodded, savoring the taste. *That's it. I'm asking her out. No putting it off.*

"Well," James began, licking his fingers and dusting off the powdered sugar from his dark pants, "I think it's a smoke screen. Somebody wanted us to think something had been stolen so they rifled through the boxes. But, what has me stumped is how someone knew they were here. You said nobody saw you over the week end and only Caroline's secretary saw you Friday night and you weren't doing any of this work then, were you?"

"Nope, and someone had a key." Derrick mused.

James sat back on the chair, holding the paper bag in his hands and pushed the napkin inside. Then, suddenly, his face lit up, "I got it, man! You said you left Caroline a phone message last night that you finished it for me – right?"

"Yes." Derrick sat up, pushing himself against his desk, waiting.

"That's it then!" James stood up quickly, smashing the bag with a loud pop, as his words toppled out and he moved to the door. "Let's go find Caroline. Come on." He pushed the papers out of the way, and led Derrick down the hall, past Eric, past the big room and into the executive offices. Caroline's door was ajar, so they pushed it open.

"She's not there," Lana said out of the side of her mouth, her eyes trained on her computer screen.

"When will she be back?" James asked urgently.

"Lunch date. *Jakes* on Alder. When she meets him, she's usually late. Don't expect her until at least 1:30 or 2:00. I'll tell her you came by." Lana's fingers continued to race over the keyboard, still not looking up.

"Lana, what's up with you?" Derrick's head clouded with surprise.

"Nothing, Derrick. You asked and I answered. I'm behind, that's all." Lana's stomach felt heavy and she refused to look at the men standing close to her desk and the strained silence echoed like a quiet night in the country.

Caroline pushed the heavy double doors open to **Jake's Bar and Grill**, and searched for Lee among the luncheon customers hunched over wine, tea, salads and any number of items from their lush menu. **Jake's** was a restaurant of long standing on the west side and a must-go favorite, attested to by the fact that there were two **Jake's** restaurants. And they were always full.

THIS *Jakes* was adjoined by the Governor Hotel, an old building that held the feeling of rich, deep and true textures, having been renovated and built to accommodate quaint and elite rooms connected to the restaurant itself. Caroline glanced around the room and took comfort in her surroundings. **Jake's** décor was conservative, the walls adorned with enough photographs of the past and present to fill a mini-museum, complete with stuffed animal heads above the long, burnished bar.

Marble floors, stained glass windows and a well-stocked bar that was hard to beat kept the place bustling. *And where else could you find a huge hamburger, fries and a giant pickle for less than two dollars during Happy Hour?* This was where they always met and she was early, as usual. And she knew Lee was probably late, as usual. For an attorney, he always had a glib answer and she always accepted it as they laughed. *Sure, fighting the bad guys in the halls of justice my foot,* she thought.

Her thought stuck there ... on their shared laughter. Their meetings were always laughter filled. They embraced it. *He's really my best friend besides Callie. And I love....* She stopped the thought mid-stream. Her eyes grew thoughtful and she tapped the rubber-tipped cane on the floor beside her as she waited near the dais.

Tall potted palms filled the foyer, offering a semblance of privacy from the sidewalk outside, where small tables were aligned closely together and interspersed with European-styled chairs filled with people.

She stood there a moment, smiling toward the hostess, and pointed to her name on the reservation list. "My window seat? I'm meeting someone." She was the first in a line of well-dressed men and women standing behind her. She glanced up and saw friends across the room, already seated, waving a welcomed hand. *Oh, why not? I'll just say hello and then he'll be here,* she thought lazily. As she turned toward them, she felt a hand on her elbow, startling her... "Oh, Lee," she said, with a teasing smile on her face. Then, her eyes grew wide in astonishment. The room closed around her and she grew still.

"Nope —- not Lee. Hello Caroline." The voice was silky smooth. His hand, firmly on her elbow, attempted to pull her toward a small table in the corner, as a muscle flicked in his jaw. She was unable to think coherently for a few seconds before realty slapped her in the face. Then, she gave him a withering stare, yanked her arm loose and pushed at him.

Backing up blindly, Caroline felt stranger's hands catch her as she fell into the waiting line of people. Her cane fell with a loud clatter and everyone in the room stopped drinking and eating as they craned their necks to watch.

The hostess, Sallie Ford, and the group around her, rushed across the small space to help Caroline right herself. Sallie had worked the door nearly two years. She knew Caroline and liked her. She was a short woman with a blonde pixie hairstyle. Her French-manicured fingernails and flowing skirt were impeccable. Sallie was used to strange encounters, off-color jokes, lover's meetings, and quick lunches but the animosity emanating from this man made her hackles rise.

Now, standing close, she felt Caroline shudder as she spit out words like a hammer tapping nails into hard wood.

"*Ste*-ven... take- your *blood*-y -hands- *off* of me!!!" Her eyes sent darts in his direction. She swallowed hard, lifted her chin and boldly met his gaze. "I swore a long time ago that no man would push me around again and I mean it!"

The restaurant was deadly silent.

Steven's shoulders sagged briefly. "Caroline, please........"

"When they discover the center of the universe, a lot of people will be disappointed to discover they are not it."
—Bernard Bailey

Chapter 8

✳ ✳ ✳

"I'm sorry, but please leave the premises immediately," the uniformed man stated with iron control, not sorry at all.

"Hey, Alex, all I wanted was to apologize to an old friend and share ....." Steven sputtered and straightened up to his full height again.

"No, Steven, you will leave now or I will have you removed. Do not make a scene and do not return again." Alex Star discovered that he enjoyed the look of consternation and anger emanating from the man and secretly hoped he would not leave without a struggle. He'd known Caroline and Steven for some time and knew Steven deserved a swift kick in the butt. He was quite disappointed to see Steven shake off his grip, his eyes on Caroline. A slow smile that showed a crooked front tooth crossed his face for an instant and he stared Steven down.

Then Steven was gone, past the potted palms, past the round-eyed guests and out the double glass doors, his shoulders hunched, and his face grim.

Caroline stood transfixed, then took the cane Sallie pressed into her hand, just as Lee walked in the door, his head twisted around, looking back down the street.

Jake's patrons returned to their conversations, Sallie began seating the waiting customers and Caroline wanted to melt into Lee's arms. "Five minutes earlier....on time, that is, and you would have been in on the fireworks," she told him, trying to regain her equilibrium. Her hands still shook and her face was still.

"What? Don't tell me that really **was** Steven I just saw when I rounded the corner?" One look at her face, off kilter with a half-suppressed tenseness about her mouth and Lee knew he'd hit the nail on the head.

"Do you want to leave or...." He said, reaching for her anxiously.

"No, I worked up an appetite, my friend. Let's eat and besides, I'd like a glass of wine." Caroline turned toward the table Sallie was nodding to, at the front window, her favorite. The woman touched Caroline's left shoulder and nodded at Lee, leaving each with a menu and time alone.

"Ok, let's have it. When you called me this morning about the ripped boxes fiasco, you didn't say anything about Steven. I'd heard he hoped for an early release, but I didn't really think the parole board would believe his promise to be an ideal citizen and continue anger management counseling. Obviously I was wrong. What was he doing here anyway? I mean......," he paused and scrunched up his eyebrows slightly. "How did he know you were here, assuming you were his reason for being here in the first place?"

"Oh, I was his reason all right. AND everyone inside **Jake's** knows it." She gazed into his clear, gray eyes and classical handsome features and shook her head slowly. Pushing her menu aside, she proceeded to tell him about her encounter with Steven Roget in minute detail from the moment he touched her arm to the dropping of her cane against the tile foyer's floor.

As Caroline studied her menu, Lee studied her.

"Warm spinach salad and Merlot," Caroline ordered, her brow still wrinkled.

"Make that two of the same." Lee said quickly, handing the man his menu.

Their lunches arrived almost immediately along with wine that seemed to match their moods. Red and dark. Savoring its warmth, their eyes studied one another in an uneasy silence as men and women rushed to and fro outside the bright window beside them. They turned to watch the passersby, trying to encapsulate thoughts of Steven, torn boxes, the merger and a new awareness of each other all neatly rolled into one confused package.

"Well, let's see what we have," Lee continued, sipping his nearly-finished glass of wine and tapping his plate quietly with his fork, spearing another piece of spinach in his quickly disappearing salad. "We don't know who is leaking info to the press. We don't know who is behind Premier's obvious knowledge of sensitive information that only you should be privy to. We don't know if it's an employee or Board member, but we should know that when James and Derrick finish rifling through the paperwork back at the office. Unless, of course, we're all wet and the clues are not in the boxes at all, in which case we have jack shit." He dropped his fork, wiped his mouth and finished off his wine in a flourish, "I know this is taking a major toll on you, dear...but just what the hell DO we know, Caroline?"

Taking a deep breath as the muscles constricted in her throat, she acknowledged everything he said with a flat, "I don't KNOW!" She rolled her eyes, shaking her head slightly, watching Lee for direction. The look of surprise on his face confused her a moment before she heard James and Derrick's voice beside them.

"Thank God we found you. Hope you're done. We have work to do. Ma'am?" James said softly, "We need to get to your house right away. I think we've come up with something. You too, Lee. "

A short time later, all four stood beside Caroline's telephone, sitting discreetly beside her living room couch, pictures surrounding it, as if hiding from the rest of the room. James held a small black cylinder in his hand as the others watched him intently.

"Here's how somebody breached the confidentiality, Ms. Phillips." James handed it to her to inspect. "Now we just have to figure out who put it there in the first place. We'll never know how long it's been there but at least it's out now. I want to check your other phones." He turned and left the room as Caroline turned the little black piece of plastic in her hand, rolling it over thoughtfully.

"But, I don't use my personal phone for the type of information Premier had in order to contact Robert or know who could........." Her face suddenly jerked upward, staring straight at Lee. "Steven. It must've been Steven," she said hoarsely.

Three pair of eyes squinted in studied anger as they added one more notch to Steven Roget's belt.

Just then, James entered the room. "There's a message on your phone machine in the kitchen and who ever it is has undoubtedly already been taped by our intruder," he finished with a serious expression on his grim face.

Caroline nodded briefly before leaving the room, tapped her message button and listened to the voice with apprehension, before calling the others to join her.

Pressing the rewind button harshly, the others heard the voice as one, "*Bonjour*, Caroline. This is Robert in Toronto. I did not want to leave a message at your office since I have not heard from you or Lee to find out if you've found the person responsible for our problem, so I chose to leave you a message at your home. Please forgive the intrusion. I'm flying into Portland Monday on the 9:45 morning flight on United. I'd appreciate it if someone could pick me up. I want to finalize the pharmacy contract next week, so I will be in town until I fly out again Thursday morning at 8 o'clock. *Au revoir*, Madame." The dial tone seemed to scream in the silent kitchen.

All knew they weren't the first to hear the message.

Caroline fought the unraveling feeling she experienced the remainder of the day, but forced herself to meet Janine Vinnier at *Sammy's* on N.W. 23rd Avenue in old town for dinner. It was in the middle of a busy sector, not far from her office.

Janine's family lived near Callie's Beauvais' family in the south of France, a fact Caroline realized during their initial meeting with the Cystic

Fibrosis Foundation. Janine was a little older than she was, but her French roots did not lay dormant, despite her living in the United States since 1990 when she married. Ever since realizing the connection to Francois Beauvais' family near Aix, Janine adopted Caroline and Callie and the three had become a threesome periodically since Francois's death.

Caroline fought for a parking space, which was a usual occurrence, but eating at *Sammy's* was worth it. The restaurant was separate from the lounge; a stained glass light fixture ran the length of the booths in the center of the restaurant and the cozy atmosphere and excellent food won the war over the traffic congestion.

Janine raised her diamond-studded hand to Caroline and pointed to two glasses of red wine in front of her. "*Bonjour,* Caroline, nice to see you." Her elegant pantsuit, new manicure, expensive jewelry and perfect makeup lent the distinct impression of money, but Janine managed to make one feel special and down to earth. Bussing each other's cheeks, they sat across from one another as Caroline tried to catch her breath.

"*Bonjour,* Janine. Sorry I'm late. I've had one hell of a day. But, now I'm here, that wine looks good even though I rarely drink it twice in one day, but today seems to be made for it." Caroline smiled at the perfectly coiffed woman in front of her and applauded her serene display of womanhood. *I hope I look that good in ten years,* she thought, as she glanced at the menu.

Almost immediately, huge salads graced the small booth along with a plate of baguette bread laced in swirls of olive oil. The women sipped their wine and discussed the upcoming auction for the CF Foundation.

Caroline dipped her bread and sopped up the golden oil before lifting it to her mouth, while listening to Janine update her on the progress for the upcoming fundraiser.

"They've already had 240 RSVPs," Janine said with a huge smile that reached her eyes. "*Bon*! I know we are going to do well!"

"Yes, I do too. Tell me what I need to do, Janine. Right now, my company is in the midst of some big changes and I will work on this because I promised, but my time and sanity might be an issue. Somebody is trying to stop me from doing something really important." She lifted the Cabernet to her lips and closed her eyes a moment.

"Well, I hope it isn't serious. Maybe we should run away to Aix, *oui*?" Janine was always ready to jet back to France, like a rich, aimless fool and having a companion sweetened the pot for her.

"Mmmmmmmmm." Caroline swallowed. "Oh yes. I'm sure Callie would love it too. She's finally starting to enjoy her life again, Janine. The family over there has been wonderful to her, knowing how hard it's been for her since Francois's death. Wish we could take you up on it!"

They laughed quietly and clicked glasses.

"To France, *mon amie*." Caroline whispered.

"*Oui*, to France." Janine's diamonds glittered as she sipped the red liquid.

Discussing details for the December fundraiser at the Hilton, Janine checked off finished items and Caroline mentally noted others. Janine closed her notebook, slid it into her bag and reached for her glass of wine once again. "Caroline." She looked across the table at her friend. "You look very tired, my dear. My prescription is to have some fun."

"A Prescription? Funny you should say that."

Janine laughed suddenly. "......Yes, let's get together with Callie to see a movie at the Mission Theater and drink beer and eat hamburgers. It's so nice to get into jeans and just hide in the dark with you two because we always laugh and it makes me happy. What do you think?" Her right eyebrow rose questioningly.

"Janine, you have such impulsive ideas!" She glanced at her watch and exclaimed, "I'll ask Callie and get back to you, but my friend, now I must run. No meetings, but I'm expecting to hear something on an important problem that's going on at my office. Wish I could just stay and chat, but....." She tossed a twenty-dollar bill on the table and got up, reaching for her cane.

"Oh, I am so sorry you have to run, darling. Well, if you must......... Maybe I'll go to the library, I haven't been there in awhile and it's so glorious since it's been renovated. It is open until nine o-clock and Vincent is working late.... So, I'll follow you back and walk over since it's only a block from your building. *Tres bien?*"

"Yes, sounds good and I'm sorry to hear Vincent is working late again. That happens often, doesn't it?" Caroline exclaimed before she could stop herself. "I wonder when I'm ever going to meet the man. We've known each other three years and I've yet to set eyes on him."

Janine's mouth trembled a moment before smiling firmly, and followed Caroline out the door. "He's promised to attend the CF auction. But, he's made promises before...." Janine said quietly.

"I'm a charming coward, I fight with words."
—Carl Reiner

Chapter 9

* * *

The tavern was dark when he entered, causing his footsteps to falter slightly on the brick steps leading down into the gloomy, smoke-filled interior. Reaching out his right hand, he descended the rest of the way down, walking his fingers along the brick wall and squinting into the low-ceilinged room to see if the doctor was already waiting inside.

Smoke circled and lifted toward the ceiling, the low lights barely illuminating the occupants of the bar and the small tables lining two walls. The Storm Den was a place where folks could meet without worrying too much about being seen, as long as they watched their back upon leaving.

The tavern, itself, shared a building with an old storage warehouse and stood just beneath the Burnside Bridge on the east side of Portland. The entire building was made of brick and the parking area was actually under the bridge itself. Police patrolled the area sporadically, leaving the area open to vandals, thieves and prostitutes to roam out in the open without much worry of containment. The city was too busy with serious criminal activity farther north to pay a lot of attention just "watching" around the Storm Den.

It seemed the perfect choice for Del Reed to choose for their quiet rendezvous, banking on lax police surveillance and a place his peers would avoid. He wore his loose-fitting business suit like a plate of armor around his associates during the day, but felt at home with some of the crowd currently surrounding him. They didn't ask questions. He was 64 years old, tired and ready to retire.

Twenty years ago he'd enjoyed his job as the Medical Affairs Director. Lately, he felt pushed into a corner trying to think about a future he'd only dreamed about. Now he was ready to walk. The 401k Plan and severance pay Premier would offer him, plus the additional income that would put him in the driver's seat from his blind partnership would help. And the cruise his wife continually talked about. She deserved it after what he'd put her through. Ah, the life of a doctor. Saving lives but making lots of money in the meantime. Right! Lorrie, we'll do it, I promise.

He watched the big man stumbling down the dark steps and he smiled. Seeing him looming in the dark entrance, his eyes darting around like a feral creature, Del again applauded his choice. I have to do it for Lorrie. He lifted his arm in invitation as the smoke continued to swirl around him and saw the man move in his direction.

The blonde man, hoping to avoid anyone he knew, hastened his stride across the distasteful soiled carpet. "Hey, almost didn't see you. What a dark dungeon. Why here and not the pub off Vista Avenue where we usually meet?" Steven looked around, nervously glancing over his shoulder.

Del lifted his arm again and a barmaid appeared at their side. Her breasts nearly fell out of her tight, constricted costume and black leotards hugged her hips, leaving little to the imagination.

"What can I do for you, gentlemen?" Her accent was strange, almost mesmerizing, her blonde hair long and fluffy around her face as it laid curling across her heaving breasts.

Del reached up with the back of his fingers, and softly caressed the woman's arm. "Oooooh. That's nice...."

She responded, purring out the words slowly, "Drinks?" Her large, heavily made-up eyes lingered on Steven a moment, then stared at Del, waiting.

"Chardonnay. Two." Del said, as a dull throbbing pounded inside his head, trying to remember when it hadn't.

She disappeared into the gloom as fast as she'd materialized; while the men began a stilted conversation, intent upon the other, smoke lying in the air like fog.

"I wanted to meet here. What have you found out?" Sweat oozed down his neck and inside his stiff collar. Reaching up, he placed his two fingers between cloth and skin, pulling outward, arching for a clear breath.

"Shelton-Kent hasn't signed the contract with Larkspur yet." Steven looked around anxiously, and then carefully studied the older man's face. Del looked older, more tired, and Steven could see strain in his eyes. Two glasses of wine were clunked down on the table, no napkins.

"Start a tab, sweetheart, will you?" Del's fluid voice filled the silence.

She nodded, left again, and Del stared at Steven.

"That's it? That's all you have?" Del reached down beneath the small, round steel table to retrieve the laptop near his feet. Lugging it around the chairs, he pushed it beside Steven. "Here, I'll be glad to be rid of this and give your job back," he said under his breath, barely loud enough for Steven's ear.

"Yes, Thanks." Steven pulled it aside and looked back at Del with shrewd eyes. "Well, what do you want? I tapped her phone. I'm following her around like a loon. Crashed into the offices and ripped boxes of papers to shreds. I didn't have a lot of time, but made a mess of things. They don't realize I still have a key to the office since I gave up my own before my days in court. Anyway, it will slow them down a bit. I thought you were going to get in touch with the Canadian in Toronto? Do I have to do all your work for you? This is making me very nervous, Doc." His voice was heaving, as he lifted his glass and gulped half the wine in two gulps. He licked his lips, and then replaced the glass in front of him.

"Hell, who isn't? That is not the way you drink Chardonnay, Steven." Del's voice was low, with mock severity as he felt the sweat roll down his face and neck. Suddenly, his eyes blurred. Damn. Not again.. His left arm jerked. He squeezed it suddenly with his right, his eyes bulged. He reached across the table toward Steven.

"What is it, doc?" Steven's worried frown was replaced with anxiety as he gulped the remaining wine. Del's hand gripped his arm. "Hey, are you all right, man?"

Del nodded and motioned to stop conversation. A full minute elapsed before Del let his hand drop off Steven's arm, loosened his hold on the tabletop and felt normalcy slowly return. The room stopped spinning, the heat subsided and his shirt sopped up the dripping sweat. Pulling his jacket off, he took another small sip of the white wine in front of him.

He saw Steven's panic. "Yes, ok now. Give me a minute. What about their lawyer?" He took a deep breath. "The one who flew up to meet with the Canadian a few days ago?" His voice sounded weak but his eyes seemed to pull back into his face and he exhaled deeply.

"Lee Carle. He talked with the Canadian, but I don't know exactly what was said. Then, after the paper's article, they hired a PI to check out people at Larkspur. My bug gave me that information. I rummaged through all the shit to shake them up and here I am." Steven sat up, proud of his latest attempt at camouflaging the issue surrounding the pharmacy contract. And he smiled.

"Well, I called Caroline Phillips again just before lunch but I missed her. She didn't return my last message. I'll try her again when I get back to the office. Until then, keep in touch. I know you have to watch your back with the probation officer, but we can do this and the money is there. We have to do it, Steven. I'm depending on you. You know we'll be paid well once we get this situation under control. He wants his own pharmacy contract in there and he's willing to pay us well to get the job done. Do you understand how important this is?" Del stared at Steven, not waiting for a reply.

He finished his wine and raised two fingers to the busty woman and lowered his voice once again. "It is 2:30 now. Let's finish this by next Friday, huh? I am ready to be done with this. You aren't the only one who could have their neck in a noose, you know? As it is, when we leaked this story to the press, the Oregonian jumped on it like a duck on a June bug. And the boss loved it. But I don't like doing that because it leaves a paper trail, you know?"

"Who is the boss, Doc?" Steven asked as he saw the woman returning.

Two more glasses appeared before them and Del reached up and slipped a $20 bill between the woman's breasts. "Thanks, darlin'." *This isn't even fun anymore but what the hell...*

Steven sat there, disgusted with the doctor and watched the woman, whose job it was to make the patrons happy. He was interested to find out how she would get out of that outfit, amusement flickering in his eyes as they exchanged glances. His eyes dropped to her breasts and back to her face.

Her eyes slid from Steven's to Del's before answering, "Well, we have lots of booze, so I'll be here to serve you whenever you want to imbibe... and my name's Julia," she said with a wicked twinkle in her eye. Winking at Steven, she turned and pranced away, swinging her hips.

They both watched her before resuming their conversation, each anxious to leave.

"So, the plan is pretty cut and dried then. We stop Larkspur from getting the Canadian contract and make sure that Premier gets it. That will force them to take Ace-Deer's offer and it's a done deal. Larkspur loses out on the drug card, Premier gets the drug contract instead, the boss gets what he wants and we get paid for it. I like it."

Steven's eyes grew dark and his fingers tightened on the stem of the wine glass. "I have some personal things to get straight......." he muttered.

"Just don't screw this up for us —- whatever it is you need to do, just don't screw it up and don't screw with me," Del clamped his jaw tight and stared at him.

"Yes, don't you worry about me, doc. I can take care of the job and myself. Just leave it to me." Steven gulped his wine down once again, ignoring Del's look of annoyance, and pushed the chair backwards. "My eyes are burning in this damned place with all the smoke. You never did tell me who the boss is. Why is it such a big secret anyway?"

Del stared at him silently.

Well, I'm out of here then," he said, shrugging and lifting the laptop as he stood up. Nodding, he pushed his way toward the brick stairway once again, stumbling upwards as slowly as he'd entered, fighting the darkness. Just as he reached the door, he felt a soft hand on his arm.

"Got a light for a lady?" The busty waitress pulled him the rest of the way upward, out of sight from the other tavern patrons, enjoying the look on his face. He reached out to touch the cleft that held the $20 bill just moments earlier, pushing softly, his eyes clinging to hers.

Julia felt a tremor where his warm flesh touched her. She reached upward, kneading his hand into her soft breast, pushing it deeper, harder. She grabbed his other hand and looked at him questioningly. Without another word, he followed her outside into the afternoon sun.

The next day, a perfect Indian summer morning dawned bright and filled the Portland skyline. Callie stood at her sink and watered the plants that flourished inside her garden window and enjoyed the sun, a huge red ball between the fir trees, and smiled. Against her better judgment, she'd accepted a lunch date from Derrick and they planned to meet at noon over at Three Lions and she was as nervous as a jittery cat.

No loose ends when there's not a man around. Pressing her lips together, she tried to be honest with herself. But Derrick is different. It's not like I'm going to marry the man, for goodness sakes. It's just lunch. She'd been friendly over the last few years with other employees and co-workers but never dated them. Until now. I feel comfortable around him. And his nearness excites me. I won't deny it!

In the past, Caroline's teasing her to get a life had always forced her deeper under the rug. Until Derrick was planted so near her office…like a giant flowering Daphne, with an Old Spice scent. His name lingered around the edges of her mind. Putting the water pitcher under the sink, she reached for a cup and visualized Derrick with a Daphne's little pink and white flowers smelling like Old Spice. She laughed aloud.

Pouring her coffee, she remembered him visiting her at the hospital. Then, why is this lunch date making me so nervous? I don't know a lot about him except he's divorced, his dad lives here and he has a daughter. Well, Mom, I could use your input on this one.

Still grinning like an idiot, she plopped down at her round dining room table to soak up the early sunshine and reached for the newspaper. She picked up the juice at her elbow and pulled the toasted English muffin, filled with strawberry cream cheese, toward her. Then, she opened the front page.

LARKSPUR HEALTH PLAN OR PREMIER HEALTH TO GET
CANADIAN PHARMACEUTICAL CONTRACT?

Discount pharmaceutical companies are trying to fill the need for less expensive health care as the amount of money Americans pay out of their own pockets increases.

A rise in the number of uninsured and out-of-pocket prescription expenses has spurred several companies to form alliances with non-American companies such as the Canadian company that is currently being courted by both Larkspur Health Plan and Premier Health Link. It is unknown which carrier will contract with the pharmaceutical company to our north and have the ability to add it to their list of enhancements in the health insurance marketplace. Maybe both?

"These particular fights for offering covered members savings between 10% and 50 % may just be the first in a long run of similar jousts we will see in the marketplace ever since Larkspur's Derrick Leander met with Oregon Senators Wilding and Amburgey to affirm the legality of such mergers," said

Lawrence Shearer, of the Consumers Union, publisher of Consumer Reports Health Magazine.

As of this writing, the name of the Canadian company in question has been undisclosed to the Oregonian; however, a spokesman at Premier assured us a decision will be made next week, when the arbiter arrives in Portland to finalize the contract bids.

Callie reached for her orange juice once again and bit harshly into her English muffin. She chewed so hard her jaws ached, and then she stuffed the remainder into her mouth. *This is becoming a real pain in the ass. Premier assured us, huh?*

Across the city, James Garnett read the article with growing concern. Struggling with impotence due to his inability to corner the unknown intruder, he growled at the paper. At the beginning, the job appeared simple but his findings were not much help, even though the bug had been removed from the Phillip's house. The big question still remained. *If she didn't discuss business information to the detail that this article inferred, then what? I'm definitely missing something.* He reached for his small, dog-eared notebook and jotted another note, waiting for Lee's call.

By the time Callie arrived at her office, the building was abuzz with consternation and loaded questions. Veering in the direction of Caroline's office, carrying her Starbuck's coffee container carefully, she jammed her thumb over the opening and gripped the cardboard jacket in an effort to avoid burning fingers. Seeing Lana at her desk, she smiled at the young woman. "Good morning, Lana. Has Caroline arrived yet?"

Lana's eyes seemed much larger in her face today, lavender shadows beneath her eye sockets; eyes that appeared sad, lacking her usual zest. As Mom would say, "she has her bags packed" Callie bent toward her quizzically, and then reached out to feel her forehead.

Lana pulled back and smiled briefly, nodding her assent to enter her employer's office. "I'm ok, Callie. Really." She whispered.

Shrugging slightly, she pushed open Caroline's door to see her slumped behind her desk, blonde head bent over the paper, a coffee cup held aloft in her right hand.

"Hey, lady. I called you earlier but missed you and your cell phone wasn't turned on. What's going on...other than the article in the Oregonian, I mean." Callie's sympathetic eyes held Caroline's anguished ones as they shook their heads at one another and exchanged looks.

"It's just so damned crazy, Cal. Who is it? I can't believe James is still coming up with blanks. This information must have come from the bug in my phone............but it states, 'Premier assured us.....'" she said, pointing to the words before her.

"Yes, I caught that too. What bug? I hadn't heard about that. Catch me up," Callie responded. She carefully removed the lid from the cup and inhaled the coffee's aroma, before scrunching down into the loveseat facing Caroline.

Caroline brought her up to date as she tapped the paper in front of her. "We are positive it was Steven who put the bug on the phone, but James assures me there's got to be another answer besides that. I mean, somebody is eavesdropping or something. I don't know how and Lee.... well Lee is at his wits end too." She hung her head, took a deep breath and resumed with a voice nearing defeat, "I guess there's a chance that what Steven tried to start, we may not be allowed to finish. Damn! I wanted that contract.... I swore after I left Paul that I'd make my own mark and this is it. Damn. Damn and double Damn!"

She sipped the coffee and pursed her lips. "Well, the other news is that Robert arrives Monday morning for three days and wants to finalize the contract during his visit. We don't have much time to figure this mess out and I thought we had all our ducks in a row." She sucked in her breath and sat back in her chair.

The women were silent as they finished their coffees, and could not think of anything further to add to the dilemma. They quietly sipped, blinked, shook their heads and repeated the litany as their minds fought to fill in the blanks.

"Well, enough of that. What's your day look like, Callie?" Caroline asked with apparent interest while closing the distasteful paper in front of her and reaching for a file on the corner of her desk.

"Well... you mean other than my date?" The words rushed out as she licked her lips over a secret smile.

Caroline's head jerked up quickly. "Oh rrreeeallllly...? I want to hear about this." She rolled out the word like a slow motion film, waiting expectantly.

Callie stood up, reached down to push the non-existent wrinkles from her green pants suit and flipped the cream scarf up over her shoulder mimicking a fading Mae West. She took a step, not answering Caroline's question, but stopping at the door to turn and grin.

"Yes, reeeaaalllly." Then she was gone.

"The future belongs to those who believe in the beauty of their dreams."
—Eleanor Roosevelt

Chapter 10

* * *

Derrick applauded his good fortune and watched Callie sip her Latte'
and pick up the soup spoon. He ordered the Hungarian
Mushroom at her insistence and ladled spoonfuls into his mouth
with alacrity, listening as she told him about herself.

"........then he was killed in a boat accident several years ago right in
front of our cottage at D Lake. That's just this side of Lincoln City in a little
burg called Neotsu. I don't drive over to the beach often.... anymore, just
pay the maintenance people and taxes," her voice petered out as she bit into
the herb stick beside her bowl, her brown eyes unfocused for a moment.

"That must have been a nightmare," he responded, sadness in his voice.

Callie didn't answer immediately, but looked out the side windows
instead. "Yes, it was. I'm not sure why I shared that with you, Derrick. I
don't usually. It's tattooed in that hidden place inside my heart."

Derrick tried to pull her back to the present, "Well, I'm glad you let it
out. That pain can't get any better until you talk about it. I've been
divorced four years. We'd been married twenty-two years. One day I
realized I felt lonely even when Millie and I were together. Then she played
house with someone else." The sentence hung in the air a moment. "I have
one daughter who is the joy of my life and of course, my Dad lives here in
Portland. So does my Uncle Ted. They're real characters and I love them
like crazy. Dad needs surgery for a gastro disease and he's waiting for
approval for surgery. The delays drive me nuts, but Dad seems to take it in
his stride most of the time. I've lived here nearly a year. Let's see, I love
the ocean, music and dancing. Not necessarily in that order. What about
you?" His herb sticks were long gone and he was pushing his spoon around
in a near-empty bowl on the table in front of him. His eyes danced as he
smiled at her.

"Me? Well," she took a deep breath. "No children I'm sad to say. I always wanted them but it just never happened. Francois and I were married for twenty years before... Well, then my mother died last year. That was a terrible blow. She was only sixty eight and always so healthy." His look of concern made her pause a moment. "Cancer."

"Oh, God, that's ...."

She quickly blinked back tears and said, "And I love the ocean, music and dancing....not necessarily in that order."

They both laughed and a tiny burst of hope kindled.

"Have you read the paper today?" he asked, suddenly serious once again.

"Oh, yes, every word." Her eyes sparkled.

"Me too...I have to tell you though, I'm stumped...All over a drug card."

"...Derrick, how well do you know Steven Roget?"

His teeth tugged at his bottom lip before answering. "Well, I thought I knew him pretty well but that was in college really. For the past year, minus the last six months he's been in jail, he seemed okay and I felt he put Larkspur first and foremost in his business dealings. He and I were college roommates at U of O and he was a computer genius... and a computer hacker. He was always getting into trouble and invited me along, but his kind of fun wasn't mine so he finally gave up on me. That's why I find it ironic that I'm at Larkspur now with the computer job and he was in management and close to Caroline and......" His eyes searched Callie's and his voice died down.

"Yes.............. Caroline." She looked down at her fingernails.

"What brought all of that on anyway? Even after all our talks when you were in the hospital, I really never got the whole problem answered.... And...By the way, did you know I clocked him?" he countered. The scent of her delicate perfume wafted toward him and her eyes reminded him of freshly ground nutmeg. His eyes lingered on the little silver streak in the midst of curls covering her forehead.

".........You clocked him?" Her brow furrowed.

"Yeh, I was so mad at him for acting like an asshole and hurting you and Caroline, I tried to knock the shit out of him. He looked worse than I did, but not much." His grin was slow and he waited for her to continue.

"Ouch!! So, you slayed the dragon for us? I didn't know that." She took a breath and smiled an instant before turning solemn once again. "Well as far as I know and based on the disagreements he and I had before that fateful day at Caroline's, my uncertainties about the liaison between the LEXUS doctors that were being pushed at us through the Midlothian Merger made him angry. When I tried to undermine his desire to force both entities into the contract, he started unraveling."

"Yes, obviously. I found Steven before the police did but that's another story." Derrick ground out.

"I'll have to hear it sometime, then, Derrick. Back to the reasons.....Ace-Deer Rx has had problems. My agents complain about them all the time. They use a very short preferred prescription list. They don't pay the drug benefit if the member's prescription isn't on Ace's preferred list. One of the agents I work closely with was told by Premier Health that the drug card only paid for generic drugs, but if the member's doc specifically requested the name brand drug, they could request an exception and Ace-Deer would fill the prescription if it was approved by Dr. Reed. For some reason, he's on the Premier's drug review board even though he's a LEXUS big shot. I know he's the Medical Director, but prescription approval too?"

"Isn't he also Larkspur's Medical Review doc?" Derrick asked, baffled.

"No. We don't employ him but he's been acting as the decision maker for the past few months until we find a permanent replacement. Caroline asked him when the LEXUS HMO issue first arose but she wasn't happy about it. She says he's fair though."

"Anyway, I balked, Steven got angry and then the Oregonian's article pushed him into panic mode. He told Caroline I was sleeping with him and she almost believed him because of their relationship and...." She suddenly realized what she said and felt a flush crawl up her neck and into her cheeks. She dropped her eyes a moment, eyelashes brushing her cheeks like a fur blanket. "Well, you know the rest."

Derrick felt her discomfort and changed the subject, moving to the article instead. "Why did it make him so upset? Things were moving slowly but they *were* moving." He urged her to continue, his soup now cold. "I remember that day all right, Callie. You looked lost and really upset and I wanted so badly to follow you out of the agent's party that day. I remember the Oregonian article only vaguely. It stated that Larkspur wanted to enhance their plans by merging with Midlothian but it had been put on hold pending the resolution of a draft of contract issue."

"I've tried to bury the memory of that agonizing day. Let's see.... Steven wanted the Ace-Deer drug plan included with the merger, so the article that the Oregonian printed had him so angry, he went nuts. What happened was that Caroline listened to me about the negativity involved around Ace-Deer. Between my input after listening to our agents and Lee's findings that the Better Business Bureau had been inundated with complaints, she asked Lee to help her modify the contract for the merger. The Oregonian article basically related Caroline's thoughts stating something like, 'We have reviewed a number of items that must be carefully defined to construct the document so it is clear and concise and easily understandable, blah blah blah.'

She sipped her latte' before continuing, "Caroline didn't identify which items in the draft report required clarification. She called the document a 'draft' as Lee suggested, but she neither confirmed nor denied its contents in the newspaper that day. She said the final report the following week would contain modifications from the draft."

"So, on that basis, he flipped out?" Derrick's confusion and distaste at Steven's betrayal showed on his face. "All over a business matter?"

"Yes. That's when Steven got really angry. He was so angry; Caroline met him over at her house to avoid a scene at the agent's party. Then she was shocked to see a gun. She wrestled it from him and God only knows how she did that. And then she shot him, and then she called me on the cell phone. It shocked him so much; he grabbed her and pushed her. She stumbled and fell part way down the stairs, breaking her leg in the process. She told me he carried her back upstairs, propped her down on the floor by her bedroom so gently... like someone else had hurt her."

"Then he kicked the wall."

"My God."

Callie nodded. "Caroline screamed at him and he slapped her face...but you know what? Somehow, she grabbed his gun and she shot him again. Two shots. God, Derrick! I couldn't believe it when I got there. I mean, he's a big man so he must have been awfully sure he had her spooked to let that happen." Callie shook her head, trying to toss the nightmarish memory out and her eyes closed briefly.

"Oh, my God." Derrick took a deep breath. "So, Midlothian Corporation owns Ace-Deer? I know it's an in-pharmacy drug card at specified pharmacies. I know several local carriers use them in the marketplace such as Premier, United Life Works, Blue Health and Group Health HMO. But if Ace-Deer is a rotten supplier and that's why you didn't want it in the merger, but Steven did.... Why, knowing about the bad rep, would he continue to push for it, I wonder?" Derrick was thoughtful.

"That deep question must have a dark answer and we haven't figured that one out," she said lightly. "We should get back to work, you know..."

"What?" He glanced at his watch quickly.

Callie snickered. She thought the time had passed too fast also and laughed aloud.

Derrick listened to her laughter, felt the sweetness of it flow through him, warming him. Slowly, he set down his coffee cup. "I suppose, Callie, that....... would you like to go out on a real date?" His eyes spoke volumes as they waited for her reply.

Callie's heart missed a beat. "What did you have in mind?" The golden moths were dancing a jig in the pit of her stomach and her chest felt tight.

"I'd like to take you to *Alexander's* at the top of the Hilton Friday night. They have a great piano bar, a small dance floor and great wine." His infectious grin set the tone and offered a challenge that she didn't want to deny.

He could see her pleasure in being asked and her hesitation in accepting.

"Well.......it sounds wonderful. I haven't been any place fun like that in longer than I can remember and it's time. That's what Caroline keeps telling me...And I would like that, but the dance floor may have to wait until I can toss these ugly shoes."

"Excellent!" Lifting one hand, Derrick laced his fingers through hers as he reached to help her up. Their warmth freed in her a bursting of sensations.

Lana Potts dialed the intercom and told Caroline that Dr. Del Reed was on the line. Her voice was strained, almost hoarse; her chest felt heavy when she hung up her phone and sat still, anxiously awaiting the outcome of the early call. She held her breath and stared at the phone. *Oh God.... Why???!*

Caroline's trepidation was matched only by her slight hesitation before lifting the receiver. "Caroline Phillips." She gripped the receiver and hitched her foot onto the edge of her chair, needing support.

"Good morning, Ms. Phillips. This is Doctor Reed." The voice droned, silky and deep.

"Yes, Doctor Reed. How can I help you this morning?" She answered with slight disdain.

"I have an offer from Premier and I'd like to meet with you to discuss it."

"I have no intention of discussing any offers from Premier for Larkspur, doctor. You can discuss it over the phone or not at all. I've heard quite enough from Premier in the news lately." Her voice carried barely restrained anger. She stabbed the pencil into the tablet beside her and watched as it snapped and flipped onto the carpet.

"Oh! Well, since you and Premier both want the Canadian drug contract with Shelton-Kent..... You can't win, you know.... So why not just allow Premier to offer Larkspur the opportunity of a joint merger, per se, and our companies can share the rewards all the way around? Then you can contract with Ace-Deer as well. It makes sense when you stop to think about it. It would give more options to your members. My people can draw up the ...."

"Are you absolutely crazy, doctor?" she sputtered. "We are miles apart in our goals and our methods. Premier uses only LEXUS docs and we use a select few. Premier uses Ace-Deer and we refuse to use them at all. Just because you sit in for our medical reviews doesn't mean you can assume we work together in other areas of our company. I believe our conversation is finished. What part of NO don't you understand? Good bye now." Caroline took a deep breath and pulled the receiver away from her ear.

"Wait —- don't hang up —- I just want to tell you if you won't agree to join us then we'll get S/K on our own, and there won't be a chance in hell............Don't forget we gave you an offer." Del Reed finished firmly.

She was horrified as the words fell like iced chips. "And I suppose you will leak this magnanimous offer to Richard Ellis at the Oregonian like you've done so many times already, right?" Before she let him have a chance to answer, her voice raised an octave, "Well, I make it a rule to never get involved with sneaky, unethical conspirators, Doctor Reed."

Before she could disconnect the conversation, she heard him say quietly but firmly, "Well Ms. Phillips what about Steven Roget?"

Silence followed his statement like an empty tomb as he heard Caroline's sudden intake of breath before the sudden click and subsequent dial tone thrummed in his ears.

Caroline's hands wavered in front of her eyes, as she stared at the phone, likening it to a coiled snake. *The audacity of the man*, she thought, angrily wiping her cheek with the back of her hand. Quaking inside, she squinted shrewdly as a germ of an idea assembled itself in the front of her mind and she untangled it step by step before she lifted the receiver to call Lee.

Del Reed gently set the phone back in its cradle and leaned back in his chair, his hands clasped behind his head and a pained smile on his face. Then he sighed and rearranged his features to place the second call. His fleshy hand held the receiver as he punched in the numbers with the eraser end of his yellow pencil and waited for the man to answer.

"Reed here. Yes. I followed your instructions to the letter. She's royally pissed." Without waiting for a response, he hung up, this time turning his head to stare out toward the Willamette River, watching the river traffic and water rushing below his window. Twisting back toward his desk in his swivel chair, he felt sweat dripping down his temples and into his shirt collar. "Shit." He forced himself to breathe evenly, reached into his desk drawer, grabbed the aspirin and then unscrewed the top to his ever-present Evian.

"The heart is wiser than the intellect."
—Goethe

Chapter 11

* * *

Moments later, Caroline's voice sounded frantic. "...........then he wouldn't stop.......he brought Steven into the conversation about....My God, Lee... it was like a movie. And if it had been a movie, I could have turned the damn thing off!"

"Start from scratch, ok? Now, breathe in with the good ....and out with the bad...like Callie tells you to do, and tell me what happened," he coaxed, his voice almost a caress over the wire.

"Lee, I was just approached by Dr. Reed with an offering from Premier with the most delightful opportunity to mesh Larkspur with Premier and of course, everyone will live happily ever after," she replied with sarcasm. "And you know what I realized after I slammed down the phone? He knows we are dealing with S/K specifically, so we know he must be the Premier intruder. He must be the one who called Robert last week and I think I've thought of something to bring this all to a head. I just don't know how Steven fits into the mess."

Lee listened with a serious expression lining his forehead, his dark features concentrating on her words as if memorizing them. "Caroline... that may work. I applaud your idea ten fold... I'm up to my neck taking depositions all day today, so get a hold of Derrick and James ok? Go over this with James and please, Caroline......... keep me posted, ok? Leave me a voicemail, no Email. Wish we could get a handle on this thing." He hesitated, lowering his voice, "By the way....this is a crazy time to ask but I just got two tickets to see Phantom at the Civic Saturday night.... Will you be my date?" He finished lamely.

"A crazy time is right," she laughed. "I'd love to, Lee. My home is feeling like a prison... between this frantic activity and Steven turning up so suddenly and... an emphatic YES! I would enjoy that very much. What time?" Caroline's only thought at that moment was to feel Lee's closeness. *Why do I feel vulnerable with him after all these years? Why now?*

"We can figure that out later, Caro.... Please call James and Derrick. A.S.A.P."

"Yes, sir." Caroline's mood lifted as she felt a fight brewing and admitted she also felt more in control than she had in weeks.

Del Reed's partner sat alone. *Profits must stay at the forefront of my agenda, regardless of my medical profession. What do I have now... twenty patients, thirty? Since I have no need to worry about the more mundane aspects of survival I can select the patients who interest me the most. Having them on an annual retainer fits my needs perfectly. I'm available for them and they keep my mind medically primed.* His mind turned to the Midlothian Merger once again, his cold blue eyes straining against the sunlight and worried the minute details impinging on his plans. He let the thoughts rattle through his brain and a problem he couldn't seem to control, namely Steven Roget.

As he'd walked east on Alder toward the Willamette River at ten o'clock that morning, he passed Nordstrom, then crossed the street dodging crowds of street kids hanging out at Pioneer Square. Thousands of bricks covered the entire block behind and below Starbucks. Stopping briefly to appreciate the architect's design, his shrewd eyes followed the deep steps directing Portlanders and tourists into the eye of the square. A platform was set up in the center and a band's music would be reverberating through the lunch crowd if this was summertime. People would be standing to listen or scooting and nudging into open spaces for seats along each tier of the brick-layered steps.

Looking upward, across the square toward Yamhill Street, he allowed himself a brief pee-warm smile as he gazed at what his wife called her 'umbrella man." The bronzed statue gave the impression he was taking a jaunty walk through the upper area; He was nearly six feet tall, dressed in a bronze suit, a smile on his face. Carrying the perpetual umbrella, he was the sign of a true webfoot Portlander and the mainstay of the block. It was their meeting place. Janine had a flair for romance. He shrugged and turned toward the river again.

Suppressing further inanities, he continued his trek down Alder Street, crossed the Tri Met bus lanes, and ignored the old post office on one side and Macy's on the other. His calculating mind was awhirl and his eyes once again pooled with intense power, as he flexed his hands, turning his knuckles white as he held the Oregonian in a strangle hold. Then, he smacked his lips and held them tightly against his dentures, and hurried his stride toward the tall KOIN tower, where his office held the papers he'd requested.

She won the first round, he thought, *but she won't win the second. I'll have my way if it kills......* he smiled slightly as the jumbled thoughts whipped through his already-mounting rage. He didn't care whether he hurt her or not. *That merger was meant to include ALL the providers AND my Ace-Deer caveat.... Not just the docs she deemed fitting to belong to Larkspur. And the drugs. Damn her!*

A cloudless cerulean blue sky framed the white-tipped crown of Mount Hood in the distance as he crossed the last lap of his daily walkabout. But not even the awe-inspiring view could relax his muscles as he pushed the glass doors open and punched the elevator button with a light snapping sound. *The bitch is ruining my walks now.*

Premier Insurance Company shared the building with the Channel 6 television station and was arranged to enclose the medical clinic as well as the LEXUS HMO corporate offices. Since he was the sole proprietor of both plus the major silent stockholder of Premier, he had to be organized, alert and savvy to the business ventures one required to stay on top of the heap. He was a very private man and didn't advertise all the pies he diddled his fingers through. Many assumed it was just a coincidence, having the offices nearly intertwined and throwing the nosy public off kilter increased the challenge. *Even my other office is ....* He smiled, mentally patting himself on the back. *Just like father instructed...never put all one's berries into one pot. Diversify. Diversify. Diversify.*

Even though his patient load was a selective few whittled down by financial-based criteria, he was always in control. He liked it that way. Many of his patients paid him a bonus annually, in exchange for being "on call" for their needs either at his office or in their homes. It worked well for each of them and it still allowed him the flexibility to supervise his HMO and insurance company. Delegate. Delegate. Delegate. His motto was well known and he inspired a strange but anxious loyalty in exchange for the money he paid his employees. The downside was that he did not allow for mistakes or failures. He made no exceptions. And he made no friends. Except for Janine.

Reaching his plush office after walking past open doorways filled with patients, doctors, nursing staff and machines whirring noisily, he closed his door with a snap.

The package lay on his desk, right where he'd left it. Things were going according to plan but he wouldn't allow himself the luxury of applauding prematurely. Pursing his pale lips, his long fingers ripped open the package as he thought of Roget again. Bleakness filled his craggy features as he dropped the envelope in the wastebasket, the Washington D.C. stamp blurred.

A damned loose cannon, he thought. *Too bad he didn't just stay where he was, but.......... He could still be of use, and the loose ends will eventually be tied into a nice, tidy bow.* He smiled again, totally devoid of humor, and began to read the papers in front of him.

Carl Leander's stomach burned. He pushed himself up on one elbow again to chew the colored Tums he'd placed near his bed the night before. The chronic, constant swallowing kept him awake off and on all night and each day dawned, a replica of the one before. His body was tired and his face, wan. After tossing and turning for hours, trying to placate the never-ending burning, he reached his hand up to turn the ticking clock's face toward him. Five o'clock. He twisted beneath the bedcovers once again, trying to force his body to relax and to sleep again.

By six o'clock, he gave up and tossed back the covers, an expletive whispered harshly in the early morning's dawn. Birds chirped wildly outside his bedroom whistling in the new day, knowing the sun was about to burst over the eastern horizon. But Carl didn't enjoy any of it. Feeling slightly chilled, he shrugged into his old flannel robe and shuffled into his slippers, tossing two more Tums into his mouth, chewing until his jaws ached. The timer had started the automatic coffee pot and he could smell it brewing. Trudging through the house, he headed outside to pick up the paper on the front porch. Bending down, he immediately felt his stomach rush upwards toward his throat.

"God, this is getting old," he said as he picked up the Oregonian, snapped it irritably against his thigh and reentered the living room. He headed for the kitchen and the enticing aroma. Within minutes, the coffee was ready. Grabbing his well-worn blue cup with the little thumb handle from its hook, he filled it with the steaming brew. His eyes felt grainy, his body ached from insufficient sleep and his stomach rumbled and churned as the coffee bit into his gut. He set down his coffee cup. He was feeling so angry; he wanted to hurl the cup against the wall. "I know," he said aloud. "Friday. One more day." Then, he slumped into the chair beside his dining-room window. *The doc said we'd know tomorrow,* he thought. *Just one more day to get through and then I can move on with it.*

In Beaverton, about fourteen miles to the west, as Carl drank his coffee and mentally calculated his future once the surgery was over, Lana Potts stood beside her clean kitchen counter, pouring her own coffee into a white ceramic mug with angels surrounding its perimeter. Her red hair was tightly pulled back in a little ponytail and her flowered robe was wrapped around her taut body. She listened for any movement from her bedroom and said a quiet prayer. "Please let this silence continue.... at least until I can wake up a little more, and start the boys rolling into their morning routine." Deep in thought, she inhaled the brew and sipped.

Pulling them out of warm beds early each morning, then into clothes, feeding them and gathering up their day-care items was never an easy task. One Lana wished she did not have to perform. She enjoyed her job, or at least she had for nearly two years. Until recently.

She gulped the coffee, burning her tongue, and pulled it back into her mouth to rub it across the front of her teeth. Leaning her hip against the counter, she raised her head upward, stretched her neck and closed her eyes against the panic that constantly swelled in her chest and throat. She hated what she was doing; facing the problem each day at work and again, worse when she got home with the boys. Her dilemma seemed tantamount to a disaster waiting to happen and she could think of no way out. She ground her left hand into her abdomen and finished her coffee, before tiptoeing into the boy's room down the hall. She woke them up gently, holding a finger to her lips, begging their silence.

The little boy's round eyes stared at his mother, enjoying the game, although his teddy and pillow invited him back into the coziness of his covers. Lana pulled them back again and patted his little butt playfully and reached down to kiss his warm neck as it curled into the pillow. "Come on, Nick. Let's get Frankie up and dressed. Please be real quiet, sweetheart, just for Mommy, ok?" Her eyes implored her son.

Nicholas nodded, eyes flickering toward the hall.

Within ten minutes, both boys were dressed and being plied with animal-shaped, sweetened cereal at the little kitchen counter that opened between the kitchen and dining room, little Frankie whimpering against the early morning grizzlies that he fought each morning. *He is definitely not a morning person, just like his father,* Lana thought as she pushed toast their way and poured milk over their Raisin Bear Flakes and sliced bananas.

It was still quiet in the back bedroom, as she backed away and whispered to the boys, "I'll be dressed and back in a minute so...... stay put."

I feel like a monster, she thought, as she gazed at herself in the large mirror over the bathroom sink, ears straining for a warning movement beyond the door. Tossing on a slim dress over underwear and pantyhose, she rushed through her make-up and ran a comb through her slightly-curly hair. *Almost out*, she thought. Quickly reaching for her earrings, she had the second one poised near the hole of her left lobe when a second pair of eyes met hers in the mirror. Blonde tousled hair and a bare chest reflected the man in the doorway. Her knuckles tensed on the counter.

"Well, darlin' you weren't planning to leave without kissing your ol' man good bye, were you?" Steven drawled, as his glance sharpened in the mirror.

Lana held her tears in check. "Of course not, Steven, we were just letting you sleep, that's all." She tried to push by him but his right arm snaked out and she felt fingers wrap around the back of her neck as he yanked her forward and clamped his mouth onto hers. She pulled away and pushed at his chest, "The boys, Steven. Please.... don't.....I was just thinking that....." she whispered, fighting against his kiss.

"What is it, Sweetness——please or don't?" His voice was warm and inviting.

"Is daddy up?" Nick called from the kitchen, his voice sounding odd and anxious.

Steven reached down and grabbed Lana's buttocks, pushing her toward the little voice and whispering, "Don't get any ideas about thinking——just remember, *I* do the thinking around here," he said in a low rumbling voice. Propelling her into the kitchen steadily and patting her intimately, before reluctantly letting her go, he winked at the boys. Both boys raised their chubby arms for his kiss. He picked up little Frankie and allowed Lana to wipe up their faces and cereal messes before she gathered their backpacks.

"I have to go now. You know where I am." Her voice was flat as she hoisted Frankie onto her hip and grabbed Nick's hand, leading down the stairs and into the garage.

Bright, unblinking blue eyes followed her departure as she rushed out of the kitchen and he knew she didn't care or notice the pain etched in their deep pools. He was getting a headache and stroked his temples. Steven went into the bathroom and took two aspirin. While he washed them down, he stared at his reflection in the mirror. He looked pale and shaken. Since his return from the state pen, he kept reliving the horror behind those bars, seeing inmates in his mind's eye standing too close or the guard's meanness, the dankness, the never-ending rattling of inmate's thrashing around him. His stomach clenched and he pushed his palm against his forehead trying to erase the memories that swirled around him day and night.

"With most people, doubt about one thing is simply
blind belief in another."
—G. C. Lichtenberg

Chapter 12

* * *

Del Reed dreaded Thursdays. He knew he'd have a list a mile long with names and surgeries begging for approval. His round face and thinning hair was rampaged as his fingers ran across his features and played with the thin strands that were combed across a balding pate.

The Medical Review Board's agenda was lying on his desk in front of him and seemed littered with patient names and diagnoses requesting surgeries, and they were all stamped '**Urgent**'. *Oh, of course. Aren't they all?* The room felt hot and sticky even though he knew the air conditioning unit had not been changed. His explicit instructions were followed: seventy degrees, no higher, no lower. He'd told the employees surrounding his office to keep a sweater handy if they didn't like it. The crisp air permeated the offices and sweaters lingered on doorknobs and chair backs. And the air conditioner was never pushed over seventy, on the dot, as he put it.

Carla, his assistant, brought in another stack of files and laid them gingerly on his desk, turning swiftly to answer the phone. She also detested Thursdays. His annoyance was reflected in his demands as the clock veered toward two o'clock. She hunched into her chair and pulled her gray sweater around her shoulders, fighting off the chill.

Del's finger followed the words of each attending physician statement and request. He had many faults but he took pride in his perusal of the medical information. However, as his job required, he also managed to postpone or stop many surgeries. Since he was hired director of the Medical Review Board for the administration part of the mix of both the Premier and LEXUS HMO, his job was to save money. He knew the HMO was a 'capitated' product, and premium dollars were paid directly to the Primary Care Physicians (PCP) every month whether they saw their patients or not. Of course, some of the files were Larkspur patients also, he noticed grimly, due to select LEXUS use.

The HMO required that the medical care remain within the clinic; preferably only PCPs performing most of the care. However, all medical professionals know that often specialists are required and surgery is imminent. His job was to coordinate specific care and see that precautions were taken. If an alternative procedure or treatment versus expensive surgery was available, it should be tried, whenever possible. *The all mighty dollar must stay here. Why share their fees with surgeons if it's unnecessary?*

He counted fourteen names with the coordinating fourteen files stacked on his desk. There were doctors both on the LEXUS panel as well as independent surgeons caring for Premier Members. *I'd like to say 'no' to all HMO docs caring for Larkspur members,* he thought harshly. *However, it's a damn shame my conscience gets in the way, and my ethics won't allow an arbitrary red check across those specific names,* He trudged through the list, muttering. "But I wish I could, just this once," he sighed. "But I won't."

As she did every Thursday, Carla knocked on his door, and held up five fingers. He nodded, pushed the files into some semblance of order and got out of his chair to walk down the hallway toward the conference room to meet both in-house nurses from LEXUS and the claims supervisors.

Three hours later, grumbling and tired, the group scattered and the files were returned to their prospective medical providers. Inside each file, firmly clipped, was a form with a notation to **'proceed with surgery'** or a red check mark in the slot that read, **'suggest another alternative. If surgery is still required after six weeks, appeal for surgery negotiable'.** Del Reed's meticulous signature was scrawled across each form with a firm hand and relieved mind.

At five thirty, Carl Leander's file was delivered to Dr. Sam James's office manager, a red -check mark in the box on the form inside, clipped tightly to the file.

That evening, the three women walked up the steps to the Mission Theater, laughing like children as they tried to escape the rigors of business and pretend carefree lives.

"This is the first time in so long that I've run out to have some fun, ladies. Thank you for joining me. I don't even know what movie is playing, I just know it begins at 5:30 and Vincent is working late. Thank you for coming on such short notice," Janine Vinnier said as she pulled the heavy doors toward them and they flanked the foyer.

Inside, the lobby was almost empty as the young man selling tickets took their $3.50 and opened the door for them. They hardly noticed him. *Not the usual crowd,* he thought, turning back to his post to get ready for the onslaught that typically drifted into the Mission's specialty movie house.

They chose the back row because it was open and a bar-type table sat snugly in front of the chairs. They were fit into a curved room, sporadically set at odd angles so the crowd could watch the movie, eat and talk with a clear view of the screen. Beers in hand and hamburgers ordered, their words cascaded over one another as they relaxed in an atmosphere made for it.

"Oh! It's 'First Wives Club' about three women. Oh good," Callie said, as she saw the list of names, "Diane Keaton, Bette Midler and Goldie Hawn. I like all of them." She slid down in her chair, rested her feet on the edge of the wooden footrest, forgetting she wasn't sixteen but appearing so.

Caroline laughed. "I saw Goldie Hawn in 'Overboard' years ago with Kurt Russell and I just about died laughing." She loved the feeling of temporary careless abandon.

Janine drank her microbrew and studied the two women closely. *My life is so tightly woven. To be that relaxed.....* "I wish Vincent liked movies and fun! He doesn't like sharing me with anyone and I need people!" She shook her head and reached for the plate the young woman sat in front of them as the lights dimmed and the movie began.

"Me too. Well, here goes," Callie whispered. She settled into the chair and grinned at the others. She gripped her hamburger in both hands and let its juice run down her wrist. "Oh Yum. It's been too long since I was this naughty and it's so good!"

"Glad we got a back seat so I can see my food," Caroline said, staring at the huge screen and squinting in the darkening room. People were moving chairs around for a better view. The food's aroma surrounded them. "Maybe we should get pop corn later too?" She gripped her beer glass and sipped the brew, waiting for an answer.

Janine continued to study her companions in the darkness, bit into her hamburger and drank more beer, contemplating what it would be like to live a different life. A long-dreamed restlessness gripped her. "We won't be able to fit popcorn inside when we're done with all this, *mon cherie*," she said with a far-away voice.

"Bet me! By the way, what does Vincent do for a living, Janine? I can't believe we've known each other so long and we've not met him. You don't talk about him very much." Callie asked, sad to hear their friend voice such discontent. "There really IS a Mr. Vinnier, isn't there?" Callie bit into her hamburger again and felt the juices running down her chin and laughed to herself.

"Oh, he's a doctor, but Vincent's name isn't.... Oh! I like the music in this movie." She answered, taking another sip, her eyes riveted on the screen, the question forgotten.

"A woman is a lion in her own cause."
— Author unknown

Chapter 13

* * *

The following morning, Caroline found Lana at her desk, staring at the monitor and typing with such speed, her fingers blurred. She afforded Caroline only a brief smile and nod as she'd watched her walk down the hall toward her.

"Good morning, Lana. I have several phone calls to make this morning so please take messages." Caroline said as she stood next to her secretary's desk, flipping through the stack of mail that looked exceedingly heavy for a Friday. A pot of purple Violets flanked a picture of Lana's little boys and files were banked up next to her computer. A hickey peeked out above a scarf tied around Lana's neck. *A romance? Then why does Lana seem paler with each day?*

Lana felt Caroline watching her as she concentrated on the letter she was typing from the notes she'd received the previous day. She sat in the chair stiffly and refused to give into her fear that Caroline might read her thoughts. *Oh God, please don't let her.............* Lana heard the mail drop back onto her desk and forced a smile to her lips, glancing upward to meet Caroline's gaze.

"Are you all right, Lana? Forgive me for intruding and I don't mean to offend but I've noticed you're in a relationship," nodding toward Lana's neck, "yet you seem so sad. Is this guy right for you?"

Caroline's concern caused the little knot in Lana's stomach to double in size. "I'm not sure. Thanks for asking. I'm really okay." She reached for the mail, hoping Caroline didn't suspect something wasn't right.

Caroline shrugged, picked up her briefcase and entered her office, still unsure how to help Lana when something was obviously taking a toll on her emotions.

Her big desk was clean, as usual, since it was her habit to clear everything off at the end of each day. She pulled out a pad and pen, as well as her address book where she had the names and numbers she needed. Then she drew James Garnett's business card from under the calendar tab and laid them all in front of her, lining them up evenly. Everything seemed in perfect order except her mind. That was doing flip-flops. *I have to do this.* Proceeding with the idea rambling in her head ever since Del Reed's call, she focused on the telephone and opened the book beside her.

James answered on the first ring and listened. "Yes, it has definite merit and it might work to Larkspur's advantage to stop the flow of sporadic interference and subsequently might tighten your grip on the S/K contract. It's an approach he will find hard to resist and I'm anxious to hear the outcome." His voice held a healthy respect and wished he'd thought of it.

The second call she made was to a Ms. Manuela Ruiz in Malaga, Spain who was in charge of pharmacy contract negotiations at *La Verdadero Pharmecia Corporation.*

"Como esta' Senora Ruiz? Me llama es Carolinena Phillips y trabajo en las Ustados Unidos." Her conversation lasted ten minutes, the answers positive and helpful.

Her third call was to a Mr. Manfred Ordsdorff in Berlin, Germany who was in charge of their drug-marketing department at *Gruggs Obelisht.*

"Good afternoon, Herr Ordsdorff, my name is Caroline Phillips and I work in the United States. I would like............"

Fifteen minutes later, their conversation ended with a hint of laughter and smiles on both ends of the phone line.

Holding her breath with steam-rolling excitement, she dialed the *Oregonian* and was immediately connected with the infamous Richard Ellis at the *Oregonian.* "Well, Mr. Ellis, this is Caroline Phillips from Larkspur and I would like to give you the opportunity to be the first journalist privy to our company's new challenge into the mail-order drug card marketplace. Can you meet me in my office at ten o'clock this morning?" She finished and sat silently for only a couple beats before she heard the man's voice respond with a mingling of questions and interest.

"Yes, ma'am. I'll be there. Where do I find you?" Richard Ellis scribbled down the information and hung up the phone, elation flitting across his features as he readied for the meeting after making changes on his calendar.

Caroline's office was open and bright. She stood at her window, clearly enjoying the morning, gazing at the bridges that spanned the Willamette River off to her right and the west hills to her left. *I never get tired of this view!* She watched a helicopter land on the helipad across from her office window and smiled. She wore a burgundy dress, matching jacket with silver filigreed buttons. Simple pearls were draped around her neck with matching pearl studs in her earlobes that she knew complimented her blonde snug hairdo. She was ready for a fight.

Promptly at ten o'clock, Lana ushered the reporter into Caroline's office.

Richard Ellis was agape at the sight of her, clearly surprised, as he saw the sun shining onto her face. He could feel his heartbeat accelerate. He'd always assumed a CEO should be matronly with horned rims. Well, so much for generalizing. Pictures definitely didn't do her justice.

Caroline turned to welcome the man. Her left arm motioned to one of the loveseats as she limped toward him, leaning slightly on her cane. "I'm Caroline Phillips. Welcome Mr. Ellis, would you like a cup of coffee?" She purred the words, her welcoming friendliness knocking his mind off balance.

"No, ma'am, I'm coffee logged already, thanks anyway." With pencil poised and a question on his face, he watched her sit down.

Caroline placed the cane beside her desk and sat across from the reporter, handed him a sheet of paper and allowed him a few minutes to read the press release.

"You mean this to be a real pharmacy war, then, don't you?" Richard scanned the rest of the page and glanced up to meet her, open-eyed, and staring.

"Yes, sir, we do." She answered, struggling to maintain an even, conciliatory tone.

Their meeting was over within fifteen minutes with his promise to print her press release in Monday morning's paper and not a day sooner. They each had what they'd hoped to accomplish and both headed in opposite directions.

Business frantically resumed as Caroline's day proceeded with a short meeting to douse some other fires so she headed toward the outer offices. That done, she stopped at Callie's office for a quick hello before continuing down the hallway to iron out some claims issues. She pushed the door open.

"Callie?" her voice called out softly, but the office was empty. She was surprised to find nobody around, not even Callie's secretary, or the sales people who typically buzzed around their desks like bees to honey. Caroline continued on down the hallway and noticed an uncanny silence where there should be noisy printers, ringing telephones and conversation. *That's odd. Where is everyone?* She stood a moment, leaning on her cane and pushed it outward on the carpet, seeing the nap darken as she stroked it. She retreated back toward her own offices, scrapping the visit to Claims and noticed Lana was missing too. Her brow furrowed.

Reaching her door, she saw a yellow sticky note with the words, "Conference Room – Quick." She grimaced a little, stripped off the note and marched down the hallway, the limp especially apparent in her right leg.

The double wooden doors were closed. She placed her ear to the door before gently pushing down the brass handle. As she stepped into the room, she was surprised to see the blinds closed. Hesitating a moment to adjust her eyes to the darkness, the blinds were suddenly thrown open and the lights switched on simultaneously.

She jumped, raised her hand to her breast and caught herself on the door frame as the group of people started singing, "Happy Birthday to you, Happy Birthday to you, Happy Birthday dear Caroline...How could we forget you?"

Laughter rang out all around her and her eyes glistened. She saw Callie, Lana, Derrick, Eric, Janet, Betsy, Elaine, the entire Claims Department, her Underwriting team, and Lee Carle all beaming at her and clapping, smiles lighting their faces.

"Oh my God, you scared the hell out of me........." Still holding her hand over her heart, she sat down on the closest chair. Coffee was put into one hand and balloons were placed in the other as someone took her cane. She blew out one candle on the large iced cake and saw it cut and doled out quickly.

"I can't believe this. You know what? I forgot it was my birthday and I have never done that before. Never! PMS maybe? But guess the days move on.......... thank you, everyone. You made my day. Even though I promised not to celebrate them, I feel blessed I've seen another one. Thank you all." Joy bubbled in her laugh and shone in her eyes.

"Hey, can't let your birthday go unnoticed so I make sure everyone knows *who's* older than *who*..." Callie teased, as she planted herself down beside her friend and scooped up a piece of cake with her fork and lifted it to her mouth.

"Well, lady, you're next," Caroline said, a teasing tinkle in her words.

"Yes, I am, but I'll never catch up to you." Callie winked and moved to the table for coffee.

"Happy birthday, my friend," Lee's voice was low and vibrant behind her, sounding like velvet to her ears. She felt her heart beat swiftly, feeling his hand on her shoulder. *Where did this come from? He's been around for years and his nearness feels like electricity snapping through me. This definitely needs to be analyzed more closely.*

Callie reached over to squeeze Caroline's hand, "I must get back to work. I'll talk to you later. Great cake!" Callie grinned at them. "Bye Lee."

The room quickly emptied as everyone returned to their desks, cake and coffee in hand, leaving Lee and Caroline alone.

His eyes never leaving her face, he turned to her.

"Is tomorrow night still on, Caroline?" Lee asked, as he stabbed another bite of carrot cake with his fork.

"Of course! I'm not letting you off the hook. I'm really looking forward to it. I saw Phantom in San Francisco and I loved it." Her voice sounded strange to her ears, and she rushed on, "Oh, and Lee, I talked to the Spanish and German folks today and just met with the journalist."

"Mmmmmmmmmmmmmm.... Good. You're a shrewd woman, Ms. Phillips." He answered, as he wiped his face with the napkin and licked the cream cheese frosting off his bottom lip. "I don't have any of this stuff in my mustache or beard, do I?" he asked, looking at her quizzically.

Caroline found herself staring at his mouth, mesmerized, and felt her throat tighten.

"Caroline?" Lee's gray eyes looked into Caroline's.

"Oh...." She laughed quietly, glancing down at her hands, "no, you got it all."

The room suddenly felt warmer as she reached for her cane. "It sure was sweet of you to come over here just for this little birthday moment," she said quietly, pushing herself upward as Lee touched her elbow. They stood apart, looking at each other.

"Well, it's not like I had far to go. I'm just over on Taylor, remember? Must go. Hate to eat and run, but I have a client coming in about five minutes," he said in a deep tone, an unusual silence hanging between them. "See you tomorrow about seven, birthday girl." Then he was gone.

Caroline grinned in anticipation.

As Lee Carle left the building across town, Carl Leander's phone rang sharply disrupting his attention from the Friday morning paper. He jumped and spilled coffee on Page A5 and all over his left hand. Swearing at himself for being so jumpy, he wiped wildly with the dishtowel hanging on the stove bar. He reached for the phone and still managed to pick it up on its third ring.

"Carl. It's Doctor James." The voice sounded tired.

"Hi Doc, are we set?" Carl's voice asked, anxiously.

A deep breath prefaced Dr. James' words, as he continued, "That's why I'm calling, Carl. Got the Medical Review Board's response and their feeling is that we should put the surgery off for at least six weeks and try an alternative method to ease your symptoms." Sam held himself erect, trying to keep the frustrations out of his voice.

"Shit." Carl answered, disgustedly. "I'm running out of Tums, doc, and every time I bend over I think I'm going to lose what I ate and............" His anger got the best of him as his voice rose sharply, "it's the HMO, isn't it, Doc? That's why they're trying to put me off. Well, I want it anyway. Let them be damned."

"Carl, that doesn't make sense. Your surgery wouldn't be covered and you didn't just win the lottery, did you? I know it's a pain in the butt to wait but please work with me on this. Let's play their game and I'll give you a prescription for some medication that might help. It's called *Prilosec*. It's about a buck a pill but it's cheaper than paying for your surgery out of your own pocket. I'll call it into Fred Meyers as soon as I hang up, ok?" Sam James' voice was urgent, but soothing.

"More pills." He blew out of the side of his mouth loudly. "Ok. I'm still with ya Doc, but just for the record, I'm damned mad about it." Carl's voice eased down in volume as he finished his sentence, waiting for a response.

"I know and I don't blame you on this one. It should be filled and waiting for you just after lunch. I'll call you next week to check up on you though, huh?" His voice tried to ease Carl's anger, even though his own belly hurt as if an ulcer was beginning. He gripped the handset until he felt bones crunch.

"Thanks, then." Carl hung up, dejected and troubled, before returning to his coffee. Stirring his Coffee Mate fiercely he slopped it over the side onto the round maple table. He grabbed the towel again and stared out into his yard and watched Alice watering her plants across the street. He wished he could calm himself and enjoy such a lazy chore.

The next moment, Sam was dialing Del Reed's number, preparing for another fight. Ever since he'd become part of the LEXUS panel, he'd had an uneasy and distasteful relationship. *I should have remained specifically with Larkspur's panel, but I knew I needed to belong to both panels to stay above water.* He knew without contracting with provider panels their patient base would drop dramatically along with their bank balance. Sam had never considered his bank account in the same breath with his patients before, but with the HMO influx and the rules guiding the medical community to join or get off the pot so to speak......... he was screwed.

He felt helplessness wrench his gut as he waited for Del to answer and it turned to unrestrained anger as he heard the voicemail message in his ear. He ground his teeth just listening to Del Reed's voice drone on about being unavailable, and crunched out a message, "Reed, this is Sam James. My medical experience and knowledge is adamantly against allowing Mr. Leander to wait another six weeks for his LNF surgery. There is no doubt that he needs it and forcing *Prilosec* on him is like placing a band-aid on a broken leg! Call me back please. 503-232-7812."

Fighting to calm himself, he called Fred Meyers Pharmacy and turned to the other files littering his desk. *Oh, how easy it used to be in the old days where patients were people and not numbers jerked around by actuaries. Having laypeople, nurses and a review board making second-rate decisions rankled and I'll be damned if I'll allow them to dictate how I run my medical offices. But what can I do??*

After driving into the garage, Lana's footsteps dragged. Helping little Frankie out of his car seat, Nicholas with his backpack and the many items that always accompanied little people at the end of a day away from home, she shut the door. Punching the button, the garage door closed behind them.

She trudged upstairs slowly, all part of her regimen, in the hopes of stalling the inevitable entrance to the apartment above. Before Steven was released from jail, she had taken the boys to visit him every Thursday afternoon, leaving the office on the pretext of visiting her sick mother in

Salem. Caroline didn't know her mother was dead. She thought she could handle the visits and tried to prepare herself for his release. Now, she wasn't so sure. *Now that he's back, I don't know if I can do it. I know he needed a stable address for the probation officer. But this other stuff is too hard. Why did he have to get out early? And why did I let him back in? I wish I had my old Steven back....... God help us.*

She swallowed heavily and took a deep breath, smiling suddenly at little Frankie when he clutched her fingers, trying to walk up the steps one at a time. *God, I love them and yes, I'll do anything for their well being. Even if it means....* The echoes of their little-boy laughter fed her fantasy and fanned her imagination. *I wish I could just grab each boy and run like hell.* Realty brought another smile to her lips as she watched them follow her upwards, slow but sure. Frankie's warm little fingers gripped hers and his feet tried to match his brother's steps as they ascended the stairs.

She'd had the boys late in life and she felt all of her forty two years.

Nicholas was seven and was an independent little imp. He was a good, sometimes impudent, child who rarely caused Lana worry other than the typical fuss a boy his age produced. He never knew his father, so Steven was the father he looked to for love and attention. He adored his little brother, Frankie. Each day when they arrived home, he'd try to pull the baby up the steps, sometimes getting behind him and pushing his butt upwards, usually knocking the poor tyke's face into the step above. Frankie would laugh, thinking it was great entertainment but it usually took them so long to get upstairs that Lana ended up doing stairs-duty most of the time.

Nicholas was quiet and watched his mother and Steven, often with a crease straining his forehead. Sometimes while watching Nickelodeon on television, he'd stop and turn his head if words were being flung around between the adults spilling tension into the air. And he watched silently.

That Friday night, she smiled at the boy's antics on the stairs and pulled herself upward by the handrail. She likened it to clawing up a dangling rope on the side of a mountain; invisible strings holding her as helpless as a butterfly in a spider's web. She remembered a long ago memory as a child, seeing a gorgeous yellow butterfly caught in a web outside her bedroom window. She'd tried to dislodge it before the spider could feast but only managed to get her small fingers covered in the stickiness of the web before she realized the butterfly was already dead. She shivered, hoping she wouldn't become the butterfly before this nightmare ended.

Reaching the top step, she turned into the kitchen and stopped a beat listening to Nick's excited chatter. She closed her eyes a moment, put the bags onto the counter and closed the door behind the children. Entering the living room, she tried to smooth her tired features, knowing the lack of sleep and recent tense atmosphere had transformed her into a shadow of herself.

The boys ran toward Steven, glad to see him instinctively stretch his arms toward them and give them hugs, equally, long and measured. He plopped a kiss on each boy's head and looked up at Lana with a lost look on his face for an unguarded moment. Then his features changed and the quiet sadness was gone. He had papers splayed all over the large marble coffee table. As he began to quickly gather them up, Frankie leaped onto his lap. He hugged the child and met her eyes above his curly head.

"Daddy... I made a bird house today." Nicholas said proudly as Frankie reached upwards with both arms after Steven placed him on the floor.

"Up... up... Daddy," Frankie's little voice begged, merging with Nick's intense explanation of wood, cutting with a saw and hammering his little birdhouse. His voice was filled with pride and Lana saw Steven reach out and squeeze his shoulder, nodding happily toward him.

Lana's brain screamed with the changes in Steven, sending different messages with every encounter. *Where's the man I fell in love with? The one who promised me a life together. A commitment? When did the changes start? How could he have hurt Caroline and Callie like that? Where's my other Steven?*

Steven's laptop was humming. She could see icons filling the monitor as his questioning look met hers. "Is it on?" he asked anxiously. His tie was tied haphazardly and he looked as if he'd dressed hurriedly, unlike his usual neatness-counts attitude. His eyes were glassy as if he'd been drinking.

She turned away from him to pour herself a glass of iced tea, listened to the ice hit the sides of the glass and swirled it around in her hand. "Yes, just like you told me to," she answered sadly.

"Good girl."

"It's love, it's love that makes the world go round."
—French song

Chapter 14

∗ ∗ ∗

Later that evening, Callie looked at her reflection in the mirror to make last minute adjustments. Smoothing her gray silk dress before snapping her beaded belt buckle, she saw her jet earrings dangling along her jawbone. They tickled as she bent to wrap black ankle straps around her ankle and latch them swiftly. A half-empty wine glass sat beside her. When she finished fluffing her hair, she grabbed the stem of the glass and glanced toward the mirror once again.

She stood sideways to the long wall mirror and sucked in her stomach. *Damn! I just have to get back into my walking routine and cut out those croissants.* She glanced down at her shoes again, hoping she wasn't being premature. Her ankle still swelled occasionally and she wanted tonight to be special. She did a slow pirouette before the glass and placed a hand over her racing heart.

Okay, half an hour and he'll be here. As she sipped more of her Cabernet, she hoped the fermented grape juice would relax her. *Or knock me flat,* she thought ruefully.

Gazing at the full moon less than five minutes later from her glassed-in patio, she heard the car drive up. *He's here! Lord...... I am feeling again and enjoying this anticipation. And I know somehow Francois would be happy for me.*

She was elated with her new objectivity as she opened the door. Derrick smiled, stepped inside, and the scent of Old Spice slapped her with memories. Francois. Kissing his neck when he wore it, she'd told him she'd follow him anywhere; same scent, different man, another time.

"Wow! You look wonderful." He reached for her hand after she closed the door, curious at her far away look.

"Why thank you, Mr. Leander. Would you like to join me for a glass of wine before we leave? " She pulled him through the living room and into her European kitchen.   Her French country blue and yellow ceramic countertops usually invited guests to linger, but Derrick's eyes were too intent on the woman to notice kitchen tiles or the room around him.

"I have Cabernet or Chardonnay… but if you'd rather have beer, I have Lebatt's Blue," she found herself rambling, the last of the *blue*, quietly spoken.   She cradled her wine glass in her palm, covering its top with her free hand.

"I'll have what you're having. I assume its Cabernet?" he said slowly. His soft gray eyes glanced around the room after dragging them away from her face. "Your home is very cozy, Callie. I like the big room here beside your kitchen and the patio all glassed in."   The wall of windows beside her wicker dining table exposed the gardens and evoked a sigh of admiration from him.   "Very nice indeed. And the hot tub is so open and inviting. Perfect. Have you lived here long?"

Callie handed him a glass of wine, fingers touching.

"Yes. Francois and I………… Yes. Ten years, this year." She finished lamely.

"Please don't feel uncomfortable mentioning Francois. It's ok," he said, placing gentle fingers on her arm.

The hard shell she'd purposefully built cracked slightly. She smiled at him and asked if he'd like to finish their wine on the patio. Her CD player changed to Michael Allan Harrison's piano, playing gently and smoothly.

He nodded toward it and murmured, "Harrison's music is a favorite of mine."

"Yes, mine too," she said as she walked out of the kitchen, expecting him to follow.

They stood just outside the big room, quietly inspecting the huge full moon in the quiet night. He reached up and lifted a lock of her hair, caressing it gently.   Touching her arm, he turned her to face him and watched her facial expressions flit like a hummingbird afraid to light on their feeder and gently touched his lips to her temple.

Callie stood still and moved her head to look at him. His nearness made her breath catch as she saw the moon's reflection in his eyes.

Torn by conflicting emotions, she whispered, "I think it's time to go, hum?"

"Yes, you're right," he answered and tipped his glass.

Atop the Hilton Hotel sat *Alexander's*, a piano bar on the eighteenth floor, high above Portland with an overwhelming view of Portland's nightlights. A smiling bald-headed man sat at the piano playing "Hey Jude" as they entered the small lounge.

Derrick led her to a window seat at a tiny table nearby. Within minutes, they were stumbling over each other's words as they began the trek of getting to know each other. They forgot work, their problems and the self-consciousness they'd felt earlier on the patio as the pianist's music swelled.

Callie's delicate perfume gripped Derrick. He leaned closer to smell her freshness and reached up to touch her dangling earrings. She automatically moved her cheek down to caress his hand, resting it there ever so slightly. The music worked magic and she closed her eyes, feeling herself moved by him more than she cared to admit. His fingers were warm and her heart jumped as he caressed her chin. *Oh God, this feels good.*

"Let's dance. The floor's small but....," he whispered.

Callie nodded, put her hand in his and let him lead her toward the piano. Steel-rimmed defenses began to slide.

On the dance floor, they watched two other couples doing the East Coast Swing on the parquet tiles. Candles flickered all around them and low lighting on the walls generated a gentle, romantic ambiance as they swayed together. The music changed suddenly to a slow moving ballad. He reached for her and she leaned into him. Moving slowly to strains of "*Yesterday*," he held her closely and his hand caressed her back. The music melted into their thudding hearts and they became immersed in one another.

This is so nice. Callie could not deny she'd missed feeling warm hands at her waist, pulling her close.

She fits so well. His thoughts were centered on her. His thumb caressed her palm and he inhaled her provocative perfume as they swayed to the music. He could almost feel the pain of Millie's betrayal begin to ooze out of his heart.

They danced until Callie whispered, "I hate to stop. I'm enjoying this so much, but my ankle is talking to me."

"Still having problems with it, aren't you?" Derrick asked with concern in his voice. He led her back to their table and felt her limping beside him. He helped her into the chair, his brow creasing.

"Yes, I just have to be gentle with it. I can go walking a little now and love to, especially on the beach. However," she said, a comical look coming over her face, "dancing is quite different than wading through sand."

They laughed and talked and laughed some more. He ordered splits of champagne. As they sipped, the bubbles danced in their mouths and tickled their noses. The lights outside the large expanse of window twinkled as they talked into a night that neither wanted to end.

A tap on Callie's shoulder halted conversation as they saw the woman beside them.

"*Bon soir*, Callie. How good to see you out," Janine whispered, smiling at Derrick.

"Janine! This is Derrick. Derrick, Janine Vinnier." Callie's voice filled with warmth before standing to hug her friend.

"Hello Janine. I know it sounds like a line, but you sure look familiar." Derrick said slowly, studying her.

"I've lived here many years, *monsieur*, so one never knows. *Abiento*, Callie. I am just leaving. We had dinner with some friends and Vincent is waiting in front." She waved her fingers and walked away. Callie wondered if friends were invented to hide the fact that she was alone.

Frowning again, Derrick picked his brain trying to recall where he'd seen the woman before. "I know her from somewhere. But I just can't place her."

"She works on a committee for the *Sixty Five Roses* fundraising campaign with Caroline. It's for Cystic Fibrosis, a disease that kills so many children. She acts a little sad sometimes and I've never seen her husband. She's very private about her life but quite sweet. She was born in southern France where my family is from..." her voice trailed off as she saw Derrick watching her lips.

"You really do look pretty tonight, did I tell you that already?" he breathed, taking a sip of his champagne, already dismissing Janine.

"Yes you did, but you can tell me again." Callie felt sweet contentment. "And you look quite handsome. We sound like a mutual admiration society, huh?"

The champagne was going to their heads; they felt vaguely, sweetly intoxicated. The music in the darkened room invited an intimacy that grew between them as the pianist watched the couple smile into one another's eyes. He glanced toward them several times and continued to play romantic ballads.

Later, Derrick walked Callie across the redwood deck to her front door, waiting while she placed her key in the lock. "I won't come in, but I want to thank you for a wonderful evening," he said, his face close to hers.

Callie turned toward him, her hand on the front door handle and studied him a moment before answering. "You know, Derrick, this is a milestone for me. I haven't dated ....I mean a real date like this since I lost my husband and you are the first person who has made me feel like I want to.........date, I mean." She said, rattled.

Derrick smiled and reached out to cradle her right cheek, then gently lowered his face to hers, barely touching her upraised lips. A vaguely sensuous light passed between them and she reached up with her left hand to cover his, her lips pushing against his in the moonlight, entranced with the moment.

"Can I call you? This could become a habit," he asked, feeling uncertainty attack him suddenly.

"Yes, Derrick, please do that," she whispered, stepping over the threshold and moving away from him slowly.

"Right, then....Have a good night," he smiled jauntily at her. Turning away, he exhaled a long sigh of contentment.

"Derrick?" She whispered.

He turned back toward her as she took an abrupt step toward him and they were in each other's arms. Contentedly, she leaned against his warm body and felt his hands rubbing up her back, the nape of her neck and smoothing her hair.

"Callie, you have no idea how long I've wanted to hold you like this."

"Oh, God. Derrick, I've tried to keep my distance but you've shaken up my world. I feel like a kindergartener learning how to get into first grade. You may have to be patient with me."

"We'll both work at trusting our feelings and we're bound to move in the right direction," he whispered into her hair, delighting in the feel of her hands on his chest as he kissed her temple. He squeezed her tightly before pushing her inside the house and his eyes bathed her in admiration.

"Good night now."

"Yes, Derrick. Good night. Thank you again."

Then he was walking away.

She stood at her front window until his taillights flickered out of sight. Then, with her fingers on moist lips, she turned and walked into the bedroom. She managed a tremulous smile. *He makes me want to love again and I feel like it's time, but is it too soon? Is it?*

"Dost thou love life? Then do not squander time,
for that is the stuff life is made of.
—FRANKLIN – Poor Richard

Chapter 15

The next morning, rain pelted against Caroline's upstairs bedroom window, inviting her to curl up and pull the covers around her like a cocoon. She beat the pillow to fit the swell of her head, scrunched down to embrace the warmth and tried to stay her whirling mind tightly against her thoughts. *Steven's arrival back in Portland at the same time as Premier's butting into our drug-card plan is too coincidental.* Tension cut her to the quick. The constant mimicry of his words and the pain at his hands only months earlier caused her heart to beat wildly in her breast. She slashed out her arm against the memory and forced her mind toward tonight's opera with Lee instead.

Lee. She conjured his face and imagined rubbing her cheek along his soft, short beard, knowing it would be warm to the touch. Her face split into a grin as she admitted how much she was looking forward to being with him, outside the office, amid strangers. She imagined sitting in a deep chair at the *Civic*, listening to Phantom's lilting voices fill the auditorium, as she sat beside him. "Strange," she said aloud. She finally gave up the quilts, pushing them aside.

Caroline's chest tightened in anticipation. *Why all of a sudden does he leave me breathless? I mean, what's changed? Where was the light switch? We aren't kids. What makes this happen? Did I miss it because I was so busy trying to make Paul love me? Why did I turn to Steven instead of Lee this past year? Why now?* She looked at the clock. *My God, I'm even counting the hours before he picks me up.* She took a deep breath and grabbed her silken robe and her cane. Walking carefully down the carpeted stairs to the kitchen for her coffee, she noticed the stairs were getting easier each day. Irish Cream coffee, her favorite, was saved to relish on lazy Saturday mornings. She ground the fresh coffee beans exactly thirteen seconds before tossing them into the filter and tapping the perk cycle button.

The sky was gray, scattering raindrops in the river and splashing across the view that was a photographer's gold mine. Paintings and photographs of The Harbor Side Restaurant, the floating pier around Newport Bay Restaurant and the boardwalk could be seen in every store window around the city and beyond. And the view was hers to enjoy every day. She loved it. Even rain slapping against the windowpane could not dispel her hopeful mood as she put her anxiety over Steven and Premier on the back burner. Placing her forehead on the window, she traced a particularly large raindrop with her finger before remembering Callie's date the night before.

Grinning again before taking a tentative sip of the freshly brewed coffee, she sat down on the tufted wicker chair and quickly dialed Callie's number. The phone machine answered and disappointment raced through her. "Hey, Cal, how was the hot date last night?" She said, flippantly, before hanging up.

She lifted her briefcase onto the round, oak dining table and poured herself a second cup of coffee. Retrieving the files that lay inside, she pulled out a lined yellow pad. Her thoughts now on a single task, she picked up a pencil, and jotted down bullet points for Monday's meeting with Robert Dubois. Gaining access to his drug card as the common denominator, she added Larkspur's actuary's name. With Jenny's number-crunching ability, she could discuss detailed financials with Robert on the spot.

She tapped the pencil on her teeth. *Let's see. Lee's picking him up and driving him directly to the office. I want to settle the contract debate without Premier's interference and he won't know about my ruse in Monday's Oregonian article. Steven really got things riled up. Dammit!!*

Feeling slightly chilled, she pulled her robe tighter and hugged the hot coffee cup with both hands. She glanced toward the window and saw rain. Torrents of rain. Fueled by the angry thoughts Steven evoked, she closed her eyes and rested her head on the back of the couch. Unable to stop the invasion of sad memories, she let them flit through her mind.

Steven Roget joined Larkspur three years earlier with a glowing resume´. When the office manager first interviewed him and reported to Caroline, she'd jumped at pulling him away from Micro*Media* Systems. His second interview culminated into an employee contract. Caroline met his salary requirements, adjusted fringe benefits to form an agreement and everyone welcomed him to Larkspur's team. She trusted the character traits she'd seen in him.

He charmed the ladies with his easy-going smile, his blonde good looks and outgoing personality. And Caroline followed suit. *Was he manipulating me even then? Why had he fought me so hard? What was his connection to the LEXUS doctors and Ace-Deer? There must be one. If only I could figure that out.* But, as before, she had no valid answers to her questions.

She grimaced. *How easy it was for him to ingratiate himself into my personal life. I'd never dated employees. And romance! He was so persuasive.* She remembered the hand holding, neck rubs, making her feel desired. *He was definitely a romantic... always arriving with a bottle of wine and a long-stemmed red rose and....* "You are my single, lovely rose," he'd said. And she'd believed him.

She tried analyzing her feelings during those four months they were involved and realized with abject clarity that they'd never discussed love. She admitted she was vulnerable. She didn't sleep around, so it amazed her, even now, that she'd allowed him into her bed. *Yes, he made me feel sexy.* After feeling like a second-class citizen married to Paul, being with Steven felt delicious and she'd basked in the knowledge of that power.

She shook her head and the anger returned again. Her coffee was cold and she shivered, remembering his hands on her. "My God, how could I have let him get that close and not known the real Steven?" Her fingers climbed around the cup rim and she pushed herself up. *More coffee is what I need.* She shivered again, shaking her head to dispel memories, and turned on the log fireplace.

She stood in the vast, empty room, looking out at the sheets of rain lashing the windows. Even on a day like this, she hadn't felt so good about her personal life in a long time, but thoughts of Steven dulled her thoughts. She clicked on the radio, hoping to drown out her mind chatter with music. Within a few minutes, she smiled as the sun slid around a cloud and streaks of light permeated the room around her. *And now, there's Lee.* "And he was there all the time. I was the one who was lost."

Across town, up on NE 79th Avenue, Carl opened the door to admit his son into the small living room, the paper folded up under his arm. Carl reached for it and hugged his son, who returned his father's embrace with an "MMMmmm. Good morning, Dad, got the coffee on?"

"Does a bear shit in the woods?" his father answered, tossing the paper onto the table, while dragging a clean cup out of his knotty pine kitchen cabinet.

Derrick laughed and sat down to join him for their usual Saturday morning visit. It was their special time together and Carl looked forward to it. He planted the large cup in front of Derrick; his favorite, with a picture of an antique poster: a woman advertising Ghirardelli's Ground Chocolate from their trip to San Francisco together. The coffee was hot to the touch and he fingered it gingerly before lifting it to his mouth.

"How are you, Dad?" He blew into the cup and sipped as his eyes roamed over his father.

"You don't want to know, son," Carl's voice sounded low and despairing.

Derrick glanced up and felt worry marks dimple his features. He sat his cup down. "What?"

"My surgery. They didn't approve it. Doc James said we have to wait six weeks to *ask* permission again. I got some high-dollar pills yesterday and I have to take them until the damned HMO gives the okay. This HMO bullshit makes me tired," he finished lamely, anger making the vein in his neck beat like a tick.

Derrick reached over and touched his father's arm. "I'm sorry, Dad. Sometimes I'm not proud being part of it but the HMO premise is to be cost effective. If they can put off surgery, they will. What does Doc James say about it?"

"Not much. I know he was pissed too but he has to follow their rules. I told him to do it anyway but he talked me out of it. Told me taking the damn pills would be cheaper than my paying for the surgery. Said something about me having to win the lottery."

Carl laughed then and pulled the tickets out of his pocket and placed them on the table. "I bought some and not one damned number came up. Ted told me I was crazy but we know someone who won over $5,000 last week when the guy had five numbers out of six. It was worth a try."

Helpless frustration choked Derrick when he saw his father look like the air was punched out of him. "I'll call Doc James first thing Monday and find out what's what."

"Well, son, I don't know if you should get involved since you work at Larkspur and all." He hunched over, arms resting on the table.

Derrick got up, poured himself another cup of coffee and snagged a cinnamon roll off the counter. He licked his fingers, sipped more coffee and watched his father's face.

"By the way, I thought since you won't invite Alice in, Dad, I decided that one of us Leanders should make a bold move. I had a date last night with the woman I told you about...Callie."

Before his dad could make a joking comment, he went on, "And you know what? She liked me. We drank a little wine, watched the lights above the city, danced a little and talked a long time. It was different than when I was with Millie. It was nice and she smells like God's gift." He finished and waited for his father's response.

"She's not married, is she?

"No, Dad." He rolled his eyes at his father and bit into the roll.

"Good. Then, if she makes your heart happy and you feel magic, ask her out again," he mumbled and his eyes filled. He wiped frantically at a tear and turned away, but not fast enough for Derrick to miss the emotion or the broken words.

"It's Mom, isn't it? You've been thinking about her and missing her again."

"Son, I think about her all the time and miss her all the time. What we had, well, not many have. I'd say one in twenty are lucky enough to have someone whose face can lift your mood, whose smile can make your heart hurt and whose love can fill you so full, you don't think you can stand the fullness. That's how I loved your mother. It's like I met her yesterday. I can still feel her lips on my neck and her body warm against mine in the night. Four years have passed but the memory is timeless and I want to see you happy like that. I can have instant and vivid recall just saying your mother's name. Millie was too selfish to make you happy and you didn't have that light in your eyes when you married her. I was always sorry you would miss what your mother and I had, so maybe this Callie.......... Tell me about her."

Carl's mood improved dramatically as he heard Derrick recount their evening and the woman he could not get out of his head. He smiled when Derrick mentioned the perfume-filled air that followed her.

"You got it bad, son," he chuckled.

"Yeh, 'fraid so, dad," he answered with a smile and lift of his shoulders.

Hours later, not having heard from Callie, Caroline was listless. Her yellow pad was filled with scribbled notes. The clock's hands moved like molasses most of the afternoon until six o'clock bonged into the room. *Shower time! I want to do this right. I may have another chance and my God... I think I'm placing too much importance on tonight. This is really silly. It's Lee, for God's sake...not a stranger. It's Lee..... And I'm enjoying every minute of it.*

The navy silk dress lay spread out on her pale quilt and the pearl and diamond necklace set waited on her dressing table. She made a moue when she pulled out the navy, flat-heeled shoes but she wanted to leave the cane behind, if Lee would let her get away with it. Her navy Victoria Secret bra and panties were draped across the back of her dressing room chair along with ecru pantyhose.

Naked, with a bottle of Sunflower Bath and Shower Gel gripped in her hand, she stepped into her shower. Hot water soon cascaded over her warm skin and face, plastering her short hair against her skull. Laughter bubbled up into her throat as she visualized images of Lee, naked in his own shower, shampoo in his wet hair and beard. *I'm mad*, she thought. "Or I've been without a man too long." She said aloud.

Once Caroline was ready, she felt like an aging but sleek fairy princess. The new v-necked navy dress followed the lines of her figure and flowed around her knees. A fabric flower on one shoulder did the rest. She pulled on the matching blue shawl from the bank of drawers near her closet. Ready and waiting, she grimaced at her cane and wondered for the hundredth time if she could leave it.

She felt like a page was turning in her book of life. Before she was hired as the CEO of Larkspur, she had worked for four different HMOs, each of them built up through her contacts and creativity over the past twenty-four years in the health insurance marketplace. She was part of the National Association of Health Underwriters and the Portland Association of Health Underwriters and worked her way from secretary to president of both groups.

Working so many years as an agent created many friendships and business contacts were cultivated in her quest to be a bright light in the marketplace. But her position as CEO was her dream job and she hoped to retire there. She'd fought her way through the early years married to a man who thought everything a woman did was suspect in a man's world and not quite up to par. That challenge inspired her loyalty to Larkspur. Fueled by their differences, she'd shied away from the aspect of politics that hounded people in her position. And their personal life suffered. He wanted more. She was happy where she was. And he'd never forgiven her, his bitterness flooding over into their children's lives and his own, for leaving him.

But she loved her job. It was exciting. In the past several years, it had been all she wanted, but the current complexities made her tired.

It's a real prescription war. She listened to the strains of a violin and piano concerto and contemplated the coming fireworks on Monday.

And now....Lee promises what's missing and I've never felt so sure of anything in my life. It feels like home.

The telephone rang loudly, bursting into her thoughts. She glanced at the large living-room clock before reaching for the portable phone, hoping it was Callie.

"Hi, Mom! I'm on my way to Paris! Dad gave me a ticket for an early Christmas gift... an airline ticket! What would you like me to bring home to you?" Elizabeth's voice cracked over the phone.

"Sweetheart! How exciting for you. Let's see, how about something totally French, like a CD by Charles Trenet, you know... sweet music?" Caroline's heart swelled with love for her daughter, who had worked so hard to excel in classes and needed a break from it all. Paul did some things right, she admitted grudgingly.

"Well, I'll look everywhere for it. How are things going with all the stuff you're working on with the drug thing?"

"Too slow to mention, honey. When will you be home again?"

"I'm not sure. Dad's friend has a house in Avignon and says I can stay there a month for free if I clean it for them. Not sure what it entails but it's free so I can do it. What do you think?"

Caroline smiled. "Go for it, honey. Keep in touch and be safe. I love you."

"I love you too. I'll call again soon! I got a chip in my cell phone so I can call you from there." Caroline felt the excitement in her voice across the wire before she hung up.

Five minutes later, the phone rang again. Caroline chuckled and answered, "Calling again so soon?"

"Caroline. Are you ready to talk to me yet? I can be there in ten minutes." His silky voice held a challenge.

She froze. "Steven? Are you nuts? We have nothing to talk about and you know it. Leave me alone!" Her voice vibrated through the room, where just moments earlier, had been a calm sanctuary filled with her daughter's laughter.

"Caroline... I told you I was sorry about what happened. And I really am. I am really so sorry, Caroline. But think about it. I was right. I just wanted to be your spokesman and help you work out that contract with LEXUS. It's not finished, is it?" His voice sounded tormented.

She couldn't assimilate thoughts as she stood, transfixed. "What are you talking about, Steven? The LEXUS situation is finished exactly as I want it."

Caroline was shaking with anger when she heard Lee's step. She walked hurriedly to the door, jerked it wide, much to Lee's surprise, then motioned to the phone and pulled him inside quickly.

Holding the receiver between them head to head, they both listened as Steven's voice continued. "Caroline, LEXUS and Ace-Deer go together like salt and pepper. You can't have one without the other and he won't let you get away with it, he just won't....." Steven's voice sounded strident, almost apologetic.

"Steven....WHO won't let me........?" she cut in.

"YOU listen to *me*, Caroline!" His voice sliced through the room as Lee and Caroline jumped and stared at each other, waiting. "There is no way in hell that Premier is going to let you off easily. They want to sell the package and that's what they'll do. Do you think they don't know that Robert Dubois is arriving Monday? Do you think they don't know that your lawyer is picking him up from the airport? Do you think you can hide anything from me whether I'm in jail or on the street? Think about it, why don't you? I don't want you hurt again... and I'm not the one that might hurt you this time. I am trying to warn you to tread lightly. Please. Please, Caro." He stopped talking, waiting for Caroline's response.

Caroline's body grew rigid as she leaned into Lee. He guided her into a chair and held his finger to his lips.

"What do you want, Steven? And who is pushing you into doing this to Larkspur and to me?"

"What I want is for you to tell Robert to bug off, you changed your mind and you don't want his prescription deal. You tell him you're sorry you wasted his time and he can take his prescription card and shove it for all I care. Just tell him you aren't interested! Ace-Deer will work! It will cost a little more to your consumer population. You can't be the saint you try to make people believe. Money is money! And I don't KNOW who it is. I have never met him."

"My God, Steven." She whispered, speechless.

His voice sounded slick, like polished varnish as he continued, "I told you before that the Ace-Deer contract was a good one. So what if a few people think it's a five or six on a scale of 1 to 10? They pay for the drugs and administer the claims just fine. The preferred list is small but I know it will be enlarged because of this S/K deal Premier wants. Or, maybe that was your plan all along.......... to manipulate Ace-Deer into adding more drugs to their preferred list and dropping their costs down before you sign on the dotted line?"

Lee made a chop-at-the-neck motion and Caroline blinked rapidly. "Steven, go to hell." Then, she hung up.

Lee took the phone from her shaking hand and replaced it beside him. Then, he fluffed the pillow in back of her and left to pour them each a Courvoisier. *The brandy will do us good and bring some warmth back to her cheeks.* He grabbed two short crystal goblets and poured the golden liquid into each glass.

"Here, sip dear." He chose the seat across from her as he bent forward with his elbows on his knees, his drink in both hands. Silence loomed between them like a heavy mist.

"Lee, what do you think about all this?" Caroline asked, her voice filled with intensity.

"You know, Caroline.... I haven't a clue in hell." He swirled the brandy in his cocktail glass and held it to his chin. "It sounds like he knows what's going on and I heard desperation in his voice. What is the issue with Ace-Deer and why is he so adamant that Larkspur include that prescription instead of the Canadian's? And who is he trying to save you from? If he doesn't even know who it is, how can we? I can't understand it and now that he's out of jail, he seems to be right back to where he was last spring. I'm just lost here. Is there anything you are leaving out that will help us understand his motives??" He saw her face close up.

"No, Lee. What would I be hiding?" She took a big swallow of the brandy and coughed, sputtering toward him.

"Sip, dear. Don't gulp." He stared at the floor before continuing. "It's not that I think you are hiding things, Caroline, it's just that there is a missing piece to this puzzle. How does he know these things? I'm god-awful stumped..." He sat there, lifting the rim of his glass to his lips, and sipped the liquid and felt a pleasant burning sensation. He leaned forward once again.

"He spoiled our evening." She looked at him sadly.

"We won't let him! We have dinner reservations at the Harbor Side Restaurant. Baked Brie awaits. Let's go."

Caroline's stomach was on fire. She took a deep breath. "Oh, baked Brie and wine," she said eagerly.

He winked broadly at her, and reached for her cane. "Yes, ma'am."

"Let's leave it, Lee, I think I can deal with it."

He looked at her steadily and said, "Well, that's all and well, but let's leave it in the car just in case. How's that, hummmm?" he insisted.

She laughed and reached for the wooden cane that had become the bane to her recent existence and allowed him to help her. On their way out the leaded glass front door, he turned to her quietly and said, quite low, "By the way, madam, you look gorgeous tonight."

Caroline suddenly felt she'd sprouted wings and her pale face brightened. "Thanks, my friend." *And I will not allow Steven to mar the evening. I won't,* she promised herself as she worked her way crookedly down the stairs.

The Harbor Side Restaurant was festooned along a wide boardwalk nearly in line with Caroline's condo across the water. Amid the ambiance of candles, the interior sported tables placed in tiers narrowing toward wide glass windows at the river's edge, allowing a clear view above the people and the river below them.

Little shops sat in tandem with boardwalk benches along the walkway just outside the doors and flowers and shrubbery lined the front, offering more than a garden - variety décor. Tables littered the walkway outside, inviting a quick drink without the rush for dinner inside.

The night was clear, and the October stars sparkled on the river like tiny diamonds, enchanting the patrons inside the restaurant, including Lee and Caroline. The rain had stopped hours earlier and the air smelled clean and fresh on the boardwalk. Her heart squeezed as she smiled at him, noting the gray speckles in his short beard and smelling the woodsy aftershave wafting toward her. She wanted to reach out to touch it.

The hot, softened Brie sat on a wooden tray among golden baked garlic and Focaccia bread and their sparkling crystal glasses were filled with Beringer's White Merlot.

Mischievously, she slid her hand beyond the cheeseboard and the wineglass toward him. "Lee, thank you for inviting me tonight. I needed it and I enjoy your company very much." Her eyes sparkled as brightly as the princess-cut diamond on her right ring finger.

Glancing down at her outstretched hand, he covered hers, enjoying their warmth.

"And I you," he said. "Caroline, I always enjoy being with you." The words were out of his mouth before he could stop them and he reveled in the smile in her eyes.

Silence reigned.

"It's an adventure with you. I never know quite what to expect."

"Pray tell, what is happening here?" she whispered, their fingers still tightly clasped.

"It's hard to keep inside," he whispered, eyes liquid.

"Lee?" Something clicked in her brain. Her gaze darted from his eyes to his lips and her heart began to pound.

"Caroline. It's ... you are the epitome of what I feel a woman should be and I have always respected you and I value your friendship very much." He disentangled his fingers and lifted the wineglass to her in a mute toast, then to his lips.

"Lee... that's the way I feel too. About you, I mean." She swallowed hard. The implication sent excitement through her.

The waiter quietly placed plates in front of them, before lifting the pepper grinder at their bidding. The chilled, fresh green salads were filled with plump pink shrimp layered among the lettuce. They ate, deeply aware of one another. Shrimp melted on their tongues, wine washed it down, the minutes slid by and the Phantom waited.

Caroline sat quietly and watched the man across from her, mind racing. *I love him.* Her heart thumped in her throat. She took a deep breath and smiled into her plate. *What was that line in Jerry Maguire? You complete me. Yes, she thought, it's been there all the time. Dear God. He does complete me.*

Lights glittered in the water, lighted boats floated by the large bank of windows, and the Newport Bay Restaurant on the floating base below was lit up like a Christmas tree.

They stared outside and the lull in the conversation surrounded them like a safety net as they ate, drank and smiled, each brimming to discuss their feelings; each hesitant.

Later, sitting among the crowd at the Civic Auditorium, Phantom's music of the night filled the air and Caroline's breast rose in admiration. The story touched each of them and the music thrummed through their high emotions.

Lee reached for her hand when the Phantom's voice whispered his love song. He laced his fingers through hers, lingeringly.

She relished the warmth and squeezed his fingers in return, feeling thrills chasing over her nerves. *Omigod, I've got it bad.* She looked up and saw him watching her, smiling. The simple pleasure in his eyes made her toes curl.

Caroline enjoyed the closeness, afraid to move for fear of dislodging his grasp..... Afraid to move for fear of losing what she realized she'd never had? A good, honest man. One who wove magic around her just by being there? She sighed.

Rubbing his hand across his dark-bearded chin, he turned his head back toward the stage, but he did not relinquish her hand, but tightened his hold.

She had the mischievous notion to twine her arms around his neck as she inhaled his cologne, subtle and sexy. She took another deep breath before raking her fingers through her short blonde hair as if to prove she wasn't dreaming. And then she turned toward the voices on stage and listened to Christine Dyea sing her magic for the Phantom.

"A delusion, a mockery and a snare."
—Lord Denmann

Chapter 16

* * *

The *Oregonian* slammed onto her front doorstop at dawn Monday morning. Caroline's heart leapt as she recognized the sound and wasted no time grabbing it and unfolding it quickly. She grinned at the headline in the middle of the front page, boldly proclaiming that two other prescription suppliers were vying for Larkspur's hand.

She laughed to herself and sat down on the couch, laying her blonde head against the pale pillow and closed her eyes. *Today will be one hell of a day.* Lifting her cup of Constant Comment tea to her lips, she quickly scanned the press release Richard Ellis printed word-for-word, as promised.

She checked the clock and started ticking away the morning's agenda. First, she'd prepare for the meeting with Robert and make sure she had everything in order. Then, she'd gather up the loose ends. Her mind was awhirl and she was as giddy as a teenager getting ready for the big prom. Her busy pencil ticked off her list of ten items, and then she laid it on top of the *Oregonian. And Lee will be there.* She smiled again.

THREE hours later found James and Lee in front of Caroline, waiting for Derrick and Jenny Lunden to join them. Heavy 3-ring binders filled the actuary's arms as she pushed open the office door. Everyone turned toward her. Jenny wore her dark hair pulled back in a French braid, balanced purple-rimmed glasses on the bridge of her nose, and held her head upward giving one the false impression of haughtiness. Caroline smiled to herself, knowing the woman hid, instead, a shyness and complex personality. Derrick followed closely behind and all five sat a moment, waiting for Caroline to begin.

"I'm sure you have all seen the paper this morning." She held her yellow pencil aloft as she watched everyone nod their heads and smile knowingly. An added vitality filled the room and she placed it on top of her desk pad, pushed up her sweater sleeves and pursed her lips. She stood up and glanced out the window before staring at them again.

"Good. Now we want Robert to make a decision. Does he want to do business with us or not, even though we haven't found the culprit in our midst. I refuse to allow Robert to control the situation. He's a nice man and has a great offer but without the contract, he must realize this is a business and we cannot stop the big ball from rolling or it will run all of us down. Agreed?"

Again, everyone nodded, still waiting, a measured anticipation lingering.

James sat quietly, flipping his small notepad onto his thigh, his eyes filled with determination as he followed her with his eyes.

"Still nothing — right, James?"" Caroline asked seriously, eyes focused on the tall man.

"No, ma'am. I just cannot figure out a way other than a treasonous employee. We know someone is accessing your information. The computer seems to be the only other way and without someone allowing confidential entrance, it cannot be done easily.

Caroline's interest was piqued and she looked at Derrick for support. He shrugged his shoulders and raised one eyebrow in thought.

"Well, James, I know the computers well enough to know that the ones I've looked at so far do not have anything on them that would allow it."

"What do you mean, 'anything' that would allow it? I'm a novice at computers, you all know that, but explain this to me," Caroline said, watching Derrick and James intently as she paced.

"Well, there are a lot of computer programs that allow access to another computer. You could activate the program and it would be an open book as the *host* computer. When you take your laptop home, you connect to your office over the internet to that *host* computer. You would be the *user* on your laptop and access information from the *host* computer in your office." Derrick finished with a sigh.

"What a mouthful. And more than my brain can comprehend." The word, *host*, jogged a memory and niggled at the back of her brain. The pencil stopped in mid air as her eyes squinted, deep in thought. "Are you saying someone else could gain access to my computer or someone else's computer here at Larkspur if someone had that kind of program and......... you mean there are no safeguards against this kind of thing?" She looked hard at Derrick, her lips pursed in dismay.

Feeling like a bug under a microscope, he felt a tickle of suspicion. "Yes, Caroline, there are safeguards. Everyone has a password. You wouldn't share the password with anyone unless you wanted others to be aware of it........... Does anyone know yours besides me?" Derrick muttered uneasily. His vexation was evident.

Caroline's face clouded with uneasiness and she turned to Lee.

He nodded his head in confusion. "Where is this going, Caro?" Lee's voice cut through her thoughts and she moved her lips as if to speak.

James answered for her. "We checked the phone bills and Emails. We didn't check everyone's computers. It must be here somewhere. He opened his notebook and started making notes, jabbing onto the paper with each letter. "Why I didn't think of that, I'll never know. Sorry, Lee. My work is not sloppy but this takes the cake. If it's there, I'll find it so help me God."

Derrick's face remained impassive as he listened to James. He waited, hoping for another piece of information to help solve the mystery.

"Ok, well. You get on that. James and I can continue my meeting with Jenny. Lee, thanks for picking up Robert at the airport; his plane comes in this morning and you have all the information?" Caroline raised her brows.

Lee nodded as he reached for his briefcase and jacket. He turned to her with a smile that she met, unwaveringly, as a warm glow flowed through her.

The unspoken interlude did not go unnoticed. Oblivious to the silent looks the others shared, Caroline glanced down at her notes once again. She asked Jenny to join them once Robert and Lee arrived after lunch.

She ran her fingers through her short hair and took a deep breath. *Host, host, host*, she thought the words over and over. *Where have I heard that before?* She drummed her fingers onto the desk top, trying to pull the thought out of the air around her. Tugging at her blonde bangs, she twisted her lips tightly in agitation.

The shiny brochure laying on top of her desk for the new agent classes caught her attention and she pulled her hands down quickly. More than mildly curious at the bend in her thoughts, she flipped it over in her hands and studied it. She smiled suddenly, and grabbed the hated cane. Limping slightly to the door, she called Lana through the door and asked her to come inside.

Lana's heart missed a beat. She grabbed her tablet and pen, minimized the program on her monitor and walked into Caroline's office. Her stomach burned and she stifled a sob as she imagined herself walking off a wooden plank. *This is it.* She sat down slowly on the loveseat and faced Caroline. *This is it!* She flushed miserably as she saw Caroline lift a colorful brochure toward her.

"Lana, I've been thinking about you a lot lately. I know things have been wild around here with the Premier situation. But, thinking back to my early insurance days, I remember needing a challenge and how goal oriented I was ...well, I see that old me in you. I wondered if you'd like to study for your health insurance license."

Lana stared at her, momentarily stunned.

"You are so involved with it daily and probably know most of what you need to know anyway. Does that interest you? Being an agent?" Caroline watched as Lana's face turned blotchy and her eyes turned glassy.

"Larkspur will pay for the classes, the test and your continuing education classes to earn credits to maintain your license. It won't cost you any money. If you like it, we can add other responsibilities and God forbid, but you could work in Sales if that's what you'd like to do too..."

Caroline became increasingly perplexed at Lana's silence and then dropped the brochure when Lana burst into tears. Hard sobs wracked her body. Caroline was at a loss.

"Lana........ you don't *have* to do it. I thought it would put a smile back on your face. Between your sad face lately and your boyfriend leaving those dreadful hickies on your.........." With these words hanging in the air, Lana lifted her hands and covered her face, the sobs louder and more insistent.

Caroline moved out of her chair and sat beside the crying woman. "Hey, Lana....What *is* it?"

Lana's shoulders shook and Caroline's arm went around her instantly. Lana turned into her shoulder and tears didn't stop for several minutes before the heaving of her body slowly began to quiet. Lana's green eyes lifted, glasses sliding down her nose, and her mouth quirked back and forth. No words came out.

Caroline waited.

Lana shook her head sadly side to side. "I didn't want to do it, Caroline." she whispered brokenly.

"Do what? You don't want to take the test? What?" Caroline repeated and stared at the wet face, inviting an answer. She rubbed her hands along Lana's arm.

Lana talked at great length. It took twenty minutes for the sordid story to unfold. Her hands twisted together as Caroline listened to Lana unburden herself.

Then Lana sat, shaking. "You can't imagine how good it feels to tell you everything." She looked imploringly at Caroline. "I'm fired, right?"

Caroline said nothing for several moments, before shaking her head. Her anger focused on Steven.... hurting yet another woman.

Lana's body shook inside her peach-colored sweater and brown slacks following the dissertation. Caroline leaned toward her, and Lana hung her head, as she allowed Caroline's arms to embrace her and they rocked as one.

"Sh........shhhhhhh...." Caroline crooned, as if she held her own daughter, Elizabeth.

"I'm so sor........ry, Caroline. I never wanted to do it. He tried to manipulate me before Frankie was born and I fought it. He said he had a plan to build a nest egg for us faster than he could with his other job. I wanted a job and pay my own way. Then ... he found me this job and said I owed him. He told me I couldn't tell anyone that Frankie was his son or that we knew each other before I came here. He said he had a big plan and I loved him. That's why I couldn't allow myself to be friends with anyone and it's been like a prison. My boys are my life, Caroline. I'm so afraid if I don't do what Steven says...........''

Lana sat up, staring at Caroline, as fear filled her green eyes. "I'm so tired of being a victim, Caroline. And I won't do it anymore. I want to fight back. Now, what will happen?" she asked, brokenly.

"We will work this out. First though, tell me......do you want to stay at Larkspur? And if you do, are you interested in bettering yourself by studying to be an agent? Whether you remain my secretary or move to Sales. You do an excellent job. He might have helped you get this job in the first place, but *you kept* it on your own. Do you want to work with me on this?" Caroline's voice was calm, steadying the silence between them.

Lana tried to dispel her shaking body and nodded her head. "Yes, Yes, and Yes......" she said with a firmer resolve than she had felt in months. "Tell me what to do and I'll do it. But, we have to get him out of my apartment and he can't take Frankie away. He loves the boys. I know it. He wouldn't hurt either of them but he knows what would hurt me most and that's taking my boys."

I didn't think he'd hurt me either. Caroline looked at the rugged shoes and the wooden cane, her constant companion for the past few months that attested to her naiveté. She tried to compose her thoughts and alleviate Lana's distress as her mind clicked into place with each note like a key on the piano.

Lana's eyes were hopeful as she waited.

"Ok, Lana. This is what we need to do." Caroline's voice said firmly, her gray eyes flashing as she reached for the phone beside them.

ONE HOUR LATER, James and Derrick again sat across from Caroline. They listened in rapt silence as their hands fisted up beside them in tandem. Hearing that Steven Roget's deceit had struck again after hurting both Caroline and Callie before, Derrick thought his head would explode.

James wrote wildly and showed the pad to Derrick, as they sat side by side. Derrick looked down and nodded before lifting his eyes toward James in agreement.

"This morning when you talked about the computer and how someone could access it, you mentioned the word '*host*' and something jogged my memory. Then, after I talked with Lana, I remembered an incident last Monday, the same day someone ripped up the boxes in your office, Derrick. There was a hum when we came in here and I realized my monitor was on but it was black... you know ... the safety thing. When we hit the space bar, there was a big, colored box on the monitor. Neither Callie nor I knew what it was. It had little boxes at the top listing words like *Be a Host, Remote Control* and things like that. Since we didn't know what it was, we thought it was a glitch or something. I thought I'd forgotten to turn off the computer the previous Friday night. So, we clicked out of it and guess we both forgot about it in all the drama around here. Now we know that Lana left the computer on each night so Steven could access the information. Since she always arrived earlier than I did each day, except Monday last, she'd click it off every day and shut off my computer.

Derrick's face paled. "Derrick, since you weren't aware of it, then it must have been Steven who installed the program months ago. How am I doing so far?" she asked, looking from one man to the other. "Of course, since I'm the one who housed the confidential information, it would have made sense to check my computer first, don't you think?"

"Yes, it would have…," Derrick said, shaking his head, disgustedly as he looked at James.

"Well, Caroline, it couldn't have happened with more perfect timing since Robert will be here a little later. He said he wouldn't sign the contract unless we had the culprit. Now that we do, what's your next instruction?" James posed the question, his pencil ready.

He watched her make her way back to her desk, limping badly when she twisted around the backside before lowering herself into her chair. He marveled at her self control and the bright red dress made him smile. She was out for blood today, her trademark to fight fire with fire? Robert would have his hands full, ready or not.

"You are right about that, James. And we have our work cut out for ourselves. With the *Oregonian's* article, I know there will be people dying to find out what it's all about. Lana is going to go home as if nothing happened today other than the meeting she knows will take place. She won't be in the meeting, which is normal and she will leave my computer on when she leaves, which is normal. What won't be normal is the information that will be on my machine. And that's where you both come in." She paused a moment before lining out her thoughts.

"Wow! That is an excellent idea. But if you want to catch him…," Derrick said as he saw her lift her hand to silence him as she continued.

"Derrick, I don't believe Steven is working alone. He told me that Saturday night when he called me at home. He also told me he doesn't know who it is. That's hard to imagine. And maybe there's more than just one other person. Someone had to set up the scam with him, right? Lee and James both said last week that there's bigger fish to fry and it must be coming from Premier. We need to find out what the real zinger is and how Steven is involved. I want to go fishing with a big worm and then I want to reel him in." Caroline's smile split her face as she watched how her words impacted the men facing her.

"While you are putting in the fake information about the Germans and the Spaniards, I will call Lee to put a restraining order against Steven for Lana. We better hurry. Lana said Steven usually logs onto my computer late at night. Hopefully, we can beat him at his own game. Then, we are going to help her throw him out on his ear and save those little boys from harm;

even though she assures me he won't hurt the children.... But you know what? I don't believe it for a damned minute."

"Heaven ne'er helps the man who will not help himself."
—Sophocles

Chapter 17

* * *

His white knuckles gripped the newspaper before he slapped it against the desk in front of him. Then he stabbed the keypad on the phone causing it to jump a few inches across the marble desk. His now-cold coffee and cinnamon roll forgotten, he spoke harshly into the mouthpiece, ripping the edge of the paper as he spit out words.

On the other end of the phone, Del felt heat rising up his neck and loosened his tie. "Yes, I've read it. I can't know every move she makes......or be all places all the time," he answered after the man's voice died down.

"Well, my dear *Doctor* Reed. That is what I pay you to do. *Be all places all the time.* Get in touch with that *idiot* you have so much faith in and get back to me with something I want to hear! I'm meeting with Robert Dubois at 4:30 this afternoon and if he's not the only fish in the sea for Larkspur, get me in touch with who is!" He slammed down the phone. He grabbed the cinnamon roll. Tearing it into pieces, he stuffed it into his mouth and chewed angrily.

A few minutes later, Steven dropped the phone on the table as he rummaged for the *Oregonian* Lana brought inside earlier. He'd heard her rush the boys out that morning amid promises of Mickey D breakfast rolls. She knew it would annoy him. He vowed to talk to her later about no breakfast as his empty stomach rumbled.

"Yes, I have it." Steven muttered into the phone as he scanned the top of the front page. The headline screamed at him mid-way down the page. "Hot damn!" he exclaimed. "Well, now what do we do?"

"You tell me, Hotshot. You said you had things under control. The boss is meeting with the Canadian this afternoon and he wants answers before that meeting, so you just better freakin' tell me what I should tell him. And don't take all day! My stomach can't take this shit." Del Reed finished his spiel with the zeal of a lion, trying to stave off the perspiration moistening his starched shirt and shiny face.

Steven hung up the phone in disgust and dragged the newspaper into the kitchen. Jerkily, he poured coffee before sitting down at the open counter, his back to the dining room window, as bright sunshine filtered in through the ivory sheers. *Well, at least she made the damned coffee.*

Gripping the steaming mug, he read the entire article with grave concern; not because he feared Del or the big boss, but because he saw the money draining from his US Bank account downtown. He'd felt part of something big and hadn't wanted anyone to stop those plans. His thoughts were crackling and he was scared.

He ran his fingers through his thick, disheveled blonde hair and rubbed his prickly, bearded jaw. Sitting on the stool, he gulped the entire cup of coffee, feeling it burn his throat. *Well, the time has come to take a little more action.*

His last thought before climbing into the shower was Caroline's barricaded views several months before and Callie's obstinacy.... and Lana's coolness. *Ah, my Lana.* Their sex life was more like friendly rape. He knew how great it could be between them. *I love her, dammit. Other women want me, why can't she?* He was still the same man she loved before she got pregnant with Frankie. *Am I?*

Random words slapped at him. *Hell, I like women, I don't deny, but I need her..* He growled, scrubbing his skin and lathering his face, neck and arms like he was trying to wipe out a wine stain off the carpet. *I love her. God, I'm so mixed up. Maybe Lana's right and I do need treatment.... But that money is just waiting for us and then things will be good again. It has to be!*

A mixture of indecision and anger fired his nerves. Freshly dressed, Steven logged onto his laptop even though his habit was to log in at night. His stomach knotted and hoped Lana hadn't closed the line yet. The program was slow to fill the screen, but was open and invited him to click into Caroline's computer. He knew Caroline had outside meetings all morning. But it didn't take him long to find out there was nothing to support what he'd read in the paper. *Well, I'll just try later. It's got to be there!*

After lunch, he called Lana to confirm Caroline was still out. Then, he tried again. *Ah ha. There it is. She is a little doll.* He scribbled down the names, phone numbers, and pharmaceutical companies quickly along with the pertinent information showing Larkspur's offers for their mail-order drug card. He worked quickly, knowing Lana would probably be shutting it down anytime. He smiled slyly and nodded his head as he clicked out of the program and gathered the supplies he would need for the morning.

Del wanted action and that's what he'll get. He literally skipped down the back stairs to his gold-colored car, smiling at the irony as he got into his Lexus; LEXUS…gold like the HMO's money filling his bank account.

During the next few hours, everyone followed Caroline's instructions and busied themselves for the meeting with S/K Pharmaceuticals. Then the waiting began.

Caroline called Callie and asked her to run across the street to Three Lions for a quick lunch and morale booster. Despite the messy happening that morning, Caroline was still curious about her friend's Friday night with Derrick. *He'd looked very content*, she thought wryly.

Callie's dark striped pantsuit and red duster, with the Swarovski Angel pinned to its lapel, stood out in the crowd. Caroline pushed the doors open and walked into the busy café, smiling at her warmly. The freckles stood out on Callie's face as they headed toward a table in the corner. A quick lunch followed and conversation slipped in between mouthfuls of soup and bites of bread sticks as Caroline brought Callie up to date.

Callie's mouth formed an 'O' when she was done and her eyes filled with fury. "I should have known Steven was in on it. And using Lana to do his dirty work by blackmailing her that way…….." she sputtered.

"I know. I know. But we will fix the man this time…. Now **you**……." Caroline's voice was clearly questioning.

"Now, me *what?*" Callie answered. "I got your phone message Saturday morning. I was actually running around Saturday Market and enjoying myself immensely even through the drizzle. I hit Starbucks early, then ran over to Macy's and just played the rest of the day. I came home and soaked my ankle in Epsom salts, ate popcorn and watched The Green Mile on the video."

"You played all day?" Caroline felt a warm glow flow through her.

"Alone." Callie slurped the rest of her soup.

"And Friday night? Are you going to tell me what happened?" Caroline implored her.

"No." She bit her breadstick with a final chomp.

"Why?" Caroline asked with mock anger.

"Because I'm savoring it, Caro. I'm just holding it close and letting its warmth cover me all over."

"Oh! It is sounding exciting." Caroline grinned.

"Yes, it definitely is."

"And that's it?"

"Yes, it definitely is." Callie watched Caroline's face with smug delight.

"Well, this is certainly a deep conversation, my friend. And I'm doing all the talking. Elizabeth is in France for a month. She called me between planes. And I will tell you that I had a wonderful time with Lee at dinner on the river and the Phantom was just as grand as I'd remembered it. He held my hand. Of course, it was a little difficult to enjoy it after Steven's nasty phone call.............." She lowered her voice, purposely mysterious.

"What? You didn't tell me!" Callie protested. Caroline's eyes smiled with satisfaction as she pursed her mouth and answered, "Nope, I definitely didn't." Then she grabbed her purse and cane before finishing her latte´ and held it high in a mock salute.

"Touche´" Callie said, laughing but curious.

Robert Dubois sat in the reception area, flipping through *People Magazine,* waiting for Caroline Phillips. Lee had dropped him off first, before looking for a parking space for his BMW. Lee told him it was like looking for a needle in a haystack around Southwest 12th and Morrison or within several blocks of Larkspur's building.

His ruddy face and delicate bone structure fought with each other but his smile was genuine. Intelligent eyes wandered around the room. He wore a navy beret and carried a brown leather bag with a long strap, similar to a woman's purse, only flatter and more compact. The large briefcase was stuffed with papers, catalogs, a water bottle and what looked like his lunch.

He saw Lana smile at him before the phone rang beside her. He saw her face pale as she stammered into the mouthpiece. Then, he watched her, quite interested in the intriguing drama that filled her face. *Americans,* he thought, *always the drama.*

Lana's breath caught in her throat. She tried to avert her eyes from the man across from her, but felt nauseous fear envelop her as she pressed the phone to her ear.

"You listen to me, sweetheart. You want those boys to live with me sailing around the world forever without their mama, just ignore me. If you want to be part of their lives, then listen!" Steven's voice carried such angst that she was sure her heart missed a beat. Her hand gripped the receiver as if it was a lifeline to hell.

"Don't take them anywhere! You know I've done everything you've asked. Why, all of a sudden are you trying to hurt me again?" she whispered quickly, shaking like a leaf.

"Something is going down, Lana. I'm sure you saw the front page of the paper, right?" He waited, knowing she must know more than she'd let on.

"No, I left too early," she lied. "Why, what is in it that would..............?" she stuttered briefly.

"Oh...... just that the *Queen* you work for is going to Spain or Germany for the drug deal instead of Toronto. I know that Canadian is arriving in Portland sometime today from S/K." His strident voice continued harshly.

Lana glanced over at Robert. He was staring at her.

She shrugged and smiled tentatively in his direction as her lips trembled and tears welled in her throat. She felt her heart thumping so wildly, anyone passing by would hear it. She couldn't remember being so afraid.

"What are you asking me to do now, Steven?" Her voice shook as she listened with dread. After another minute, she quietly replaced the receiver, again turning to smile at Robert. Then she dialed Lee Carle's cell phone as Caroline had instructed.

Within thirty minutes, the restraining order had been placed on Steven Roget for Lana and both boys. The police were headed over to the school on Scholl's Ferry Road and to the Christian Daycare on Southwest Jefferson Street.

Since Steven had not committed an offense, they would not put an APB on him, but he would be under surveillance at the school parking lot or daycare yard until Lana picked them up... as a special favor to Lee. That was all they could do. Lee understood putting two of their team watching for something that *might* happen was not money well spent by the city.

Lee relayed the news to Lana when he walked into the office a few minutes later, trying to allay her fears. His overcoat was loosely trailing behind him and his briefcase slapping against his thigh as he approached Robert.

Caroline walked down the hallway to see Robert chatting with Lee and her heartbeat sped up. Looking at Lee's soft beard pumped her imagination. She could almost feel it rubbing against her neck, then her jaw. She shook her head to dispel the image and took a deep breath.

Her professional face was in place as they looked up and nodded. She invited them into her office, and hesitated as she noticed Lana's pale face while opening her office door.

"Go in and sit, gentleman. I am sure Jenny will be here any moment, I'll be right with you." Caroline turned back to Lana.

"He called and he's mad as hell." She whispered, with eyes full of fear. "Lee has the police watching the school and the daycare but they can't actually pick him up unless he does something wrong. What good is a restraining order?" she finished, as she looked at Caroline and gripped each end of her keyboard.

"Oh, God. What next? It must have been the newspaper article and someone's pushing his buttons. Let me finish this meeting. I have an idea that I've been mulling around in my head. I think you need a vacation at the beach with the boys, don't you?" she winked and watched surprise lift Lana's face as she slipped into her office.

Jenny, Lee, Callie and Caroline all watched Robert remove the sheaf of papers from his briefcase and lay them onto the glass-topped table between the loveseat and the big desk. Robert appeared more relaxed, knowing they'd found the traitor. He pulled out contracts to discuss the negotiating criteria, full of expectation.

"Premier also wants this contract. I told you from the beginning that I would be happier to place it into Larkspur's hands. I want everything out in the open," he continued, his French accent evident. "It is my understanding that we will fill your member's prescriptions as your benefits require and our facility in Toronto will comply with each order. *Bon?*"

"There will be two CoPays for each 90-day supply. The first prescription order goes through the member's local pharmacy. That activates our card when the pharmacy's computer reads the implanted chip inside the ID card. All drugs will be covered; no American list of preferred drugs will be used. Name brand and generic will be filled as ordered and the same cost would be applied. That is correct so far, *oui?*" Robert saw nods all around.

"And in place by January 1st?" Caroline drilled him.

"Yes, madam. Now we come to the financial part of our contract. If it were up to me alone, I would sign this immediately. Unfortunately, I have stockholders who hold me responsible for their dividends. Premier Insurance Company has just offered us an additional ten percent per order above the cost of the drugs." Robert watched as the faces in the room turned stony.

"Ten percent per order?" Caroline said, askance. "Can you tell me who you are dealing with at Premier, sir?"

Robert nodded solemnly. "No, Madam. He has asked for how you say... anonymity."

"Yes, I'll bet he has." Caroline pursed her lips.

Lee turned to Caroline.

Caroline looked at Jenny.

"We can't do it, Caroline. We can't beat their offer." Jenny said flatly.

Crestfallen, Caroline asked quickly, "Would you accept five percent per order incrementally over a period of two years to increase to ten at that time?"

Robert's eyes looked thoughtful a moment before replying. "Ah...I say, *Oui*, madam, but I must discuss this with the Board members. They will be meeting this morning. I must meet with the other gentleman at 4:30 today. Then, I will give you the answer. Is that acceptable? Madam? Monsieur?" He looked quite discomfited and very weary.

"I won't play games with you, Robert. This is important. I want our members to have the drugs from your company. We have looked long and hard. Shelton-Kent has the best reputation and I like the way you do business. If you must take Premier's offer, we will be subjected to keeping our current supplier. We have refused the Ace-Deer prescription contract and no matter what you decide, that is not a contingent plan. I would appreciate a call immediately once your Board has made their decision. I want this settled tomorrow or we can just forget the entire deal. Is that understood?" Caroline's blonde hair glistened as the sun shone through the windows behind her. Gray eyes snapped.

"*Oui*, madam. I will call you immediately. Again, I am most sorry that money must be so involved. However, as much as my personal feelings wish to sign here for you, money will be the final point and I need the stockholder's approval." Robert smiled apologetically and gathered his papers. He stood and shook hands with Lee and Jenny. Then he slowly walked toward Caroline.

As she reached out her hand, he held her shoulders with each of his hands and briefly touched his lips to her cheeks, one after the other, in the French fashion. Slightly flustered, she smiled and bid him goodbye.

"Whew........." Caroline lifted her brows, "Those Frenchmen." and briefly smiled, before expelling a deep breath and looked at Lee and Jenny. "Ten percent per order. Crap," she muttered through clenched jaws.

"Let's wait and see. We gave them an offer. Let them do the math. Quick thinking, by the way," Lee said, his voice filled with admiration as he winked at her.

As soon as he found a quiet minute, Derrick called Dr. Del Reed. He knew he shouldn't, but Del *was* in charge of approving surgeries. But his Dad was more important than this breach of ethics as far as he was concerned. He waited on hold for several minutes and finally asked to be put into voicemail. Doubly frustrated, his voice carried all the anger he'd felt when Carl first told him of the denial.

He was determined to talk to the man and wished he could talk with Caroline about it as well. *That's all she needs is this too. Guess I'll see how the medicine works for dad first.* But he wasn't so sure about that either.

Eric popped his head in the door and held up three fingers. "Sophia's on the phone."

Derrick grinned and picked up the phone. "Hey, darling. It's great to hear from you. Yes, I know. What did the doctor say?" he prodded.

"I am going to have in-vitro-fertilization and the doctor may implant three instead of one in case one or two don't take," Sophia said hurriedly.

"Do you have any idea what that could mean?"

"Yes, triplets, but the doctor really doubts it."

His eyebrows rose. "Triplets? Lord in Heaven, Soph, you will need six hands. Does your mother know what she's in for?" Derrick laughed, and then Sophia explained the procedure she and her husband would soon begin.

"Well, sweetheart, I support your decisions and I'm excited for you. Yep, Pop's doing ok. He's very disappointed because he needs that operation and the insurance company won't approve the surgery....Yes, I know, I'm going to find out as soon as I can." Derrick spoke into the phone hurriedly as he saw Callie walk by his office. "Have to run, sweets. Call again soon and keep me up on all the news about it. Yes, I can handle it, smarty pants. I love you too. Bye now."

Derrick got up and went to the door, but Callie was out of sight. "Did Callie want to see me?" he asked Eric.

"No, boss. She stopped just a moment, but someone needed her down the hall."

Derrick felt unreasonably disappointed. He returned to his office, shoved his hands into his pants pockets, and sat at the computer to let the web pages pull him into its depths.

The rest of the day was a blur of activity. Lana drove her Taurus wagon into the school's lot off Scholl's Ferry Road and looked carefully for Steven's Lexus. She leapt out and ran into the school where Nicholas waited in the principal's office. Getting out of school early was like a vacation and he was grinning from ear to ear.

She drove downtown again quickly, crossed Patton Road, followed the sharp curves down Jefferson and drove slowly by Frankie's daycare. After studying the entrance, she pulled into the front area and waved to the woman waiting for her just inside.

Within minutes, Frankie was in his car seat, the map was beside her and new Fred Meyer bags littered the back end. Food, pajamas, jeans, t-shirts, socks and underwear for all three of them were stuffed inside. Caroline cautioned her about going home to pack and she'd taken the advice. She sped along the Sunset Highway, followed Hwy. 217 toward Tigard, then turned west onto the Old Pacific Highway toward the ocean.

Fingering her cell phone, she remembered Callie's instructions to answer it only after it rang twice, stopped and rang again. She constantly checked her rear view mirror for the gold car that could break her spirit once again.

The boys played and laughed along with songs they loved to hear their mother sing, delighted in the changed routine. Neither asked where daddy was.

Lana stared out the window at houses, trees beginning to turn rust and the small towns as she headed west away from the city and into the woods. Her mind was a jumbled caldron of conflict as she swerved through the northwest forest toward sanctuary.

Steven's calls to Spain and Germany had been met with frustration. The operator told him to dial again, as the number he dialed was no longer in service. His anger erupted again as the minutes ticked by, waiting for the operator to look up the names of the pharmaceutical companies he'd accessed off Caroline's computer.

The companies were not listed in either Malaga or Berlin. Would he please check the names and try again? *Hell, no, I won't try again.* His brain screamed as the realization that he'd been outwitted began to slowly sink in when he hung up. His hands were sweaty and he was breathing hard.

He endured the panic attack and jerked into the parking spot near his probation officer's office. The meetings made him angry but he entered her office, looking as if he hadn't a care in the world. Yes, he had a place to stay. Yes, he had a job. Yes, he had some money he'd saved and no, he lied, he had not approached either Caroline or Callie.

The dark-haired woman studied Steven. "Well, why is there a restraining order in effect then? You can't go near Caroline Phillips, Callie Beauvais, Lana Potts and children."

"What?" He stared at her, stunned.

"What part did you *not* understand, Steven?" She asked, shaking her head sharply.

"That is crazy. Those boys are my sons!"

"Well, you better talk to the courts, then. There is nothing in the courts that says they are. That's all I know and you better watch yourself. You are walking a thin line here." She closed her file and watched him storm out the door, eyes burning.

Minutes later, he pulled beneath the Burnside Bridge and entered the **Storm Den**, looking for Julia and finding her quickly. He waved to her and watched her remove a white lacy apron and nod his way. He remained on the brick stairs in the near-darkness as he watched her speak to the bartender and walk toward him, her hips swaying in tune to the music.

"Hello, big guy," she whispered sexily.

He reached out and pulled her upstairs, touching her all the way to the door. Her breasts surged at his intimate touch and she didn't seem to mind his roughness. "Hello yourself," he said urgently.

At 3 o'clock, Steven parked in front of Frankie's daycare, ignoring the ten-minute parking sign. Five minutes later, he rammed his fist into the front door, tearing the skin off his knuckles, anger at the forefront of his brain. He ripped the Lexus car door open. Vehemently twisting the key, he shoved the gearshift into drive and squealed tires as he pulled into traffic, barely missing the Tri Met city bus as it lumbered beside him.

He called Lana's number and another woman answered her phone. Lana had gone home ill. He called home and got the answering machine. He called her cell phone. No answer. Driving toward Beaverton, searing pain stabbed through his head. He ran upstairs and found the apartment empty. Then, driving to Nicholas' school, his disbelief was confirmed. Lana had disappeared with the boys. He slapped the steering wheel and cursed as if hell just reached up and squeezed the life out of him.

Del Reed had four messages on his desk when he returned from lunch. They were all from Sam James regarding Carl Leander. He decided to get the call over with as he waited for Steven's call. He reminded Carla once again that if Steven Roget called to put him through immediately even if he was already on the phone.

It was his fourth request and her nerves were shot. "Yes, sir. I will put him through right away!!"

"Okay. Okay, just wanted to make sure..........." He strode back into the office.

Sam James' voice held barely-restrained anger. Del listened as Sam described the HMO struggle. He allowed Sam to vent his frustrations, made notes, scribbled and drew cartoons on the pad beside his phone. When he was finished, he answered, laced with partial understanding.

"Sam.........Sam. Hold on. You know I'm only doing my job and it's a hell of a job. I can't always *yes, yes, yes* to all surgical requests. You know the PCP angle and how they pay for the surgery. Let the member pay for some measly drugs while we wait it out. If the Board sees you've tried alternatives, they are more apt to approve an appeal." More cartoons and squiggles filled the paper and he shook his head trying to wind down the conversation.

"The *Board?* You mean *you*, don't you? Don't give me that shit, Del. I know the bottom line is money and this man needs the surgery *now*. Why not compromise for surgery in *three* weeks instead of six,?" he cajoled.

"Sorry, Sam. The decision stands." Del dropped his pen, ripped the page off the pad, wadded it up and tossed it in the wastebasket, missing it by a foot.

"Sure. You're sorry all right..this isn't the last of *this* one," Sam retorted ad the line went dead.

"Disappointment is the nurse of wisdom."
—Sir Boyle Roche

Chapter 18

* * *

Speechless, Robert Dubois wove his way down the corridor, through the lobby and outside. *Portlandia*, the huge bronze bust perched above the entrance to the Portland Building, watched his disjointed departure as autumn wind swayed the trees and blew thick leaves around him.

After walking a few blocks in a daze, he stopped on a tree-lined street abuzz with activity. Standing still a moment, he inhaled deeply and studied the high-rise buildings around him. *These strange Americans.* He shook his head, zipped his coat against the cool breeze and tried to lasso his mixed thoughts.

Robert had never imagined his trip to Portland would generate such stress. He knew pharmacy administrators, like Shelton-Kent usually met directly with the corporate headquarters of each pharmacy chain to procure prescription contracts. *But that's too complicated,* he'd thought months earlier. *When Ms. Phillips approached me with the idea of dealing directly with us, it was a nice challenge Alors!*

Robert rammed his hands deeply into his pockets. *I wanted to step outside the box and where did it get me?* He ran the scenario around in his head. The fees are typically based on Brand Name or Generic. *But not ours!* The pharmacy has the acquisition costs, so it is imperative to get the best price from large chains because when they buy in volume for the best rates. His head hurt.

He stood still, wondering what had actually gone wrong. Premier said they wanted the contract and they were willing to pay high dollars plus the normal fees and discounted drug rates. But that was yesterday.

He knew the ten percent-per-prescription incentive was a tough one for his CFO to pass up. After making the call two hours earlier, he'd argued finances versus ethics to no avail. Robert had their answer. He had been grimly disappointed that the financial aspect won, but not surprised. *Money.*

At 4 o'clock, he'd reached the impending meeting with a dragging gait and heavier heart, knowing he'd have to accept Premier's offer. But, the meeting went south.

So now what? He sat down hard on the wooden bench near the street corner, amidst a mixture of casually dressed adults and squealing children. His beret and the long-strap dangling off his shoulder made him fodder for curiosity seekers, but he didn't notice them or the wail of a tiny girl trying to get out of her mother's arms.

He replayed the meeting in slow motion, one piece at a time.

"Our Board changed their mind, Mr. Dubois. I'm sorry to have wasted your time." The big man stared into Robert's gentle eyes, daring the Canadian to don boxing gloves, while an insincere smile crept into his face. Robert knew he wasn't a bit sorry.

An icy chill had crawled around Robert's scalp as the man's cold eyes bored into his, ending the meeting abruptly. Robert had no option other than to turn to go. The meeting was over.

After a few minutes of further contemplation, Robert shrugged his shoulders in defeat. *Watching people and traffic isn't getting me anywhere.* It didn't take the Canadian long to realize that cabs weren't 'flagged' down on the streets of Portland like they were in New York City. "Come on, monsieur. Give a guy a lift," he shouted as he jumped back, barely escaping a cabby who nearly ran him down.

French slang rumbled in his brain like shooting marbles as he shook out the little street map Lee Carle had given him that morning. He traced the minute lines with his finger and started walking down unfamiliar streets leading him toward the river and the Marriott Hotel. Blue blanketed the sky above him and a slight breeze caressed his face. He looked ahead and felt Mount Hood lure him eastward as he teased out some answers for his problem.

Or is it a problem? Sudden clarity rejuvenated his mood and a smile cleared his brow. He stopped and stared at the ground as if counting the cracks, as his clicking thoughts calculated the irony. *Oh my God. What am I thinking? The challenge is back*, he thought. *Bon!*

Despite butterflies dancing in her stomach, Caroline stood at her office window, staring at the vehicular and pedestrian traffic below, thinking idly that they reminded her of Ben's childhood metal cars, about three inches long. *What were they called?* She couldn't remember and grimaced at the way her mind kept forgetting things. *PMS*, she thought, grimly. *Oh..Matchbox cars*, she remembered, suddenly feeling better. She thought of her son again and his toys a moment before she shook herself.

"Why am I at odds over Robert's call?" she said aloud as she gazed across the tops of nearby buildings. "It's a pharmaceutical war after all!" She tapped the wooden window frame before running her fingers through her hair. *Why am I not more relieved to have that contract?*

Callie's voice broke into her thoughts. She was leaning casually against the door frame, purse firmly in hand. "Come on. Let's celebrate. I know it's only 4:45 p.m., Ms. Phillips, but let's sneak out and go to *Jakes* for a glass of wine and a two dollar burger, what do you say?" Callie's curls bounced and her jubilant mood filled the air. "Lana's safe, we got the contract and I'm hungry."

Butterflies paused and gray eyes studied nutmeg brown. Caroline reached for the distasteful cane automatically and wondered when she could burn it. Not yet. "Yes, ma'am. Let's go play and.....just do it, as they say." Caroline laughed, crinkle lines around her eyes triggering her friend's laughter as well.

"Just because we are over fifty doesn't mean we have to act like old ladies."

"When do you ever act like an old lady?"

Caroline shrugged and her eyes smiled.

Outside her door, the phone rang. Caroline hesitated and turned to ask Lana who was on the phone... but Lana was gone. A knot wedged across her abdomen again. The temporary receptionist, Sarah, jotted down the name and held the pad up for Caroline to read. Laura Amburgey.

Both women's eyebrows rose. "You mean, Laura Amburgey, the *senator?*" Callie asked, clearly surprised.

"The one and only, I'm sure. Wait for me. I don't want to miss my two buck dinner and fine wine," she winked as she reached for Sarah's phone.

"Hello, Laura? This is Caroline Phillips. What have I done to rate a personal call from you?" Caroline teased, sitting in the chair beside the receptionist's desk. Caroline's face turned to alarm, then anger.

"You have *got* to be joking! I can't believe this. We were told this was a legal process and......... oh. It is. But someone has gotten to Senator Wilding and he's asked ... Well, how long do we have before it goes before Congress? And does that mean if a contract is already signed and then the law goes into effect afterwards, we'd lose the contract all together?" Caroline's lips tightened and she raised her eyes to Callie, rolling them and shaking her head, as she listened to the senator.

"Yes, thank you, Laura. I will definitely call Tillie immediately. If I have to come to Washington, I will. Thank God you gave me a heads up. Can I count on your support on this issue? Excellent! Thanks again. Now I'm going to *Jakes* to get drunk." Her stomach twisted.

Callie and Sarah exchanged glances. They both waited for Caroline to explain, but Caroline grabbed Callie's left arm and said, "Lead the way, my friend. We are going to hit the booze tonight. Sarah you can go home. We're done for today." And with that, they both walked down the corridor toward the elevator, each with broken strides that many feared might be permanent.

Jakes enveloped them into the wooden cubicle before the old wooden bar like a lover's embrace. Wine glasses sat on the table and fattening cheeseburgers and fries were ordered.

Caroline put her elbows on the table, folded her hands under her chin, and looked Callie straight in the eye.

"Let's quit this party and head for the hills. This is giving me a pain in the ass." She lifted the wine glass to her lips and gulped.

"That's it? No explanation? C'mon, Caro, what did Senator Amburgey say? It sounded ominous and I know it was about the drug card." Callie braced her chin with one hand and reached over to squeeze Caroline's right shoulder. "Come on."

"Ok, you want it? You got it. Some jackass has obviously *bought* Senator Wilding. There is no doubt in my mind that's what happened and I know Premier is definitely behind it. I just don't get it! Laura said the Senate Health, Education, Labor and Pensions Committee (HELP) held a hearing to discuss pharmaceutical importation and Wilding wants to rescind the law making it a Black Market issue, just like the old days. We can kiss the contract good bye if it's passed, she said. She said it is just in an embryo stage but it is definitely something to worry about because it could negate our contract after the fact. She told me to get in touch with our lobbyist A.S.A.P."

Callie's mouth fell open. "No kidding."

Caroline lifted the wine glass to her mouth again and drank liberally. Bringing her fingers to her temples, she rubbed them, laid her head back on the leather backboard and sighed. She glanced above the bar and stared at the stuffed buffalo head that graced the wall before focusing on Callie. Her arms stretched toward the table, fingers splayed. "That's our next move and Derrick has her number." She slurped more wine and motioned for another.

"Whose number?" Callie asked, curious.

"Tillie Tooter, the lobbyist Laura told me to call." She snorted. "What a name."

"I see this may be a long night. It's unusual for you to drink more than a couple glasses, Caroline. Are you sure you don't want to wait for your food?" Callie cajoled.

"Nope. I think if I drink two or three, I can figure this one out." She screwed up her eyebrows in thought. "Why in the hell do you think Premier would fight the legalities of Canadian drugs when they tried so hard to beat us out of the contract with Robert? He didn't explain anything when he called earlier. He just said, "*Mademoiselle, the contract is yours.* It was odd. Why would Premier change tactics?"

"No, it doesn't make sense. Maybe it's not Premier at all. Let's think this out, Cal." Another gulp, her glass was empty and a second one took its place.

Callie shrugged and drank her own as she listened to Caroline muse.

"I need to call Lee. He might be able to.........." Caroline stopped. "Well, speak of the devil... he just walked in."

Callie turned slightly in her chair to see the bemused smile Lee sent in Caroline's direction.

"The devil, huh?" He loosened his tie, tugging it back and forth to ratchet it loose. "Do you care if I join you ladies? I just left a contentious partner's meeting and I have a sour taste in my mouth. Robert took a cab to the airport. Hey, what's going on here?" Lee stared at Caroline closely as he loosened his tie another few inches.

"We are having one *helluva* party, Lee," Caroline said, her eyes slightly askew.

His brows lifted. He bit the inside of his cheek to keep from laughing and turned to Callie to find her much the same as Caroline. He pulled the wooden chair toward the table and said, "Ok, spill it. What's happened? This isn't normal for either of you. Celebrating Robert's contract or something else?"

Their words spilled over one another. The waiter shook salt on a napkin before sitting down Lee's microbrew and accepted a menu. Pursing his lips, he waited until Caroline finished her last sentence, lifted the menu to the man standing beside them and pointed to the Chicken Strips. The waiter quickly left to turn in his order.

"We thought you could help us figure out this puzzle." Callie said, wiping the table with her napkin where she spilled some wine.

"Oh, you have? Sounded to me like you were talking about the devil.... Well, let's take what we know. Premier obviously found out about your pharmacy deal from Steven. It may be because you refused to sign with Ace-Deer? He was against your going outside the dotted line to sign directly with an outside drug firm, am I right so far?"

"He didn't know about Shelton-Kent then but otherwise, it sounds right."

"So now that you have the S/K contract....... and we still don't know why Premier didn't get it with that extra ten percent offer... somebody wants to stop you from using it."

Both women nodded, sipped more wine, and slumped back in their seats. As Lee ticked off more obvious facts, both women slowly hunched forward again with their chins braced in their hands, looking less like professional women and more like the Bobsey Twins.

"So, Premier wanted you to go with Ace-Deer. Steven wanted you to go with Ace-Deer plus the entire LEXUS HMO panel. Premier uses the entire LEXUS panel. It's common knowledge that they also use only Ace-Deer. I never could figure out why they wanted the other contract........"

Lee stopped suddenly, his eyes lighting up. "Unless.... Ace-Deer keeps popping up. Let's shine a light in that corner. Premier uses them. We know of three other carriers who use them here in Portland and in Bend. We know they administer the drug programs, but don't wholly own the rights …. Or do they?" He drank his beer. "Do we know who owns Ace-Deer?"

Caroline watched the foam settle into Lee's mustache and lost her train of thought.

"Good question, huh?" Lee continued.

Caroline and Callie leaned closer, eyes on Lee. Caroline turned to Callie at the same moment Callie's lips started to move and the words slid out as one.

"Premier Health."

Lee made a steeple with his fingers and shook his head slowly. "You know, ladies, it's surprising how clear things look through an alcohol haze, isn't it? I wonder if that's the answer. Premier owns Ace-Deer. They want you to be part of it. You refused, went elsewhere. They tried to cut you off at the pass by grabbing the contract and probably wouldn't have used it at all, thinking to force you back to Ace-Deer. I think we have something." He reached for his beer glass and finished it off.

Moving aside for the three plates to be set in front of them, Lee glanced up between bites. His fork stopped in mid air at the look on Caroline's face.

"Caroline, what............?" His voice trailed off.

Callie stopped chewing to look at Caroline and Lee, trying to decipher the conversation as the wine swirled around in her brain.

Caroline's face was strained as she reached over and touched Lee's hand. Then her voice said quietly, "Where does Steven fit into all of this then?"

"Life is a game of whist. From unseen sources. The cards are shuffled,
and the hands are dealt.
—Eugene F. Ware

Chapter 19

✳ ✳ ✳

Callie's head was heavy on her pillow, still spinning slightly. It felt like
a bowling ball that should be put somewhere nice and dark and quiet
and forgotten. And she knew Caroline's must match hers in
intensity since they'd imbibed steadily, matching each another one for one.
Oh, Lord help me. She struggled to open her eyes against the sun as it
squeezed through her blinds. *Why couldn't this be Saturday instead of
Friday?*

She forced her thoughts back to the night before. Both cars were in the
parking garage. *Thank you, Lee.* He drove them home the night before,
long after happy hour ended and the night crowd grew to a roaring rumble
around them. Their conversation continued into the evening, as each tossed
their thoughts into the brainstorming bowl, unable to answer Caroline's
question.

Steven. Callie was at a loss. She didn't have a lucid answer, nor did she
particularly care...She just wanted to put one foot in front of the other.
Dragging herself out of bed, she moved slowly, holding her head with one
hand and reaching for the phone with the other. She'd promised Caroline
to get Tillie Tooter's phone number from Derrick. She smiled as she
remembered the sly remarks the night before from Caroline, as they'd
discussed who would call him at home this morning. Heads won, tails lost.
Right.

Derrick picked up the phone on the second ring, sounding much too
cheery and very loud. She pulled the receiver away from her head in slow
motion.

"Derrick, this is Callie," she said softly, for fear of losing her head as it
rolled off her shoulders.

"Good morning, Callie. What a nice surprise," he answered, sounding
as if he'd been given a rare gift and smiled loudly into the phone.

She pulled the receiver away from her ear once again. "Not so loud, Derrick, okay?"

"Oh, oh, do I detect a headache or a hangover?" he said, immediately interested.

"Yes...... no....... yes ...." she answered.

"Well, what is it?"

"Yes, yes, YES!" She said, more sharply than she intended, feeling her stomach roil.

"Ouch! Sounds like a bad one." He whispered, trying to keep the grin out of his voice.

Callie nodded, immediately sorry, and groaned.

"Are you ok? "

"No, I'm *not* ok. But I'm on a quest. Two questions actually. One I'm embarrassed to ask, but would you please pick me up for work this morning on your way in? I would never make the walk up to Dosch Road to catch the bus." Before he could answer, she quickly added, "And I need Tillie Tooter's phone number for Caroline. We have encountered quite an interesting development," she finished.

"I take it your car is not there...Can you be ready in thirty minutes?" he asked, trying to talk quieter.

She groaned once again, thinking. "Aaarrrgh. Yes, I guess so. Ok."

"Then you can tell me...slowly of course....and you can whisper. Sorry, don't mean to tease you. I've been there too. Do you want me to stop at the Starbucks?" he asked, plying her with sweetness.

"Uhmmmm... yes. That would be good. Thanks, Derrick. I'm hanging up now. See you. Uhmmmmm... and thanks." She hung up the phone, setting it down gently to mute the sound, a tiny click and the dial tone disappeared.

Thirty minutes? Oh God. Why did I say ok? I hate feeling this lurching hideous emptiness in my belly. Her eyeballs felt like Brillo pads behind her eyelids. Her mouth tasted like cotton and her head felt like it was the size of a watermelon. She sat down slowly on the couch without moving her head. Turning in slow motion, she lay on the cushion and gently held her stomach. She groaned again before forcing herself up, padding into the bathroom and turning on the shower. The water swished into the tub, beating against the porcelain. She turned away, the sound hurting her ears. *Was the shower always that loud?* She grimaced, closed her eyes and kneeled in front of the toilet.

Derrick rang the doorbell exactly thirty-three minutes later to find Callie's pale shadow answer the door. Her curly hair framed her face, devoid of makeup. His instinct was to put his arms around her, but instead handed her the cardboard cup and gently closed the screen door quietly. He caught the semblance of a grateful smile as she motioned him into the big room.

"Still feeling like shit?" he asked.

She smiled only slightly and nodded her eyes slowly, with minimal movement of her head. "Yes, good definition." She murmured.

Holding the coffee between her hands and letting the cup lead her to the sofa, she told him what Laura Amburgey had told Caroline the night before and the content of the conversation between her, Caroline and Lee afterward.

His brow wrinkled as he sat back, holding a cup of coffee of his own, watching her.

"And you didn't invite me. I'm hurt."

She tried to smile but couldn't manage it.

"Your car?" he asked.

"In the garage. Lee drove us home."

"Good man." He said, sipping coffee as he watched her over the rim of the cup.

"Yes, we thought so." A little color was beginning to reappear in her cheeks.

"It was good of you to give Lana your cottage for a while to get away from Steven. That whole thing is more than I could have imagined. And her littlest boy is Steven's on top of it all? What a mess he's made of his life and it sounds like he's still in it up to his butt. We know he's involved with Premier. That must be where he got the job when he got out of jail. But he must have been involved before! Whew. Is Lee following up on that?"

"We have several things going on. Lana's been running like hell, trying to keep her boys and herself out of his way. He's obviously looking for her but there's no way he can find her unless he followed her. She's watching constantly." Her eyes felt like they were being tugged out of their sockets and she pushed the silver bangs out of her face.

"Have you talked to her recently, then?"

"Yes. I reminded her yesterday afternoon when she called to keep a trained eye out. The cottage faces D Lake and anyone can park in back away from the lake side, hidden. She's staying inside this morning with the boys but it's rough since she said the weather is gorgeous. Telling them it's too cold has worked for her so far. I told her once we know Steven is still here, I'll let her know. I don't think I've ever heard her sound as relieved as I did once she got there. She's been going through hell. I know Steven was a friend of yours, Derrick, but I think he's despicable.

"I never thought so before I met him again here in Portland." He sighed deeply.

"Lana said he's addicted to sex and he's surprised when she fights him, then he's all sweetness. She's baffled. But you know what? I think she loves him. She said he isn't like this normally....drugs maybe? I asked Caroline about the sex thing and she was dumbfounded. She said he'd evidently been on his best behavior or she didn't turn him on." She grinned at this. "Fat chance, she's beautiful."

Derrick smiled at the turn of conversation. "Well, if you can go to work, I'll take you. I have Tillie's number at my office." He didn't take his eyes off her pale face.

"Oh, it's not in your little black book, huh?" she teased, keeping her head still and sipping the latte´ that seemed to ease some tension behind her eyeballs.

"Well, I can see you are feeling *much* better," he countered, knowing full well she didn't. "Besides, all I see in my little black book is under the Bs for Callinda Beauvais."

Her throbbing eyes glanced up slowly, heavy head forgotten a second. Meeting his gaze, her eyes warmed. "That's nice," she said, "very, very nice." Then, she got up, turned green again, attempted a smile, and purposefully made her way into the bathroom. "I will be ready in ten minutes. There's more coffee on the counter," she said as she hurried to the commode again, praying for a false alarm.

"Compromise makes a good umbrella, but a poor roof; it is a temporary
expedient, often wise in party politics,
almost sure to be unwise in statesmanship."
—LOWELL

Chapter 20

* * *

Four days later, the sun rose above the marble and brick buildings over
Washington D.C., casting the promise of blue sky as a warm breeze
skidded between the heart of the city. Caroline watched cars careen
around her taxi, each fighting for space, racing through yellow lights,
sometimes red. The license plates varied from Washington, D.C., Maryland
and Virginia plastered on new models, rarely older ones.

Her heart skipped a little as she enjoyed the views encapsulating the
political bed of the nation. The taxi skidded to a stop after jerking around
a limo paused in the lane ahead of them at the last minute. Her head lolled
on her shoulders and slammed her against the seat. She quickly paid the
driver, gathered her stuffed briefcase and got out.

Caroline found the Hart Senate building easily, with Tillie's directions.
Standing a moment before entering the building, she looked up and down
2nd Street, NE. She hugged herself with the knowledge that she was in the
city where laws were made and the President of the United States of
American nearby.

She summarized the points she and Tillie Tooter had discussed earlier
that morning. She understood exactly what she must get across to the
Senator, intent on standing her ground. She was not going to let a man
walk over her again, even if he was a Senator from Oregon. Paul taught her
well enough how to fight back and win after he'd treated her like a stupid
woman. *Well, I'm not a stupid woman!*

Gripping her burgundy leather briefcase tightly, her cane guided her
into the marble building. Her eyes scanned the inside of the foyer. She was
mesmerized, feeling like a country girl who'd just entered the big city and
she laughed a little to herself. *Well, that is exactly what I am. Sure, I run an
insurance company. Sure, I have employees on three floors of our building in a
city dominated by bridges and two grand rivers. Sure, I'm a mother of two*

grown children. Sure, I'm a taxpayer. I may be a country girl living in a city, but I know what is right and what is absolutely wrong.

After watching her belongings pass through the security checkpoint, she glanced at her notes again.

Prescriptions purchased abroad: Canada, Switzerland. France, Germany, Spain, England

Concrete resolve strengthened her stride as she searched for Senator Arnold Wilding's office. Her appointment was for 2:00. It was 1:40. She slowed her steps to read office plaques as she passed doorways, seeing young Interns scampering around, phoning, writing and talking to others. She smiled again, enjoying the ambiance of the judiciary world that surrounded her. The underground tunnel railway was closed to the public since 9/11. She would have liked following the steps of congressmen and women as they scampered to the Capitol Building to vote every time the bell rang.

Concentrating once again on her impending meeting she was oblivious to admiring glances as she stared at the round blue plaque in front of her, surrounded by gold; an eagle above and a team of oxen below, pulling a covered wagon.

Arnold J. Wilding
State of *Oregon.*

A smiling intern welcomed her and led the way through a massive wooden door to the senator's office.

The man in front of Caroline looked at her through hooded eyes. He stood for a quick handshake, before motioning for her to sit.

Then they sized up one another.

Within five minutes of the senator's patronizing welcome, he launched into overused stump statements.

"I am happy you are in Washington, Ms. Phillips. I'm sure once you think about the exceptions you are requesting for your insurance plan; you will find that it is in your best interest and in your... what do you call the people you insure?" He asked, with an artificial smile.

"*Members*, senator." Her answer was clipped.

"Yes, thank you. You will find it is in your best interest and in your ah... *member's* best interest to keep business in America. That is what I constantly strive for. You see, I truly listen to America and they are talking loudly about their anger over NAFTA and ...."

Caroline detested the pompous ass in front of her. "......I'm not here to discuss NAFTA, senator. And I'm not asking for an exception. That drug importation law passed several years ago that decriminalized people who purchased prescription drugs outside America." Caroline countered.

Arnie Wilding's egotistical nature did not see intelligence in women. He gave a practiced smile to the pretty woman in front. "Ms. Phillips." He watched her as she sat across from him, ankles crossed neatly at the foot of the black leather chair that made her appear much smaller than she was. He sat all constituents in that particular chair purposely built lower to the floor than his own. She was forced to look up at him, just the way he liked it. She didn't appear to be discomfited by the distance between them.

She counted to ten slowly with crossed arms, listening politely, lips pursed.

Arnie Wilding spoke, as if to a child. "The Trade Laws differ in each country, Ms. Phillips. Of course, there is a disparity in costs for drugs in other countries. They have national insurance coverage and their governments lean heavily on the pharmaceutical companies to force them to charge the consumer lower rates for their drugs. But, remember, in those countries, there is less research and development. What's their incentive to come up with wonder drugs if they won't be paid accordingly? Do you know America's pharmaceutical companies retain a 17-year patent on their drugs? In America, we aren't heavy handed by forcing low drug prices on these companies. American business has the freedom of enterprise, the ability to recoup the millions of dollars that are spent annually on the research and development that other countries ignore."

"But this is a prescription crisis," she cut in boldly.

"Of course, it's a prescription crisis. I don't deny that. I never have, but the policy analysts for insurers and drug companies alike know that these millions must come from the consumer since, obviously, they enjoy the benefits. I'd like to take this outside the box so to speak, but my position is relative to choice and America demands that the drug choices stay in America." He finished, reached for the water glass near his hand and emptied it.

Then, he turned toward her, waiting for the response he expected. He wanted to show her out and get to his next appointment and still have time for a quick whiskey in his back bar before heading home.

However, Caroline Phillips was atypical. Her voice was firm and she looked straight into his eyes when she responded, "Senator Wilding. That was a lovely scripted over-long statement in what I admit may be your best political speech, but it didn't move me one damned bit from my stance or my argument. You are wrong. American people are not going to sit back and let you or other politicians tell them what and where to buy their prescription drugs. They've already spoken. They voted for the law you are trying to stop. This isn't the dark ages. I'm sick of playing the bad guy in this scenario while you hand out cigars and kiss babies. Larkspur is fully capable of charting its own course and our actions should be illustrative of the promises we have given to our members ...."

".....But, Ms. Phillips, I wouldn't ...."

"Please do not interrupt, senator. You had your say. I want mine. I pay your salary along with everyone back in Oregon. Our promises to Larkspur members are based on yours and Laura Amburgey's support several weeks ago when you met with Derrick Leander. That conversation gave me the authority or legalese if you will, to go across the border and sign a pharmaceutical contract directly with a Canadian supplier to save our members money. We intend to stop the bureaucracy forced upon us by our American pharmaceutical companies. We must stand up and fight and you can be damned sure that is exactly what I am going to do no matter how many pharmaceutical companies write threatening letters across the border."

With that, she stood up, pulled her cane off the edge of the chair's armrest and pointed it directly at the simpering man in front of her. "That is not a threat, senator. It's a promise and you better believe I'm not the only person you will hear from if you try to block this law. You are right, America has spoken but you certainly are *not* listening. Good day." She turned away from him abruptly, twisted the doorknob and was gone with a swish of her skirt as she walked out, straight and tall.

Arnie Wilding's chubby jaw went slack as he stared after her. Less than a minute later, he was on the phone. "You didn't tell me she was a lioness bitch with sharp teeth. We are going to have a fight on our hands and if she gets to the press here in Washington with that Tooter woman, we are going to have our asses in a sling unless you stop her. Yes, yes yes.... I'll still push the bill."

He canceled the rest of his afternoon appointments and went straight to the Jack Daniels he'd been promising himself since lunch. *To hell with them.* He got up and locked his door.

Later that day, Tillie and Caroline were in a deep discussion with the other senator from Oregon, Laura Amburgey. She was a no-nonsense woman in her late fifties who held her office to a strict code of honesty and fairness. The media loved chasing after her. Laura had bright red hair that was a tangled mass of tightly woven curls like a knit and purl afghan. Her bright green eyes sparkled as she spoke.

A widow, she found it amazing how many male senators hovered around her door, fully expecting her to fall into their arms, like a wilting flower. It didn't make any difference whether they were married or single. The men amused her. She enjoyed them as dinner and theater companions but she drew the line there. Single, yes, but she had been raised to believe in the sanctity of marriage and her own marriage lasted nearly thirty years before her husband succumbed to a dreaded cancer laced through his abdomen.

Now, living in Washington, far away from Portland, she enjoyed lavish dinners, shows and all that her adopted city offered. She rode the little red bus that transported tourists to and from the city sites she was so proud of, as often as possible. So proud of her seat in the city, she was determined to make sure the woman in front of her wasn't run over by political schemes. Therefore, she dug her heels into their dilemma and made it her own.

Caroline laughed at the women when they'd first suggested eating at the **Hard Rock Café** but joined in their escapade and the thrill of the city. She stared at the gigantic guitar above the bar and the memorabilia that lined the walls from floor to ceiling. Sitting near the front windows of the restaurant, she viewed the large room. Music blared and she wondered how on earth they would be able to discuss her crisis in the melee.

It didn't take her long to realize why the restaurant was chosen for their meeting. Laura moved her chair around one side and Tillie moved hers nearer the window. The vibrant sounds all around them muted their conversation. Laura said she lived in a fish bowl where the news was concerned. "Just watch, ladies. Expect to see your names in print tomorrow, if not your pictures."

Laura glanced at the menu and studied it as Caroline and Tillie exchanged looks.

They ordered Hard Rock hamburgers and wine. Laura said, "We aren't driving and we can think better...wine or not, right?" She pushed a ketchup-covered French fry in her mouth.

Caroline groaned, remembering her last visit to **Jakes**, as she lifted the wine glass to her lips.

"We fought long and hard to remove old laws that kept us America-bound and it's wrong to throw it into the ring again, to watch politicians do their constituent's thinking for them. We are in Washington to serve our fellow Oregonians, not to serve duck." Laura said, with a grin.

Caroline groaned again. "Duck...you're an Oregon alumni?"

"Yes, ma'am." Laura and Tillie answered in unison.

"Lord, an Oregon State Beaver and two Oregon Ducks at the same table. That's rough." She raised her glass of wine in a salute. "So many years between college classes and still the age-old Ducks and Beavers competition lives."

"That's right." Tillie laughed.

"Well, back to Wilding's senate bill proposal. Imagine planning your day around a glass of whiskey as a simpering puppet instead of a helper America begs for?" Laura bit off the next French fry, tiredly.

"He started out in very good form but for some reason, he's slipped the last year like he doesn't care anymore. Someone wasn't pushing his buttons when we met with your Derrick Leander a few weeks ago, Caroline. He and I agreed your idea made sense, filled with a logic we found hard to dispute. We met Derrick together."

"Yes, that's what made me so angry," Caroline sputtered.

"We were making progress but he's made an about face in the last month. In fact, lately he's acted vague and distrustful. When I heard about this senate bill he wants to bring to the table, I was staggered. I've had lingering doubts about what's making him tick for some time."

Laura looked at the others, waiting for comments. She picked up her burger, its aroma making her mouth water as she bit into it. She was glad they'd chosen **Hard Rock Café,** even if it was busy, crowded and noisy. The delicious juices ran down her fingers as she listened to Tillie.

"We've been pushing for change for longer than a few weeks, Laura. The Oregon Association of Health Underwriters work closely with all insurance agents, carriers and their legislative chairs to make sure that we don't miss anything crucial to our goals," Tillie said earnestly.

Her auburn hair swung around her animated face as she spoke, her plate untouched in front of her; her fingers wrapped around the stem of her wine glass. As if just noticing the red liquid inside, she lifted it to her lips.

"As a contracted employee for OAHU, I have a stake in this too. You know I have other clients and some of them are very big. Several of my clients are on your side. We all want drugs that are financially feasible, especially if it's covered by insurance plans like yours, Caroline....." Tillie took another sip. She winked before continuing. "I mean pharmaceutical drugs, of course, and remember, this drug situation is still fluid, it moves all the time."

Caroline studied her painted nails a moment before looking at both the women, trying to set a timeline to a solution. "So, the fact that Robert has assigned the S/K contract to us, the issue is can we keep it? Of course, if Wilding has his way and the bill actually gets to the floor, our main thrust should be to contact other senators and beg them to vote against it. Am I right?"

Tillie and Laura nodded agreement as they munched on their burgers and washed it down with wine.

Laura turned back to Caroline. "Tell me, Caroline, is there anyone at Larkspur you feel confident can work with me... someone who is close to your agent community? I really want to pursue this fight for you. I need to know what the agents are saying now, other than annual meetings during their Capitol Conferences. Otherwise, I'm at a loss."

Callie's name rose to Caroline's lips immediately. "Callie Beauvais. She's the head of marketing and works closely with the agents. Her representatives are some of the finest in the city. I'm proud to have them on board. They know their jobs and keep up with legislation through continuing education. They have to, or they'd lose their licenses. They keep up to date not only on federal and state legislation but also have some very good contacts in the Portland metropolitan area. I know she'd be delighted to work with you. Here or at home?"

"Both, actually. She'd be my personal resource and spokesperson. Also, working with Derrick Leander was a plus. If I could have both of them, I think there's a war to be won and we have to be ready." She smiled again, eating the last French fry and sipping the last of her wine.

Caroline's face was thoughtful. *Derrick and Callie working together might prove quite interesting.* "Just tell me what you need and I'll discuss it with both of them, Laura. Your valued support and willingness to work with us on such short notice proves that you care." Caroline reached across and patted Laura's hand.

Laura gave an answering squeeze. "I'm here for you. I know it's a political cliché but I happen to mean it," she answered solemnly and cringed as loud music screamed across the room. "How do these kids stand that stuff?"

Tillie sat her glass down and looked at Laura earnestly. "Laura, as I've done before, I will be happy to do again by setting up the legislative meetings that we have on the first Tuesday morning of each month with the association's board members and interested agents. I'll move it to weekly until this crisis is met. Do you think that would help?"

Tillie Tooter wanted to mend what she felt was a monstrous disservice. The medical community didn't seem to care about where the drugs came from and the insurance carriers typically contracted with pharmaceutical administrators. This new concept of surpassing the middleman was an entirely new idea that would mean financial savings for everyone. She knew drug companies earned millions of dollars from the backs of the little people. Their needs must get into the agent community's hands to effectuate a change.

"Caroline's pursuit in this genesis experiment will set a precedent, and I am adamant to continue my pledge to the community. I'm proud to be part of it and refuse to allow one man to stop me for all the wrong reasons. Senator Wilding's sudden, treasonous change only drives me farther into a war that I will fight to the bitter end." Tillie took a deep breath and slapped the table in front of her.

"Wow. You're hired!" Laura laughed.

Caroline shook her head in wonder.

As the music surged louder, they sat in a tight circle around the small table as darkening skies invaded the room. They continued their brainstorming when they were startled from a flash as bright as lightning. They turned as one as another flash caught them unprepared.

A young man in bulky jeans and a long sweatshirt caught the women's faces, wine glasses in hand with his camera, and then looked at Laura expectantly.

"Damn. What'd I tell you, ladies?" Laura looked at the man in mock anger as he approached the table.

"Ms. Amburgey. Sorry to surprise you but can I have just a few minutes?" The man was looking directly at Caroline, then over at Tillie before Laura answered calmly.

"Joe Smith, meet Caroline Phillips and Tillie Tooter. They are my Oregon constituents enjoying dinner and conversation. No more. No less," she replied and turned to look out the darkened window, ending the conversation.

"Come on, I know there's a story here. You were tangled up like a football huddle, Ms. Amburgey. Can't you tell me anything? You know my budget depends on...."

"Oh good Lord, Joe. Get out of here and leave us alone. I'll tell you what though. You will be the person I call when and if there is a story on one condition." Laura replied, winking at the two women beside her.

"Sure! What is it?" he said, breathlessly.

"Don't print that picture if my eyes are closed or my mouth is open or... if I look like a lush," she said, laughing. "But, Joe, I will have a story for you soon," she said, a sincere smile lighting her face.

"You got it. I'll Email you both pictures before they go to press. How's that?"

Joe Smith's job came first. And Laura knew it. They'd had run-ins before but his articles were usually fair and he reminded Laura of a younger version of her late husband. She decided if she told him the story, she could depend on reading facts. Other stories would be hearsay, fed to the paper anonymously. She was curious how the rest of the month would play out.

"Now, go away and leave us alone," she said, dismissing him with a wave of her hand.

"Laura. Do you have to put up with that kind of thing all the time?" Caroline asked, incredulous.

"Oh yes. My bread and butter, actually," she said. "Many times the press helps more than hinders."

"Why do you do it, Laura?" Caroline asked the senator seriously, very interested in Laura's reply.

"The commitment to run for elective office is more than just an emotional and intellectual commitment. Time, energy and stamina are equal partners in the effort. But it's also exhilarating when I can make a difference." She took a deep breath. "Well, we have this started. Now, let's get to work. You go back to Portland tomorrow?" Laura asked, as she handed Caroline her business card and gathered her sweater and purse.

"Yes, I leave at 4:30. Laura, you are amazing. May I ask what surprised you most about Washington?"

Laura Amburgey looked at Caroline thoughtfully. "I don't know if anything surprised me, since I think I was pretty well-prepared. But there were some things that definitely took some getting used to."

The other women nodded.

"There is so much going on, from legislation to meetings to committee hearings to conference meetings. It is challenging to get everything done properly. That is why the Hill is so staff-heavy. You have to be very particular with your staff because they handle quite a bit. This issue, however, I will have my finger on its pulse from the get go."

Satisfied, Caroline nodded and reached to shake the woman's hand. "Excellent! Laura. I'm so thankful you are on our side," she said, firmly. She glanced at Tillie. "You stay the rest of the week, don't you? If we can get this in place for January 1st, I owe you." She pointed at her with the business card before dropping it into her purse.

"Yes, I'll be back in Portland on Friday and then let's get to it. The first of the year isn't that far away and we really have work to do. I'll set up the next meeting on Tuesday and if you get Callie and Derrick lined up to work with me and Laura, we are on a roll."

At the end of the two-hour meeting, Caroline was excited, encouraged and confident.

"No one can disgrace us but ourselves."
—J.G.. Holland

Chapter 21

✳ ✳ ✳

About the same time Caroline got into her cab in front of the Washington Plaza Hotel heading for Dulles Airport, Steven Roget was sitting in a darkened corner of the *Storm Den* waiting for Del Reed.

He rested his head on the wall, and held the beer bottle to his lips, glazed eyes watching the stairwell. His shaking hand belied any semblance of outward control as he swallowed the remainder of his microbrew. As he set the bottle down on the table and wiped his lips with the cuff of his sleeve, his thoughts centered on Lana's disappearance. His fist closed around the dark brown bottle, squeezing the glass as he stared into the room around him. *Five days already. God, I miss her and my boys. That's what I get for having an act first-think later mentality.* He grimaced.

Suddenly, Del was standing in front of him, a stricken look on his face, reaching toward Steven cautiously.

"What the hell are you doing, Steven?" he implored.

His mind was blank and his head throbbed as he stared Del.

"You! Steven. What have you done?"

He followed Del's gaze. He saw blood dripping down his wrist and onto his shirt cuff. The bottle was lying in broken, jagged chunks inside his hand on the table, now sticky with blood. He stared at his hand, and then lifted his eyes to Del. He saw the doctor sit down beside him, grab his handkerchief to stem the flow and heard him hiss under his breath.

"Hey! Bring a towel over here … quick. This guy just cut his hand on a beer bottle," Del yelled toward the bar. He held Steven's arm down on the table while gently removing shards of glass from between the cut hand and fingers, still slick with blood. Del moved into doctor mode, his face a mirror of concern as he grabbed the tossed towel.

"Stop crowding around me," he muttered to the people closing in on them. He wiped at the blood to figure out how severe the damage was before calling for an ambulance. He found the gash, in the fleshy web between Steven's thumb and forefinger, extended nearly to his wrist. He called out again for ordinary soap and water, but stopped the bartender when he decided he'd take Steven to Providence Hospital ER himself. "Never mind, forget it."

He reached toward Steven urgently. "Come on, you're coming with me," Del said, angrily. *I don't need this shit.* "What the hell's wrong with you, man?" he asked. Del felt heat rushing up his neck as he hauled the bleeding man toward him.

Del pulled Steven out of the chair and across the room, dodging curious patrons. Fighting the lunch crowd coming down the steps, Steven held the towel tightly around his injured hand and followed Del, stumbling and erratic.

The nervous bartender and new hostess watched closely, glad the two men left without yelling lawsuit.

Del pushed Steven into his red BMW, being careful that Steven had his bloody appendage well covered. Priding himself on the cleanliness of his car, he didn't want blood dripping on the leather seats or carpet. He threw the little car into reverse, backed out quickly and headed toward Burnside. Driving too fast and barely squeezing through green lights as he headed up toward the five-corner intersection at Sandy Blvd., he ran a red light just before angling onto Glisan on his race toward Providence Hospital.

Steven groaned and laid his head against the headrest.

Del quickly followed the sound. Despite the seriousness of Steven's injury, the sooner he could get him out of his front seat, the better. An eye on Steven every few seconds, he wove in and out of mid-day traffic, moving his eyes from the road, over to Steven and then back again.

Quickly twisting his Beemer around the Joan of Arc statue at Laurelhurst Circle, he slowed a moment before belting up toward NE 47th, through the light and twisting to the left, shifting down as he eased into the ER parking lot.

Del turned toward him, wondering why he'd been in such a daze earlier. "Steven?"

Steven did not turn toward Del, nor did he show any sign of hearing him.

Del hurried around and opened the passenger door, anxious to pull Steven out, but was hindered by the man's size. Steven stumbled forward as Del yanked him toward the door. "Come on, I can't carry you, man!"

Within ten minutes, Steven was being wheeled into a cubicle and a blood pressure cuff was wrapped around his good arm. An efficient-looking nurse took over and pushed Del out of the room. "Hey, I'm a doctor," he said as he stood near Steven. "And I know something's wrong with this guy."

She looked at him sternly, "Well, *doctor*, it doesn't take a rocket scientist to tell me that. I don't know you. Do you have privileges here?" The short, heavyset nurse pinned him to the floor with her stare.

"Well, no. I'm at Meridian Park but...." Heat rushed upward again, his heart racing. "But, that's ok. I'm leaving. I meant something is *mentally* wrong besides the injury..." He reached over and patted Steven's cheek. "Hey, buddy. They'll take care of you. Your car's still at the **Den**. I'll wait outside to take you back when they're through.

Steven lifted his face to look at Del and murmured, "It really doesn't matter anymore."

"What doesn't matter any more......?" Del asked, shaking his head.

"Nothing does. I don't know where she went and she took my boys with her......" He mumbled, then caught his breath in surprise as the nurse jabbed him with a needle.

Del left him, trying to make some sense out of Steven's words. *Where's the macho businessman?* He wondered. *I trusted him to get a job done, hired him at LEXUS because he was good. Dammit. He really was good. We have to get this taken care of before..........* Del stood in the ER waiting room, debating about whether to call his partner or just wait. *Oh, hell.... I'll just wait, read the Oregonian, and watch the kids playing around.* He sat down. A soap opera blared on the television. He tried to ignore it as he watched the clock tick each minute out of the day.

By the time Steven emerged through the double doors two hours later, Del had worked himself into a frenzy. Seeing Steven with a big bandage around his hand, he turned his anger toward him as he walked unsteadily toward him.

"Hey, thanks for waiting, Del. Let's get out of here." Steven's voice was dull as he turned toward the outer door without waiting for Del's response.

"Ok, now you're *fine*. You want to tell me what in the hell happened back there? I don't have all this free time to spend the entire afternoon babysitting you anyway, you know?" He spit the words out as he opened his car door, jumped in and revved up the engine, barely allowing time for a sluggish Steven to swing his feet inside before roaring out of the lot.

As he drove up the ramp to the Banfield Freeway at 58th Avenue, white knuckles gripped the wheel as he headed toward the Lloyd Center exit.

"I don't want any more to do with all of this. I just wanted to do my job and I didn't want any more trouble. I've made a goddamned mess of my life and it's time I fixed it. I did something bad and don't know how to get out of it." Steven stared straight ahead, holding his bandaged hand up near his temple.

"What? What did you do that was so bad? All we're trying to do is force Larkspur to use Ace-Deer and drop their drug quest outside America. We will do whatever we have to do and you've already been paid. Very well, I might add." Del sneered shortly.

"That's not what I mean. My kids are off somewhere with their Mom and I don't know where. My probation officer is on my butt because Lana put a restraining order on me... and...." Steven said with a grim voice.

"What? What? I'm not in the mood to play charades here, Steven." Del slipped in and out of traffic like a slithering snake following it west until he could get off at the Lloyd Center ramp and slip back to the *Storm Den.*

Steven twisted in his seat, placing his right side and part of his back toward the passenger door and looked directly at Del. "I was mad as hell at Lana and I was a little rough on Julia."

"Who is Julia?" Del asked in confusion, shaking his head. He deftly maneuvered his little car beside Steven's gold Lexus under the Burnside Bridge and turned off the ignition.

"Julia is the barmaid with the big boobs that you drooled over at the *Den*, remember?" Steven said snidely, and then fell silent.

"Oh.....yes. I remember. What do you mean you were a little rough on her?" Del's curiosity got the best of him. "You've seen her since then?" he coaxed.

Steven laughed quietly, a slightly *mad* laugh filling the car. "Oh, I've been seeing her all right. We've had sex a few times...." He enjoyed the look on Del's face, so he went on. "She pushed herself at me that first day when you stayed behind and that sexy body had me going back for more. Wouldn't you?" he teased.

Del stared at him. "You sly fox. You said you were too rough on her. You never answered me. What'd you do?" he finished, his patience running thin.

"I nearly killed her." Steven said, his eyes lifting toward Del's once again.

"You did what?" Del sputtered and spewed spit.

"You heard me. I got a little to....shall we say, amorous? ...but this time..........." Steven's voice suddenly choked. "I was angry at Lana and took it out on her.... I went a little nuts."

Del stared at him. "A little nuts?" He wanted to get as far away from Steven as possible. "Well, you're on your own, bud. Get out. I'll figure out this mess without you. Don't call me and don't expect any help from me. There's your car. Drive." Del reached across Steven's lap, turned the handle and tried to push the door open but could only unlatch it slightly, waiting for Steven to get out.

"Not so quick, Doctor Reed. My bank account doesn't tally up to $40,000 yet. You promised." Steven quietly closed the car door again with his good hand, and pushed Del's outstretched arm down.

"Who do you think you are that you can make demands of me? You got over $25,000 already and you haven't finished the job you were paid to do. Now, you've made such a mess of your life, do you really think we want to have anything to do with you at all? You're already a criminal, remember?" Del pushed on, ignoring the heat that he knew was turning his face blotchy red again. It was becoming harder and harder to ignore.

"I am the man who has taken all the flack, gone to jail and lost my job, you dumb ass. You're going to do whatever I say because you know what? I did everything I could and she still got the contract. I'm done and now you can finish paying me or I will go to Lee Carle and spill my guts. I'm tellin' you. I am done with this shit and I want OUT." He stared down Del as an idea formed in his drugged head. "You're in deep...just like I am," he said quickly.

"In deep? Like hell I am. I'm just a doctor with a job to do. I do what I'm told and retirement is just around the corner. All I want to do is make sure Larkspur's contract goes with Ace-Deer and I'm in like flint as far as leaving and living a life of leisure. There's something else going on to stop her now. And that's that. I have my heart set on less work and more relaxation. It won't be long now," he told Steven, smiling at him suddenly. *When my investment pays off, there will be years of recreation to look forward to.*

Steven's eyes bored into Del's and the two stared at one another. "You've got it all wrong, Del..."

"No, YOU have it all wrong, Steven. Now get out of here." Del whispered sharply, his breath short. He tried to get his breathing back under control, but it was a slow maneuver. Doctoring himself was getting harder to control. He needed to take his Metoprolol to bring his blood pressure down and a glycerin tablet, but wanted privacy.

"Well, doc, don't you want to know where Julia is residing now?" Steven rubbed his good hand up and down on his navy suited thigh, still agitated.

"No, I don't want to know. I don't want to know anything about her."

"Well, I'll tell you anyway. I left her on your patio's garden bench by the Rhodies that surround the white, brick pathway from your garage to the water garden. She's just sitting there waiting for you. I'm sure your wife will enjoy chatting with her when she goes out to feed the birds." He said smoothly. Steven felt a sudden rush of enjoyment at the stricken look on Del Reed's face before he opened the door and slammed out of the car.

Steven's thoughts ebbed and flowed around his brain, while remembering his first encounter with Del Reed, the promises, the anger he felt toward Caroline for taking sides with Callie and having to put Lana in the middle.

He'd told Steven urgently, "It will be easy, man. Just push the Midlothian Merger, force her hand subtly and the money's yours." Steven could hear Del's voice slide into his head like creamy butter rolling off a fresh-baked roll. "The Ace-Deer contract must be part of it and LEXUS too, you got it?" Steven remembered thinking about all the money for the boys and Lana even though he had to get enmeshed romantically with Caroline. Lana tried to understand but it went all wrong.

Oh, God, Lana. Lana. She always stood by me no matter what I did and I treated her like poop. He closed his eyes and laid his head against the headrest, letting the past slide through his mind. Lana when he first met her. Lana's sweetness. Lana pregnant just after her 40th birthday. She was willing to have Frankie anyway! Lana's laughter and the way she played with the boys. Her sense of humor. Her hair brushing against his face when he held her. The way he forced himself on her last week, as if holding her responsible for all the times his life turned from sugar to shit.

Suddenly, Steven's mind jumped forward and remembered the way he'd treated Caroline, forcing Lana to keep quiet about their relationship. He couldn't tell her why. The money was the surprise. *I hated telling her she'd get fired if Caroline knew about our son. Caroline was a good woman and I liked her but didn't love her. Callie wasn't the bitch I tried to make her out to be either but God~ I needed that money Del promised. Too late to make it up to her now.*

Steven scowled and remembered the look on Del's face when he laid the last joke on him. Julia had hurt feelings but that's all. He'd fallen all over himself apologizing, trying to make things right. *But, dammit! My playing with Del's mind was exactly what he deserved.*

He felt heavy as the drugs took effect and his head felt fuzzy. The doctor at the hospital told him he shouldn't drive but that was a laugh. He could hardly ask Del to take him home and where was home anyway, without Lana? His mind skated around the past few weeks and always came back to Lana. An empty throb pounded in the pit of his stomach.

Acting on impulse, he lifted the cell phone and dialed home again. He didn't know where she was or when she would check messages but he had to beg her to talk to him. He spoke into the phone and his heart galloped with the thought that she might soon be listening to him.

"Lana. I'm sorrier than I can say well ....about everything. I've been stupid. Irresponsible. An asshole. I would never hurt you or the boys. I love them. I love you. I always have and always will.... Really. It was just too much money to turn down. It was for us but I became obsessed with it and made... oh...I can't think." He sniffed and caught the tear slipping down the side of his nose and he finished, brokenly, "Please Lana. Please give me another chance to be the man you once loved. I need you and the boys. I........money isn't everything. I know that now. And I will see a counselor just like you begged me to do. I will. I promise." He shut the cell phone down and felt his head loll.

Then, he remembered his mother telling him that God loved him no matter what he did. *Even failures?* Steven challenged as he fought off another wave of dizziness. *Mom's God has probably written me off too.....*

He held his injured hand close to his chest and prayed for the first time in years. He prayed for himself. He prayed for his boys. He prayed for Lana. And he prayed Lana could love him again. His hand throbbed and he knew he'd have to drive slowly onto Barbur Blvd. *I'll go the back way and take Multnomah Blvd. I can go slower and pull over if I have to. Now concentrate, you asshole!!*

He twisted his left arm around the steering column and started his engine. Suddenly, a feeling of peace flooded over him after making a deal with his mother's God, hoping He was listening.

He allowed himself a rueful smile as he turned the wheel to avoid the jogger in his path. That woke him up and he expelled a long breath. Everything seemed to be moving in slow motion. He sat up straighter, shook his head again. He needed noise. He turned on the radio and stopped to listen to Faith Hill. He breathed deeply. His injured hand throbbed but his mind felt clearer than it had in a long time, even with drugs floating through his blood stream. And he felt a kernel of hope ingrain itself among his chaotic thoughts.

He didn't notice the red BMW around the corner, engine idling, as he headed toward the nearby Hawthorne Bridge.

"Wise men argue causes, and fools decide them"
—Anarcharsis

Chapter 22

* * *

Doctor Sam James sat in his deep blue LaZBoy armchair, hunched beside the tree lamp, its light focused over his right shoulder. He rustled the file with his thumb absently as he read the sheaf of papers in front of him. Despite the company rule not to remove files from the building, Carl Leander's file lay beside him; But those same rules shaped his mood and future actions as he wondered if his days as a doctor were numbered, albeit over.

The page in front of him was titled, "Operational Policy." The topic was "Grievances and Appeals" and it was dated the month before. His frustrated brow crinkled as he read the words, his glasses tucked on the bridge of his nose.

'Larkspur understands that at times our members, agents, and providers may have questions or concerns about decisions made by our staff. Our policy is to document, investigate, resolve, and notify all affected parties in a timely manner. Fair consideration and timely resolution are the goals of our grievance and appeal process.

Larkspur has a four-level system for addressing and resolving inquiries, requests, concerns, complaints, and grievances. When issues concern our members and providers, we adhere strictly to this four-tiered system.'

He thumbed through the definitions for "concern" "inquiry" "complaint" and "grievance." *Well*, he thought *they want four steps....they'll get four steps.* He wondered briefly if he had the guts to approach Caroline Phillips. He thought idly; *Why not start at the top? She always seemed accessible. Why not? No*, he told himself, *she has so much on her mind......... Well, I begin the first step that way... it says here........... His finger ran down the page once again.

"Concern" means any expression of dissatisfaction with Larkspur, whether verbal or written. He penciled her name beside that area and decided an email might work. He would write it precisely and to the point, leaving no doubt about his disgruntled state and Carl's obvious surgical need.

Good. I'll do that tonight. He slapped his palm against the stack of papers and file beside his chair and promised himself he'd follow this to the end. *No more playing around with Del Reed. This is serious and I'm sick of being dictated by the HMO.. It's forcing my Hippocratic Oath to the back burner... I'm a doctor, dammit. And I want to treat my patients!*

Two hours later, Sam finished his letter to Caroline Phillips, reread it twice and clicked the send button. *What can she do..... fire me? It would be better than what I am up against now. Why can't I work out the last few years before I retire doing what I do best, practicing honest medicine?* Satisfied, he folded up all the files and replaced them in his worn-out brief case and went hunting for something to eat.

Marianna was bowling. She'd left him a note about some meatloaf. He quietly contemplated a glass of beer, looked down at his growing paunch and decided he didn't need the extra calories. He tried to wait her out but his rumbling stomach beat her bowling game. *Damn. Well, I'll wait on myself. I know I can do it. It's just so much nicer when she fixes it.*

Munching on a meatloaf sandwich laced liberally with ketchup, he found some potato chips and gave in. He opened a bottle of MGD beer. *I'm nearly sixty- two years old, in pretty good health and I want a beer. So, I'll be boss and just have one.* Taking another bite and washing it down with the beer, he suddenly stopped that thought. *Boss? Why not? Maybe I should just withdraw from both the LEXUS HMO and Larkspur. No, I can't do that. What am I thinking of? I wouldn't be able to take care of the patients who have Larkspur insurance, like Carl Leander.*

He took a deep breath and sat thoughtfully, the rest of the sandwich uneaten.

That is how Marianna found him half an hour later as she stepped into the door, her bowling ball leading the way.

"Sam?"

"Yes, hon. I'm here. Just thinking."

Marianna walked to him and placed her hands on his shoulders. "Glad you found something to eat, dear. What are you so deep in thought about anyway?" she asked as she put a cup of water into the microwave to heat and punched in a minute. Then, quickly, a high-pitched ding announced the tea was hot and she reached toward the microwave door.

"I decided I wanted to be boss." Sam mumbled.

Her arm stopped in mid air as she removed the cup. "You want to be boss?" she repeated, a question in her voice.

"Yep. I do."

She looked down at him and realized he was serious. She stamped her foot to get his attention and said, "No, Sam, *I* want to be boss."

They both laughed.

"Fat chance, lady." He reached for her hand.

She squeezed it quickly, grabbed her hot tea and joined him at the table. "What?"

"Well, it's like this. You know how sick and tired I've been, led around by the nose on this HMO? I know it's basically a good idea. The importance of preventive care, networking with all a patient's doctors to avoid drug overdoses and that kind of thing. But, dammit, when I know someone needs an operation, then I want to do it. Now that the boys are doing well and the house and cars are paid for, what do you think about me pulling away from the LEXUS HMO panel?"

Marianna looked at Sam and shook her head at him. "Sam, it's sweet of you to ask me, but sweetheart, you have always supported me in anything I wanted to do and I will support you the same. Do what you have to do. You know I like hot dogs and beans." She smiled and sipped her tea, winking broadly.

"Right... You have enough stuff in the freezer to feed us until I go onto Medicare," he responded.

She smiled her agreement, laughter quietly mixed with his words. "So what's the plan, dear?" She asked him, feeling the hot tea sear her tongue.

"I just sent an email to Caroline Phillips, the CEO at Larkspur. She is fair and is known to listen to anyone I've ever spoken to about any problems within the system. It's an HMO but I trust her. I do not trust the LEXUS Corporation, nor do I like their CEO or the doctor in charge of the medical reviews. Well, I got it off my chest and I'm going to fight them this time. My patient is covered by Larkspur and uses me because I'm a LEXUS doctor. He needs an operation and he's become a friend and you know what? I'm on his side like I always was in the old days and money be damned." He took a bite out of the sandwich and finished his beer, setting the empty bottle down like a punctuation mark.

"So *there*!" Marianna said and they shared another bout of laughter.

"Mystery is the wisdom of blockheads"
—HORACE WALPOLE

Chapter 23

* * *

"I NEED TO DO THIS *my* way, Lee. I don't agree with you this time." Caroline's voice rang out sharper than she intended, and her gray eyes sparked. "Why should we retain our current drug card benefit and postpone the S/K card since we have the contract? It's being processed now. I am certain that Wilding's bill will be killed. I know it's just my woman's intuition but I just feel it."

Lee's unhappiness was evident in his voice. "But Caroline, what happens if it gets to the floor and the vote changes the course of your actions? What happens if, after all the time, money and efforts go into the new contract with S/K, you have to dump the whole damn thing? It's not a good business decision and it's my job to tell you so!" His voice rose as he finished speaking and stared at her, eyes unblinking as he listened deeply.

"I've always followed your legal recommendations with regard to Larkspur in the past, Lee," Caroline's measured words were slow and defined, "but I feel compelled to move on and take the final steps I've promised everyone. The implementation of the new drug card **will** roll January 1st and I'm nearly giddy with my coup. Lee, I'm a small vineyard. And I'm not willing to sacrifice the way I make my wine to get into the supermarket. And I will not wither in defeat. You know what I mean?"

He chewed the inside of his cheek and gave her a questioning look. "Who knows what they'll throw at you next?" His gray eyes were troubled and his tenseness was evident as he sat on the edge of the chair, waiting for her rebuttal.

"Lee, have you ever played Pinochle?"

"Yes, years ago, why?" He was having trouble following her line of thought.

"Did you ever play shoot the moon?"

"What?!" He was completely lost.

"You know....Shoot the moon. It's when you and your partner lay down all your cards and the meld isn't enough to win the hand unless you can both pull all the points during the play off. It's like you're thinking, 'it's all or nothing....... win or lose. Shoot the moon is what I may be doing here. I want that drug card and I'm willing to gamble that I can do it and win by pulling in all the cards that count." She took a deep breath.

"And if you don't?" He said quietly.

"I WILL. I can *fight* it. You *will* support me on this, won't you? Deep down, you know I'm right. We can't keep charging our members more as each year rolls around just to keep up with the drug costs that suppliers keep handing us each year their contract is renewed. You *see* that don't you?" she asked, eyes pleading and brows furrowed, trying to read his mind.

Lee just shook his head and admitted conciliatory defeat as his eyes swept over her face. He resigned himself to losing the battle. He shook his head again, and then rolled his eyes. "Do you know how beautiful you are on that soap box?" he asked quietly.

Caroline dimpled and smiled at him, looking at the small mustache above his mouth and the way his neatly-trimmed beard covered his chin. She inhaled the scent of his aftershave sliding across the expanse between them. No response could clarify her feelings, so she remained mute and forced herself to concentrate on the matter at hand. "Thanks, Lee.......I think?"

They laughed together knowing their hearts were knitting together quietly there in her office.

It was going according to plan. Shelton-Kent's liaison, Robert Dubois, delivered everything he'd promised and the prescription cards were being generated. A chip would be imbedded into each plastic card and Larkspur's bold logo would be on the right-hand top corner. Caroline's letter was being created for a mass mailing to insurance agents the following week and Larkspur's members the week after that. The members would receive a 30-day notice along with their new drug cards with complete instructions on its use.

She watched misty rain drip off the window ledge. The rain had been increasingly depressing all week and she was anxious to see the sunshine beat through the glass and into her thoughts. Now, feeling restless, she tried to slough it off as she turned to the papers strewn across her desk and tried to concentrate.

Caroline had always prided herself in her ability to separate her business life from her personal life but Lee's face continued to spill over. Ever since the night of the Phantom they'd held their own counsel. She laughed at that. *Their own counsel. Ironic. Do I really want to pursue a personal relationship? Should I ask him how he feels? Why don't I just wear a sign that says ASK ME, MISTER.* Caroline laughed.

She tossed her pen down, feeling like a nervous teenager instead of graying and turning flabby in areas that had once been firm. She got up, returned to the large window and leaned against the frame frowning at the ever-present raindrops pattering against the glass. She tapped her fingernails along the ledge and stared outside.

As she watched the cars travel down Morrison Street she admitted the romance would be welcomed. "Dammit" she whispered. She returned to her desk, the bright blue suit a blur as she thumped down into her chair and lifted the pen once again.

She heaved a sigh and leaned back in her chair. *I must get Lee out of my head.* Forcing herself to focus once again, she shook her head and began the letter with studied, careful thought.

Drug Benefit Transition Update
A letter from Caroline Phillips

Dear Larkspur Members:

We are battling the rising cost of pharmaceuticals. Whether you blame it on an aging society, aggressive drug marketing or new and improved drug therapies, no one disputes the sharp upswing in pharmaceutical costs.

Drug representatives note that trends in prices and new drug introductions are likely to continue and likely to keep rising. No efforts are under way to limit the direct consumer advertising that is prompting patient demand.

We have fought the tide of the prescription war and have listened to you. Larkspur has dedicated extensive resources the past few months to making a smooth transition to a more robust and efficient prescription card system. No more preferred list of prescriptions. The only differential will be Generic vs. Name Brand drugs. While the transition is still in process, we are excited about the enhanced service we will soon deliver to you.

As we complete transferring the data to our new prescription supplier, Shelton-Kent, we are also auditing to verify accuracy. New ID cards should be in your hands around Christmas for a January 1st implementation.

There is a motion in the legislature to rescind the law currently in place to disallow drug importation. However, we are moving ahead, because I am very optimistic that the bill will not stop our quest to fight this prescription war. With you in mind, I remain,

Caroline Phillips
CEO

Caroline smiled. *That should do it.* She ran her fingers through her short hair and saved the letter to a disk.

I'll sure be glad when Lana returns. Her thoughts wandered to her secretary, wondering how she and the boys were doing. She'd hoped Lana could keep her mind busy studying for her health license while she was gone but visualized the boys and chuckled. Caroline made a mental note to call her later and proceeded to take the disk out to Sarah to process.

That project finished, another issue took its place and weighed heavily on her mind. She wondered, idly, if she should retire early as her days continued to fill with chaos.

She went over in her mind, once again, the Email she'd received from Sam James. Her research told her he was fair and honest, a good surgeon and a nice man. *It's ironic that the patient he's worried about is Derrick's father.* Even though HMO rules made good sense, sometimes member's needs didn't. This was one of those times.

She lifted the phone and dialed Sam's phone number. She wouldn't delegate this time. Besides, she had a brainstorm that just might kill two birds with one stone and she was anxious to act on it.

The phone began to ring on the other end. "Sam. Caroline Phillips."

"Good morning, Ms. Phillips. You read my Email?" Sam inquired, speaking in an odd, yet gentle tone as he felt goose bumps rise over his skin.

"Yes, Sam, and I have weighed every word. I may have come up with a solution. I have been bombarded for weeks trying to finalize the new drug card and I'm afraid I haven't had much time to think of anything else. Your worries are not the first ones I've heard though and you are not the first doctor to approach me with your concerns."

"Well, now. It's a relief to know I'm not alone. What issues appear to be the most prominent?" Sam asked seriously, breathing slowly.

"Most of them. Sam, would you do me a favor? I want two other doctors and our attorney to discuss this at the same time, preferably first thing Monday morning around 7:30. It's before the day begins to fight with the masses. I can answer all your questions then. Can you make it?"

"I'll be there. At your offices, then?" He tried to hide his apprehension, but glad he got the ball rolling.

"Come to my office on the top floor and someone will direct you to the conference room. And Sam, thank you for bringing this to my attention. It's something I've been putting off for some time and your Email pushed me into action. I'll have coffee and rolls. See you then." She said firmly and hung up.

Sam remained in his swivel chair; foot propped up on the bar beneath it and thought over the conversation, wondering why an attorney would need to attend the meeting. *Well, guess this may be it. I wanted to retire anyway,* he thought grimly, *but I wanted it to be my own idea, not Larkspur's! I'll just figure out a way to work on my own if that's what it is all about.*

Lana was feeling increasingly stir crazy. After nearly two weeks holed up in Callie's cottage even though it was cozy and beautiful, it wasn't home. The weather turned dreary and the boys were running around inside like wild Indians. *These videos are driving me a little nutty too. If I see Toy Story or Jungle Book one more time, they'll begin to take on a life of their own. I can only take Buzz Lightyear and Woody so long!*

"Nick, get down off that. You know better than that."

"Frankie.....leave the remote control alone. I've told you already!"

She stood before the large floor-to-ceiling windows looking at the expanse of water before her. The boys chattered and jumped around the huge log coffee table in front of the stone fireplace behind her.

This would be such a lovely place to spend some time with........... Lana tried not to think about the time when Steven thrilled the very essence of her being. *Oh, Steven why did money have to come to the forefront of your life and push us out?* She sipped her steaming coffee and stuffed her left hand into her jeans pocket. Inhaling the coffee-bean aroma, she let her mind wander back to the man she could not shake, reliving the laughter and promises. Her mind lingered there.

Nicholas pulled on her sweatshirt a moment later, jerking her back to the present. "Can we watch Jungle Book mama?"

The CEO of Premier Health scanned the business section of the *Oregonian* with a shrewd eye. The stock market was erratic. His daily perusal of the page, after noting each of the closing figures made him so angry he could spit. Rolling his tongue around his mouth, he lifted his dentures with a snapping sound. *Damn*, he thought. *This time last year...........* He quickly calculated that he'd lost another $7,500 in one day.

It'll bounce back. It shouldn't be long now. He reached down, pulled out the bottom drawer of his massive desk and pulled out the small flask he kept there. He walked over to the door and locked it, after telling his secretary to hold his calls. *Nothing is going to stop me. When my investment pays off....* He smiled and swallowed the whiskey, feeling it sting his throat. He took another long sip, wiped his mouth and idly looked out the window. But his smile was calculated and short-lived as a cloud of uncertainty bounced across his hopes and blinded him momentarily.

He thumped his jaws together and slapped the paper. *The Midlothian Merger was my ticket. Without Ace-Deer aligned with the docs, I might just as well throw the damn thing in the dump. It was perfect with that young buck, Roget, ripe for extra bucks. He'd been sure he could get the Phillips woman to do his bidding. What a joke.*

There were four messages from Arnie Wilding. *To hell with him. Laws take too long. Can't I trust anyone???* He got up and leaned against his desk, deep in thought. *And now Del is turning into a wimp. God Almighty, do I have to do everything myself?* He paced back and forth behind his desk. Unfortunately, the success of his scheme depended on his partner. Doubting him was burning his gut as fiercely as the whisky he'd just swallowed.

He lifted the flask and drank, savoring it. He was so close now. Adding the other carrier in Colorado they'd been talking with added to the current member count, the stocks would jump even higher than the current $242. He knew actions and solutions paid off, not suggestions and promises.

He could almost feel it coming his way. But not quite. It was either get Roget to come across or go after the Phillips woman himself and that's what he'd done. But, she was a hard nut to crack. And she gave him heartburn.

He reached out and gave a mighty push with his hand and knocked everything onto the floor. The paperweight slammed into the wall. The stapler and heavy tape dispenser hit the windowsill, barely missing the glass and the papers were gently swooping around, looking for a place to land. His gut hurt.

The phone rang on his desk and he ignored it.

The sky was darkening already and he didn't have any more idea than the man in the moon as to what to do next and that's what made him angrier than everything else. He felt control slipping and he wouldn't accept it. *I'll think of something.* He lunged forward to grab his suit jacket and left his office, snapping the door closed behind the mess.

"It is always darkest just before the day dawneth."
—Thomas Fulller

Chapter 24

* * *

Del Reed left the curb slowly, angling around the same jogger that Steven barely missed. His thoughts were black and he was sweating, bushy eyebrows slowing the trickle only a little. Rolling the window down for fresh air, he followed the Lexus weaving in and out of traffic heading for the bridge. His mind was awhirl with anger.

Abruptly, his doctor-heart switched to concern as he saw the gold car cross the white line and veer close to other vehicles, a white jeep in particular, then an SUV, then a Dodge Van. Del hit the gas and took a deep breath. "Damn," he said. He pulled alongside Steven and made a jerky rolling motion with his arm to get Steven's attention.

Steven was rapidly blinking to fight the drug that infiltrated his system, as it worked to stifle the throbbing pain in his hand. A red car filled his peripheral vision and Steven glanced over and saw Del's angry face. He scowled. *Now what?* He blinked hard again and shook his head before rolling down his window. "What?!" he yelled.

"Pull over, dammit! You're going to kill yourself," Del screamed at him.

"No!" he yelled back, "I'm just fine."

"Fine, sure you are.......... " Del answered. He hurriedly cut Steven off in front of the traffic light before the bridge.

Steven's reaction was slow to stomp on his brake and nearly caused the cars to collide. Del parked at the curb and was out of his car and moving before Steven could react.

"Move over." Del yelled at him.

"Del, I'm ...." Steven's tongue wouldn't work.

"I said move over, Steven. You are too drugged to drive. Tell me where you live and I'll take you home. I'd like to strangle you but Hippocrates wouldn't like it, so screw it. Where do you live? I know it's in Beaverton, so tell me the way. Don't be an idiot."

Steven stared at Del a moment before answering. "Well, I can't move over unless I straddle the damn gear shift," he said sluggishly. Then, he got out and shakily walked around to the passenger seat and Del took the wheel.

Twenty minutes later, Steven was lying on his bed in the empty apartment and Del was gone.

*   *   *

Tillie Tooter pushed the papers toward Callie and watched her read the information she'd received that morning from Laura Amburgey. Callie's eyes raced over the text before looking at Tillie and smiling.

"So, it sounds like you've approached a lot of the congressmen and women about this. This survey shows they would vote against Wilding if he manages to get it on the floor. Am I reading it right?" Callie's heart raced.

Tillie grinned and shook her head. "You know, I have never seen anything like this. It spread like wildfire. As soon as these folks heard that Wilding was trying to negate an existing law by trying to push his weight around with nothing to support his forum, they gave me their support. That's twenty-three to four so far. I have two lunches and six coffee dates set when I return to Washington.

Callie greeted the information with a chuckle.

"Can you and Derrick meet me Friday when I see the Senator from Ohio? She's a senior member. She's wavering. With her clout, I'd like her on our side. Can you manage it?"

"Yes, of course I can. I can move my appointments, but I can't speak for Derrick." Callie smiled at Tillie and reached for the phone.

She got Derrick's voicemail. "Call me when you get back, would you, Derrick? Tillie wants us in Washington Friday." Then she hung up.

She and Derrick had exchanged calls all week and she enjoyed the exchange on a personal as well a professional level. They worked well together and the magnetism they shared only served to enhance the project. She looked directly at the woman in front of her and adjusted her calendar. "I'll cancel my Friday appointments. You'll want us there Thursday I'm sure. Do you have a hotel that you'd recommend? I've been to Washington twice, but both times have been business conferences. The hotels were arranged for me. I'd like to stay over the weekend. I'll ask Derrick, unless he has other plans." She finished, lamely.

Tillie smiled as she reached for her briefcase. *Yes, right...and pigs can fly.* "The Hilton. I'll make the reservations. Two rooms, right?"

Callie's head spun around.

"Just kidding, Callie. Just kidding." She met Callie's eyes and broke into nervous laughter.

Callie's face colored, but Tillie just shook her hand in front of her face. "Enjoy it, dear. Just enjoy it." And then she was gone.

Thursday morning, the plane lifted off at 10:45 a.m. The Portland sky was bright blue. No rain for a change. Callie craned her neck to catch the breathless wonder of Mount Hood as the splendor of the mountain's snowcap came into sight. Derrick bent over her to see it and she laughed in his ear. "This will be fun."

Derrick reached over and grabbed her hand, nodding his head and winking at her.

During the next few hours, they talked about their lives, murmuring quietly and chewing nuts that passed as a snack. They laughed at the hard roll with the cheese curling around the edge and ham wedged between lettuce leaves. The cookies were eaten quickly and washed down with coffee.

A driver met them at Reagan National Airport and whisked them to the Hilton downtown. The tall, white Washington monument rose above the city and the capitol building's dome shone brightly. Callie's neck hurt and eyes ached as she tried to catch it all.

"I'm glad you suggested we stay the week end, Callie. I've never enjoyed Washington as a tourist. When dad and mom were here a few years before she died, she gave me a list of *have-to- see places*. I got it from Dad before I left." He glanced toward her and grabbed her hand. "I know it might sound corny, but it will be so much more fun sharing it with you." He pulled the small tablet out of his suit pocket and flipped it open, showing a list starting with the Air and Space Museum.

"Not corny at all. And even if it is, let's be corny. I feel the same way," she whispered, glancing at his list and pointing to the Library of Congress and Supreme Court. She saw the cab driver's eyes look at them in the rear view mirror. He grinned at her before returning his eyes to the streets, narrowly avoiding the cars racing around him.

Thirty minutes after reaching their spacious rooms, Callie headed for the lounge to find Derrick, as planned. He was sitting in an easy chair beside a fireplace, a bowl of nuts in front of him and a glass of wine in his hand. Another glass was filled and waiting beside him.

His chest tightened as he saw her walk through the lobby, noting that she'd changed into a black-fitted pantsuit. A brightly colored jacket was tossed over her shoulders. He saw her glance at the potted palms and talk briefly to strangers passing by. *She is so pretty.* He took a sip of wine with his right hand, and waved his left to get her attention.

Callie's head spun around. She saw him and the fireplace beyond. She felt as warm as spun honey. *Dear God, he is so darling.* She wound her way around the railing and up the stairs, smiling when she saw her wine waiting. *I could get used to this. Yes, there IS a God.*

The next morning, Callie's phone rang at 6:30. She groaned. *What? I'm not ready to get up.* She reached for the phone, knocked it off its cradle and barely caught it before it hit the floor. "Hello?" she answered, unfinished sleep making her voice hoarse.

"Put on your tennis shoes and let's see if they work. The sun is up and I found a Starbucks only four blocks from us. How's the ankle?" Derrick's voice was smooth and wide-awake.

"Are you nuts, Mr. Leander? My ankle's still asleep. It is 6:30 in the morning!!"

"No I'm not nuts... and yes, I know. I don't want to miss any part of this day and we have to be back, showered and dressed up like fancy folks by 11:00 to meet Tillie by 11:30 so up an' at 'um."

"Aaarrghhh....... "

"Callie Beauvais. You know you want to get up and have coffee. The sun is shining brightly. The air is crisp. Your Latte´ is waiting. I'll buy you one of those giant orange and cranberry muffins you like with lots of nuts...."

"Oh? Food too? Why didn't you say so! Ok..." she gave in. "Give me fifteen minutes and not a second less." She hung up, groaned again and tossed back the covers.

The room was extraordinarily furnished with cherry wood Colonial renditions of antiques and none of the details escaped her eye. The little television on the bathroom counter made her laugh. And the telephone beside the toilet. *Really. What a life.* She tiptoed onto the cold tiles and stepped into the shower, feeling the minutes ticking. Unbelievably on time, sixteen minutes later, she met him in the lobby and he made a show of staring at his watch and up at her, then down to his watch again.

She gave him a mock slap on the arm when she reached him making a show of pulling her jacket around her body. Clamping onto his arm, they walked out the swinging doors in tandem, headed for Starbucks and the beginning of their Washington day.

Senator Nancy Christine Donofrio literally filled the room behind her desk. She watched the trio shown into her office by an intern at 11:30 sharp. The furniture suggested an antique lover with a sense of humor. The old oak and cherry pieces were dustless, shiny and nearly empty. Callie looked at each table with a wrinkled brow. Nothing was on any of the tables except rocks. Little tiny rocks. Gold rocks. Black rocks. Lava rocks and smooth, shiny rocks. And petrified wood from the Petrified Forest in Arizona?

"You like them?" the senator asked, watching Callie's expression with derision.

Callie jumped imperceptibly. "Yes, I guess I was staring. Sorry, I find it quite an interesting display but frankly wondered, are they from the moon or someplace equally wonderful or do you just like rocks?"

Nan Donofrio's healthy laughter joined the others. She nodded to the rocks and invited them to sit down;

Callie had managed to break the ice for a meeting none of them could guess the outcome of.

Tillie shook Nan's hand and introduced her to Callie and Derrick. An intern brought coffee on a large, antique oak tray with brass handles and slid it onto the desk so everyone could reach cups plus fresh Petit Fours.

Derrick grinned at Callie. *See? Food awaits*, his eyes spoke volumes.

Callie laughed at him, knowing he read her mind as she reached for a sweet and coffee. Tillie poured and Nan began to explain her position before the others had a chance to say a word.

"I know......." She took a bite of cake between her words. Callie thought she clearly must weigh over two hundred pounds naked, and she didn't waste much time talking with food nearby. She chewed swiftly and continued, "..... that you want to stop a motion Senator Wilding is trying to put to the floor. I know it's a law that is already in place that has decriminalized consumers from their pursuit of buying prescriptions out of the country. I know you want me to help you move mountains in your direction and that you have been approaching many of my peers for the same reason. Until you can educate me with enough supporting information against Mr. Wilding's cause, I will cling to my neutrality." She popped two more sweet cakes into her mouth, washed it down with her coffee, then folded her hands, waiting for someone to proceed.

"Well, first of all, we want to thank you for seeing us on such short notice, Nan," Tillie started.

Nan waved her words away and looked, instead, at Derrick and Callie. "Where do you two fit into this equation?" She asked, seriously.

Callie nodded to Derrick and his demeanor changed from jesting to serious instantly.

"Ms. Donofrio, we know the prescription drug coverage issue is at the top of Washington's agenda and never far from ours at Larkspur. As you know, a recent poll conducted for House Republicans by David Winston of Smith-McLain revealed that prescription drugs far outrank managed care as a voter concern and that voters want a plan that will take effect immediately. Over the past few years, we have seen a steady incline in drug prices because pharmaceutical companies are afraid they can't recoup all the money they spend to create the drugs in the first place. They either stop making old drugs and replace with new ones or they buy out competitor generic pharmaceutical companies."

Nan nodded and he proceeded. "**Families USA**, a national organization for health care consumers, predicts that drug bills for Americans will more than double in the next 10 years. Drug costs grew nearly 116% between 1999 and 2008. Caroline Phillips, the CEO at Larkspur, made a startling discovery not long ago when her friend was diagnosed infertile. Her Infertility Physician ran various tests and she was given prescriptions for drugs that cost enough to knock your socks off. The physician suggested she purchase the drugs in Germany or England to save nearly 60% over American costs. He gave Caroline's friend the information to order the drugs by mail. Caroline was horrified and excited at the same time."

Callie added, "We are talking hundreds of dollars difference, Ms. Donofrio, enough to make our heads swim. Our insurance agents have begged for relief when they receive their client's renewal figures each year. They have to explain to employers why they've received 25-50% rate increases. So, Derrick went to work," she said hurriedly, smiling toward him.

"She gave me the opportunity to clarify and confirm the drug importation law that governs the FDA so I met with Senators Wilding and Amburgey three months ago. I was told, and they both agreed with me as to the validity of the law, that it is legal and decriminalizes the use of imported drugs. I got on the Internet, which is what I specialize in since I was hired as a web designer." He paused.

The senator nodded and urged him to continue.

"Seeing all the graft and greed with my research, I developed a burning desire to do everything in my power to fight this pharmaceutical robbery. Well, once on the web, it was easy to find the noted suppliers all over the world. We chose a company in Toronto, Canada based on criteria that particularly met our needs." Derrick stopped to catch his breath and eyed the senator for her reaction.

Tillie Tooter shifted her position and grabbed another sweet. Her movement and the plate caught Nan's attention again. She reached over and grabbed the last one on the tray, then sat back and folded her arms across her generous chest. "Go on, Derrick. I'm listening." She popped the sweet into her mouth.

"Well, one thing led to another and we've had a rough road trying to finalize our contract because another insurance carrier has been competing with us in unethical ways but we won't go into that. We need support. We want the current law to stand.

"So, you are working with the Canadians."

"Yes, we are senator. The drug contract is signed. Our insured population deserves to receive their drugs at a cost-effective stop point. The current system is choking all of us and if Senator Wilding has his way, we'll be right back to square one. If the law is rescinded, we won't be able to use the contract. We've already fought red tape and voted it into law already. Why do it again? Since we've already created a viable solution, we need your vote to sustain it."

Nan looked at each of them. "Do you mean to say, buying the prescriptions in Canada keeps the cost down for your *company* or your company *AND* your insured people?" She stared hard as she waited for their response.

"Our insured population too," Callie and Derrick responded in unison.

"I see. Then what we have is Wilding trying to stop something that has already been studied, changed, voted on..... and your Canadian contract with Larkspur is already rolling?" she asked, pursing her lips.

"Yes." Derrick answered, holding his breath.

"You mean that Larkspur marched ahead and signed the contract, ordered the ID cards? Your CEO isn't afraid there is a chance this bill could become law and stop the works?" Before anyone could answer, she said, "That woman may have her ass in a sling, but she has guts. Or brass balls. Either way, I am impressed, but wonder at her lack of fear with regard to what the law could do to her." She licked her lips, wiped her face with a napkin and pushed her coffee cup away from her.

Callie crossed her legs and waited for someone to speak. She glanced at Tillie and back at Nan.

Tillie knew from past experience that Nan Donofrio thought out loud. She motioned to the others to be silent.

Nan's brown eyes turned inward for an instant. Suddenly, she looked at the group and asked them if they'd heard about the Maine drug law putting price controls on prescription drugs. She pinned them with her statement, mollified to see them weigh their answers.

Derrick and Callie studied the woman, but Tillie looked diffident.

Nan's voice was filled with censure when she stated, "I found some pretty heavy evidence that pharmaceutical companies are motivated by only one thing... profit...since I read about the Smith-Kline Beecham announcement, one of the major drug manufacturers. They stated they would fight the Maine law. In their effort to circumvent the law, the company says it will shift its supply routs, shipping drugs directly to wholesalers based in other states. According to the Maine Commissioner of Human Services, this could cause prices to increase for Maine consumers because reshipping the drugs from other states would cost more. That law was designed to negotiate lower drug prices for thousands of uninsured residents as well as thousands in Medicaid and the elderly population."

The others listened intently.

Nan continued, "I am livid over their sidestepping the law and what you've told me today just amplifies the need to find an alternative. It sounds like your Caroline Phillips has found a way to slow down the mighty dollars being funneled into drug companies. You have, therefore, found a recruit for your venture. I promised to work diligently and tirelessly for the good of the people. Stretching beyond my constituents in Ohio on the state level to the federal level gives me a rush. I will speak to others and pray for all of us."

With that, Nan stood up and smiled. "And with your approval, I propose a coalition to involve others in this prescription fight. I will call Laura Amburgey since she's been involved with you from the beginning, I understand. Wilding won't push me around."

Callie's eyebrows danced and Derrick's lips turned up at the corners, showing even, white teeth as he stretched out his hand to shake Nan's. The large woman pooh-poohed their thanks and walked them to the door. Just before they reached the outer sanctum of her offices, Callie spoke again.

"Nan. May I call you Nan?"

"Of course, and please keep in touch with me, Callie." Her brown eyes knew Callie had more questions.

"I just wanted to ask you, before we leave..... about the rocks....?"

Nan laughed and looked at Tillie. "Well, each of those rocks is a memory. One is from the time I walked down from the north rim of the Grand Canyon, in my skinnier days, of course. One was from the Meteor Crater in Arizona. One from the furthermost tip of Washington state where the Indians still fish in canoes like their ancestors at Neah Bay. One is from my last trip to Hawaii with my husband before he died. One from my honeymoon trip to Orcas Island in the San Juan's. One from the south of France when I was in college. The list goes on and on. Guess I started the rock collection when I was a little girl when I spent my summers on Lake Erie in Ohio. They don't keep me warm at night but they sure take the edge off some of the days that are pure hell here in Washington."

"The south of France? You went to Aix?"

Nan was startled. "Yes, I did. You know it?"

"Well, I have family near there. Aix is one of my favorite places." They exchanged warm glances.

Callie was touched by the woman's down-to-earth attitude. Thoughtfully, they left the building and ended up at the Union Station, each with a glass of wine in their hand toasting to another coup and Washington.

Tillie looked at her watch a third time before gulping her Chardonnay and scraped back her chair in the midst of the group surrounding them. "Must get moving. I have a date." She smiled at them, winked at Callie and grabbed her purse, promising to be in touch with them during the following week. "Have fun, you two.... I'm sure you'll find lots to do." Then she was gone.

"There is an hour in each man's life appointed
To make his happiness….."
—Beaumont and Fletcher

Chapter 25

* * *

The allure of Washington, D.C. invaded Callie's soul and Derrick's mind as they planned their two days in Washington after studying the street map minutely.
"6:30 coffee date again?"
Callie rolled her eyes.
"We can stop at Starbucks again for an all-you-can-eat stop and a latte´. Then we walk to the White House." Derrick cajoled as he held the White House tour tickets in front of her face, they'd received from Nan Donofrio.
Callie expelled a deep breath while she thought about it.
"I'm sure glad it's open to the public again since September 11th."
"Ok, you're on, but Starbucks is definitely first."

A blustery wind blew along 16th Street when they left at 7 o'clock the next morning. The refreshing, brisk walk was a short one as their adventurous souls blended. They wanted to see it all, even with the threat of snow. Derrick watched the cold breeze lift Callie's bangs off her forehead and her nose start to run, but the excitement of being in the city fueled their anticipation.
The chill chased caffeine-deficient tourists and locals inside Starbucks, enveloping them in warmth like a cozy blanket. Chairs waited as people ordered coffee and grabbed sweet rolls and Callie's eyes closed a moment to inhale the aromatic coffee beans like a starving nymph.
Derrick rubbed her shoulders, pointing her toward a chair and went to order. She smiled after him and wondered when it became so natural having him share her heart. *I've found someone I can't throw away easily…but I'm scared..*

Derrick placed a fat muffin and a hot paper cup in front of her, and then joined her. His eyes motioned for her to eat up, time was wasting. They shared a look and sipped their hot brew.

"Where first, Monsieur Tour Guide?"

"I know it will take quite awhile to see the Smithsonian. There are so many buildings and I want to see the Castle, although there's not much in it. I'd like to see the dinosaurs and the space ships. It's near the union station because I saw them when Tillie drove us by after our meeting. Remember?"

Callie nodded. "Yes, and the other way is the Capitol Building, the Supreme Court and the Library of Congress. I'd like to see all those but you know what? I'd like to get one of those tickets she told us about to ride the little red buses and just get on and off as we want." She sipped more of the latte'. It was hot and she pressed her hands around the cup. "Glad I wore gloves and a hat. Brrrrrrrrr ——- it is cold but at least it's not raining like it was in Portland all last week."

"Well, we have both days and I think the list may take it all —- but I'd like to walk around the white house after our tour —- that's at 8:15. Then we can grab the little bus across the street from there. Do you think your ankle will hold out?" He asked, concerned.

"To be honest, I'm not sure. But as long as I walk on a flat surface and don't twist it, it's really doing great. My shoes are sturdy, but the bus will be a life saver."

Five hours later was another story. Callie's ankle throbbed and her legs felt like burning sticks. She tapped Derrick as he was sailing around the dinosaur exhibits and motioned to the bench along the wall.

"Oh, you want to go? We don't have to spend so much time here..."

"No, look around. I think sitting *now* is better than going somewhere else to sit. I'll wait right here. Just don't forget where you left me, huh?" She felt a warm glow flow through her.

"I promise never to forget where I leave you," His eyes held a sensuous flame as he touched her cheek before returning to the ancient bones along the passageway.

The Air and Space Museum was Derrick's favorite and Callie could tell he ached to linger. "I enjoy just people watching... if you don't mind looking at all these exhibits without me? There's a bench away from the cold draft."

A probing query came into his eyes. "Right, lady." They walked over to the bench and sat down. "I know what you are doing and I'm touched. But I don't have to see all this stuff."

"Yes—- you——do," she said as she heaved an affronted sigh.

Derrick pushed the silver bangs off her forehead and kissed her temple. He made no attempt to hide the fact that she mattered to him and the answer was a rapid thud of her pulse. His touch was soft and caressing as their eyes met.

"I have the hotel's city magazine in my back pack... why don't I find a lovely place for dinner while you're into your Star Trek mode." She answered with a laugh and pushed him toward the space exhibits, refusing to take no for an answer.

An hour later, Derrick returned with a look of wonder on his face. Words tumbled out a mile a minute as he proceeded to tell her about everything he saw.

"Whoa horsy," she said, her mood suddenly buoyant.

They both laughed and she handed him the magazine, pointing to the picture in *A Taste of the City* portion of the magazine. "Remember I told you that my heart is still in France when I'm at my loneliest and most thoughtful?"

"Yes.... What'd you do, find someone to fly us there for dinner? Hot damn! You are good, Ms. Beauvais!"

Callie snickered and pushed the magazine toward him again. "It's in Georgetown but I'm not walking. It's too cold and crisp outside..... even if my ankle was up to it."

Derrick snorted, read the advertisement and pulled out his cell phone. The *Chaumiere's* hostess made reservations for seven, her French voice lilting. "Oui, pour deux personnes, monsieur. Il est sept heures du soir.. tres bien. Merci." Callie's lips twitched, watching Derrick's face.

"I hope someone speaks English when we get there or I'm in trouble," he said ruefully.

"Not to worry, Monsieur Leander," she responded with a chuckle.

The remainder of the day was spent gazing at the Washington skyline, jumping on and off the Tour mobile and ending at The Library of Congress. They stood on the sidewalk to stare up at the massive old marble building.

Tour book in hand, she read aloud as they wound their way up the steps. Derrick pulled her upward with a gloved hand, feeling her fingers curl around his.

"It was erected in 1897 and the library occupies the Thomas Jefferson Building and the new James Madison Building. The library administers the American copyright system and has over 14 million books and 36 million manuscripts with a total of more than 88 million items."

"That's awesome. Wonder how long it'd take us to read all of them, hummm?"

She snickered behind him and placed her backpack onto the scanner. Once inside the building, they stood in the center of the main lobby and stared upwards, awestruck. The inside of the foyer took their breaths away and noting the stairs gave Callie pause. But, she wanted to see it all, so they grabbed the balustrade and touched the chiseled cherubs as they pulled themselves upward higher and higher, their eyes struggling for a panoramic view.

The exhibit room included a headset with cassette players; each exhibit was numbered. A voice explained the contents before them when they punched in each number.

Derrick lost Callie in the jazz section and then she lost him in the Civil War. The room was filled with people, despite the cold weather and she watched others listen with their earphones and shared some head-shaking and rolling eyes at the abundance of facts shot through their earpiece.

At 5 o'clock, Derrick and Callie barely managed the walk from the bus stop to the Hilton. The lobby was busy as the friendly doorman ushered them inside and noted their dragging feet. "Washington doesn't seem so large until you try to see it all at once, right, ma'am?"

Laughing, she rolled her eyes. "How could you tell?" Her gait was crooked, back and shoulders tight and her shoes felt two sizes too small.

Derrick reached for her hand and they walked to the elevators, Callie limping noticeably. *It's like a sweet dream,* He squeezed her fingers.

She broke into a wide smile, glorying briefly in the shared moment. *He makes me want to dance and I'm ready...but this foot isn't!* It ached like a toothache. She was anxious for the hour's rest that waited before leaving again.

Chaumiere's could only be described as a French country inn with a caressing romantic atmosphere. The central grey stone fireplace was surrounded by a solid stone hearth; a dark wooden shelf about six feet from the floor housed various old wine bottles. Small wooden tables, each covered by a French blue-flowered print and topped by a square of white linen. Empty wine glasses waited.

Derrick could feel Callie's joy as they were led to a table near the fireplace. Burning candles flickering against the windows and the aroma from the kitchen made his stomach ratchet up in anticipation.

The European ambiance seemed to change her earlier limp to a smooth glide. "This is wonderful," she whispered, glancing around the room and audibly drinking in the paintings, copper pots. She smiled at the other diners and back at Derrick.

Once seated, he responded, "Yes, if this is anything like the south of France, I know I'd love it," he answered. Holding the menu in front of him, he stared at her. "I love seeing you light up like that."

She turned her face toward him and the beginnings of a smile tipped the corners of her mouth. "You mean happy? Yes, I am."

"I'm glad. I'm enjoying myself more than I have in longer than I can remember. Putting our work behind us and you know...... I haven't thought about that drug card all day?" He reached over and covered her hand with his. "You bring out the best in me and I'm not one who knows how to say things right nor am I one who can be really movie-type romantic but you make me want to be both."

Featherlike laugh lines crinkled around her eyes. "And I haven't felt this alive in longer than I can remember either." She placed her other hand over his and began to say something, but was interrupted by the waiter standing beside them.

The man was friendly, dark haired and tan. "Voici la carte et la carte des vins monsieur-madame"?

Callie smiled and glanced at Derrick. "Shall I order for both of us just this once?"

He nodded, mesmerized with her lips as the French words were spoken in that lilting fashion he'd heard in movies as she leaned toward the waiter.

"Apportez-nous une bouteille de vin rouge a une carafe d'eau s'il vous plait." Callie's eyes slanted upwards and then back to the elegant menu. She pointed with her neatly trimmed nails to hand-written words in neat European script asking what he would recommend.

The Frenchman noted her choices, bowed toward them, and smiled appreciatively. "Oui, madame. Je vous recommande les escargots et après la selle d'agneau." With that, he left quietly.

Derrick studied her.

"Well, you certainly are full of surprises although I'm not sure why I'm surprised. I know you lived in France. But it is refreshing." He looked at Callie's beaming face, her hair a halo of darkness gentled with the silver strands fluffed above her well-defined eyebrows.

She didn't answer.

A few moments later, they gently tapped their crystal glasses of Cabernet Sauvignon.

"To Washington and sweet moments," He whispered, looking into nutmeg-colored eyes that revealed promised enchantment.

"To adventures and laughter." she answered, matching his mood and savoring the fluttery emotions his nearness invoked. She lifted her glass, barely tasting the dark red liquid.

"I envy your fluency in French," he said, admiration evident on his face, while he held the stem of his glass and rubbed his finger across its base, watching her.

She laughed and her eyes spoke volumes.

He felt emotion choke him and sipped the wine.

"Oui, monsieur," she said, lifting her glass once again before taking a small sip. She found herself enjoying his company so much that a slice of fear nudged its way into her mind. *Oh, take a breath....*

He wondered at her thoughts, his voice carrying an alluring softness across the table toward her. "Do you still have family in France or friends that you spent time with before you came to Larkspur? I remember during the last agent's meeting. Lord, was that only one month ago? Anyway, I remembered Caroline saying you'd taken a sabbatical in France...you said your family lived there?"

"Actually, yes. My family is from Pertuis, a lovely little village outside Aix En Province, in the south of France. Well, correctly put, it is Francois's family but they adopted me and love me like their own." She was lost in memory a moment before her attention swung back to Derrick when he spoke again.

"How could they help that?" he asked, softly urging her on. He reached for her fingers and she watched them curl around hers, feeling warmth engulf her heart.

Her voice stumbled. "Well....Francois and I spent a month outside Pertuis every summer of our marriage, so I had to learn French or miss all the good stuff! We bought an old farmhouse close to his parent's vineyard. Each July we got together and boy! Did things get done when Francois was there to lead the way! Things move very slowly in that part of France or at least the part where we were... and unless there's someone to get the ball rolling, well, it might never have gotten done."

"Sounds fine," Derrick murmured, sipping his wine and nodded for her to continue.

"Anyway, the farmhouse is an old stone building, just four bedrooms with a huge kitchen and eating area and the end of the house has a bathroom like none you've ever seen. I fell in love with it and it digested our money like a hungry cat at the milk bowl. My favorite part of the house is the big dining room off the kitchen where two huge black-grille gated doors face the mountains. They're arched and swing outward so they butt up against the outer gray stone wall and the doorway is completely open to the most spectacular view. It steps down from the kitchen....."

Derrick watched her face soften in memory.

"We spent a lot of time at the dining table, whether with family or just the two of us. Yes, my heart is there because of the farmhouse and lovely memories but it isn't my home..... so I returned to Portland where I grew up, my home holds me... And my job. And Caroline. But since Mom died last year, well, I could probably live anywhere now." Callie stopped talking and looked at the man across from her. "I went there to lick my wounds after Francois died.......... Oh, Derrick, I'm so sorry. I'm babbling."

"No you are not! Tell me, do you still go back? I mean is the farmhouse still there for you? It must've felt like sanctuary.... peaceful and I hope it helped you mend."

"Yes and no. What I mean is I still go back for visits every year. The farmhouse is taken care of and it's still mine. Since Francois died, his niece Cendrine lives there with her family, Oliver and two children. They work the vines with Maman and Pere Beauvais. My room is still mine. It's a lovely, lovely place. Wild poppies grow everywhere." She kissed her fingers as she said, "Bon..... You should try their wine. *Beauvais Cellars Vineyard* is not available in America and so much better than many American wines..... No fillers. There's nothing quite like it for me. Tell me about you now." She leaned her elbow on her linen napkin and placed her chin in her hand, urging him to take the reins of the conversation.

He sighed. "Well... right now, I've been trying to fight our HMO system. Dad needs surgery but the HMO won't approve it. I was mad as hell and Dad was too. I tried to tone it down when I spoke with him, but it's ironic though. He's seeing a preferred provider with Larkspur but the medical director they use also works for Premier. Go figure. Guess it's the LEXUS HMO connection. Anyway, I'm fighting it and so is his doctor. ...."

"And the rest of your family?" She waited for more.

"I have a grown daughter and she's the light of my life. She lives in San Diego so I don't see her often. With new plane fares so high, she can't fly up often since she always wants her husband to tag along." He laughed at Callie's look.

"Derrick!" Her cheeks dimpled.

"Just kidding. Her husband is great. They've begged me to visit but with everything that's been going on here, I can't. Wait until she hears I spent a week end here in Washington." He finished his wine and caught the waiter's attention to bring a second glass, still waiting for their lamb. The salad plates were empty in front of them, but neither could remember eating.

The fireplace hummed behind them; Callie removed her red bolero jacket. His Old Spice cologne wafted across the table and she felt the stirrings of a long-ago need. Sighing deeply, she stared into the fire and then over at Derrick. She found herself fighting the fantasies that were created by the mood, the atmosphere, the wine and the softness in his eyes.

He wondered at her facial expressions but as he built up courage to lay his heart on the table, the waiter appeared and the moment was lost.

The snails and lamb were positioned in front of them, their water glasses filled. To Derrick's eye, the servings weren't enough to fill up a bird. He remembered his mother telling him nouvelle French restaurants had beautiful presentation, but very little substance and dad was happy with meatloaf and mashed potatoes. He smiled at the memory and picked up his fork.

"The only time my parents ate in a French restaurant was in Napa Valley on their twentieth anniversary. Dad tells the story about being ravenous and Mom wanted to eat at a little restaurant, Le Petite Zinc, so dad agreed. When the dinner arrived, she couldn't quiet him down." He chuckled.

The bite of wild rice remained suspended on her fork. "What happened?"

He grinned, showing a deep dimple in his left cheek. "Actually, she was happy as a little Lark and started eating. Dad started grumbling and he threw his napkin down and said he was going to find a fast-food place for a burger."

The rice fell off her fork. "You made that up!"

He laughed and shook his head. "No, I swear it's true....but dad was only teasing her. He did end up stopping later though, since the plate was nearly empty when it was put in front of him." He shook his head, thinking about his dad's laughter with each storytelling. He knew that's how memories kept moving along; he enjoyed his father's reminiscences through each story.

Callie toyed a moment with her glass of white wine, a smile lingering.

They ate the remainder of their meal in silence, enjoying the camaraderie; the wine warmed their throats and calmed their thoughts.

His eyes kissed her with promises.

And Callie pressed her hand to her hammering heart, anxious to be part of them.

As their plane lifted off the runway Sunday afternoon, they were thoughtful, teasing, relaxed and comfortable with each other. Their hands touched repeatedly.

The evening before, there had been a sweet uncertain moment at her door. He'd keyed it open for her and then stood aside as she stared at him with longing and in one fluid motion she was in his arms. The long-awaited kiss was lingering and his arms held her closely as she was crushed in his embrace. Then he'd pushed her inside the room and blew her a kiss before closing the door.

Mentally, Callie felt the memory of his soft lips and caressed his qualities. Despite her fears, she felt a hot and awful joy. They both felt cheated but knew this was bigger than both of them. It would keep.

Now, flying west, they skittered away from the conversation that might bind them and yet the need to do just that kept their minds busy but their words at bay.

She reached over to pull his shirt collar outside his suit coat. She jerked away, surprised at how natural it felt.

His eyes studied hers before catching her hand and holding it to his lips. He kissed her palm.

Callie drew a deep breath and he kissed her hand again. "You know, life can be so good if we just let it."

"Yes, I'm beginning to think it could be."

"With you, I mean."

"Yes, can you hear my heart bonging clear over there?" She smiled wanly.

"No, mine's too loud to hear yours," he exclaimed with intense pleasure. He cradled her hand in his and they both laid their heads back and closed their eyes as his thumb caressed her fingers. "Callie?"

"Yes?" Her chest was so tight; she thought she should unclasp the seat belt.

He turned toward her, eyes brimming with moisture, "I love you," he whispered.

The fringe of heavy lashes cast shadows on her cheeks as her eyes met his. She sat motionless, torn by conflicting emotions. "God, I'm so afraid I'll hurt again........ Mom used to say if we try to avoid the dance we'll miss the music. And I don't want to miss the music.........." She paused before answering in a suffocating whisper, "I love you too."

Derrick let out a long audible sigh before reaching toward her and she felt the heady sensation of his lips against her neck. "God, laying our hearts out on an airplane surrounded with a sea of strangers is not my idea of a romantic moment!"

Callie's eyes twinkled and she looked at his lips a moment before gazing upward to see the glint of wonder in his eyes. She admitted there might still be a chance to grow whole again as pleasure radiated outward. And the clouds buffeted them toward Oregon and home.

"——That this nation, under God, shall have a new birth of freedom."."
—LINCOLN —- Gettysburg Address

Chapter 26

* * *

Monday dawned bright, a promise of sunshine and hope. Hot coffee and doughnuts were perched in the center of the long conference table as Lee opened the door to find the others already sipping and munching.

"Good morning, Lee," Caroline saw the inherent strength in his face as she greeted him with a warm smile. "Let me introduce you to Doctor Sam James, Doctor Ray Marling and Doctor Karen Des Jardins," she gestured toward each person as she spoke.

Lee's friendly nod encompassed the group as he shook their hands and reached for the cup of coffee Caroline lifted toward him. Her perfume filled the air as he gripped his briefcase and told himself to concentrate.

"Before we begin I want all of you to know how much you are valued at Larkspur. Without our providers, where would we be? "She glanced toward Sam. "Sam, would you please relate your concerns as you relayed them to me?"

Sam James took a deep breath before rehashing his consternation with the HMO process, Larkspur and his patient-doctor relationship in between it all. He summarized his frustration with the medical review board and Del Reed. He left nothing, detailing the flaws he disliked as well as the advantages he believed in. His face flushed as he finished and he looked at those around him, wondering if he'd overstepped his bounds.

Drs. Marling and Des Jardins nodded in agreement.

Caroline looked at them and said, "See? I told you that you weren't alone. Is there anything either of you would like to add to Sam's dissertation? This is the opportunity to open up. I'm all ears." Caroline looked at each doctor with an intelligent understanding and compelling encouragement.

"That's a very good encapsulation of my feelings, Sam," Karen Des Jardins said. "Thanks. Your thoughts mimic mine. I'm sick to death of asking permission to operate on a patient that needs my expertise and I've taken it as a personal affront. My gut wrenches when this happens and I'm glad you had the gumption to do something about it because all I've done is whine." She grimaced.

Dr. Marling nodded agreement. "Me too. Big time. What do you have in mind, Ms. Phillips?"

Lee finished his doughnut, wiped his hands and washed it down with coffee, waiting for Caroline to continue. Proudly watching her, he studied the doctor's faces as they listened.

"As you know, Larkspur is an HMO with specific guidelines. We are accredited and proud of it. However, with your frustrations added to others I have heard from other doctors, my staff and patients, I've done some serious thinking about Larkspur's future. I've heard grumbling from the agents already and we've set a precedent by going outside America for our drug benefit." She took a deep breath.

Lee nodded and exchanged glances with the doctors.

"I've heard your frustrations. Now, I propose we go outside that damned box again. I've explained my thoughts to Lee Carle and he's made me aware of the problems we may encounter. However, I would like your input and Sam.... this will involve a serious consideration from you." Caroline looked at everyone and began an explanation that left everyone agape.

"You mean Larkspur would change their forum to a PPO and allow an office-visit co-pay benefit to all providers without a referral to specialists?" Sam James stared.

"Yes," she said, eager to hear their responses, fueled with their delight.

"What about pre-authorization for surgical requests?" Sam asked, attuned to the idea but skeptical about his biggest frustration.

"Well, Sam, that's where you come in," Caroline responded, with a look of mystery. "You all know it is absolutely necessary to have the pre-authorization process in many cases. I certainly cannot budge on that, but we can raise the bar."

Sam's eyes fell for an instant before snapping up again with Caroline's next sentence.

"How do you feel about providing medical direction for our current physicians? You could retain your patient base and oversee our Medical Review Board for surgical pre-authorizations and receive a salary directly from Larkspur..... Sam?"

Sam sat, thunderstruck, and his mouth went slack. Before he could answer, she continued. He felt his heartbeat accelerate; creating an excitement he hadn't felt in years.

"Sam, we are excited with the level of experience you bring to the Larkspur team. We believe your professionalism and strong commitment to quality patient care will make you a valuable resource for our members and other participating physicians." She pointed to the other doctors at the table. "And these doctors heartily agree."

Watching the doctor's face gave her the impression he'd just been given a piece of pumpkin pie spiked with rum and covered with whipped cream. It was intoxicating to make things happen and she knew this was one of the best parts of her job.

"Oh Lord. My wife will tell you I'm never speechless but today I am. Caroline, I don't have to think about it for more than a second before giving you an unequivocal, adamant, YES!" He gripped the table and grinned.

Everyone laughed and took turns pumping Sam's hand.

Caroline's eyes looked at Lee above the papers in her hands and they traded looks. *That was great*, his eyes told her and she nodded in agreement.

"Sam, Lee will draw up the paperwork for you to sign and we can work out the particulars during the week. Is that acceptable to you?"

Sam grinned again. "When does this begin, Caroline? I mean... what about giving Del Reed some notice? The patient I wrote to you about... I want to approve his surgery now." Sam asked straightforwardly.

"You're the boss, Sam. If you feel the need outweighs alternative treatment, do it. There's no contract with Del Reed for giving him notice, it was an interim situation only. Let me worry about Doctor Reed."

A HALF HOUR later, Lee watched Caroline sign some legal forms when the subject of Thanksgiving arose.

"Are the kids flying home for Thanksgiving?" Lee asked Caroline, a thoughtful look stamped on his face.

"No, it's their year with Paul so Ben's flying to L.A. Elizabeth is in Paris! I get them for Christmas," she said, as she scribbled her signature on each page where little colored sticky tabs were attached. Her glasses slipped. She pushed them up automatically, with no break in her stride.

"Well, some friends told me their traditional Thanksgiving is always downtown at *Hubers*. I'd like to make a reservation us. Do you have plans? I'd like you to join me," he said quietly.

She looked up swiftly. "I'd love it. I'd miss the smell of turkey in the house, but then again, I do get tired of eating leftovers for days afterwards. Callie and I talked about sharing the day. She always cooked for her mom and this will be her first Thanksgiving without her. I haven't been to *Hubers* in years....not since I drank two Spanish Coffees. Oh God, what a lovely hangover *that* gave me," she finished, sarcasm dripping eloquently.

Lee laughed at the facial expression her memory generated. "It will be a nice change. No Spanish Coffees though, promise?" He smiled and watched her. "I'll set it up once I get confirmation from you...about Callie," he said, chuckling.

"Thanks for always being here when I need you, Lee." Caroline's silver-gray eyes pooled a moment before handing him the sheaf of papers, their fingers touching a moment longer than necessary.

"It goes without saying, Caroline." He answered, like-gray eyes watching her, holding raw emotion in check. He found it hard to walk toward the door.

"I'll talk to Callie today. She and Derrick were in Washington meeting with our lobbyist and a senior Senator Friday and they stayed over the weekend to explore. They flew back late yesterday. I haven't seen her yet but with the meeting so early, I'm not surprised. I will get back to you soon though." The phone rang and she turned toward it.

Lee gathered up the papers, slipped them into his briefcase and saluted her gingerly. He saw her wave toward him before pinning the receiver to her shoulder.

That afternoon, Caroline knocked on Callie's office door before slowly pushing it open. It wasn't a large office, but sat in the corner of the building with an ample view of the river and the fir-covered hills. A dark green leather couch swamped one wall and a huge Asparagus Fern sat on the window sill, pictures of France and her family on each side.

Callie was leaning toward the window, one arm on her keyboard, with a dreamy look on her face. She swung her head around and her face lit up with a welcoming smile.

"Hey, lady, what's going on in that pretty head of yours?" Without waiting for a response, Caroline leaned on Callie's desk, hiked her tweed skirt up a couple of inches and then lifted her hip to sit on the edge.

"I'm getting ready to launch into a sales meeting with Betsy and her team. You know, just trying to get my head together. That letter you're sending out about the drug card has the staff in a tizzy. They are excited, but at the same time, answering hundreds of phone calls. I know the letter will mollify the members and staff." Callie answered.

"Well, your face sure didn't look like it had the sales team or the drug card on your mind. What else?" Caroline waited expectantly as her friend pushed a silver curl off her forehead with a brief flip of her hand.

"Oh, really? I love my job. Why wouldn't I have a smile on my face with things moving in a positive direction?" Callie answered evasively as she felt her flesh color.

"Come on, Callie. Spill it."

Callie laughed noncommittally. "What's on your mind, my friend?"

"Thanksgiving. Lee's invited me to *Hubers* for turkey day. You and I talked about sharing the day. Please join us…he's making reservations and I wondered if there's anyone else we should invite?" The question hung in the air.

Callie moved her mouth as if to speak, then she just smiled and gathered a pen and tablet to her chest. "I can let you know later today. Will that be soon enough?" her voice was like silken oak.

"Fine," Caroline said as they walked out together, eyebrows lifting to study Callie's dreamy expression.

"Oh, by the way," Callie said, "I just got off the phone with Lana. She's homesick and wants to come back to work. She can't take another kid's video for fear of turning into a pumpkin or Tarzan or Bambi. And she can't study that insurance book with all the chaos anyway." They laughed at the image.

Suddenly serious, "What do you think, Callie? I haven't heard anything from Steven. Has she?" Caroline looked worried.

"No.... nothing. Well guess no news is good news. I'm not sure what she's going to do but she said she'd call you."

The hallway suddenly filled with people. Their conversation was cut short as each headed to meetings and the busy day that awaited them. Callie welcomed the diversion because she wasn't ready to reveal the excitement mounting within her, even to Caroline.

Just before closing time, Callie called Derrick's office but received voicemail. She left a hurried message and asked him to call her, inviting him to *Hubers* for Thanksgiving. She asked if his father and Uncle Ted could join them if they hadn't made final plans yet. Then, she began thinking of a nice long hot-tub experience and headed home.

Gripping a large green bath towel around her body, Callie had just opened her sliding glass doors, when the phone rang. She picked up the portable handset and proceeded toward the patio and the hot tub beyond. The jets were thrumming and water bubbled over the surface, lights shining from the inner sanctum of the pool. She answered the phone and dropped the towel simultaneously onto a large hook and stepped into the hot water, holding it aloft.

"Hi Callie. I got your message and I've already spoken with Dad and Uncle Ted. They liked the idea of not having to eat my cooking so we'd love to join you with Lee and Caroline. Thanks for thinking of us. Just need to know the time and location.....what's that strange noise? What are you doing?" Derrick's voice was soft and Callie could feel her body melting with warmth, wondering if it was his voice or the water she felt pelting her naked body.

"*I* just stepped into a bubbling hot tub. What are *you* doing?" She grinned in the darkness, adjusted her legs on the ledge across from her and stretched out one arm, dropping her head back and staring up at the sky.

Stone silence met her statement.

"Derrick? Are you still there?" She inquired, smiling knowingly. She felt a tightening in her belly as the steam rose around her.

"Yes, I'm here. I'm just imagining you in that hot tub. Don't suppose I can drive over and join you?" The audacity of his question sounded nonchalant to his ears even though he was anything but.

"Mmmmmmm....sounds nice. But if I waited until you got here, I'd look like a dried up prune, but I'll give you a rain check. Ok?"

"Yes, Ma'am. I'll look forward to it. Can you fit in lunch with me tomorrow? I found a little British Tea Room around the corner from the Mexican restaurant on 10th. They serve a mean Shepherds Pie and their tea is great....real English tea. English accented employees...I thought you'd like it there........." His voice trailed off.

"I'd love to. It sounds wonderful. Come by my office and get me when you can, would you? I have tomorrow free from meetings because I'm working with Betsy. We're updating the forms for you to input onto our web site. So, we should discuss it... and what better way than over lunch to avoid phones and......" She smiled as she adjusted her hips on the curved bench to get closer to the hot rushing jets.

"Good, although I had more personal stuff on my mind....... But for now, enjoy the hot tub," he teased. "Next time I'll join you."

In the city, Del Reed sat slumped over his desk. He sighed and stretched, then caught his reflection in the mirror near the coat tree. He studied himself shrewdly, and then turned away to sit in silence. The lights were strewn across the city, while the night deepened beyond his office window and the empty building creaked and sighed in the autumn wind.

The fright Steven gave him had lingered all week. His personal life mottled in his mind as everything ran together. Dusting off his memory, he realized how difficult it was, in the past few years, to face himself in the bathroom mirror each morning during his ablutions. He was sick, knowing he'd lost himself in the fracas, admitting he was taking Lorrie down with him.

He'd flirted with women for years. *I don't know what I'd do if another woman responded.. The only one I want is Lorrie. Damn. What a mess.* At least he hadn't done anything stupid. Not finding the **Storm Den's** barmaid in his wife's flower garden made him faint with relief. It had slapped him out of his recent stupor with a sharp dose of reality.

His business life was another story. Del reached for his Evian and took an aspirin. He leaned his elbows on his desk, pushing files and papers out of his way and covered his face in his hands. *Maybe Steven was right. I am in too deep....and so close to my retirement.* His skin felt clammy and he rubbed his cheeks and eye sockets with the palms of his hands. The end of another week and he still didn't have the answers to get out from under his partner's thumb. *When had that happened anyway? Partners? Like hell.*

"If the pursuit of peace is both old and new, it is also both complicated and simple. It is complicated, for it has to do with people, and nothing in this universe baffles man as much as man himself.
—ADLAI STEVENSON * Speech, October 24, 1952

Chapter 27

* * *

Lana stared at Devil's Lake through the wall of glass and pressed her warm cheek against the window. Numb and shaken, she wrapped her arms around herself. Calling home for messages had been a leap of unadulterated hope. She wanted to return home. She wanted to live her life again…to allow the boys structure and peace. But, listening to not one, but three messages from Steven caused her eyes to mist and tears choke her throat. In an instant, the emotions tumbled together: joy and pain, relief and sorrow.

Shakily, she'd replaced the receiver. Then, she'd proceeded to pack all their bags, clean the kitchen and push at the boys. Their two-week hiatus was over.

One last look at the lake and the long drive back to Beaverton began. It was icily precarious, as the weather had changed to snow through the Van Duzer Corridor's forest roads that morning. The windshield wipers struggled against the snow, but she was determined. She kept her eyes glued to the road with darting glances between Nicholas and Frankie from her rearview mirror.

"Mommy, the snow looks like silky stuff," Nick whispered, awed and wide eyed.

"Yeh, silky stuff," Frankie mimicked.

She answered with a nod as she gripped the wheel, trying to define her lane by measuring the distance from the snowy ditch. Her arms hurt and the boys argued. Only after they were asleep, did she feel any relief flood through her body and mind. The roads began to clear and her arms finally relaxed on the wheel. She felt drugged, numb.

She replayed Steven's voice in her head. The first message brought tears as he professed his love and begged forgiveness. She felt his desperation and sadness reach across the line.

The second call frightened her. His words didn't fit, filling her with a sense of foreboding, over the edge...on the brink of insanity, not wrapped too tight. Her mind swelled around the man she admitted still held her heart captive. And she'd rushed away from sanctuary toward a home filled with disturbing uncertainty.

"Oh Steven," she sobbed quietly as she swatted at the tears that pooled and rolled down her cheeks, pushing her red hair behind her ear.

Mile markers pointed toward McMinnville. She knew she was on the home stretch. She wound her way through the little village of Dundee and past the Argyle Winery. Nearly-forgotten memories triggered her mind as she sped by, trying to retain the 35 mph speed. They'd driven to the beach when Nicholas was a baby before Frankie came along. She smiled, slapping tears from her face.

His third message tore away the fearful barrier he'd forced around her as she'd listened to his broken words. She'd been right about his going over the edge and she hoped the doctor he mentioned would help him. She hadn't heard of a Doctor Berger but he obviously had. *Where will I go first*, she thought, frantically, watching the boys sleep as her mind raced into the lunatic range.

The snow on the roadside cleared as each mile ate up Highway 99. She repeated Callie's mantra as she headed east. Breathe in with the good. Breathe out with the bad. Breathe in with the good. Breathe out with the bad. Breathe in............ And the trip seemed unbearably long.

AS LANA headed home, Sam James was speaking to Carl Leander and an operating room was reserved for surgery. He could hear the relief in Carl's voice and felt a doctor's contentment steal over him.

"So, it sounds like you have made things happen, doc. Having the review board axe our request really frosted my onions." Carl told him, chuckling now that the end result was in sight.

Sam snorted, "Yes, Carl, I got that idea and again, I apologize. The hoops that are required sometimes frost mine too, although I must say I've never heard it put quite like that. You certainly have some interesting sayings, you know that?" He marked his calendar. "And Carl, have a good Thanksgiving. I'm sure I don't have to warn you not to eat anything too spicy.

"Right, doc. I'm sick of mashed potatoes and yogurt, I'll tell ya. I'm going with my son and brother to a place downtown called *Hubers* for turkey. My son got out of cooking...he got the short straw for the cook....and we're celebrating *that* too. He's no cook but he tries. We're going to meet his girl. I'll try to be a gentleman and eat what I should. But, I got Tums in my pocket. Glad to know it's just another week. I'll be at Providence at 6:15 next Tuesday. See you then, with bells on." Carl felt spry all of a sudden and took a deep breath as relief spread through his body.

After Carl hung up, the phone rang again almost immediately. Carl reached for it half way expecting it to be the doc again.

"Hey Pop, how are you doing up there?" a female voice inquired.

"Sophia, girl. What a treat. How are you, darlin'?"

"Well, I'm very, very good; thank you and I've got news. I told Dad we were trying to get pregnant. And I am! I just found out and I'm so excited I could bust, but he's out to lunch. I was splitting a gut to tell someone besides Mom. AND it's more than one. That's all we know. I'll have an ultrasound soon. I'll keep you posted but I'm so happy I am flying on air without wings. I don't think our feet have touched the floor since I left the doctor's office this morning." Sophia rushed on, words tumbling over each other. As each word flitted into Carl's ear, they got louder and ended in a mighty crescendo.

Carl was grinning from ear to ear and chuckled. He couldn't get a word in edgewise. He kept nodding with eyes like spun glass as he heard his granddaughter's voice give him the gift her grandmother should be sharing.

"Oh, my dear heart! I can't tell you how happy I am for both of you. Are you doing ok? The doctor says you're fine and all that?" Carl questioned her earnestly.

Sophia gushed another five minutes before hanging up, after gleaning Carl's promise not to tell her father the news.

"It'll be tough, young lady, so you keep trying to get him. We're going to have Thanksgiving in a restaurant for the first time in our lives tomorrow. That's all I can promise without bursting my buttons and he'll know something is up." After professing love and sending cyber hugs, he hung up feeling the world was turning in their direction at last.

Farther west beyond the many bridges spanning the Willamette River, Callie drank her Earl Gray tea in the British Tea Room. She felt the stress in her neck and shoulders lift as she pushed away the empty china plate. Her tea sandwiches had been filled with cucumbers and cream cheese, cut into quarters and presented in such a delightful way that she vowed it was her new favorite place.

The room was deep and narrow with a gray stone wall surrounding a private patio along the back. Two trees, green plants and ivy slithered across the expanse on all three sides. One would never know it was in the heart of Portland, instead of the faraway English hills.

It was too cold to eat outside on the patio tables but she vowed to enjoy it in the summertime. She noticed others sipping tea and talking quietly to one another and welcomed the peacefulness of the room and her companion.

Two long walls were covered with built-in bookcases and filled with English items to purchase, such as tea, cookbooks, linens, china, teapots and miscellaneous English tea biscuits. Pulling herself back to her tea, she saw Derrick watching her.

"You like it then."

Feeling suddenly self-conscious, she lifted the teapot and filled her cup once again. She lifted it toward him and nodded. "I certainly do."

He sighed. "Good. I guess we can talk business, Callie. The website is waiting for your input. As soon as I get approval from Lee and Caroline, I can dig in. You know, I really like that part of my job best. It's like I'm creating something that reaches so many. Now that I have the providers listed and links to all the insurance benefit summaries, we are really on a roll. With the addition of this new drug card, I feel like we are tops. You know, Premier's site doesn't include half the information ours does and we are peanuts in size compared to their consumer base."

"Yes, and you should pat yourself on the back. Betsy and Elaine told me the agents love it. When they receive quotes, they just pull up the website and know exactly what benefits were quoted. It has really cut down on phone calls and the FAX machine isn't smoking.. Do you have any idea how much we needed you, Derrick?" she asked, playing with her teacup and watching him.

His face had been animated as he discussed the web design and she was mesmerized with that aspect of his personality. She watched his gray eyes and found herself trying to count the gold flecks that surrounded the iris.

"Do I have my hat on straight?" he asked, enjoying her.

Callie laughed and dropped her eyes a moment.

"Ok, better get back to work. Dad is looking forward to *Hubers* and thanks you from the bottom of his heart because I'm not cooking after all." He winked and pushed his chair back as he reached to help her with her coat.

"You know where it is, right? Just four blocks south of Burnside on Third Avenue. It's an old place that is filled with wonderful Portland history and burnished wood and an elegance that isn't really elegance."

He laughed, shepherding her toward the front.

She wrinkled her face. "That doesn't sound right, does it? Well, you'll like it. I've never been there for dinner, let alone Thanksgiving. But Caroline is right. All that turkey at home makes us sprout feathers and clucking after weeks of leftovers."

He laughed at the image. "I'm looking forward to it. Thanks for thinking of us." She touched his arm as he opened the glass door toward the street and grinned.

Hands linked, they walked back to the office. The naturalness made her wish for more and they remained firmly clasped all the way past Three Lions Bakery. But as their office building came into view, their fingers regretfully untwined as they crossed the street.

Derrick grinned at her flushed face and she bit her lip in response, fighting a smile.

"To climb steep hills
Requires slow pace at first."
—SHAKESPEARE —- - *Henry VII.* Act I. Sc.1

Chapter 28

* * *

THE APARTMENT WAS EMPTY AND COLD as Lana and her sons entered the kitchen. Her heart thumped wildly as silence greeted her. Nicholas and Frankie ran ahead of her, rushing through the rooms squealing, singing their happiness at returning home once again. Lana's footsteps were slower, her thoughts in sharp expectation. *Where is he? The apartment is empty...he's not here.*

Judging from the temperature, he's not been here for some time. The third message he'd left was nearly a week old. Her chest hurt.

Later, heat permeated the rooms. The boys stared at the television. A cup of hot coffee was gripped into the palm of her hand. She called her office, intent on working Monday, after another four days off. *What a life,* she thought. *I need to get a small turkey and...........* Her mind wandered.

She pulled out the huge phone book and flipped to physicians in the yellow pages, her finger followed down the page to the Bs. Belden, Bendura, Berger. *There it is. Mental Health.* Her hand shook as she dialed and a moment later, she hung up. *Stupid. Stupid. Of course they aren't going to give me any information,* she fumed.

A short time later, after riffling through the papers on the bureau in the bedroom and ransacking drawers that still held Steven's clothing, her fear escalated. *Where could he be?*

*   *   *

He shook his head, refusing the phone call, and his secretary bit her lip as she lied to the man on the other end again. "Sorry, Mr. Wilding, he is in a meeting. Would you like his voicemail?"

"I've left several messages with you and I'm sick of leaving messages that he doesn't return. What is going on there?" Arnie Wilding was angry and didn't waste niceties on the woman fielding her employer's calls. He reached for his whiskey glass and gulped the liquid.

"I will certainly tell him you called again, Mr. Wilding. I am so sorry you two aren't connecting." Her voice was steady, sounding sincere.

"Well, he wants me to help him with a serious issue but won't talk to me about it. Just tell him there's a coalition being created to fight the drug issue we talked about. I won't call again. If he wants me, he knows where he can find me." With that, he slammed the phone down so hard the woman's eardrums rang.

St. Vincent Hospital was a massive modern structure with outbuildings and separate parking garages that littered the surrounding property. It sat parallel to the MAX light-rail tracks and Sunset Highway leading to the coast. It was the largest hospital on the west side of the city and housed an inpatient mental health wing as well as offices for outpatient visits and personnel.

Dr. Michael Berger was head of the department, supported by six associates and two interns. He was proud of the accomplishments St. Vincent Hospital had attained during his leadership, equally proud of major steps many magazine articles attested to.

The newest case on his agenda was a 55-year old man, a voluntary admittance who'd arrived ten days earlier. His main intent, as always, was to make a difference in the man's life, to create a feeling of comradeship and he was anxious to see him.

Holding the file loosely in his hand, he opened the door leading into the patient's room. The man was tall, blonde and showed an amazing capacity for intelligent conversation. He glanced toward the door constantly, as if waiting for someone. Today was no different.

He watched the man's face jerk around at his entrance; then watched his face register the usual intense disappointment. He sat in the stuffed chair near the window with his coffee, refusing to remain in bed; He appeared to be on a working-man's schedule and didn't intend to deter from it even now.

"Hello. How's the coffee this morning, Steven?" The doctor watched him silently.

Steven Roget watched the white-coated doctor enter his room and his eyes strayed to the file. He gripped his coffee cup with one hand and set it down smoothly into the saucer held in the other. He clicked it together and blinked. "Good."

"Well, that's fine. And you ate all your breakfast?"

"How does drinking coffee and eating my breakfast make me better, doctor?" he asked, his voice holding a sadness that caused the doctor to regroup and start again.

"Just idle conversation, Steven. Tell me what you'd like to talk about today. I don't have to be anywhere else at the moment. I'm all yours.

Then, the day room expects you to gather with other gentlemen to join in a group chat. Do you think you'd enjoy that?"

Steven looked slightly depressed and a little sullen. "I don't know."

"Well, we won't know until you try it. What is troubling you this morning?" the doctor asked gently, touching Steven's arm, urging him to join in the conversation.

"Well." Steven was thoughtful a moment. He tipped the coffee and drank the remainder of the brew before turning toward the doctor.

"You make me feel safe. I don't have to pretend with you. I've had to pretend with so many people for so long that it's nice for a change..... to be myself. I've been trying to figure out who I really am. I've been beating myself up. I've hurt a lot of people. I just want to get better. I want to see my boys......."

Dr. Berger's head swung up to meet Steven's gaze. "Your boys? I didn't realize you had a family, Steven. It's not listed on your chart," he said as he flipped through the pages in the file on his lap, scanning the notes.

"Yes, I do. And Lana.... That's the boys' mother. She had Nicky when we met and then she had my little boy, Frankie, even though she was past forty. We didn't want to raise Nicky alone and we were a family, he's like my own son too....but......." He made an effort to smile.

The doctor's pen scribbled into the file pages as Steven spoke quietly. "You are married then?"

"No. I'm not married. I should be but.......I was stupid.... Made money my priority. I want to put my family first and hope it's not too late. I've screwed up so much... she may not give me that chance. That's why I'm here. I must get well. I need to fix myself first. Do you understand? Can you help me?" Steven's voice beseeched the doctor as his cup rattled against the saucer, his grip tight, feeling desperate shame.

Dr. Berger reached out and removed the cup from his patient's hand gently. "Let's go one step at a time. None of our file notes show any indication that you have a family and there's been nothing noted about Lana calling the hospital about you. What am I missing?" The doctor's eyes bored into his patient's troubled face.

Steven became agitated and stood up quickly. Thrusting his hands in the pockets of his gray corduroy pants, he moved to the window and stared at the trees that lined the back of the property behind the hospital. The fancy rungs at the windows reminded him of bars and being back in jail; a deadening knot bit into the pit of his stomach.

"She doesn't know where I am, doctor. And I'm not sure if she should or if she even cares. She had a lot on her plate for awhile. Being a single mother isn't easy and I've made her life hell the past couple of years." He turned back to the doctor, his eyes pained, tears pooling in the corners. A single tear from one eye ran slowly down his trembling cheek, unnoticed by the big man as he returned to his chair.

"Do you want to talk about it, Steven?" The doctor put away the file and pen. He could see Steven's eyes dart from the file to the pen and back again, noticeably upset.

"Yes, I'd like to." Steven said slowly, in a deep wavering voice.

Dr. Berger sat back and folded his arms. He crossed his gray-suited legs, waiting silently until his patient was ready to unburden himself. The room was quiet and the trees outside the high window slapped against the pane. It was the only noise in the room.

Steven's disjointed words changed from agitation to a quietly defined oration outlining his past two years. His voice was flat and lifeless. The only sign of animation was when he discussed Lana and her sons. His words were measured, thoughtful. His money-hungry actions were filled with delusions of a grandiose future that he believed were more important than life. When he was finished, he looked up at the doctor and sagged in his chair, gripping his knees with fists.

Steven saw understanding and compassion in Michael Berger's face and the tide broke with his loud, wrenching sobs. He bent over and put his head down, clenching his jaws and pushing at his eye sockets. And he cried out all the bitterness, sadness, grief and guilt. Then he cried some more.

The room held an equal mixture of fear and hope as the two men mentally reached out toward one another: Steven, re-living the past that threatened his sanity and a doctor willing to help him step beyond the past and learn how to cope with a future. It wouldn't be easy and wouldn't be fast. The doctor touched the back of Steven's head in confident sympathy. He smiled and remembered again why this job was so important to him.

*   *   *

In Washington, D.C., Nan Donofrio and Laura Amburgey shook hands, promising to meet the following day before the other congressional members to discuss the prescription agenda. Each felt confident in their need to slow the wild ranting of a senator they no longer respected. Then, Thanksgiving and the quiet week with their families was a promise they looked forward to with anticipation. It was long overdue. The coalition was welded together with intelligent members and it was owed largely to Tillie Tooter's work in Oregon. The two senators complimented each other.

"I think we did it." Nan crooned, to the tune from My Fair Lady. "My dear, I think we did it. We did it. We did it." She laughed at Laura's reflection in the mirror as she reached for her coat.

Laura turned around and laughed. "Yes, by jove, I think we did it....." she finished the song and grabbed her purse. "............almost."

"I'm happy with the results. Do you want to call Callie or should I?" Nan asked.

"You did it with your clout, lady. You should be the one to call her. It's just after lunch on the west coast. You'd probably catch her in the next couple of hours. She's delightful. I really like her...real and sincere. She and Caroline make a good team. We're going to get together during this long weekend while I'm home for Thanksgiving and I'm looking forward to it." Laura smiled in anticipation as she shrugged her arms into the big coat and began buttoning it up to her neck.

Nan handed her the brightly-colored scarf as Laura headed for the door.

"Caroline invited me to her home Sunday for a Dessert and Coffee Soiree to meet some of her friends. She has a home in Southeast Portland that is built on a small bluff above the Willamette River. Callie said there is a delightful view of the bridges on the river and it's on a dead-end street. Sounds fun. Call Callie and let her know about the mass-migration to our side, ok?" With that, Laura wrapped the wool scarf around her neck, pulled on her leather gloves and was gone.

Nan smiled thoughtfully. *This is the part of my job that I like best. The feeling I get when I can make a viable difference to PEOPLE and not bank accounts makes it all worthwhile. Laura, it's not clout...it's working together.... so let the fireworks begin!*

Lifting the phone, she dialed Oregon and for a moment she wished she could take the plane west with Laura.

"When I demanded of my friend what viands he preferred, He quoteth:
"A large cold bottle, and a small hot bird!"
—EUGENE FIELD —- - *The Bottle and the Bird*

Chapter 29

✳ ✳ ✳

Lee knocked on her door as the clock chimed two o'clock, holding a small bouquet of daisies wrapped with green paper and entwined with raffia.

She threw open the door but words died in her throat as she saw them in his hand. *Daisies in November?*

"Well, aren't you going to invite me in?" he teased. Intense pleasure bit into his heart as he pushed the flowers into her smooth hands.

"Yes, of course, Lee. Come in. I'm sorry. You just surprised me... and you remembered daisies were my favorite. Thank you, my dear friend." She led him into the kitchen, reached for a vase on the top shelf of the cabinet and proceeded to fill it with water.

He removed his coat and enjoyed the look of her backside as she stretched and began arranging the petals.

"Thank you," she breathed.

"You are welcome."

She looked at her watch, moving the pearl bracelet away from its face. "How much time do we have?" Wisps of hair framed her face as she twisted the flowers.

"Well, it depends on what you had in mind," he moved forward and looked at her intently, pulling out the words like taffy.

"What?" She twisted around in a lightening fast motion, spraying water on the counter.

"Caroline.... I'm joking...." He followed her into the living room to see her place the vase near the couch.

"Lana's back, Lee. She called me and said Steven left her some phone messages that told her he's mixed up. What else is new? Anyway, she packed up the boys and drove home. The apartment was freezing cold and empty. She doesn't know what to make of it except she thinks Steven is under a Dr.

Berger's care. She'll be in on Monday...which will be wonderful. She sounded worried about Steven. I was right. She really cares for the man and she assures me he's sorry for everything, etc, etc, etc....." She leaned forward in the chair facing Lee, inviting his response, her head shaking.

"Well, maybe he's finally on the right track. You and I thought before that the man had a screw loose. Maybe now he can tighten it up and get on with his life. I hope Lana looks at all her options and weighs the odds. Those little boys are her life but I also know that life is empty without someone you love to share it with." He smiled his mercurial smile.

Caroline hugged her knees and stared into eyes that seemed to have a sheen of purpose. She nodded her head, eyes searching. "Yes, I think so too."

He continued to look at her, his fingers drumming his thigh.

She saw a man she desired as well as a friend and her heartbeat increased. She took a deep breath. "Lee, life *is* dull without someone to share it." She blundered on, "You fill me up when you walk into a room. I've just recently noticed this happening.....What do you think about that?" Not wanting her brain to stop her soul from reaching out to him, the rush of words whooshed out on their own.

"What do I *think* of it? There's nothing to think *about*, Caro. I've felt that way about you ever since I met you over twenty years ago. Are you saying a mere friendship isn't enough anymore?" He waited, chest held taut, half rising from the chair.

"Yes, that is exactly what I'm saying." Caroline stood up at the same time Lee moved in her direction.

They reached toward each other. The prolonged anticipation turned their kiss and embrace into a soul-searching, bone-crunching hug that marked the first page in their step-beyond friendship. They pulled back, their hands roving each other's back and smiled at one another with longing, both quite breathless.

The heart-rending tenderness of his gaze caused Caroline's throat to close.

"Oh, my God Caro, I've wanted to do that for so long. You are so, so beautiful," he murmured, holding her closely.

Caroline turned into his arms, pressing her face into his neck and smoothing her hand over his heart. "Oh, Lee, why didn't I see it all these years? I started thinking I was going nuts the past few months because all I could see was your soft beard and smelling your aftershave drove me to distraction." She laughed, huskily and squeezed him again. "It was hell during Board meetings." She laughed and he kissed her again.

The clock chimed two-fifteen. "Damn that clock," he whispered. He pulled away from her and held her hands, looking at her as if he were photographing her with his eyes. "Reservations are for two-thirty. Guess we should get going...."

She lifted her lips to his once again, and met his kiss, slow and thoughtful. "Yes, I guess we should," she responded against his warm lips.

Lee leaned forward and lowered his voice, "Can't believe we're trading this for turkey," he mumbled, turning her smile into a chuckle.

"Come, my knight." She laughed and stood apart from him, "Our friends await and the turkey will be eaten without us," she answered, playfully, as she pulled him toward their coats and out the front door. "I can't believe the tradeoff either...." Her voice softly answered.

The first thing that caught Callie's eye as Caroline and Lee walked into *Hubers* was their clasped hands. They were fastened like morning glories entwined around a rustic fence post. Their faces glowed.

Callie glanced over at Derrick for his reaction, but he was talking with his father, and hadn't noticed their arrival. Callie reached up, waving her hand in their direction. Caroline's eye caught the movement and they wound their way toward the large round table in the corner. Flowers were everywhere and the room was jumping with intensity, people laughing and talking all around them.

"Well now......" Callie murmured, catching Derrick's attention and conversation stopped. All heads turned toward the two latecomers.

"Caroline...... Lee." Derrick stood to shake Lee's hand and smiled at Caroline, and then he introduced Carl and Ted. Chairs scraped and everyone got situated, beer and wine delivered and the conversation took on a life of its own.

The room was filled to capacity and the tables were littered with food, drinks and people. The festive air embraced the diners and for the day, troubles were forgotten, blessings abounded and the smell of turkey had stomachs rumbling.

Callie tried to catch Caroline's eye, who clapped a hand to her cheek, ignoring the questions scampering across her friend's face. Then, she saw Caroline lift her toddy, and look at Lee over its rim. *There it is again,* Callie thought. *Fireworks. Definitely big fireworks. Well...well.*

Callie's mouth opened for salad as her stomach yawned for food, but her heart hungered for more than turkey, especially seeing her friends across from her. She watched them as the others shared conversation. She lifted her drink to her lips and sipped it thoughtfully.

Derrick also felt the electricity in the air as his thigh touched Callie's and his fingers caressed her forearm. He grinned at her and surreptitiously watched Caroline and Lee, before turning toward her when his father's words waylaid him.

"So, you're the lady who gave my doctor a boost up the ladder?" Carl asked Caroline, after sipping the foaming beer in front of him. "He's mighty proud and he deserved it. I thank you." He saluted her with his beer glass.

Caroline smiled in his direction. "Glad I could make some positive changes, Mr. Leander....I mean, Carl." She saw the man's eyes crinkle at her, remembering to use his Christian name as he'd asked her to do. "And I can assume surgery is already on the docket?"

"Yep, Tuesday and I'll be God-awful glad to have it over with. Oh, pardon me, ma'am. I've been around Ted and Derrick too much and forget my manners when I'm with ladies." Carl dropped his eyes as Derrick punched his shoulder.

"Hey, Dad! I'm glad to hear surgery's set. Lots of good news in our family, right Dad?" Derrick waited expectantly.

Carl Leander looked at his son, gauging whether he'd heard from Sophia or not. "Yes, I guess so........"

Derrick glanced around the table and told them his daughter was hoping to make him a grandpa. Smiles lit up all around him and he saw Carl take a slow, shuddering breath. Derrick looked at him questioningly before being interrupted by another question from Lee.

Suddenly, aromatic plates of steaming turkey were placed around the table with all the typical trimmings; pineapple-Jello salad, sweet potato pie and peanut-butter stuffed celery. The golden gravy was rich and hot over fluffy white potatoes and the cranberry sauce was sliced to perfection. Forks clicked against crockery and conversation lulled.

Carl reached for Callie's hand and squeezed it. "You are just what my boy needs," he whispered to her when Derrick was in deep conversation with Lee as they wound down their meal. He pulled the package of Tums out of his pocket.

She blinked at him and said, "Thanks, Carl. We enjoy being together and we laugh a lot. It's so nice to talk with someone and not run out of things to say. He's a lovely man." She finished, watching him slip a Tum's tablet into his mouth.

Carl nodded and thought, *Thank you, God. She's a far cry from Millie and she's local so my boy will not be running back to California any time soon....or at all?* Carl watched his son and saw the look he gave the petite woman beside him. Carl's heart flipped with delight. He touched his brother's hand and motioned toward Derrick with his head. His brother smiled and they traded a look.

The busy waiter rolled a dessert trolley over to their table, filled with pies. A groan rose as one as they found it dripping with temptation. Pumpkin, Pecan, Mincemeat with rum and Apple pie slices with ice cream were delivered with hot coffee. Nobody knew how they'd fit it in, but it was Thanksgiving, after all.

As the day ended and everyone grumbled about eating too much, the party slowly subsided. And the long weekend stretched ahead.

"Now you two forget about work. And I don't want to see your faces at her office until Monday. I mean it." Caroline said firmly. She also reminded them about the open house Sunday afternoon for Laura

Amburgey and told them she expected both of them. "Just dessert, coffee and a good time," she said as Lee hurriedly propelled her toward his dark green BMW.

Callie and Derrick watched them as they drove away. "What do you think?" she asked.

"Something…..definitely something," he answered. Then, he walked her to her car. He'd promised his dad and uncle that he'd play pinochle with them afterward, a Leander tradition. "Hope you don't mind…..?"

"Of course not, but I'm never going to speak to you again…," she laughed. "Maybe I better learn how to play pinochle. It's Caroline's game too."

Callie was caught in a bear hug from Carl and a more genteel hug from Uncle Ted. She turned to Derrick as the men got into the Explorer, parked behind her Audi. Derrick grabbed her hand and pulled her to him gently, breathing in the scent of her hair and kissing her hard on the lips. "mmmmmmmmmm… I don't want to go though…" The warmth of his laugh sent shivers down her spine; her lips tingled.

She grinned impishly at him as he opened his car door and sent her a twisted smile. His mind was definitely not on a card game.

Twenty minutes later, Callie opened the door to her empty house and stood in the foyer. The house was quiet and felt lonely. *I'm really getting used to having that man around.* She walked in slowly and dropped her coat on a living room chair on her way into the kitchen. The phone machine light was blinking. Two messages. She punched the button as she kicked off her shoes and heard Lana's voice fill the room.

"Callie! I can't find Steven. I mean, I'm sure he's not lost, but he's on my mind so much I can't stand it. The video you gave the boys is nearly worn out even though they watched it over and over, entranced. I'm getting ready to put a new one into the machine but they're begging for the old ones…. Guess I'm lonely. I can have the coffee on in ten minutes if you feel like having some gloomy company and don't mind the sound of animated characters looming in the background. I'm a mess and I wanted to thank you so much for letting us stay at the cottage. It is a fabulous place and just what I needed. My number is 646-4374. Bye now… oh, and I hope you had a happy Thanksgiving." Lana's voice sounded lost and sad.

She removed her earrings and listened to the second message. Cendrine Benoit's voice filled the room. *"Bon jour, Callie. Qu'est-ce que tu voudrais faire? Jous voudrais un….."* Click. *How odd. Why would she ask what I would like to do without an explanation? I hope the family is ok. I haven't talked to Cendrine since the last harvest, she sounded so strained…...like I knew something I don't?*

Callie glanced at her watch. Nearly six o'clock. *It's three a.m. in Pertuis. I'll be sure to call her tomorrow.* She sank down into the padded dining chair and looked at the gardens behind the house. The quiet slammed into her.

A minute later, in re-wind mode, she slipped on her shoes, put on her coat, tapped out the number and told Lana she was on her way. *I'll be a Good Samaritan to her and she will unknowingly be one for me.* She backed down the long driveway and headed to Beaverton.

Ten minutes later, the sounds of little-boy laughter could be heard as Callie opened the outer doors of the fourplex and walked up the carpeted stairs to apartment #3. After a gentle knock on the door, the sounds were replaced with running footsteps followed by bantering arguments over who would open the door. Lana won, and the boys stood back and watched as Callie entered the room. Their arms clutched around their mother's legs.

"I'm so glad you came," Lana whispered, sounding ragged. She had the sad, frightened eyes of a stunned bird and it was obvious she was swamped with anxiety.

Quickly losing interest, the boys returned to their video. Eyes unblinking, they mentally jumped inside Toy Story 2 once again as Lana led her toward the kitchen.

Lana put the pot of coffee onto the open ceramic counter between her small galley kitchen and the dining room beyond. She handed Callie cups, Irish Cream Coffee Mate and a spoon....and offered her pumpkin pie.

"Oh, dear, I can't fit anything else into this poor over-stuffed belly. Thanks, Lana. Coffee will be just perfect. I'm glad you called. It was so quiet when I got home. Tell me what's going on with you, huhmmmm?" Callie poured coffee into both cups and Lana sat down, fidgeting all the while.

She brought Callie up to date quickly. Over much discussion without solutions, their coffee disappeared. The little boys ran into the room, their movie over. Slipping and sliding around the women, they paused to ask for more pie.

Callie reached out and ran her hand through Frankie's fluffy head of hair and patted Nicholas's hand as it rested on the table beside her. *Oh, if only*, she thought sadly.

"I loved the cottage, Callie. It has such a nice kitchen; all open to the rest of the main room and that little utility room with the washer and dryer is perfect. Of course, keeping the boys from flipping over the upstairs railing was quite a fete, but we arrived home in one piece after all," she laughed. She pushed the boys up to the table with pie and a cup of milk.

"Yes, we liked the lake. And we saw birds and boats too," Nicholas told her, his eyes dancing as he shoved his spoon into the whipped cream topping.

"And what about you, Frankie? What did you see?" Callie questioned the baby.

"Birds and water and boats too," he mimicked his older brother. "And we saw fire in the firebox."

"That's a fireplace, silly," Nicholas said, reprimand in his voice.

"How long has it been since you were there, Callie?" Lana sipped the last of her coffee. Her red hair was pulled up in a pony tail; her make up long gone. The freckles over her nose stood out against her pale face as she waited, interested.

Callie's brow furrowed. "Too long actually......"

"Why don't you just take off and go then? The weatherman said the snow's melted off and it's supposed to be warmer. I got caught in a snowstorm when we left yesterday. I left the heater at 62 like you told me and there is lots of wood in the alcove outside."

Callie smiled. *It probably is time.*

After spreading hugs all around and plopping kisses on little chubby faces, she left happily, noting Lana's sadness had lifted just an iota.

"I cannot tell how the truth may be;
I say the tale as 'twas said to me."
—SCOTT —- - *Lay of the Last Minstrel*

Chapter 30

* * *

The next morning, imbued with an ambitious desire to leave the silent house, Callie tossed overnight clothes and clean underwear into a tote bag and headed toward her car. *I can stop in Lincoln City for food. Yes, it is definitely time... and Derrick helped me see it. Maybe Christmas will be a happy time once again.*

She was consumed with a ripple of urgency to get there. Half way to the beach, just passing the casino in Grand Ronde, she realized it had been nearly three years since she'd stepped a foot into the beach house.

Setting her jaw, she vowed to make changes in her life. *I've got to stop running from life. Mom's gone. Francois' gone. Caroline is in love and it's my turn. Francois would want me to live again.* At the thought of Francois, her lips quivered slightly and she felt her throat constrict but she tightened her fingers around the wheel and forged on.

Damn. I forgot to call Cendrine. Damn. Damn.

Two hours later, groceries in tow and her overnight bag slung over her shoulder, she wrestled open the side door and walked into the cottage. It was exactly as she'd left it so long ago. *The caretakers did a good job of keeping it up and bless Lana.* It felt clean. Its sanctuary enveloped her. She put the bag into the large downstairs bedroom, the food into the fridge. After opening the bottle of Cabernet, she poured herself a glass to say good bye to the past and contemplated her jump into the present.

Bright blue sky greeted her as she snuggled into her deep stuffed chair. *No haze or drizzle for a change. A gorgeous autumn day fits my mood.* Far off, a boat drew a wake on the lake and the sound of an airplane carried across the water. After yanking some logs and starter kindling off the pile near the huge stone fireplace, she had a bright fire crackling in a matter of minutes. With an audible sigh, she reached for her wineglass. Plopping down into deep cushions again, staring into the fire and swallowing the red liquid gave her a feeling of sanctuary. Then she closed her eyes and thought, *now what?*

Oh! Cendrine. She reached for the telephone. *Midnight there but I'll try anyway.* Perplexed, she heard the phone ring several times with no answer.

Two hours later, Callie was stretched out on the couch; the fire burned low and the wine glass sat empty. One glass had put her to sleep and dreams skittered across her brain, eyelids fluttering. Thoughts of Francois and Derrick blended and her mother was pointing toward her and telling her something. *What?* She kept asking. *What, Mom?* Then, she was with Derrick....outside the cottage and they were in a boat racing across the lake. She tossed and turned, groaning.

Callie's heartbeat accelerated and she woke up abruptly, her breath quick, feeling the brush of angel's wings. She sat up and rubbed her hands over her head and massaged her temples. "My God. What was that all about? That was Francois' boat but it was Derrick inside it instead of Francois' and Mom........ Oh, Mom." She whispered into the empty cottage as tears slid silently down her cheeks.

A kaleidoscope of emotions, fading and disappearing and feverishly close enough to touch walked through her body. Within seconds, she was crying. Deep undulating sobs and she couldn't stop. She knew what her mother was trying to tell her. She must put the past behind and open the door to the future or lose what she'd found with Derrick. She whimpered like an injured puppy and pulled herself into a ball, staring into the dying flames. Pulled to her cottage for so many reasons and finally seeing through them all, she felt herself begin to finally heal. *I guess Mom was right; people are put in our path as signposts sometimes, to point us in the right direction.*

The tearful release was a long time coming and it took Derrick to open up the dam, she admitted. She built up the fire again and pulled out the book she was reading, *Angela's Ashes*, delightfully written from a child's point of view. She settled into the cozy, overstuffed chair with a decided plop and felt the springs bounce. Pulling the reading lamp closer to her chair, the warmth from the fire turned her cheeks pink. Then, she began to regain her humanity as she read about Malachy and Frankie and little Margaret. She closed her eyes a moment and laid her head back, and savored the peace, the quiet and the solitude.

*   *   *

Earlier that morning, Friday's Portland *Oregonian* was tossed onto Caroline's front steps, as usual. She filled the coffee pot with her special Irish Cream blend from Millstone, as usual, and started it cooking. Hugging her thick, bright yellow bathrobe around her, she walked outside to pick up the paper and waved at the neighbor as he walked by with a Great Dane on a leash, walking proudly beside his master.

She hugged herself and smiled at the sky: rich blue, clear and crisp. She hugged her thoughts and padded back into her kitchen to pour the hot brew into her cup even though it wasn't quite finished.

I'll just lounge around this morning and enjoy the day, and spruce up the house for Laura and Lee......... His name inspired a smile again, lighting up her freshly scrubbed face, remembering his kisses the day before.

Caroline popped a giant blueberry bagel into the toaster and pulled the butter out of the fridge. Then, she changed her mind and replaced it with the cream cheese. *I'll just splurge all over the place today,* she decided as a dimple creased her cheek. The toast popped up, she smeared it thickly with cream cheese; the coffee was hot and steaming. She gathered it all onto a bright-colored tray and carried it out of the kitchen and into the adjoining room. As she sat down beside the large, back window facing the Willamette River, she inhaled deeply, enjoying the silence. Laziness overwhelmed her.

"Oh, God. It feels good to relax.," she said aloud. The scent of nearby cinnamon-scented candles filled her nostrils. She moved them, fluffed her pillow before folding her good foot underneath her and scrunched down to get comfortable once again.

The *Oregonian's* front page showed a picture of a group of missionaries who'd been killed. She grimaced. She slid past that headline and followed the next one as she bit into the toast and washed it down with her coffee. Then, her heart skipped a beat. She spit coffee in her haste to pull the pages closer. Her hands started to shake and she pressed her hand to her mouth, eyes wide. Blood drained from her features and she felt numb as her own face stared back at her.

An Old Lover's Scam still dogs Larkspur's CEO

The fallout from Larkspur's scandal continues, amid pressures that are currently building steam in Washington, D.C. to address the pitfalls and problems exposed during a hacker's scam.

Caroline Phillips, CEO of Larkspur Health Plan, still marches down her company's corridors with a slight limp imposed on her from an attack nearly a year ago by her former employee and lover, Steven Roget. But, her noted leg injuries were only the beginning of her troubles. Mr. Roget's current whereabouts are unknown since his release from prison.

Since her attack, subsequent hospitalization and return to Larkspur, Ms. Phillips has controlled Larkspur's reins with an iron spirit; She introduced a drug card for her members utilizing a Canadian drug supplier, Shelton-Kent, while ignoring American economical needs. But that remarkable genesis into the drug-card marketplace has also opened the door for a fight in Washington to rescind the current law that decriminalizes those who purchase prescription drugs beyond our American borders.

The measure Senator Arnold Wilding has submitted is designed to revise regulations to ensure FDA approval for American-purchased drugs. The National Association of Health Underwriters along with their lobbyist, Tillie Tooter, is actively fighting Wilding's bill with the creation of a coalition that has a mounting membership that negates Wilding's claims. They are trying, instead, to clarify the measure and "let America speak" as the vote has already confirmed.

Senators Laura Amburgey and Nancy K. Donofrio, her firm supporters, told The Oregonian last week that the mission of their newly formed coalition is to educate legislators and public opinion leaders about the dangers of a monopoly in our midst and to develop constructive measures to improve prescription care delivery and access through outside suppliers; In other words, consumers pro-choice for prescription drugs.

Caroline's fingers shook as the words slapped her face and stabbed at her heart. She blinked away tears and held her breath. Putting down the paper for a moment, she reached for her coffee, the bagel forgotten. The paper blurred before her eyes but each damning word compelled her to continue. She slipped her feet up onto her coffee table, and stretched the paper onto her lap, glaring at the article, her breathing short, staring at the journalist's name —- *David Perkins, Oregonian staff.*

Alas, Ms. Phillips is still reeling from the brunt of Steven Roget's long arm of deceit. It has recently come to light that he managed to infiltrate Ms. Phillip's company by hacking into her PC to access sensitive and confidential information from Larkspur.

As Caroline Phillips fights the battle to hold onto her new drug card program from Canada (to be implemented January 1st) for their 40,000 members, she's allowed her old lover to breach the confidential records of those same members, across the board. It's obvious that Ms. Phillips is dancing through a proverbial juggling act. She wears the white lace dress of the good fairy on one hand, while internal scandals fan the fears of her covered members with the other.

My question is, "How safe is the confidential medical information within the Larkspur Health Plan offices?" And can Caroline Phillips hold her head above water long enough to see her new drug-card baby lift her above the onslaught of what is sure to be a storm of massive proportions? Can her lobbyist and senators that are listening to her justifications rise above the steam that mounts daily?

In the stunned silence the doorbell chimed, but Caroline sat stiffly on the couch, feeling like freshly made taffy hardened in place. *Go away. Just go away.* Numbness clouded her head and a heavy haze controlled her mind. The doorbell buzzed again.

"Shit." Her initial horror had passed. Now she was angry, frustrated and hurt. As the doorbell continued its harsh invective, she limped into the hallway, feeling lifeless. Her legs felt like waterlogged balloons sloshing across the carpet and her head felt too heavy for her slim neck. Squinting, she peered through the peephole, unlocked the door and opened it slowly. The morning sunshine filtered onto her face, lips quavering.

"Caroline." He stood there with eyebrows drawn together in an agonized expression.

"Oh, Lee." She began to tremble. Still determined not to cry, she tried desperately to hold herself together and couldn't do it. The tears rushed out like a torrent with no warning.

Comforting arms, hard as steel, wrapped around her and she collapsed against Lee Carle's chest. Her head fell onto his shoulder as she crumpled against him. "Sh...sh...Honey, oh honey. I got here as soon as I could. I just read ..."

"I know." Her voice faded to a hushed stillness. He felt safe, steady and warm.

Leading her into the living room, he was greeted with the remnants of the roll, empty coffee cup and the newspaper. It was spewed across the table and couch, a wad crunched up and thrown toward the fireplace. Grimly, he guided her into a chair, folded up the papers and left her there as he proceeded to the kitchen. *Lots of black coffee, that's what we need and God only knows what else after this.*

Caroline hadn't moved when Lee placed another cup of steaming coffee into her hand.

"Drink, dear. Let's talk. We will work this out. Never fear." He felt tears behind his eyes as he squeezed her shoulder and drank his own hot coffee and waited.

Five minutes passed before Caroline lifted the cool coffee to her lips and moved her head to acknowledge Lee's presence. Then she smiled.

"A hell of a note, huh?"

"Yep. A hell of a note," he agreed.

"Well, my knight in legal armor, how do I get out of this one?" She licked her lower lip trying to quell her anger. "And only a month away from my drug card coup!"

"Let it out, Caro. For God's sake. Blow steam. Throw things. Scream. Do something."

Raw hurt glittered in her eyes as she looked directly at him. She lifted the coffee and drained the contents, then lifted the cup for more.

Lee jumped up to do her bidding, his worry evident. He paused to lift the short blonde curls from the nape of her neck and kiss it gently before moving toward the kitchen.

A moment later, holding another cup close to her chest, she rubbed her little finger back and forth on the cup before she spoke with dazzling determination. "I will not let them win. Whoever is behind this, they have met their match. After Paul and Steven, whoever this is will be sorry they started waging this stupid war with me. You are right. I don't believe it is only Steven. Who ever he works for is not giving up easily and neither will I! You'd think the paper wouldn't print this crap .... But Lee, the words are basically true in context but my God, it reads so horrible. I feel like I've been stripped and pushed naked down the street.

Lee rubbed her arm in sympathy as she continued.

But," she looked at Lee, "I know better of course. What do you think we should do first?"

They exchanged a subtle look of amusement. "That's my girl."

The phone rang before either could say anything. She looked at it and halted Lee from reaching for it. "Let the machine get it. I have a feeling it's going to be ringing off its hook today and I won't like what I'll hear. Thank God my kids are both out of the city."

Suddenly, her greeting ripped through the room before a man's voice came on the line. "Caroline? This is Sam James. Let me know how you want me to handle the newspaper article. I mean, how should we tell them to go straight to hell? Whatever you decide to do, I'm with you. And I won't be the only one. They are stupid jack asses. Call me if you need me, my number is 503-236-7798. We'll see this through and....You are not alone, ok?" Click.

Caroline felt tears prick her eyelids again and her chest heaved. Putting her hand to her face, the tear slid over her fingers as she looked at the newspaper again.

Reaching, Lee pulled her to him, pushing his fingers through her golden hair. He felt her shaking as he rubbed her back. "Go ahead, sweetheart. Let it out."

Pulling him down toward her, she pushed her lips into his neck and began kissing him; breathing in the scent of him. His arms tightened around her. When she tried to speak, her voice wavered, "Lee, please don't let go."

"My darling woman, it's taken me twenty years for you, how can you imagine I'd let go now?"

She chuckled quietly. His words smoothed her thoughts and she felt her dormant wits renew themselves. "This won't be easy. I have Ben's boxing gloves in the coat closet. I just don't know who to use them on."

"Not now, we won't." He pulled her toward him as involuntary tremors of arousal began, leaving no room for misinterpretation.

Caroline's head came up. Her eyes, wet and glazed, met his. He pushed a damp tress of hair from her eyes and pushed it back from her forehead. "Feel better?"

In response, she touched his cheek and smoothed his slight beard with her fingers, rubbing them softly, before pulling his lips toward hers boldly.

As the phone rang again, they were already walking up the stairs with hands entwined and hearts melded together, each step leading them exactly where they wanted to go.

SOMETIME LATER, as the sun struggled through the clouds just in time to set, Lee stood at the counter in bare feet with his shirt hanging outside his slacks. He licked his lips, trying to focus on pushing sliced ham and Swiss cheese onto the rye bread. Reaching across the counter, covering it with lettuce was nearly impossible as he felt Caroline's hands caressing his bare back and dropping kisses along his spine. "Are you hungry or what?" he laughed.

"Or what...." She danced around him and grinned up into his face.

"Well, my dear, food is served." He kissed her quickly and swung both plates toward her. She grabbed them and placed them on the table to join the chilled water and a sliced orange.

"Sit." She motioned toward the end of the table and re-belted her robe.

Lee sat down at the table, eyes never leaving hers as he watched her walk slowly toward him and press herself into his embrace. His arms surrounded her waist and his face pushed into her breasts as they held tightly, swaying into one another.

"Lee, I have never felt so full."

He pulled his head back to look up at her and his eyes brimmed with tenderness. "I love you, Caroline Phillips."

"And I love you Lee Carle, beyond a shadow of a doubt, but I am scared as hell."

"Don't be. Just enjoy us. I am." He exhaled a long sigh of contentment. "Now..... let's eat."

"Yes sir." She laughed aloud and then joined him at the table, pulling the plate toward her. With a glint of wonder in her eyes, she watched him bite into his ham sandwich hungrily before she reached for her own.

"A press release."

"Hmmmmmmmmmm?" she managed with a partially-filled mouth.

"I'm going to call Mike Mahone at Channel 6. He's a friend of mine through a business men's club that I attend once a month at the MAC club."

Caroline sighed. "How soon can we set up a press conference?"

He jumped up and had the Channel six news's anchor on the phone before she took her last bite and marveled at his competency as she grimaced, thinking about the newspaper again.

"Yes, I know........ I can have that to you this afternoon.....Perfect. See you then." A look of satisfaction showed in his eyes.

When she lifted her face, the pain still flickered there.

He moved toward her and placed his hands on her shoulders, rubbing her neck and feeling her move into him. She laid her head on his stomach and closed her eyes. "We can have you on the air Monday prime time. We might even get national coverage and it would sure as hell help you shoot that moon."

"Then, God help me, let's do it." Her courage and determination were like a rock inside her and left her aching for the fulfillment of his lovemaking.

"Adversity introduces a man to himself."
—Anonymous

Chapter 31

* * *

On his way out the door to get his morning's *Oregonian*, the ringing phone caused Derrick to abruptly change direction. He grabbed the phone before the second ring.

"Dad! It worked and I'm pregnant and there's more than one baby. We don't know yet how many but they think it's twins or maybe three......" Sophia's voice rang with laughter, excitement and the first-mother fear.

"A baby. No....babies. Plural. Grandpa Leander. No .....Pop......Gramps.....My God. I'm going to be a grandpa and my baby is going to be a mommy." His lips lifted in a smile that made his eyes mist in memory as he re-lived Sophia's homecoming. *Tiny little head and fingers all accounted for. Wispy hair, soft sweet skin and bright blue eyes. No bigger than a mite. Now it's her turn.* He struggled to tell her his feelings but couldn't find the words.

"Oh sweetheart, you can't possibly know how excited I am for you. When will you know for sure how many are in there?" he teased.

"Dad, we don't know any more than I did on Wednesday. Grandpa didn't say anything to you, did he?"

"What? Pop knew already? Well, I'll be damned. That old curmudgeon! I thought he acted funny at dinner yesterday. Well, I'll be damned. No, not a single word. Did he tell you his surgery's on Tuesday?"

"Yes, I shouldn't be worried, should I, dad? I mean, do you think I should come up there and be with him when he gets home? I have some vacation coming and I know Jack won't mind unless the doctor thinks I shouldn't........."

"No, honey. Wait until after the three month's mark. You know that's important. Besides, I can handle it and Uncle Ted is here too."

"Sure, Dad.... If you're sure."

"Hey! Wait a minute....Of course, there's Alice across the street."

"Alice? Are you dating someone?"

Derrick laughed. "No, I'm not dating Alice," he answered evasively. "She lives across the street from Pop and she's sweet on him but he won't hear of it. Guess maybe I'll play cupid and ask her to check on him when he gets home. What do you think?"

"Well.... I don't know. You didn't really answer me."

"I didn't?" He hedged.

"Are you DATING?" Her voice sounded exasperated.

"Yes, I am." He said with quiet emphasis.

"Oh! That's wonderful. Who?" Sophia spoke eagerly.

"Her name is Callinda. Everyone calls her Callie. She's a few years younger than I am and works at Larkspur. She's gorgeous, smart, quite funny, speaks French.... and she likes me too. It's time, don't you think?"

"Dad.....she's not married is she?"

"Damn. That's the same thing Pop asked me when I told him about her. I've never dated a married woman. Where's this coming from?" He knew the answer but got devilish enjoyment out of saying it.

"Well, Mom............"

"Honey......, I'm not your mother. She has her own life and way of living it. I never played around. She's the one who wanted more. But, we've discussed this before and I shouldn't have mentioned it. I'm sorry."

"I know, Dad. Did you know they broke up?"

Derrick's mind reached for words.

"Dad?"

"No, honey, I didn't but it doesn't matter. She'll find someone else."

"Well..... Anyway! Tell me everything about Callie........"

Fifteen minutes later, he hung up the phone bursting with emotion. *A grandpa.* He dialed Callie's number and was disappointed she wasn't there, so left a message, and went in search of the paper.

*   *   *

Mr. Rogers was singing through his neighborhood to Frankie and Nicholas on the television when the phone rang. They both looked up but didn't move to answer it; they knew better. Lana's voice got their attention, though, as she stood braced against the refrigerator. "Yes, I'm Lana Potts. Yes........." she responded in a hushed voice. "Yes. .... No.......... Where?" Her voice raised an octave with each response and she pressed her hand to her heart.

The boys listened to their mother, distracted only a moment, before resuming their perch on the edge of the couch, impervious to the rush of emotion bouncing around in their mother's chest. Mr. Rogers put on his shoes and hung up his coat and a cat darted around him.

Lana's hand shook as she hung up the phone. She'd just left a message at Callie's house after reading the paper and now....... She closed her eyes.

I wish I still smoked. I could use one now. "Now, what do I do?" she whispered.

She checked the clock and rapidly calculated the time it would take to get to St. Vincent Hospital. Dr. Berger said it wasn't urgent but he wanted to talk with her. *He has Steven!* At least she knew where he was. Her body sagged. Shaking her head at the boys to sit still, she opened the door and gently knocked on the apartment across the hall.

*   *   *

The skyline toward the river was amazing from the 15th floor of the condominium on Southwest Vista near the park. Mount Hood stood starkly to the east beyond the sunroom windows. The west hills, thick with trees, looked up from their shadows into the living room and kitchen. Mount St. Helen's flat top and surrounding panorama filled their bedroom. Overall, he had a birds-eye view of all the little people he avoided in his cold quest for money and power.

Janine had designed the apartment with a skill that both amused and surprised him. Interior design had always been her first love. Without children, she had to focus on something. She was no longer the quiet, unassuming woman he'd met and married so many years earlier. Oh, no, not Janine. She was the only person he valued above his surroundings; she enjoyed what money could buy but she didn't want to hear how he got it. And he found that facet of her character quite incredible. He allowed himself a moment of thoughtful contentment.

He filled his pipe and tamped it before lifting the match and smiling, enjoying the distant panorama out the windows. He breathed in power that morning and enjoyed it more than he had in a long time. David Perkins surpassed his promise. He was elated with the spread across the front page before him. *Oh, yes. Good job, Perkins. Good job.*

As Janine left that morning, she blew a kiss in his direction as she rushed toward the hospital for her volunteer work. He'd lifted his eyebrows in response. He chuckled after the door closed and re-read the article, digesting each word and nodding approval. Janine rarely read the paper and that astounded him too. At least he didn't think she did. He stopped a moment to ponder on that thought. Sometimes he wasn't sure who she was or what she did anymore. They'd lost the ability to understand one another. When did that happen? He admitted he missed the camaraderie and shrugged. She seemed aware of the world around her, oftentimes amazing him with her knowledge and he knew she resented his workaholic personality. But he hadn't changed. She had.

Dismissing the small interruption in his mind, he stared at the article again. *This should do it. The woman needed to be stopped and by God, I did it.*

The aroma of cherry tobacco surrounded him as he sucked on the pipe and allowed the smoke to fill his mouth and rush out his nostrils. *Oh, yes. Nice.* He puffed and stared out the window, his thoughts matriculating his next agenda when the sudden pounding on his front door jerked him around. Grimacing, he walked toward the noise but after pulling the door open, he immediately wished he'd ignored it.

Del Reed stood there, his face red and angry as he pushed inward like a steam engine.

"What in the *hell* do you think you're doing?" Del's voice attacked him before he could close the door. His eyes bulged and the few hairs on his head looked like messy spun honey.

"Del! I told you never to come here. How did you get into the building anyway? There's a security code and I would have had to buzz you in…." Vincent hissed.

"I just walked in behind a little old lady and you know what? I don't give a damn what you said about not coming here." He slapped the paper against Vincent's chest. "What's this all about? I can read your name all over the freakin' thing."

"It's all true. Your point?"

Del glared. "You are one bad-ass human being."

"Slow down, Del. Those facts weren't pulled out of thin air and to tell you the truth, I was sick and tired of waiting for you and Roget to take care of this. I learned a long time ago if I wanted anything done right, I should do it myself." His nostrils flared as he squinted at the man in the doorway.

Del's face was contorted in anger. Dripping agitation, he snapped, "Well, shit. Is that right?" He pushed against Vincent and paced back and forth in the foyer; feeling like his bowels might loosen themselves any minute and satanically wished they would. *It would serve the dumb ass right to clean up the mess after I left.*

"Sit down, Del. Let's talk about this like adults." Vincent said through gritted teeth.

"Like adults? Your definition of an adult and mine are pole lengths apart, man. I'm out." Del stabbed the end of his finger into Vincent's chest pushing the point of his visit home.

Vincent's countenance became hard and he stared at Del Reed with undisguised distaste. "You're out? You mean you're leaving?" His voice dripped sarcasm and eyes squinted.

"You know exactly what I mean, Vincent Bertrand. Ace-Deer can go to hell and so can you. I'm out and I want my money back. I – AM – OUT. O-U-T… OUT!" he yelled, gripping the rolled-up paper as if he was preparing to swat a fly. He jerkily turned toward Vincent.

"No." Vincent Bertrand stared at Del as a nervous tic danced in his neck.

Del stared at the man. "No? We had a deal, Vincent. A partnership! I'm ready to retire and I'm tired of this cat and mouse game. I don't like myself anymore and I'm going to fix it. I'm dissolving our partnership and I want my money. You know there's a paragraph stating we can buy the other out upon request."

"No." Vincent stated matter-of-factly.

"You shit head!" Del stormed.

Vincent grabbed Del and pulled their faces nose to nose as he spoke evenly, his voice in tight control. "You are not going to dissolve our partnership and I am not giving you back your money. We had a deal and I keep my word, even if you don't. The *Oregonian* will force her hand and that's that. If you can't live with that, then you can go to hell." He let go of Del's arm and pretended to remove a piece of lint from his jacket. "And now get the hell out of my home. I intend to read my paper in peace and you are no longer welcome." With that, he turned abruptly toward his front door.

He didn't see Del link his hands together and raise them in the air behind him.

The shock and pain of Del's blow knocked the man to his knees. He closed his eyes a moment before twisting around and sucker punching Del in the stomach. Hard.

Del let out a whoosh of air and doubled up, placing both hands on his knees, fighting for breath. He tried to fill his lungs but they felt stuck, like something was crammed inside his chest. A deep pain shot through him and his eyes blinked rapidly.

"You stupid idiot! What the hell's gotten into you with this holier than thou attitude anyway?" Vincent pursed his lips as a remnant of cherry scented smoke filled the air between them.

Del straightened up halfway, fighting for breath, his hands on his gut. He stared at the man in front of him. A muscle quivered in his jaw. Stabbing fear enveloped him as moisture dripped off his face and neck. The pain in his chest reached out, throwing tentacles of pain down his arm and slowed his movement. Gripping his chest in agony, he lost his breath again and reached out for help. "Help me, Vincent. It's my heart. My Glycerin pills.....they're in my suit pocket. Get them for me...."

Vincent lowered his voice to almost a whisper, "Like hell I will."

Del blacked out and fell to the floor.

"I know where there is more wisdom than is found in Napoleon, Voltaire, or all the ministers present and to come —- in public opinion."
—TAALLEYRANT —- *In the Chamber of Peers*

Chapter 32

* * *

After a shower Callie felt renewed, encouraged and vibrantly alive. She opened her closet doors and quickly surveyed too many clothes swaying on hangers. *I need a change..... The black? The green and white? Striped? Hmmmmmmmm... maybe the navy?* Deciding on a wool skirt and black silk top, she tapped a brass buckle in place and walked into the kitchen. She'd skipped lunch and now felt hunger pangs snap at her insides.

Wrinkling her nose, she shut the fridge door after grabbing an apple and checked the machine. *Maybe Derrick called while I was gone. And Cendrine?* Five messages blinked at her.

Biting into the Red Delicious, she heard Derrick's voice. "Callie.... Damn. I hoped to catch you. Where are you?" Click.

Another bite of the apple brought juices rolling down her chin. Swiping her face with a napkin, she concentrated on the next message.

Caroline's quivering voice filled the room, "Callie. Call me. Things are terrible and wonderful all at the same time. It's Friday night and I wonder where you are? I'm sure you've read the paper so why haven't you called? Call me, hon." Click.

Goosebumps covered Callie's arms and legs as she set the apple down, half eaten. *My God, now what?*

The third call was Lana. "Callie. Poor Caroline. Her line is busy and wondered if you've talked to her yet? I just got a call from a doctor at St. Vincent and Steven is there ....as an inpatient. Steven put himself in! Anyway, I'm going up there now. The doctor wants to talk to me and then he thinks *maybe* I can see Steven. I'm relieved and scared as hell, but at least something is happening." Click. Her voice held a rasp of excitement.

Callie sat down in the chair, quaking.

The last call was Derrick again, sounding a frantic, "I'm sure you read the paper and wonder if you're at Caroline's already? It makes me sick. Please call me."

Callie's hackles rose with foreboding.

Fear crusted the edges of her mind as she grabbed all the papers off the porch and laid them open. *Oh Lord – There it is. Friday, Front page.* She scanned the headlines and nearly vomited when she saw Caroline's picture. Inhaling deeply, she scanned the article and probing certain parts, she sighed. *Shit! Who is doing this? Well, I hope her open house for Laura is still on. That will be good for her. I wonder what the <u>wonderful</u> part was....*

She started talking to herself. "It will be okay. Everything will be okay. But damn. What is someone trying to do? And why did the Oregonian allow this article?" Her questions rankled and rambled as she jerked the paper toward her again. Then, she dialed Caroline.

"Caro? Hi. I'm so sorry. I was at the cottage and didn't know....."

"You didn't tell me you were leaving town and I was damned worried, Callie."

"Even in the midst of this mess you can still worry about me? Darling, thank you. I love you, you know that?"

"I love you too, Cal, hurry over, ok?" Caroline's eyes blurred as she replaced the receiver, relief evident in her voice.

Thank God Laura's so understanding. She really doesn't pull any punches, Caroline thought wryly as she eyed the rooms to make sure the pillows were puffed, chairs were in order and lights set low. *Oh, no. Not Laura.*

"What do you mean you think you should cancel?" she'd said when Caroline mentioned her fears and dubious reluctance to open her house to everyone, knowing they'd read the news article.

"Well, I....."

"Well, nothing. You have a lovely day for it. You have the food and drinks ready and your legs aren't broken. What other excuse can you give me?" Laura was firm.

Caroline laughed. "*Touche'*. So what you read about me doesn't matter to you?"

"Why should it? You're fighting for something you believe in. A crap-ball is trying to stop you. You cut them off at the pass and now we're moving again."

"Yes....But, I mean the lover part. It's not something I'm proud of and certainly not something I wanted to see on the front page of the paper," she said, sounding exasperated and furious.

"Well, my friend. Why not look at it another way. Just think how many of those readers would have liked Steven Roget in *their* bed. I saw a picture of him and he was extremely good looking. A Nordic God." Laura chuckled.

"Laura!" Caroline felt steel bands loosen from around her heart and she sighed.

"Come on. I will help you combat the forces and I'm going to be there at two o'clock ready or not and that's that." Laura promised and hung up.

A short time later, Caroline stood studying the river and felt the air sizzle with uncertain expectancy. Glancing at the clock hurriedly, she walked downstairs, the Oriental rug muting her footsteps. Stopping here and there, she adjusted the plates of cookies, muffins, petite fours and her beautiful Vienna hand-painted plate filled with chocolate truffles. She popped a piece of chocolate-covered orange slice into her mouth. She envisioned strangling a journalist as she chewed with ferocity.

Soon, Lee applauded her calm appearance as soft music greeted her guests. Over thirty people sauntered around the room, standing, sitting, chatting and drinking everything from hot tea spiced with rum, coffee, black or laced with Bailey's Irish Cream. And wine. Caroline drank Evian, nodded, and answered questions meant to ease her discomfort, relishing the beehive of conversation.

Laura Amburgey was in her element. Meeting Caroline's friends and business associates had been uppermost in her mind when she accepted the invitation, but it turned out to be a rally-around-a-friend day. The amazing grace of the woman intrigued Laura as she watched her flit between guests. And Lee Carle was very obviously more than just her attorney. Her eyes grew misty with memories of her late husband. She swallowed her Earl Gray tea thoughtfully and answered questions posed to her, trying to gauge the atmosphere.

"So the coalition is making strides to fight Senator Wilding's wrench in the works?" A tall, intent-looking man asked from beside her.

"Yes, we have taken some major steps in the right direction. Of course, with the presidency still up in the air, there isn't much chance of his bill getting to the senate floor before the new president is sworn in, but we are right there fighting it anyway," Laura answered with conviction.

Caroline smiled warmly as Janine approached her.

"Caroline, the newspaper is not important. You are the one who is important and what you are doing is a good thing. I applaud your tenacity and creativity. You will make what they call ...your mark. I would like to do something real with my life too.... I just need to tell you, I am very impressed by you." Her face flushed in the rush of words.

"Janine, thank you. You must know how very much I appreciate your coming today and your sentiments sure help heal my bruised ego and public wounding. I'd hoped to see your husband today," she said, glancing around the room.

"Oh *non*. He never misses his golfing Sunday. I am usually on my own so I was happy to have your invitation. Senator Amburgey is delightful. She invited me to Washington when I see my sister in Alexandria and I told her I would do it. My sister is involved on Capitol Hill and I always love hearing about it. And she offered me a job but of course, I couldn't leave Vincent. But, to know and visit a real Senator will add a feather in my cloche. "

"Your bonnet...?" Caroline said with a laugh, happier than she'd felt since shedding all the tears.

"*Oui*.... My bonnet." Her impish smile was welcomed.

Later, Caroline watched Janine share the truffles dish with Marianna James as she stood surveying her friends.

Lee pulled Caroline aside and whispered, "Well, didn't I tell you?"

Strolling by his side, they entered the dining room and grabbed a roll. "Yes, you were right. Everyone seems to see me as the victim, not the harlot." She perused the grouping along the dining table and heard bits and pieces of conversations that supported her statement.

She smiled at her new Medical Director.

Sam James returned her smile and dodged arms and shoulders to join them. "Caroline, Lee. Please meet my wife, Marianna," his voice filled with admiration.

Marianna James was a handsome woman, with fading auburn hair curling around ruby-studded ears. Her face was friendly as she reached to shake Caroline's hand and cover it with her own. A faint scent of lavender lingered in the air.

"What a pleasure to meet you, Caroline. And thank you for making my Sam smile again. I've had to hold him down like a wild stallion since he read Friday's paper. Coming here today made him feel so much better... Your house is quite beautiful." *And so are you*, she thought. *Wow. This is the CEO?* Marianna shook her head in wonderment.

Soon, Sam and Marianna were joined by other guests and the circle warmed the atmosphere.

Lee pulled Caroline into the kitchen. "Hey, nobody's in here. How'd that happen?"

"Not for long," she quipped.

"Well, while we have a moment.........."

Caroline dodged his questing hands feebly. "You are a naughty man. We'd be missed and then the newspaper would really have a heyday. I can just see it now," she said as she lifted her arm, pretending to write in mid air. "Local Harlot Seduces Lawyer in Kitchen."

Lee snorted and waved his arm as if erasing her imaginary line, then scribbled one of his own. "How about "Lawyer Marries Local Harlot?"

She gasped. "Oh my God, Lee, that sounded like a proposal."

"Mmmmmm. Yes, it did sound like that didn't it? And I meant every word.....except the harlot part," he added in a lower, huskier tone. His eyes burned into hers. "It's not like we've just met. And it's not like it hasn't been on my mind for so long, I can't remember when it wasn't." Lee reached for her hand to draw her close, linking her fingers with his.

"Hey you two, the candy's gone," Callie trilled from the doorway. "Oh.... oh.... I interrupted something." Callie's fingers clutched the empty plate and sat it down on the counter as she retraced her steps quickly.

Caroline turned toward her with shining eyes. "Candy?"

"Later, honey," Callie whispered, then disappeared, shutting the door behind her.

Lee's eyes studied Caroline's face. "Come here, sweetheart. You didn't answer me."

Caroline's gray eyes brimmed with tears and her lips trembled. "Lee, I'm sure I've never wanted anything more."

"The candy or me?" His laughter joined hers as their arms became entangled. The kitchen was the only room in the house in a city devoid of anyone else. Caroline had heard about love the second time around but it had only been a wisp of a song. Now she was living the song and her lips trembled as Lee snuggled her closely.

Callie backed out of the kitchen quickly and slammed into Derrick as she came around the corner empty handed. "I thought you went in there to fill the candy plate?" He looked around him. "What'd you do with it?"

She put her finger to her lips and tiptoed away from the door, pulling him along with her. "There's something going on in there and the candy didn't seem important. I'm not sure but I think something is **really** going on!" Her lips quirked upwards and her eyes danced.

"Who's in there?" He glanced toward the door and back at her.

"Caroline and Lee and they're all alone." Her face crinkled in a smile.

"Let's leave this party then. You never did tell me why you flew the coop Friday morning... It's cold outside but not raining so how about driving up the Vista loop to the Japanese Gardens? You can tell me all about it then."

"Isn't that a lover's lane, Derrick?" Her voice slurred dramatically with laughter.

"It is if we want it to be." He matched her mood and grabbed their coats.

Laura hugged Caroline goodbye shortly after Callie and Derrick made their exit, wondering about her fresh glow.

"It's been marvelous. I will be in touch with your friend, Janine. She is perfect for a project I'm just beginning. Please continue what you're doing," she whispered into Caroline's ear.

"What's that, Laura?" she said, impishly.

"Kicking butt, lady…. And don't let that man out of your sight either!" Laura laughed at the look on her face and squeezed her hand. She wrapped her coat around her body and walked out the door.

Alone at last, the evening yawned before them as they rehashed the day and smiled into one another's eyes.

"That wasn't so bad now, was it?" Lee whispered.

"No it wasn't and I have a feeling it can only get better," she whispered with an encouraging smile.

"True eloquence consists in saying all that is necessary, and nothing but what is necessary."
—LA ROUCHEFOUCAULD

Chapter 33

* * *

The Channel 6 television van was parked at the curb in front of Larkspur's offices when the staff arrived Monday morning. Curious employees, thoughtful neighbors and interested bystanders watched men go in and out of the building, carrying lights, boxes, and black speakers. Then Michael Mahone arrived.

Mike was a prominent anchorman for Channel 6, had been their newscaster for years and he got smarter, wiser and better as he grew older. Barely 61, married with two daughters, he was best know as a fighter for the underdog, the victim. Preparing for the news conference with Caroline Phillips emphasized his desire to see justice was served.

His light blue eyes, sandy brown hair and easy smile matched his friendliness and sincerity on and off camera. He'd grown up about 75 miles south of Portland, in the small town of Albany. He'd spent all his school years there; all his schoolmates had liked him. As a man, his stature grew in the same vein. He was a well dressed and well-loved Christian man and his longevity at Channel 6 attested to that visage.

One of his schoolmates, Patty Bettencourt, commented during an interview that he'd always made her feel special; always had a ready smile, sensing her shyness. Helping her avoid the fear of rejection that ripped through her at the thought of reaching out to schoolmates she didn't know well, he always said the first hello. And she never forgot. She was just one of many schoolmates who watched their friend on television and reaffirmed their beliefs in him with each newscast.

Today, he shifted his briefcase, opened the door for a friendly young woman and hastened into the elevator.

"You're Mike Mahone, aren't you?" She asked, hesitantly, as she punched the button.

"Yes, I am." He noticed his floor button was lit. He held the case and stared at the floor, imagining the conference ahead of him. He'd gotten the call Saturday; he'd prepared briefly. Sundays were his family day and work didn't impinge there, so he'd work with what he had.

I'm just a figurehead here today anyway. Dear God, she *needs some support after what the Oregonian did to her.* He sputtered to himself and noticed he must have made a sound because the woman was staring at him.

They laughed and the elevator doors opened into a lighted, carpeted hallway. He looked both ways, unsure where the men had set up the lights and microphones.

"That way is the conference room, Mike. I'll show you," the redheaded woman pointed assuming he'd followed.

"Thanks, Miss........."

"Lana Potts. I'm Caroline's secretary. She's expecting you." Her voice was protective.

"Yes, I'm going to help her get started and film the conference. It will be on the 5 and 6 o'clock news tonight. I haven't talked to her yet, but talked with her lawyer."

"That would be Lee Carle. I'm sure he's already there." She pushed heavy wooden doors inward.

Mike could see a blonde woman in a bright red suit standing by the window talking earnestly with a man a little taller than she was. He was bearded and appeared deep in conversation. "Is that her?" he pointed.

Lana swung around and nodded. "Yes, that's her. I'll be back in a little while." She left as quickly as she'd arrived and Mike joined his assistants to make last minute changes to their normal routine by moving some lights and asking them to re-do the microphone so she had it clipped tightly to her jacket during her speech.

"She's starting and finishing. She'll give a speech and then I'll close it off and ask her a few scripted questions. Then we're out of here. Got it, Ben?"

Everyone nodded, curious about the change in the normal agenda. Holding the tall light, the shortest man pointed it toward the dais. The other moved the microphone away from the dais and adjusted the camera while Mike walked over to the couple still in the midst of whispered conversation.

She clipped the mini-microphone to her lapel.

Mike watched her smile at Ben as she adjusted it tightly at his instruction.

"Caroline Phillips?" She turned and smiled at the man she'd seen on television so often.

"Mike. You look just the same as you do on TV. Thanks for fitting this in at the last minute. This is my attorney, Lee Carle. He suggested a press conference for obvious reasons. I've decided to focus attention on positives rather than negatives and that awful article. Is that ok with you?"

Mike grinned. "It's exactly the thing to do, Ms. Phillips."

"Caroline, please." She reached out and guided him to the dais and felt Lee at her elbow.

The conference room barely accommodated the crowd. Board members, staff members, some doctors and the television crew waited, watching. The air was tense with silence. A helicopter landed on the helipad on the next building. Caroline's eyes strayed for a moment, and then stepped up on the dais, feeling her leg misbehave an instant before allowing her to stand tall.

Lana and Callie stood at the back of the room watching Caroline with bated breaths.

"What do you think of the red suit?" Callie grinned, feeling her stomach go taut.

Lana smiled. "It's just like her, isn't it? Meet fire with fire so to speak?"

They laughed quietly. "It's so serious in here. It's like someone died, for goodness sakes." Lana whispered.

"Yes, I know. She's tough though. Let's see what she has to say about that damned article." Callie clasped her hands in front of her, eyes strained. "*Mon dieu.*"

A hushed silence preceded Caroline's wan smile as she nodded toward Mike. Apprehensive curiosity filled the room.

"Good morning." Without waiting for a response, she continued, feeling her knees shake. "Today is the beginning of a solution to a problem, not as a rebuttal to Friday's *Oregonian* article that I'm sure you have all read." She stopped a moment to take a breath and heard murmurs surround her.

"The solution I'm addressing is our fight to retain a law that allows us to get our prescription drugs outside America. Yes, we've fought long and hard. All of us at Larkspur consider this a pharmacy war. Yes, I'm a proud American. Yes, I'd like to trust and buy drugs in America. But, I am going to find drugs for our members without cutting off their grocery budget and because I refuse to buy into the big-business creed where greed has become a cultural value in healthcare."

Nodding heads heightened her confidence as she continued, "The *Oregonian*'s blunt description of the happenings in the past year as we've fought to safeguard the law and push for our new drug card to be on the market January 1st is fraught with distortions of the truth. The reasons are unclear to me and to those who have fought beside me. I've thought long and hard about why someone would stand in the way of helping us find a solution that is long overdue. The only answer is maximizing financial assets for themselves. I am telling you today what is vitally important to me, to Larkspur and to you. Like any war, there are always two or more competing forces. In a war, there is always a winner and a loser. In a war, there is always a significant prize. That prize is freedom to go outside the box."

The board members and the staff nodded agreement and clapped, silencing her a moment. She looked up and smiled as her eyes encompassed the people sitting and standing around her. She felt compassion, friendship and agreement. And her heart swelled.

A friendly aura surrounded Mike Mahone as he lifted his microphone. "Ms. Phillips, are you saying that the drug card you managed to add to your benefits from Canada is moving ahead then?" His face invited her to lay it out just as Lee and Mike had discussed Saturday.

Caroline smiled into his blue eyes, nodding her thanks for bringing up the very point she had been trying to make. She reached into her suit pocket and wrapped her hand around the plastic card and lifted it up for everyone to see. "This is Larkspur's gift to the community. It will save everyone money and everyone who has Larkspur drug coverage will have access to it. The cards are being printed now and should be in everyone's hands around Christmas time."

She took a breath and stared directly into the camera.

She spoke with a fierce and determined force. "We have a formidable opponent in our midst. One who remains hidden? One who shoots in the dark with a secret agenda? Whoever you are, we know your aim must be the almighty dollar. Profits to line your silk purse will not stop us. This is a mighty war and I intend to make everyone a winner. I am not giving in to your tactics like a week-kneed coward." Caroline's throat swelled with broken tears.

Then she marched forward with words meant to stop the tide of criticism. "As far as the computer hacker described in the paper, Mr. Roget voluntarily entered a mental rehabilitation program because he was ill and he knew it. He's getting help. He is not the unfeeling monster others perceive from the Oregonian article. I have forgiven him and wish him only the best."

Whew. That hurt to spit out. She reached for the water glass. She glanced at Lee, inviting a proud smile before catching Laura Amburgey's wink beside him.

She hadn't realized she'd been holding her breath until she let it out. "Confidential health information was never accessed by anyone, especially Mr. Roget. The only information he stole pertained to our drug card contract. We do not know who employed him to do that...........yet."

"In closing, to assure you how serious we are to make changes, we have implemented our own Medical Affairs Director, Dr. Sam James. We have cut all ties with Premier. Now, we stand alone. With our member's support we will continue to be the best damn insurance company you expect and deserve." She licked her lips and glanced at Mike, who joined in the applause that ripped through the room.

Stepping toward the dais, he lifted the microphone again, but the noise interfered with any possible interview or question. He raised his eyebrows to his cameraman and centered himself in front of the dais. "Caroline Phillips, CEO of Larkspur intends to keep her drug card and she has met the challenge from a rogue competitor. Mike Mahone. Channel 6. Good night and thank you for joining us."

Callie felt a touch at her elbow as she inched toward Caroline. *Boy! She really kicks butt*, she marveled as she pushed her way toward the end of the room. The crowd was rushing in the same direction, inadvertently causing her to stumble. "Oh!" The air whooshed out of her as she was gathered around the waist and lifted upright.

"...You okay?" Derrick breathed close to her ear and felt her ribs beneath his fingers.

"Derrick! That was close... Thanks." She didn't want him to let go of her. "Guess I'm not going to get up there, so I'll talk to her later. She really hit them between the eyes, huh?"

"Yes, she did that. And more power to her. You know, I keep thinking about your friend that we met at Alexander's. I saw her at Caroline's yesterday and it is driving me nuts trying to remember where I've seen her.... I'm headed back to my office. Can I walk you back to yours? I assume that's where you're going?" She nodded and took his arm to work their way out of the crowd, thinking it reminded her of the maze in the countryside beside Leed's Castle in England.

Warmth enveloped her as she met his stride and contentment washed over her. "Janine's married, Derrick."

"Huh?" His head swung around in surprise, and saw she was teasing him. He snorted.

"I suppose Carl is nervous about surgery tomorrow?" She asked.

"No, and we're having a Tums-burning party." Chuckling, he said, "any chance you can have a drink with me at **Wilf's** later?"

"Oh, that lovely old train station! I haven't been there in ages. Is the piano bar still there?" The smile reached her eyes and sat there.

"Yes, and it's so cozy with those over-stuffed chairs and no sports on a blaring television. Just music..."

His voice sounded like velvet.

Her heart raced as she checked her watch. "I have meetings off and on all day and a deposition to do at a client's office later this afternoon. Why don't I drop by your office if I get back before 5:00?

As they neared her office, Derrick felt reluctant to leave her.

"Perfect. If you're already out and about, why not just call from the car and I'll meet you there?" The gold flecks danced in his gray eyes as he caressed her forearm, before backing down the hallway waiting for her reply.

"Sure." Looking around to see if anyone was within earshot, she waved him on his way. *"And* I look forward to it." She whispered loudly.

The afternoon dragged as Derrick sifted through notes and clicked his keyboard. Designing the website was just the beginning. Changing, updating and daily maintenance was his core competency, his pride and joy. And he liked having only one company to focus on. The daily frustration he encountered at his previous job was a far cry from those he encountered now. In San Diego, he'd contended with over twenty clients. He was responsible for daily changes, on call constantly, and the stress alone tired him. He loved his job at Larkspur, but he kept looking at his watch, willing the day to end.

Eric grinned from the doorway. "Telephone. I need to go down to accounting. Be right back. Good news, Grandpa," he said.

He heard Eric's laughter and welcomed the interruption as he picked up the phone. "Hey, sweetie. Another call so soon? I like that."

"Dad! There are three babies. I am having THREE babies." Her voice was tremulous and excited.

"Oh my dear girl. I am having trouble swallowing. Three?!"

"I wish you were closer, Dad. I want to share this with you so much."

At that moment, Callie hurried into the corridor trying to beat her self-imposed deadline. *We can drive to **Wilfs** together. Oh, these feelings are sweet. It seems like my heart is beating too fast all the time. The sky is brighter. The people are friendlier. The music is more beautiful. Life is wonderful. I love him. I LOVE him.* She mentally hugged herself as she approached his office.

Eric wasn't there so she rushed toward the doorway. She watched Derrick as he sat in his chair facing the window. She smiled toward him in silence. Then the smile froze on her face.

"I miss you too, darling. I think about you every day." Derrick's voice softened. "Okay, bye Sophia, I'll call you again soon."

Callie stiffened and immediately shrunk back from the doorway. Feeling as if a shot of lead pierced through her, she reached for the doorframe and caught a sob. *No. No. No.* A sharp headache slashed into her temples as she retraced her steps and got back onto the elevator. *Wait!* She jumped back off, went back to Derrick's office and jotted a note on a slip of paper near Eric's phone. Then she left the building.

An hour later, Derrick was surprised that Callie hadn't called, so he dialed her cell phone. *Damn. No answer.* He dialed her office. No answer. Swiveling around in his chair, he closed his files and started to clean off his desk when he saw Eric come in the door.

"Derrick. When I got back from accounting, I found a note on my desk from Callie. He handed the piece of paper to Derrick.

"I'm leaving for the day. See you tomorrow. Good luck with your Dad's surgery."

Derrick nodded and looked at the note in his hand. "Derrick —- Can't meet you tonight. Callie"

"That's cryptic," he said aloud. Stuffing the note into his jacket pocket, he dialed her home. The message machine picked up.

"Callie, this is Derrick. Sorry you had to cancel *Wilfs*. What's up? I'll call you later." He put the receiver down, lost in thought and not just a little troubled.

Callie sat on the couch with her feet curled beneath her. She warmed her hands with a cup of hot tea. Feeling sick and for the moment, beyond tears, her mind in turmoil. She listened to Derrick's voice cut through the living room and shook the fuzz from her head. *Why did I allow myself to get involved? It's the same old thing… Are there any honest men left? I don't think so.*

She sipped her tea and felt tears brewing close to the surface, but forced them back. *I won't allow my naiveté to spoil my life! Thank God I didn't sleep with him. Oh, God.* She put down the cup and covered her face, falling onto the couch as great quaking sobs shook her. *I really thought he felt the same way. Damn. Damn. Damn.* She hit the pillow and pushed her face deeply into the afghan, letting it capture the salty tears. Her chest hurt and her throat was clogged, causing short, sharp breaths to escape. *Oh damn.*

After she felt capable of moving, she lifted the tea, now cold. Dragging into the kitchen, she heated up another cup and switched on the news. *Caroline's press conference should be on.* She haphazardly returned to the couch and felt a heavy numbness return.

Suddenly, Mike Mahone's smiling face filled the screen, followed closely by a view of the bridges across the Willamette River, lights dotting the waterway like diamonds tossed from a mountain of glass.

Then, Caroline's voice spun its web of sincerity. *She sounded so good. I never did talk to her today. In fact I haven't talked to her since I left yesterday when she and Lee were holed up in the kitchen.* She sniffed, blew her nose and turned up the volume to finish the news; admiring her friend and feeling pride swell within her.

As Caroline finished and Mike Mahone ended what started out to be an interview, his voice cut in immediately for a breaking piece of local news.

"The dead man found behind **Zupan's** on West Burnside and S.W. Vista Avenues late Friday night has been identified as Dr. Delbert Reed, the Medical Affairs Director for Premier Health. The coroner's report stated he died of a massive heart attack but the Portland Police are investigating the circumstances surrounding his death. It appears that he was pushed into a corner behind the dumpster and the time of death is estimated at sometime Friday morning. His wife, Lorraine Reed was unavailable for comment."

Callie's eyes grew wide. "Del Reed? Is this an eerie coincidence or am I looking for ghosts?" Heart hammering, she dialed Caroline's office number.

"Caroline Phillip's office." Lana answered.

"Hey, what are you still doing there?" Callie asked.

"Oh, I'm just leaving, Callie. Caroline's inside. You want to speak with her?"

"Yes, please." Callie waited on the line, listening to Mozart .

"Hi Callie! What a day. Are you in your office?" Caroline sounded tired.

"No, I'm home.......... It's a long story. Have you heard about Del Reed?" Callie answered evasively before turning urgently toward the television again.

"No, what about him?"

"He's dead! I just heard it on the Channel 6 news just after your press release. I figured you'd be watching it. Anyway, they say he died of a heart attack but he was stashed behind a dumpster in **Zupan's** lot."

"No kidding! My God. How awful, Callie." Caroline's stomach lurched. "A terrible coincidence in the middle of all this mess, don't.... you.... think?" she asked her friend slowly.

"Yes, that's what I thought too." Callie took a deep breath. "Well, how are you, Caroline? Haven't talked to you since you and Lee............"

"I'm wonderful," Caroline's voice turned silky and warm. "Just wonderful. I admitted my feelings to Lee and guess what? He feels the same way and....he........"

Callie cut in, "......That's fabulous, Caroline. I'm thrilled for you. I know it's crazy and last minute, but I need to take a week off. I'm going back to the cottage... to get away to think about some things and I've put off my vacation and......" Her words rolled out to silence.

"What happened?" Caroline's voice was suddenly alert.

Callie took another deep breath and closed her eyes a moment, "Caroline, I really can't talk about it now and especially not on the phone. I'll send an email to cancel my appointments. There's only three and I'll be back a week from tomorrow. You have the number there. I won't leave my cell phone on. And Caroline?"

"Callie, I wish.........?"

"I am so happy for you. Hold onto it and don't let go. I'll check in later. I love you."

Caroline frowned after Callie hung up. "Now what is going on? If it's not one thing, it's another. When is life just going to ease up and just let us enjoy it?" she mumbled to the empty room. Hearing the helicopter vibrating outside her window and centering on the terrible news about Del Reed spun her into action. She grabbed her cane and left her office.

*   *   *

"Where is she this late?" Derrick asked himself as he hung up the phone for the fourth time that evening. "It doesn't make sense and it's so unlike her.... Just when I thought I was turning a page in my life."

The phone jangled again and he picked it up quickly.

"I'm nervous as hell, son. Can you bring dinner over tonight?" Carl asked.

"Sure, Dad. I don't have any plans," Derrick answered flatly.

"Good. Glad to hear it. Ted's bowling."

"Well, how are you doing?" Derrick asked anxiously.

"Everybody I can. You're next." Carl said with a light-hearted chuckle, missing the troubled tone in his son's voice.

"Thanks, Dad. I needed a laugh. I'll be there in half an hour." Heading for his father's house, he stopped at KFC and picked up dinner and another package of Tums.

"It is a misery to be born, a pain to live, a trouble to die.
—St. Bernard of Clair-Vaux

Chapter 34

* * *

"I don't care. I will pee on my own!" Carl Leander stated loudly. The nurse stared at him, hands on hips, unmoving. She pursed her lips as she held the replacement catheter near the bed, and then flounced out of the room in search of a supervisor.

Derrick walked into his hospital room, aghast. "Dad. Good Lord. What's going on? Can't you just let them do what they need to do for you?" His son lounged at the bedside and touched his father's wrinkled hand lying on top of the covers.

"Have you ever had a catheter stuck up your............." Carl stopped suddenly as he saw the shadow of a woman standing in the doorway.

"Alice?"

"Yes, it's me, Carl. Just thought I'd see how you were doing." His neighbor walked in timidly and smiled shyly at the men. "Don't want to interrupt but wanted to let you know I made a nice pot of Italian Lasagna and froze it in three nice packages for when you get home. And a Carrot Cake...all ready for you. Now, I'll be leavin'. I just wanted to see you with my own old eyes that you're ok." She said as she backed toward the doorway, feeling flustered.

"No, wait." Carl's voice rose and a weak smile lit his face. "Son, you've met Alice, haven't you?" he asked Derrick, his eyes pleading with a no-jokes look.

"Yes, a few months ago." He reached out to shake Alice's hand and pulled her back into the room. "Actually, I was just heading back to work, so I'm glad you're here to chat a bit. This old goat is giving the nurses a hard time. Maybe a woman's touch..." He winked at his father and saw the old man roll his eyes. "I mean a woman's *point of view* will give him some clarity."

Carl glared at Derrick and pursed his lips, as Alice sank thankfully into a chair and scooted it toward the bedside.

"Well, Carl. What are you doing to push the envelope around here?" she said, as she watched Derrick leave, an impish smile accompanying her words.

Derrick laughed all the way to his car. *Just what the old man needs: A woman.* Suddenly, his face grew serious.

In the corridor, he saw the woman again. *Now a volunteer handing out magazines in the hospital? Where on earth? This is driving me crazy... even though Dad always says that's not a long putt... Hmmmm...*

After starting his Explorer and driving slowly away from the hospital, he dialed Callie's number as he sat at the red light on Glisan Street. He was stunned when her secretary told him she was out for the week.

"What? A week's vacation? When did she decide *that?*"

"Yesterday afternoon, Derrick." The woman's voice answered apologetically.

"Well, do you know where she went?" his voice raised an octave, staggered.

"No, she didn't explain. We just cancelled her appointments for the week."

"Ok. Thanks." He took a deep breath before punching in Caroline's number.

"Lana. This is Derrick. Do you know where Callie is?" Feeling himself lose momentum, he pulled over to the side of the road to talk and mull over the conversation.

"No, I don't, Derrick. I'm surprised too, and Caroline's not here. Do you want her voicemail?"

"No, I'll call again. Thanks." He hung up the cell phone and sat in his car a few minutes, trying to figure out what to do. "Damn. This is too crazy. What in hell happened and why...?" Choking on his disappointment and frustrations, he set the car toward the office and tried to minutely dissect the last time he'd seen Callie.

*   *   *

TUESDAY'S Oregonian had a picture of Del Reed, with an ominous headline.

Premier's Medical Affairs Director Found Dead

Vincent Bertrand scanned the article; his cold eyes alight with morbid curiosity. His thumb rubbed back and forth on the page as he read that the police were investigating what looked like a heart attack but questioned the circumstances.

Well, they don't have anything on me. He was about through here anyway. I'll handle Ace-Deer without him. He pulled out the contract he'd signed with Del four years earlier and dismally noted the caveat naming his wife as beneficiary to all his proceeds. "Well, she's not getting his money back either. Dividends only. Period." He snorted and wished he had his pipe.

"Detective Childs is on line one, doctor." His secretary told him.

His heartbeat accelerated as he picked up the phone. "Hello, this is Doctor Bertrand."

"Yes, doctor. I'd like a few minutes of your time this morning if I may. I am working on the Del Reed case and........."

"I didn't know him socially; he was the Medical Affairs Director for Premier but....."

"You were his employer, were you not?"

"Yes, of course, but.........."

"Will 10:30 work for you?"

"Well, it cuts into my patient load, but if you must, come ahead so I can get it over with." Well after hearing the dismissive click, Vincent stared nervously at the receiver he held in his hand. Finally he set it down, chewed the inside of his lip and swore, "Damn. Well, I'll just play it cool and they'll go onto the next person. Del was a stupid idiot. Why'd he have to come to my place anyway? He was such an asshole; I should never have gotten hooked up with him in the first place." He put his elbows on his desk and rubbed his face, sighing loudly in the room.

And then he kicked his trash can across the room.

There was a gentle tap on the door, and Sally poked her head in the office. "Doctor Bertrand, is there something wrong?"

"Well what could be wrong? My Medical Affairs Director is dead and the police want to talk to me about his death."

"Oh, yes... the murder on Friday." She said simply, shaking her head.

"Nobody said it was murder, Sally." His tone was more abrupt than it warranted. She slipped out and quietly shut the door.

Caroline returned to her office to find a Federal Express letter waiting for her from Laura Amburgey. Ripping it open, she pulled the letter out, amused at the little happy faces that littered the borders. Short and sweet. The letters were spread out across the page in big, bold capitals.

> **YOU WON.**
> **THE BILL WAS KILLED.**
> **WILDING'S LOCKED IN HIS OFFICE WITH HIS BOTTLE**
> **MY HAT IS OFF TO YOU. YOU HAVE GUTS, LADY**
> Laura

Caroline lifted her skirt a few inches and danced a jig, babying her leg and wincing slightly, but still holding the letter out in front of her with both hands. "Lana!"

Lana popped her head inside the door.

"Read it!" Caroline tossed it into Lana's hands and watched her, eyes sparkling.

Lana read it quickly and raised her eyes, "Well, that's that. Thank God. And you already have the prescription identification cards done, right?"

"Well, no, not exactly." Caroline hedged.

"But I saw you show the ID card to everyone yesterday at the news conference......." Lana's eyes questioned Caroline as a light dawned. "That was a fake? Oh my God, and you pulled it off. I didn't even realize it. Guess that's why you're the CEO and I'm not, huh?" She laughed at Caroline's look, hugged her and headed for the door.

"Well, wish I could show Callie." Caroline murmured.

"Where is she anyway? Derrick was looking for her and he sounds so concerned. I really felt sorry for the guy." Lana stared at Caroline for an answer.

"Well, something odd is going on and I really don't know. But I know if she wanted him to know where she was, she'd tell him, so guess mum's the word for now." Caroline raised one eyebrow, "so I'll keep it to myself. That way, you won't be forced to lie, ok?" Her gray eyes looked sad.

Lana shrugged. "Okay, but I hope she's all right." Her red hair swayed against her neck as she left the room, her thoughts jumbled with her own issues. *God help us,* she thought. *Steven has to get well and I just have to make things better for all of us.* "Just let it happen," she whispered as she pulled out her office chair and nodded at the girl rushing past her desk.

And, oh, Callie —- where are you??

"To err is human, to forgive divine.
—POPE – *Essay on criticism*

Chapter 35

✳ ✳ ✳

The morning of Del Reed's funeral dawned bright and clear. Stilted atmosphere moved through Zeller's Chapel of the Roses. People assembled quietly, shaking hands and nodding to acquaintances and co-workers from Premier. Neighbors, acquaintances and Master Gardeners lined the pews as they listened to the pianist play *In the Garden* magically through the chapel.

Inside the small side room, Lorraine Reed sat quietly, staring into the main chapel through a privacy screen. She saw the casket and knew Del laid quietly, hands folded over his impeccable navy suit and he would never be on that cruise ship with her. He'd never share meals, gardening, laughter or her bed again. Del was gone. Her head hung down and her eyes were closed tightly as she tried to hold in the tears. She gripped the black purse on her lap and the large white handkerchief squeezed between her fingers, allowing the large marquee diamond on her left hand to shimmer from the light above. She moved an iota, opened her wet eyes and stared at it, seeing the tiny lights sparkle. *Oh, Del, what am I going to do without you?*

Lorraine and Del had planned a cruise to Italy when he retired. The brochures were scattered all over the coffee table in the den, as they'd mulled over the booklets and talked for hours about the life of retirement. It would have been only two months away. She struggled with the recent memories as she'd watched a new Del emerge from the workaholic he'd been for so many years. *The last couple of weeks or maybe longer… He'd been like the man I married so long ago. Warmth had emanated from his face and his kisses and hugs more prolonged. Oh, God, what am I going to do?*

Always an independent woman, she'd leaned on her husband more and more as they'd grown older. She spent hours in her flower garden and he'd spent time at the office. They'd pulled away from each other over the years and she'd turned to volunteer work and writing. "But lately, he was so much........." her lips quivered and she felt the tears run into her mouth, dripping down her chin.

Piano music was playing softly. She could hear a door open on her right and she glanced up to see the funeral director talking to her. She stared at him, seeing his mouth move but her mind was a blank dull throbbing unit of pain. Leaning down, he reached for her hand, "Mrs. Reed. It's time to begin. Would you like to remain here or would you like to move forward? We can certainly keep the privacy curtain pulled, if you wish." He waited for some life to come into the woman's face and she just stared at him.

"I want to stay here, if that's all right. I can see him from here and ...." Lips trembled once again and she raised the handkerchief to her mouth.

The black-suited man nodded, understandingly. "You have several nieces and a nephew who would like to sit with you."

"Please tell them I will see them later. I need solitude right now."

He nodded again and backed out of the room, clicking the door shut quietly after squeezing her shoulder in sympathy. *Family could help her right now, but all I can do is suggest,* he thought sorrowfully.

The next thirty minutes passed in a blur but she didn't move, nor did she look toward the large room except once. *It's filled with so many people and I don't know any of them except my garden club ladies.* She allowed herself a small smile. *No kids, just friends. No parents. Both of us cursed to be only children. We only had each other. Everyone is gone now. I'm alone and everyone is gone. I could use a brother or sister right about now.* Her heart lurched at the thoughts and she fought against the onslaught of the tears that pierced her eyelids. Nieces and a nephew? Where were they before? She smiled scornfully. Why come out of the woodwork now? She knew they were Del's step-brother's children and never paid them any attention while Del was alive. And she refused let them intrude into her feelings now.

There was no funeral procession and no burial. As Del requested, he would be cremated and his ashes tossed into the Pacific Ocean just outside Rockaway Beach, where their cabin sat high above the surf. She promised to do it herself, alone with her love and sadness.

LATER, she could hear his voice in her head when she returned home after shaking hundreds of hands and forcing a fledgling smile once the room emptied and she could move. Everything went round and round in her head endlessly.

"Lorraine, when I die, I want you to toss my ashes off the ledge in front of the cabin on a clear day so I can fly with the seagulls that litter the beach. I want to fall into the sand and be left there to rest."

Now, what do I do with the letters? She absently removed her coat, dropped her purse and stared at the wooden box atop the cruise catalogs. There were three of them. One was addressed to The *Oregonian*, c/o Richard Ellis. One was addressed to The Portland Police Department,

Homicide and one was addressed to her. The last one was open and well read, dog-eared and stained with her tears.

Her brow furrowed tightly again as she looked at the box. She'd never seen it before in all their thirty-five years of marriage. *Another secret*, she thought, remembering the contents of his letter to her. The box had been under her side of the bed with the edge sticking out from beneath. She'd found it the night before but he must have put it there Friday. The night he hadn't come home.

Thinking back to that terrible day, she remembered Del reading the paper and then exploding in some sort of maniacal tantrum as he spilled his coffee and hit the table with his hand.

"This is ludicrous," he'd shouted.

Lorraine's lips lifted in a small, sad smile, remembering how she'd nearly dropped her own cup, when he slapped the table. Her memory of leaning over to read the headline about a local CEO for Larkspur and scrutinizing the article came to mind. *I didn't know who the woman was but I recognized Larkspur Health Plan. I wish I knew why it made him so angry...........* She swallowed hard. Her mouth had gone dry.

The last thing I remember is that I lifted my arms and embraced him afterward. He hugged me back with such ferocity and buried his face in the crook of my neck. "If anything unusual happens to me, Lorrie, you will know what to do. I love you, honey, you know that don't you?" He'd said in a muffled voice. Then, he'd looked deeply into her eyes before kissing her forehead and left the house. That was the last she saw of him alive. That was it. He never came back home. She'd called the police but they told her they couldn't put in a Missing Persons Report until he'd been missing at least twenty-four hours. Then, when they found him, his pockets were empty and he was dead. And it had been a nightmare all weekend.

Her eyes brimmed again.

Shaking her head stolidly, she reached for the box again, inhaling the pleasant cedar smell that reminded her of her long-ago childhood. Inside its felt-lined depth, she lifted the stapled papers and scanned them. She'd only read the letters previously. *Why, it's a partnership contract for something named Ace-Deer.* She glanced at the last page, filled with signatures. One signature was Vincent Bertrand's, and below listed her name as beneficiary. And Del's was beside Vincent's. *Hummmmmmmm*, she studied it carefully and saw the $200,000 figure and her eyes grew wide.

"Two hundred thousand dollars!?!" Her chest grew tight and she took a deep breath as she lifted out another smaller envelope. Del's Last Will & Testament. The embossed envelope had a return address listed as Lewis, Carle & Henry. Silas Henry's note was inside and Del's scribbled words across the bottom caught her attention. She set it aside. I'll try to figure out the cryptic words later.

Her hand was shaking as she smoothed out the letter and opened it once again. It was dated one month earlier. *Funny how tears make paper all crunch up,* she thought, sniffing loudly.

My dear Lorrie:

If you are reading this, I am missing or dead. First of all, I ask your forgiveness. I love you and I haven't always let you know that. I've been a first class ass so often and I really wanted us to take that cruise you always talked about. There is something I must explain to you and after you read this, please, Lorrie, BE CAREFUL. Watch your back. I do not trust Vincent Bertrand. He is a nasty character and I'm ashamed I was in business with him at all. You MUST get the letters in this box to the paper and to the police. I would prefer you get the police letter out first. Deliver it yourself. Don't mail it. Do NOT go see Bertrand —- promise me!! No matter how damned mad you are. Do NOT do that. I am serious, honey. Please believe me. Now, I must tell you what I have done and hope you can still think of me with that sweet smile on your face that you manifested no matter how unforgivable my actions have been the past few years.

Lorraine finished reading it again and rubbed her thumb on the words, *I love you,* at the bottom and the capital D beneath it. *I love you too,* she cried. "I love you too........." She debated only a second before her anger propelled her to move.

"Ok, now it's my turn to fight the rest of your battle." She stood up and gazed out toward the pine trees and birdhouses that littered her back yard and started calculating a mental list, numbering them one through five.

Straightening her black-clad shoulders she lifted her head, sniffed again, wiped her nose and stuffed both letters into her purse. "Watch out Vincent Bertrand. I know you may have been the last person to see him, and that means ...."

She stumbled a little, then she stopped to gaze at the cruise brochures. Suddenly, with a new determination, she headed out to the garage and the car beyond *I need to finish this before I go to Rockaway with his ashes.* She pushed the words around in her head like marbles.

Slipping inside Del's BMW seemed to give her the confidence she needed as she drove toward the Police Station in downtown Portland. She parked, and then sat unmoving. Her limbs felt heavy. She adjusted her sunglasses. She looked toward the Willamette River. *It doesn't seem real. I can't believe he's gone. Now I know what eternity really means.* Mentally changing gears, she forced herself to buy the ticket from the meter kiosk, stick it onto the inside of the window of the car and walk up the brick steps. She gripped the letter in her hand.

She got into the car again thirty minutes later, a firmer step leaving the building than when she'd begun the ascent, with her heart beating wildly in her chest. She reached forward to start the car, shifted gears, and pulled the little car out, focused on moving toward the *Oregonian.*

"Ellis, there's a Mrs. Reed here and she needs to give you something personally. She says it's important and wouldn't let me take it for you. Can you come up front, please?" the young blond receptionist spoke into the phone as quietly as she could. Watching the woman across the lobby, she saw her wander to the walls to look at the framed pictures and news articles that covered the area in between.

Richard Ellis scanned his memory. "Reed........Reed........why does that name ring a bell?" He wove his way between desks and computer monitors on his way downstairs and toward the front of the *Oregonian* building. Forehead creased, he hit the bottom of the stairs and walked up to the pacing woman. She was dressed in black and barely five feet tall. Curious bright blue eyes turned toward him as he called her name, appearing large and immensely sad.

"Mrs. Reed?" He extended his hand toward her. His boyish face invited a small smile.

"Yes, I'm Mrs. Reed. Mr. Ellis?" Her voice was soft and low as she looked up into his face.

"What can I do for you?" Shaking his head, he led her to an empty cubicle just around the corner from the front desk. He could feel her sadness permeate the small area and his curiosity grew, inviting her to explain.

"My husband died recently and he left something for me to give to you." She reached into her purse and drew out the long white envelope.

Richard leaned over and took the envelope and turned it over in his hands. "Did I know you husband? I can't recall the name but........."

"Del Reed. He was found dead behind **Zupan's** a few days ago. His memorial service was this morning." The handkerchief reached upward and she blew her nose again.

"Oh I am so sorry. Now I know why your name sounded so familiar." Richard slipped the letter opener under the glued flap and opened it quickly. He looked up at her again, "Do you mind if I read it now in case I have questions for you?"

"No, not at all. Actually, I think I know what's in it." Her hands fidgeted on her purse handle and she moved uncomfortably in the wooden chair. She watched his lips move slightly as he read and saw his eyes open wider.

He scanned two pages, neatly-typed and double-spaced. Lorraine saw his look of surprise and then he glanced toward her again. "Wow. One hell of a mess. So you know your husband's death might not have been natural? I mean, I'm sorry, Mrs. Reed. This explains some fears he had and something that could really answer some big questions that have been spirited around Portland the last few months. Are you prepared to read it because I would like to do your husband's bidding and see this in print?" He released his breath and stared into her face.

"That's why I'm here. Do with it as you want. What's a few words when it's caused my husband's death? I mean how much worse can it get, right?" Her sarcasm wasn't lost on him and he shook his head.

Hurriedly folding the papers, he walked her to the front door, shook her hand and watched her blink rapidly. "Again, please accept my deepest sympathy, Mrs. Reed."

Lips quivering, she quickly turned and pushed the large doors open.

Standing in the near-empty lobby, he stood quietly and leaned against the wall, pinching the letter tightly. His shoulders remained still for another second before he shifted gears and jogged back to his desk.

*   *   *

Vincent Bertrand returned to his office, glad to leave the funereal atmosphere behind. *Okay, I've done my duty. He would've died soon anyway,* he argued. *Hearts are like that. Fickle organs—— and Del had shown signs of a a heart problem. It's not like I actually killed him. He must've seen it coming. What an ass to goad me that way. Well, now I just need to straighten out the Ace-Deer contract and ....Maybe I'll just let it ride. No sense in upsetting the good widow. She probably doesn't even know the contract exists.* His ice blue eyes revealed a sinister reflection in his office window as he reached for the pipe in his pocket. *This damned no-smoking law!* He placed the empty pipe between his lips and sucked on it harshly.

I should have just pushed him inside his car. It would've looked normal. Since I couldn't find the damn car, I had to get him downstairs and into my car... That crazy Mrs. Loring believed he was just drunk. Nobody would believe her if she said anything different... Why I thought Zupan's would be a good place, I'll never know. It was close and I wanted to be home when Janine came back. No questions that way. Dammit. He really screwed up my day.

Pulling his pipe out of his mouth, he told his secretary, "No calls today, Sally. And move all my appointments to next week, would you? I have a splitting headache." He stuffed the pipe back between his teeth and bit down hard. Closing his door firmly, he pulled out the Ace-Deer contracts and mused over the beneficiary caveat.

Vincent scrutinized the signatures, and realized the last page could be changed a little with some ingenuity. He refused to let his planning go awry. A fearsome grin split his face and he tossed the papers into his bottom desk drawer and locked it.

"It takes two to speak the truth —- one to speak, and another to hear.""
—THOREAU

Chapter 36

* * *

allie blinked awake when the phone beside her bed jarred her loose from the bedcovers. The room was bright with sunshine. Nerves taut, she picked up the receiver and heard Caroline's strident voice.

"Callie? My God, I woke you didn't I? It's after noon. What is wrong with you?"

"Please....Caro. I......." she answered, groggily.

Caroline heard her intake of breath, then silence and felt a knot in the pit of her stomach. "Were you asleep, Callie?"

"Yes, I was. I took a sleeping pill. I'm on vacation, remember?" Callie rolled over and sunk down deeper in her bed.

"When are you coming home?" Caroline's voice was strident.

"Probably Sunday morning. I thought I'd just laze around here until the last minute. I have food and lots of wood. It's nice and quiet and I'm walking through my mind and erasing anything that hurts." Callie squeezed the receiver. "I'm ok, Caro."

"Yes, sure you are. Wish you'd talk to me...." Scribbling a note for Lana, she reached for her purse and hand lotion, stuffing it into her briefcase. Clicking off her computer, she locked her desk and finished with, "What happened to talking over problems with your best friend?"

"Caroline. I'm not ready, but I will be soon. I promise. I'm going back to sleep now. Thanks for worrying. Love you." She clicked the phone into its cradle, thumped the pillow again and burrowed into it. It had been one of the longest weeks in Callie's life. The thrill of returning to the cottage the past weekend, the warmth that had enveloped her with Derrick's entrance in her life and the subsequent hurt kept her mind in a tail spin and she had stepped a million paces backward, into the heart-hurt time when Francois left her alone and lost. Numb and frightened as she tried to hold her heart in one piece, she realized there would never be enough masking tape to hold in the pieces. She shuddered involuntarily and pulled the covers over her head again and fought for surcease she knew only sleep could offer.

Four days and I'm still as screwed up as I was when I got here, she mused. *I'm in mourning all over again. The only time I think about Derrick's betrayal is when I'm awake, so I'll fix that and go back to sleep. It's like when Francois died, like I've lost a part of me all over again. Only this time, there are no shirts to smell in the closet or shaving kit to stare at me from the bathroom counter. This time, there are only memories to force out. I'm better off alone anyway. I'm fine with myself.* She held her lids tightly over her eyes, praying for sleep.

When Callie woke up the next time, the room was bright with sunshine and her bed was a tangled mess of sheets and covers. Screaming mind chatter slipped in and out of her consciousness and forced her to close her eyes into temporary forgetfulness.

As Caroline prepared to leave her office, she found Janine tapping on her doorframe.

"Hey, come in." Caroline invited, as she put down her purse hurriedly.

"*Mon cherie.* Can you slip away for *café au lait?*" Janine asked, hopefully.

"Oh, dear. I can't today. I'm just leaving for the day. Can I get you a quick cup here??"

Janine's eyes lit up and Caroline felt a heavy sadness for the woman. "Actually, no coffee, just a quick visit will make me happy."

"Tell me, Janine. You told me you were interested in doing something other than volunteer work and I know you've done a lot of interior design. Would you be inclined to help plan a wedding? It would be like designing a beautiful room, wouldn't it?"

"Oh my," her eyes welled with moisture. She clapped her hands and smiled. "You?"

Caroline nodded, sharing the glory of the discussion. "I will keep my professional name since it's on all sorts of contracts and nobody would know me if I changed it but..... yes, me!"

"Oh *oui,* I would love that very much. I kept my family name when I married too. When is it planned and where do we begin?" Excitement crossed her features.

"I'd like to get together next week and Callie will be back by then. She will be my Maid of Honor and we can plan it all. I am very happy. Maybe we can finally meet that husband of yours. Sometimes I wonder if he's just a figment of your imagination." Caroline said, laughter meeting her eyes as she watched her friend's troubled face.

"*Non,* V.B. is quite real." Janine's eyes skidded away a moment.

"V.B.? I thought his name was Vincent?" Caroline said, looking confused.

"Oh yes, his name is Vincent and sometimes I call him V.B. for……… I know you are leaving and I won't keep you now. Call me and we can begin the planning, *oui?*" She lifted her purse and stood, leaving a breath of French-perfume in the air behind.

Caroline stared thoughtfully after her.

A couple hours later, the sound of hammering wiped the lingering sleep from her body. *What is all that noise? Who's beating on something?* Callie lifted her head. *What?*

"Callie…………. Callie……….. Open up!" Caroline's voice filtered through the walls and Callie jerked up to a sitting position.

"Damn." Yanking her thick robe around her, she tied the belt and stood in her bedroom doorway, staring into her friend's eyes as she pressed her face against the glass in the Dutch door across the expanse of the galley kitchen. She thumped over to the door unhappily and opened the door without a word.

Caroline plopped her overnight bag onto the bottom of the stairs, took off her coat and returned to the door. Reaching around on the deck, she retrieved the two large bottles of Chilean wine, fresh Brie, warm baguettes and cluster of grapes that she'd purchased from Lincoln City for the duration.

Callie stood and watched her move through the cottage as if she owned the place. "What is this all about? I think my being alone was best, Caroline. I'm God-awful company right now."

Caroline continued to unload the paper bag, reached for plates, wine glasses, knives and the bowl for the grapes. She hummed to herself … *Love is a Many-Splendored Thing*. She turned, finally, and faced Callie with a laden tray and worried smile on her heart-shaped face. "Let's eat first and talk after."

"Well, let me get some clothes on and I'll be out then," she answered flatly, knowing she had no other choice.

A few minutes later, Caroline had the fire built up and opened all the window blinds. The view of Devil's Lake was awesome as she watched the water lapping on the sandy beach where the end of the green grassy slope fell into the water. The boat dock was empty and geese swam in small groups around the boat ramp even though it was quite cold. She hugged herself and waited.

A noise alerted her to Callie's presence but she remained standing in front of the wall of windows, articulating her thoughts and trying to lift her spirits before she turned around.

"Well, let's eat then," Callie's voice invited, soft and low. Her purple sweat pants fought with the bright red sweatshirt but her face dared Caroline to say so.

The women looked at one another a moment, then walked toward each other with arms outstretched. Caroline's arms held tightly as she felt Callie's body shake within her embrace.

"Oh, dear heart. Please talk to me." She pulled Callie toward the thick couch and the tray that waited for them on the big coffee table before the fire.

"Let's sit on the floor in front of the hearth like we used to do years ago, Caro. We can reach the wine and Brie easily." She pushed her butt onto a cushion and sat cross-legged, reaching for a hunk of bread and cheese as Caroline popped a juicy grape into her mouth.

Callie's brown eyes blinked and she swallowed the wine, pushing the cheese and bread down into her clogged throat. "I read somewhere how someone's soul could be as thin as a playing card." She was silent a moment. "That's mine. The only thing I can say is that I am going to give up any semblance of love in my life. I've made that decision just like I did after Francois died and I think...........\""

Caroline laughed. "Oh come on, Calinda Beauvais. Get real, would you? Where's the stamina you lob at me all the time? Good God. What brought on this wild display of practical clarity after our serene dinner at Thanksgiving when we were at *Hubers*?"

Callie finished the wine and lifted it for Caroline to refill. Ripping off more bread and carefully placing a piece of white French cheese across it, she stuffed it into her mouth and held the full glass to her chest. "Oohmmmmmmmm.... I was hungry. Thanks, Caroline." She looked across the hearth, a little apologetic smile on her lips.

"Me too. That was a long drive and I left at lunchtime.... I was too mad at you to eat. That would be a great way to diet, you know?" Caroline said, munching between words. "Just stay mad at you and I'll get into that old Talbot's jumpsuit in no time."

They laughed and drank more wine.

Caroline was full of questions she feared to ask.

"Okay, you first. I'll tell you what's going on with me after you tell me about you and Lee." Another grape followed the bread and more wine washed it down. She watched Caroline's face brighten.

"Well, I never dreamed love could be so ....so......... well, gripping. Perfect. Warm. Complete. And Lee told me he's felt that way about me for years. During my marriage and all the unhappiness, during my divorce, during all our meetings and he never let on." She shook her head in wonder. "Even during Steven and all that....."

"Well, what brought it to a head, then?" Callie asked, curiously.

"During this entire prescription card thing, I started to notice his eyes, his beard, and his aftershave and when we went to see Phantom, he held my hand and I knew I never wanted to let go. It was like someone opened a door and let the sunshine in. I love him, Callie, and he loves me! He asked me to marry him." She finished in a rush of words.

Callie jumped up, nearly spilling the remaining red liquid out of her near-empty glass. Laughter bubbled from within as she hugged Caroline until their laughter turned to happy tears.

"This crying stuff is getting old! But at least they're good tears. Oh, Caroline, I'm so happy for you I could burst. When? Where? All of it. Let's have it. I'm so happy to think about good things for a change."

Caroline linked her hand with her friend's. I'll tell you later. It's your turn. We promised each other a long time ago to always be honest. Through thick or thin, remember? And I almost blew it a few months ago. I won't let you shut me out like I almost did to you." Her face grew serious.

Callie nodded and shook her head tiredly. The fire started to burn down as Caroline listened to her relate what she'd overheard Derrick say, while unaware that Callie stood in his doorway, listening.

"You are telling me you are tossing away something that could be so perfect based on a one-sided conversation he had with someone?" Caroline's voice sounded shrill.

"He told me he loved me!" Callie said, angry at Caroline's statement. "He and I shared so much. It was like we knew it was real, so we were just waiting in wild anticipation for the right time to make love, you know?" Callie's eyes misted again. "I really thought he loved me and I *love* him! Thank God I didn't sleep with him. I would have felt like an idiot," she finished lamely and bit another piece of bread, teeth ripping it off raggedly as if it was taffy.

"So you just rushed out without talking to the man. He has been like an injured puppy. He's been barking at Eric who just tries to keep out of his way. I've never known Derrick to be so short, yet he's still getting all his work done. In fact, he stays shut up in his office working on the web pages like there's nobody else around. It's like he has a toothache that nobody can fix and nobody wants to get close enough to try! You should have talked to him. There might be another answer to what you heard."

"No, there can't be. I can hear it as clearly as if it were yesterday when he said, 'I miss you too, darling. I think about you every day.' His voice got all soft and sweet." She stared into her wine glass.

Caroline looked pained. "I can't believe he's involved with someone else. I just refuse to believe it."

"Oh, you can believe it all right," Callie said, angrily. "Maybe if I get drunk enough, I'll wake up tomorrow and it will all go away. But I'll get back to work on Monday and there he'll be again." She stretched her legs outward, her feet nearly touching the gray stone hearth. "And, I've been missing Cendrine's calls all week. Something is wrong. This might be the perfect time to fly back to Pertuis to lick my wounds. I can see what's going on and help with whatever it is. That way, I could just......."

"...........run away?" Caroline struggled with her anger.

Both sets of feet were lifted up on the edge of the heavy coffee table, their backs to the stone hearth.

"Yes, maybe.......I can't...." Her eyes turned to Caroline with mute distress.

Caroline stared back. Pursing her lips, she pushed herself up to sit on the couch, looking into the bright yellow and orange flames, thinking hard and staring at Callie. "What else?"

Callie remained seated. "And when he said her name in such a syrupy, sweet voice..... He just said, *bye Sophia. I'll call you again soon.*"

Caroline's head jerked and she sat forward on the edge of the couch. "What did you say her name was?"

"Sophia. I remember it as plain as day." Callie watched Caroline's face turn a mottled red before laughter suffused her features. "Why?"

"Oh my God, Callie." Caroline's blonde hair swished around her face as she shook her head back and forth. She beat her feet against the floor and pounded the coffee table with the flats of her hands, as if she was keeping time with bongo drums.

"What?" Callie asked again, staring at her and shaking her head in confusion.

"Sophia." Caroline repeated the name and laughed again.

"Yes. Sophia..... That was her name!" Callie's brow furrowed as Caroline turned toward her and placed both hands on each of Callie's shoulders.

Caroline stared into her eyes and said, "Sophia is Derrick's *daughter*, you knot head!"

Callie felt the air close in around her and felt suffocated. "No——I surely would have known. No..............Oh God. In all our conversations about his daughter, I never heard her *name*. He just always said his daughter.... Oh no! I reacted without thinking there could be any other reason than he................" She covered her face with her hands and started laughing hysterically. "Oh Shit! What have I done to that poor man?"

Caroline studied her, mouth pulled down. "Well, it can't be too late to make things right, darling." She rubbed Callie's back and shoulders, trying to soothe the despair.

"Ya think?" Callie's hopeful smile and quaking body fought in tandem with one another as she tried to visualize Derrick's face when she explained.....

Later, the wine bottle and plates lay empty. Both women sat staring into the banked-up flames; the fire mesmerizing them. Darkness settled over the lake through still-open blinds, the geese slipped into open coves and lights twinkled across the water's far shore. The cottage was dark; the fireplace's illumination shot shadows across the walls and embraced them.

Silently watching the flames lick against the stone, the air crackled around them as they rubbed their bums and complained about the hard floor. Each silently contemplated their worlds and what waited for them when they returned home the next day.

Callie reached out to squeeze Caroline's shoulder, "Thank you, dear friend." Her eyes blurred again and she wiped her cheek. "I feel like such an idiot, more like a teenager and I'm flooded with such a feeling of......" She didn't finish.

Caroline smiled dreamily and nodded as she patted Callie's hand. "I love the timing of all of this, you know? With the craziness of the office finally showing some semblance of order, and my heart tripping with excitement over Lee and now you finding someone special after losing Francois..... I haven't felt this good for so long. And you'll have the fun of going back to Portland to face that man," she finished, as she hugged her knees toward her and gazed at Callie. "Don't ask me to help with that one, dear heart."

"Damn! And Derrick is going to shake me until my teeth rattle when I tell him why I just closed myself off....and ran away from him." She swam through a river of emotions and stared at the twinkling lights across the lake. Raking her hand through her hair, she let her curls spring free. "And I'll deserve it."

"Well, that one I don't envy. You're on your own —- that is for sure. I, on the other hand, would like you to get it all ironed out. I need your mind clear, you know? Janine is going to help plan the wedding. That poor woman needs something to do. She seems so unhappy with that husband of hers or lonely or something. I got the oddest feeling this morning when she stopped by." She shrugged.

"And I couldn't have chosen a nicer man for you, Caroline. I've always liked Lee."

Caroline felt giddy and Callie could see her mind was far from the cottage on D Lake.

"Yes, ma'am. A wedding it is." Callie answered solemnly.

"Guess your trip to France will be put on hold?" Caroline chuckled.

"Yes,.....but Cendrine has left several strange phone messages for me and we're trading phone calls. I'm at a loss to know what's going on." She paused. "Frankly, I'm worried."

"Well, maybe after you talk to Derrick, he'll go with you to France......after the wedding, that is."

"....Which makes me ask the obvious question, Caro.... Have you and Lee set a date?"

"A-S-A-P but I want to put my drug card to bed and shoot that moon first."

"You shouldn't worry about it now. It seems to be set on GO." Callie told her as she pressed her hands to cheeks and watched the fire spit sparks.

"Maybe my wedding plan can be used as a stepping stone for a second one?"

Callie grinned. The thought-provoking silence that followed filled her head with mind chatter again as she started to compose her apology to the man she loved.

"The great are only great because we carry them on our shoulders; when we throw them off, they sprawl on the ground
—MONTANDRE'

Chapter 37

* * *

S ilas Henry showed Lorraine Reed to a ruby-leather tufted chair facing his desk.

"Thank you for coming today, Mrs. Reed. I know it is a difficult time." He smiled at her and saw her eyes fill a moment as she pulled out a hankie. He watched her shaking a little, but knew she was firm in her resolve to straighten out the legal issues surrounding her husband's death, even though the funeral was so fresh. His thinning red hair looked like a beacon as it barely covered his pale head, but his eyes were gentle and his gaze returned to her again and again.

"May I call you Lorrie?" he asked her kindly.

"Lorrie is fine. I know you asked me here about Del's Will. He left me a copy of it. So I realize there are some peculiarities. Is that the rush to get in here so soon after his funeral?"

Noting a look of uncertainty in Lorrie's eyes, he explained. "Yes." He cleared his throat and continued. "It should be very clear since there are no children from your marriage. Del left everything to you. For some reason, he wanted me to meet with you immediately upon his death. Maybe you could shed some light on that?" He shuffled through the blue file on his desk. "Let's see, two cars, your house here in Portland, your cabin in Rockaway, various stocks, CDs, his shares in Premier Health Systems."

"Not really.....except... What? I didn't realize he had shares in Premier," she said quickly.

"Yes," he tapped his forehead with the rubber end of his yellow pencil. "Today those 5000 shares are at $242 a share. He purchased the shares when they were at $90 so he saw a marked upswing in its worth. You can either sell them or retain your stocks and allow more growth. I understand the health insurance market is doing well but with the stock market's volatility, I can't promise you that, nor can I suggest what you should do. A tax accountant would be the man to talk to about that." He saw her face undergo rapidly changing features.

"Another one of Del's little surprises then…. So, I would have some power over Premier Health with these shares?" She smiled grimly and tightened her hold on her purse strap.

"Yes, you do."

Her face became thoughtful. "What about Ace-Deer?" Her voice sounded angry.

"Ace-Deer?" Silas flipped through the papers inside the file. "I don't find anything about Ace-Deer. What is it, Lorrie?"

"It is a prescription corporation of some kind. I have a copy of the contract right here and it shows his partner was Dr. Vincent Bertrand, the CEO of Premier." She handed him the folded papers and watched him study them.

After reading the contract, he mused, "So it seems the fog is clearing. I wonder why he didn't mention this to me. Well, it is very concise and you are his beneficiary. I'm concerned about this two hundred thousand dollars though. It looks like he added a caveat with a significant back-up plan if anything happened to him and it's been notarized." He glanced up, waiting for an explanation.

She was trembling. She grabbed a Kleenex and wiped her nose. Then, she handed him the copy of the attorney's letter that was inside the envelope with the Will. There's a signed statement at the bottom of this letter that might explain that," she said, pushing it toward him.

Silas read the notation, saw the notary validation and raised his right eyebrow. "Well, the signature is definitely Del's compared to the other articles I have here in his file as I'm sure you agree. It looks like he made sure his money retained value regardless of the solvency of Ace-Deer as a corporation. If you would like me to take care of this exchange, I will be happy to do so. With this, you would own another 9000 Premier shares to add to your current 5000 shares. Your husband's financial acuity is very impressive." He placed the papers into the file.

"You mean *was* very impressive, don't you?" she asked with misty eyes.

He nodded solemnly across his desk and made notations on the file. Pushing it toward her, he said, "Would you please sign where I've indicated, Lorrie. It gives me the authority to transfer the funds into stock and lists you as the owner."

Lorraine Reed's lips turned upward as she signed her name to the paper that would give her husband's partner pause. *I just wish I could see that man's face. Then I'll sell all of it out from under him or ……..*

Silas Henry looked at Lorraine Reed. "If I can help you at all during this transition, Mrs. Reed, please call me."

"I want to go vegetate somewhere so I don't have to think about Del being gone," she told him, blinking rapidly. "And I want the man responsible for my husband's death to pay....."

Silas stopped suddenly. "I knew he had a bad heart... and I share your distress and curiosity as to why he was behind **Zupans**, but do you think someone....?"

"Yes I do!" She whipped around to face him as her purse slapped her hip. "Can't you see that with all the secrets and these papers?" She nearly shouted.

He grasped her hands and held them an instant before she spun away.

"I have to do this for Del. I've followed his instructions to the letter but now I have one of my own and Del isn't here to stop me." Her heart felt sluggish as she headed for her car and the job waiting in front of her.

SIX BLOCKS south of the Lewis, Carle and Henry law offices; Vincent Bertrand was getting ready to leave his office. He looked out the window and saw another beautiful day. *Cold but what can I expect? It's nearly Winter, for God sakes. Janine said to meet her by her umbrella man, as usual.... so I better get hoofing it downtown.*

Pulling his scarf around his neck, he stepped off the elevator and started his brisk walk westward. *It's a great day.* He passed **Rock Bottom Brewery**, glanced into the bookstore and walked alongside the light-rail train as it lumbered up Morrison Street. *Yes, a real nice day. I don't have to worry about Del or Steven or that blonde bitch. It's hard not to admire her just a little though. She's one smart woman.......*

He chuckled into the wind. He pulled out his pipe and bit down on the tip as he stood on the corner and opened his leather tobacco pouch. Looking around at people crossing against the light, he joined the throng as he filled, lit and inhaled deeply. The smoke filled his lungs and the air as he continued toward the square, wafting the scent of cherry tobacco all around him.

*   *   *

Detective Childs entered Premier's building ten minutes later, looking grim and focused.

Sally was just leaving for lunch when he stepped off the elevator.

"You're Dr. Bertrand's secretary, aren't you?" he asked, tipping his hat at the young woman as he stuffed his hand into his jacket pocket.

"Yes, I am. But he's at lunch. Weren't you here yesterday morning?" She said, making it sound like an apology.

"Yes I was. Is there someplace I might wait for him?" He stood quietly as he held his foot in the door to stall the elevator door.

Sally looked strained. "Well, he just left and you might have a couple hours' wait. But if you want to, he has a two o'clock appointment down on the 6th floor. You can wait in the waiting room inside Room #602 if you'd like." Her hesitancy was obvious and he could see she immediately wished she'd kept her mouth shut.

"Oh, that would be fine. I'll just grab some lunch then. Thanks ma'am." Again, Detective Childs tipped his hat, moved his foot aside and rode down the elevator with her, each parting in different directions after they left the brightly lit lobby.

Vincent reached the umbrella man early. He watched people huddling in and around the statue, on the steps and across the square filled with name-encrusted bricks. The sun, suddenly hidden behind the bulky cumulus clouds, put the area in shadow. He watched the doorway to Nordstrom; sure Janine would be arriving from that direction, undoubtedly carrying something new. *It's surprising how many things that woman can't live without.* A rare smile softened his beak-like face as he pulled his scarf tighter around his neck.

"Well, if it isn't *Doctor* Bertrand," a woman's voice broke into his musings.

He swung around and saw a short woman standing a few feet away from him and his eyes narrowed slightly in recognition.

"Mrs. Reed, isn't it?" He hid his surprise with the nonchalance of a practiced businessman. He briefly skimmed her with his eyes, not quite able to hide an expression of exaggerated disdain.

"Yes, that's right. Lorraine Reed. I followed you from your building." She stated, flatly.

Taken aback, he answered swiftly, "Why? Was there something you needed from me? I was sorry to hear about Del's death. I didn't have a chance to tell you personally at the Chapel yesterday morning." He studied her again before quickly glancing toward Nordstrom one more time. He sucked ferociously on his pipe.

She laughed and answered with obvious sarcasm, "Yes, I'm sure you *are* sorry." Her eyes glistened, teeth bared in a faint, but unmistakable sneer.

"Mrs. Reed. What on earth?????" His shackles rose and he squinted at her.

She walked closer to him and spoke quietly, with a force that stunned him. "I just wanted to thank you for the Ace-Deer contract I found in my husband's papers that I'm sure you hoped I didn't know about."

His mouth dropped. Stunned, he had to struggle to find his voice. After glancing around for Janine again, he looked straight at her. "I don't like your implication." He said. "What are you talking about?" Blue veins protruded from his temple and smoke drifted around his head. He shook his pipe at her, "What contract?"

She laughed again. "The contract that spells out my destiny, Doctor. The money my husband put into that corporation now gives me some control of Premier Health Systems. I just wanted to be the one to tell you." She was trembling, knowing she'd gone too far, but rage and anger propelled her. "I know ..... I know you did it and I'll see you in hell for it..."

He grabbed her arm tightly and pulled her abruptly around to face him, his mouth nearly frothing at her words. "What in the hell are you talking about? Lay it out because you are really pissing me off," he seethed, his tone sharp as he leaned very close to her

Lorrie's fear was evident in her eyes and the pain was excruciating.

"Vincent?" His wife's voice sounded afraid and confused. Her perfectly coiffed hair was arranged neatly, her makeup immaculate and jewels covered her neck, wrists and ear lobes. Both hands held large Nordstrom bags but her eyes regarded her husband with shock, her purchases forgotten.

He whipped around and found Janine standing next to him, looking from him to the short woman, her eyes fastened on his tight grip. He immediately released Lorraine's arm and felt a hot blackness surround him.

Lorraine rubbed her arm and grimaced before she reached out to Janine. She shook the limp, extended hand that automatically shot upward as Lorraine held hers aloft. "I'm Lorraine Reed. My husband was Premier's Medical Director before your husband killed him," she snapped. Her tight smile wavered a moment. "Now you both have a good day." She turned on her heel and walked down the brick steps across the square feeling sick, as her heart thumped against her rib cage. She could only pray she wasn't being followed.

"Vincent? *Mon deux*." She said slowly, watching her husband's eyes glaze over.

"Oh, she's gone nuts since her husband died. I have no idea in hell what she's talking about. Let's eat." He turned and pulled her along by one elbow, his long angry strides forcing her to nearly run to keep up with him. He forced himself to calm down as he dragged her past Starbucks and across the street. He wouldn't lose control of his company. He'd do anything to anyone before he let that happen. Anything!

"*Alors*! Slow down, Vincent!" Her heels tapped along the sidewalk and people stared at them as she jerked out of his grasp. They breezed by the big, ancient clock on Broadway Street embedded in concrete, where it had stood for nearly a hundred years.

He turned around and looked at her as if he'd seen a ghost. "I'm sorry, dear. I just remembered an appointment," he lied and began to retrace his steps.

"Vincent, I already talked with Sally this morning. Your appointment isn't until two o'clock. Come please. *A dejeuner, Vincent......*" She pushed him into the **Red Carriage**. "I want a big hamburger and milkshake. They're the best here. You promised......"

"Yes dear, come along then." Vincent grasped her bags and followed her up the old stairway. His mind was clicking as they slid into a booth, very aware that his wife's eyes were filled with questions that he had no intention of answering. But a calculated agenda brimmed at the edge of his mind. He watched the clock tick away the minutes, wanting to think in silence as he sipped the ice water, wondering how this all happened to him.

The sandwich felt like sawdust in his mouth as he avoided Janine's subtle inquiries.

She finally gave up the one-sided conversation as she'd tried to fill the spaces with a jumble of words. She gave up after awhile and chewed silently. Her hands shook slightly and she knew something had changed in their lives and didn't seem to really care. Why and when had she stopped caring?

By the time Vincent returned to the office an hour later, he was in a steaming frenzy. *Her chatter will drive me insane one of these days.* He stabbed number six on the elevator.

He reached the office, walked into the private entrance, donned his white coat, wrapped his stethoscope around his neck and walked into the nurse's station, still calculating and angry. *What in the hell am I doing in here?* Abruptly, he stopped, removed everything and retraced his steps. He felt his heart accelerating and sighed heavily as he stood a moment in thought before jerking the door open.

Walking down the six flights of steps to the street usually cleared his mind but they wouldn't today. Today, he had a mission. He skipped the elevator, trotted down the stairs anyway and left the building. He had something to do that he couldn't put off.

Detective Childs looked at his watch and noted it was 2:05 pm. *Where is the man?* He walked up to the glass portal and stuck his face into the window. "Didn't you say the doctor was due for a two o'clock?"

The nurse looked at the appointment book and nodded. "I don't know where he is but he should be here any minute, sir. He has an appointment right now. Do you have an appointment?" She asked quizzically, the glasses sitting in the middle of her bridge, questioning eyes staring into his.

"No, I don't." He flipped his wallet open to show his badge and her eyes grew wide. "Just let me know when he arrives, will you?" He asked impatiently.

"Yes, sir," She turned to the other woman in the office and rolled her eyes significantly as she slid the glass pane closed.

Lorraine returned home, quickly parked Del's BMW in the driveway and let herself into the house. Purposefully striding straight through the hallway, into the living room and out the back sliding glass doors, she proceeded into her back yard. She stepped through her garden, following the round rock steps leading past the bird habitat and the carriage-style garden shed toward the back of the property. Robins flitted around her head and landed in the forlorn lilac tree as she sped by. Her heart hammering in her chest, she hurried inside and locked the door. Quickly jerking an old wicker chair close to the window facing the street and driveway, she sat down and took a deep breath. Then she waited.

An hour later, her legs nearly asleep and her neck cramped, she saw the car moving slowly down the street, inching past the driveway and parking under the neighbor's large oak tree. Squinting through the windows, she held her hand over her chest trying to slow her speeding heartbeat and grabbed for her purse. Never leaving her perch or pulling her eyes away from the silver Mercedes, she flipped open her cell phone and punched in 911; still waiting, frightened but focused.

James Child's beeper went off at 2:30 p.m., just after the rumblings in the waiting room became a quiet roar, since the good doctor had never arrived for his 2:00 p.m. appointment, nor his 2:15 or 2:25. He'd hitched his pants up, left the office and headed outside. While looking at his car, trying to decide his next move, the high-pitched beep cut into his thoughts. He ran across the street, jumped in his car and dialed in. Within one minute, he was headed toward Hillsdale and the Reed home.

Vincent sat inside his car, running several plans through his head, trying to make a decision. *I need that contract so I'll just go in and hold my gun on her——just enough to scare her. I'll get it and be out of there. No, she's a gutsy broad. Maybe I ought to just tie her up and grab it, when she's least expecting me to come knocking. Ha. Like hell, I'll knock.* He opened the car door and contemplated his third option and decided he'd surprise her from the back of the house instead of knocking on the front door. *Yes, that would be good. Maybe I should ring the front doorbell and then go around to the back. That way, if she tries to run, I'll be waiting.*

Lorraine's heart skipped a beat as she saw him start around the back toward her. *He can't see me. He'll never guess I'm here but——— oh my God. Why didn't I listen to Del?* Her voice screamed inside her head. *No, I want this man to pay for......... Oh Del. Dammit, why did you have to get us into this? Why did you think money was so damned important? Why? Why? Why?*

The man stopped abruptly and turned toward the front of the house again, pivoting on his foot. He disappeared from her sight suddenly.

"God, that was close," she sighed in relief. "This old heart isn't what it used to be..." *Should I wait for the police or...... go in.... or?* She reached inside her purse and wrapped her fingers around the small gun, loaded and ready. *I need to get him inside the house. Del always said if an intruder is inside, we'd be in a better position if we ever had to shoot anyone than if he was outside just trying to get in....* Yes, her mind answered. *He also said to stay away from him.*

Her legs ached and her neck burned. Shooting pains were going up into her head and down her shoulders. Stretching to loosen the kinks, she inadvertently knocked a bag of potting soil off the shelf beside her. The clatter sounded like slapping a silver spoon against a metal pan. Cringing, she froze in place and held her breath.

Vincent had just rounded the corner of the house again when he heard it. Wrinkling his brow, his head jerked toward the little building at the back of the flower garden and he studied it, staring and cocking his head to listen again. His hands clenched and unclenched, and his stomach coiled into a knot. *My God —- this is ludicrous. I'm jumping at every little noise now.* He exhaled deeply and walked swiftly to the glass doors on the patio and peered in the corner, shading his face with his hands. *Nothing. No movement. She should be at the front door by now. She must have heard the doorbell!* He could see the front door and the car in the driveway out the front window from where he stood. *Come on! Come on!*

Lorraine stared in horror as her cell phone rang. She flipped it and whispered, "Hello?" Her hand was shaking so badly, she nearly dropped it onto the wooden bench.

"Lorrie?" A young voice asked.

"I can't talk now!" she whispered quickly before pressing the power button.

Vincent swiveled around and peered toward the little building once again. *What was that?* Then, he looked closely inside the house, still discerning no movement from within. His eyes squeezed half closed. *Well, do we have the little mouse caught in her own trap?* He moved his head back and forth, between the house and the back of the garden.

Lorraine couldn't see the back of the house from the window, since it faced the street side and now she was sorry. *Where is he?* She pushed the phone onto the shelf and held the little gun tightly in her hand. Moving her face as close as she dared to the window, she nearly fainted when his face crept around the corner and stared into hers. Her heart nearly stopped.

"Well, Mrs. Reed, fancy finding you here. Would you like to come out and join me or do I have to come in to get you?" his voice was silky and smooth, sickening and frightening.

She held the gun tightly in the folds of her wool skirt as crumbling nerves turned her legs wobbly. *At least they aren't asleep,* she thought haphazardly. *I'd play hell trying to walk with pinpricks jabbing at them. Please hurry. Oh! Please hurry!*

She moved away from the window and decided she might have a better chance outside the close confines of a 12 x 12 garden shed. Lifting the latch with her gloved hands, she opened the door a crack and slipped out. Small pebbles littered the walkway and a pair of blue jays darted past her to land on a nearby limb as if ready for a theatrical event.

He was standing six feet away, leaning against the bird feeder post that Del had installed. It was a solid black shepherd's hook. The large, wooden feeder had a very thick rope holding it in place. The man's head was about six inches below the bottom of the feeder and it gave Lorraine an incorrigible idea. She kept her eyes on his face and held the gun firmly in her right hand, hidden. *Thank you, Del, for forcing me to go skeet shooting with you. Guess you knew I'd need it. Now, let's pray to God I remember how to hit the mark.*

"You have some papers that belong to me. I want you to give them to me, now! Then I'll leave," He said sternly, his cold eyes never leaving hers as he studied her beneath craggy brows, and pointed a small dark gun in her direction. His hand was pale, but unwavering.

"Like hell I will," she answered, equally severe. She could not know the irony of those words as being the last ones her husband heard before he died.

"Oh, won't you?" His voice sounded oily as he stood up, pulling himself upright onto both feet. He glanced toward the street a moment to make sure nobody could see them. It was a very bad idea and realized, too late, his hesitation was his undoing.

A shot rang out above his head and he jerked at the blasting sound a second before the birdhouse crashed down onto his head. He was stunned and screamed, "You bitch!"

Police sirens broke through the red haze of his thoughts as blood trickled down his temple. He stared at the short woman in front of him, still pointing what looked like a toy gun at his head. Blood was running into his eyes as he stared at her in disbelief.

"Don't move or I WILL kill you," she whispered and he knew she meant it.

James Childs and four uniformed policemen crashed through her rhododendrons, camellias, and winter cabbages. The rose bush snagged one officer as he rushed to her side, while his gun held a bead on the man.

"Well, we meet again, doctor. Do you realize you have patients waiting for you back at the office?" He snickered.

Vincent stared at him in a daze as he tried to wipe the blood from his face.

"You have the right to remain silent. Anything you say can and will be used against you in a court of law……," he began as he grabbed Vincent's gun. Then, he twisted him around to lock his wrists in silver handcuffs behind his back as he finished reading him his legal rights.

He stared at the doctor as the officers led him away before turning back to the woman in front of him. He just looked at her and shook his head, "Mrs. Reed, I presume?"

"Yes, sir," she whispered, shaking uncontrollably.

"Do you have any idea what could have happened here today, Ma'am?" His voice was slow and smooth, reminding her of the south.

She nodded, tears welling inside her clogged throat.

"Well, let's just say, your little plan turned out ok after your 911 call. But how did you know we'd make it? My boss was livid. You're not trained like we are but you know what, lady? That was one helluva a good shot." He laughed and looked at the gun. "You DO have a license for that, right?"

"Yes, sir," she answered again, voice clogged, sounding stifled and unnatural. Contradictory expressions flit across her face: relief because it was over, sadness and anger for all the reasons putting her inside her garden with a gun, memories of the past and fear of the future. Taking a deep breath, she straightened her shoulders and nodded toward the man.

"Well, you can leave it to us now. We have found signs that your husband was inside the doctor's condo the day he died. His wife was gone for two hours and the coroner's report specified the same two-hour window to pinpoint his time of death. So, with that and all the other evidence, I'd say we have a good chance of getting a jury to find him guilty. He might not have killed him but with all the other evidence my office is gathering, he sure as hell pushed him toward a heart attack that might have been circumvented. I am real sorry, Ma'am."

"Yes, I thought so." Her voice was soft but firm.

He surveyed her kindly and guided her to the glass doors and opened them for her. Warmth slid toward them and touched their cold faces. He tipped his hat and smiled at the sad woman in front of him.

"I'll be going now. We will need to ask you some questions and sign a statement but it can wait a bit until you can get yourself together. Are you ok alone?" He waited a beat.

Lorrie nodded mutely and watched him walk away as she widened the French doors and stepped inside to a house that now seemed to embrace her like a warm shower on a cold day. Her body still shook as she closed the door, locking it behind her. As she turned to enter the living room, her eyes fell on the wooden box and the ocean cruise brochures. Then the rage of tears broke loose and her much-needed mourning began.

"The sweetest joy, the wildest woe is love.
—BAILEY – *Festus*

Chapter 38

* * *

Derrick pushed in the screen door and heard voices in the dining room. "Knock —-knock,"" he said as he entered the house.

"Come on in, son." Carl hollered toward the front door.

Rounding the corner, Derrick came to a full stop and a grin lit up his features. "Hello, Alice."

The woman's apron was splattered with flour and her cheeks were pink. "Well, hello Derrick. I'm just fixing your father some dinner and we had a little party here a minute ago. We should have waited for you." She said shyly as she looked over at Carl and smiled.

Well, well, thought Derrick. "What was the party for, an early Christmas celebration?"

Carl chuckled and looked up at Alice. "No, but we found another package of Tums in the kitchen drawer so we had another Tums-burning ceremony." His eyes crinkled and laughter bubbled out as he swung back to smile at the woman behind him.

Thank you, God, Derrick thought. "Well, what's for dinner? I'm starved."

Alice made clucking sounds and pushed him into a chair at the end of the Maple table and returned to the kitchen.

Derrick raised his eyebrows and his dad only smiled back at him, as they waited for plates and cutlery to join the steaming potatoes and baked pork chops. Then, a cold green salad joined the dishes and little pots of jiggling Jello.

Alice sat down and she looked at Carl expectantly as she reached for Derrick's hand.

Carl glanced quickly at his son before reaching for her other hand and grasped Derrick's.

Derrick's interest was piqued, and then they closed their eyes as his r began a prayer of thanksgiving and his heart smiled.

"Dear God, thank you for this day and for the hands that prepared this good meal. Thank you for my friends, my family and especially for the good health you have bestowed on us. Thank you also for all the good things and for each day of our lives. Please let us be thankful for all that we have and not take anything or anyone for granted. In Jesus name we pray, Amen."

"Amen," said Alice, squeezing the men's hands.

"Amen to that," Derrick said in an odd, but gentle tone.

The Metro section of the newspaper was open on the couch as Derrick went out the door after hugging Alice and his father. *It's her!* He grabbed the newspaper and saw Janine Vinnier's picture beneath an advertisement for a fundraiser for Cystic Fibrosis, called *Sixty Five Roses.* Standing beside her was Vincent Bertrand, her husband. Derrick felt the hair stand up on his neck. *Janine Vinnier's husband!!?* He shook his head, eyes wide.

It was snowing as she traversed the mountain pass. Drivers slowed down and traffic was at a near standstill. She could see Caroline a few cars ahead of her, drifting as if in slow motion. It was a slow drive all the way with frequent stops; traffic was snarled in Sherwood and later in Tigard before the road began to clear and she no longer felt she was traveling inside a cloud.

Callie found five messages on her machine, experiencing a complicated mingling of emotions when she heard his voice.

Four of the messages were from Derrick and one from Cendrine again. They'd played phone tag for over a week. This message sounded more strident than the others.

"*Bonjour Callie. Appelle moi vite s'il te plaît. Je ne peux pas parler des vins à maman et papa. Tout ça concerne Olivier. Il a saboté la compagnie et il est à Paris. J'ai peur et je ne sais pas quoi faire. Je t'en prie. Il faut que tu viennes m'aider à Pertuis. Quand pourrais tu partir? J'ai un nouvel email : . Olivier revient le 4 janvier et il ne sait pas que j'ai découvert les problèmes du vignoble. Je t'aime Callie, je suis désolée de rater tes appels. S'il te plaît, essaie encore de m'appeler ou écris moi vite. bonne nuit.*"

Callie's head was a riot of questions wondering what Oliver was doing... embezzling the vineyard funds? Poor Cendrine. She couldn't blame her for not wanting to tell *Maman* and *Pere*...I must talk to her. I must go, but not yet.

Derrick first.....

"You can do it," Caroline had told her. "Just pick up the phone and ask him to come over. Tell him to his face. No stupid phone call explanation, promise?"

Yes, easier said than done. She shook her hair loose around her face and felt grimy. I think I'll just take a shower first. She got up. *No, you don't,* she reprimanded herself. *Call him, you big coward!*

Derrick's answering machine. *Damn. That was close.* She laughed at herself and hung up quickly. *Now, why did I do that?* She dialed again and waited for the tone, "Derrick, this is Callie. I'm home and I have been very unfair just ripping out of town like that without an explanation. Can you please come over? I really need to talk to you. Give me a call, huh? Oh, and........soon please."

She hung up again and tried to swallow the lump that lingered in her throat. *Lord, I sounded like a nut.* She looked at her watch and saw the dial pointing to seven. *Now, a quick shower, but I'll take the phone in with me,* she thought, as she began pulling off clothes and headed into the bathroom. *It's 4 a.m. in Pertuis, so I can't call Cendrine until early tomorrow. Oliver? He adores her. What on earth could be going on??*

She stepped into the tub and pulled the curtain. For a long while, she stood beneath the spray, head bowed, letting the hot water drum against her skull while rising steam swirled and invaded the bathroom around her.

Twenty minutes later, a towel wrapped around her head and nothing on but a short terry-cloth robe she was trying to decide what to put on when the doorbell rang. *What? Oh no!* She still hadn't turned on the living room lights, so she went to the window and tried to see the car in the driveway. *Derrick! Oh my....*

"Callie?" His voice drifted toward her.

"I'm not dressed, Derrick."

"Open the door anyway!" he said gruffly, his voice filled with exasperation.

"Well, damn." She turned on the porch light, pulled open the dead bolt and felt the door push toward her, none too gently.

"Are you okay?" he asked, nearly frantic with worry.

He saw her hand reach upward to feel the towel she'd obviously forgotten was wrapped around her head and the naked legs peering beneath her short cerulean robe still looked damp.

"Hi." His eyes blinked and an uncertainty crept into his expression, his throat clogged.

"Hi." Her composure was a fragile shell around her. But smiling, she pulled him into the house and pointed him to the big chair in the corner. "Let me get you something to drink and I'll put on some clothes and brush out my hair."

"No." His voice was quick and final. "Come here." He pulled her to him and kissed her with a fervency that surprised both of them as she tried to throttle the dizzying current racing through her.

Their eyes locked as their breathing slowed in unison. "Now, go get something else on if you have to. I'm not moving until you tell me what in the hell chased you out of Dodge."

Callie swayed a little, as the sweet intoxicating musk of his body overwhelmed her. "Yes sir. I'll be right back. Get yourself something to

. Did you eat dinner?" She yelled from the bedroom, racing around to find something she could slip into quickly.

"Yes, as a matter of fact, I went by to check on Dad and his neighbor lady was there and she was fixing him dinner, so I joined them. It was great." He finished, a grin exploding on his face again, remembering the looks on their old faces.

She returned from the back room in her purple sweat pants, pulling her T-shirt down over her waist and still barefoot. She managed to slip past him and grab a bottle of water and the crackers and cheese she'd set out before he arrived. "I'll share," she said, coaxing him with the food. She snapped on the CD player. Piano and violin music quietly filled the room.

"Seriously now, Callie. What in the hell happened on Monday? I want to know everything that sent you hauling buggy out of here from the time you broke our date at **Wilfs** to right now." His eyes slid to her midriff as she reached for the glass in the cupboard.

"Don't beat me," she whispered, as she put the plate on the counter and sat down at the dining room table. The nearness of him gave her comfort.

Derrick laughed quietly. "Is that why you left? You thought I might beat you?" He held up both hands in a claw-like stance, "like this?" He lunged at her and she grinned.

"All kidding aside. What in the hell sent you running?" he asked, once again experiencing the lump in his throat that now was threatening to undermine his composure.

His unblinking stare brooked no argument.

She took a deep breath and rolled her eyes. "I came by your office Monday to tell you I'd ride to **Wilfs** with you instead of meeting you there......" She hedged and took a deep breath.

"But, instead....you broke the date and....," he said, egging her on.

"But, instead, I............. eavesdropped on your phone conversation. Eric wasn't at his desk and I heard you talking to someone and I..." Her cheeks stained peach.

"And you what?"

Under his steady scrutiny, she couldn't think.

"I was talking on the phone and you what?" he asked again, baffled.

"I heard you telling someone you missed them and you thought of them all the time and would call again soon and ....I thought the worst. I was so upset when I stepped away from your door, I nearly knocked Eric's monitor off his desk."

Derrick stared at her. His dark eyes showed the dullness of disbelief. "Do you mean to say you left for almost a week, making me feel like an idiot for falling in love with you and thinking you were faking and playing with my feelings all because of something you *thought* I said to —— - *who*? A *lover* somewhere?" His face closed as he stared at her, unspoken pain alive and glowing in his eyes.

She sat in lonely silence. "I felt betrayed. I'd been so afraid to let any man close to me again that maybe I used it as an excuse to run away. I never wanted to feel the pain of losing anyone again." Her eyes implored him to forgive her as she made a miserable attempt at a smile. "I didn't know Sophia was your daughter." She wiped the tear that filtered down her cheek with her forearm and sniffed loudly.

Derrick's eyes softened. He got up and pulled her into the big room near the glass doors and yanked her down on his lap. She could feel his uneven breathing on her cheek as he held her. "Let's make a deal to always talk to each other, right? I am really pissed that you thought my feelings were so shallow. I love you, Callie."

He pulled her thighs closer to his and buried his face into the hollow of her neck. "After my divorce, I was afraid to hope again. I didn't want to be hurt again either, but if we don't enjoy the music, we'll miss the dance. You said that, remember what your Mom said?" he whispered as he moved in an instinctive gesture of comfort.

The mere touch of his hand sent a shiver through her. She pulled his face toward hers and her eyelashes fluttered against his cheek. "I missed you so much. I tried sleeping the whole week." She kissed his nose. "I love you too and I am so sorry I didn't trust what was happening between us." Her trembling limbs clung to him.

Something intense flared within him and she didn't protest when his hands spanned her waist and inched the T-shirt upward. She could feel his hands caressing her back and she leaned toward him, wrapping her arms around his neck and meeting his kiss with pent up emotion.

"Do you think I could cash in on that hot-tub rain check?" he whispered as he covered her neck with kisses and tugged at her bra straps."

Callie's smile was his answer as they pushed themselves up off the couch and moved toward the glass doors. "It's starting to snow. I love being in the hot tub when it snows!"

He flipped off the house lights, stepped outside and lifted the spa cover. She turned on the jets and the lights inside the pool. Then, she ran back inside the dark room, discarded her clothes quickly and stood naked before him, shivering. His warm hands caressed her cheek in the dark, then moved slowly toward her neck, her shoulders, and cupped her breast.

"Hot tubbing in the snow, huh? Well, let's get in. You're freezing," he whispered as he pulled her outside onto the deck again. He reached toward his zipper as snowflakes swirled around them. He didn't waste another minute, wanting the warm water and Callie next to his bare skin, intoxicated by his imaginings.

She rapidly reached over and helped divest him of his jeans and sweatshirt and they both stepped over the side into the bubbling water, their faces only inches apart. Their breaths steamed above the bubbling spa and they reached for one another as a hungry child reaches for candy. Soft, warm skin collided and met as he pulled her head close, his palm on the back of her neck. Comforting warm bubbling water beat a tattoo on their skin.

She couldn't get close enough as she arched into him feeling his chest hair tickle her breasts. Their lips touched, parted and she felt his questing tongue touch the corner of her mouth. Her arms slid around his neck, she squirmed closer and wiggled her toes. Their waiting was over, their feelings raw and vulnerable. And she was ready.

Their pleasure was pure and explosive as their hands continued to touch and learn one another. Moonshine watched as night sounds rose and fell in partnership with the lovers as her body melted against his and she felt the world fill with him. And giant snowflakes covered them as contented peace invaded their feverish bliss.

The End

* * *